THE SILENT RAGA

ameen merchant

A
N
O
V
E
L

the silent raga

Douglas & McIntyre

D&M Publishers Inc.

Vancouver/Toronto/Berkeley

Douglas & McIntyre
A division of D&M Publishers Inc.
2323 Quebec Street, Suite 201
Vancouver BC Canada V5T 4S7
www.dmpibooks.com

National Library of Canada Cataloguing in Publication Data
Merchant, Ameen, 1964–
The silent raga / Ameen Merchant.

ISBN 978-1-55365-309-7 (cloth) · 978-1-55365-405-6 (paper)

I. Title.

PS8626.E7528S55 2007   C813'.6   C2007-903698-8

Editing by Steven Beattie
Cover and text design by Jessica Sullivan
Printed and bound in Canada by Friesens
Printed on acid-free paper that is forest friendly
(100% post-consumer recycled paper) and has been processed chlorine free.
Distributed in the U.S. by Publishers Group West

We gratefully acknowledge the financial support of the Canada
Council for the Arts, the British Columbia Arts Council, the Province
of British Columbia through the Book Publishing Tax Credit
and the Government of Canada through the Book Publishing Industry
Development Program (BPIDP) for our publishing activities.

For *Ma* Parin
And for Madras

We shall not cease from exploration
And the end of all our exploring
Will be to arrive where we started
And know the place for the first time.
Four Quartets, T.S. ELIOT

A work of art is a corner
of creation seen through a temperament.
"Salon of 1866," EMILE ZOLA

THE SILENT RAGA

Varnam

A drawing out of the colour of a raga or scale

IF I COULD return to that time, I would choose the mornings.

Especially the mornings after my mother's death, when my days began very early. In fact, to the short, piercing whistle of the Rockfort Express at four. Sometimes I would already be up, drawing water from the well at the back of the house, and I would hear it call. My body would go still for a few seconds. The bucket would shake and splatter as I hesitated in midreach for the handle. It would slip halfway into the well again, completely drenching my dhavani and blouse.

At that time of morning, when the crows and mynahs and parrots were still nursing their voices and not a single light shone in any of the neighbourhood houses, in that deep star-lit darkness, the solitary cry of the train was a despairing call. A strange music.

I would feel the cool morning air against my wet skin, and then a quick, feathery warmth would spread through me, as though someone had rubbed eucalyptus oil all over my skin.

I wonder now if Amma thought of it in those terms. Did she even hear the train as it rumbled by only five miles away?

With the bucket of water in one hand I would grab the broom and the *kolapodi* tin with the other and walk around to the front of the house. I would sweep up the dried leaves and dust from the path leading to the front door, scoop it neatly into the pan and empty it into the big, rusty metal bin beside the gate. Then I would moisten the ground with fresh, cold water sprinkled from my cupped palm and level it smooth.

The kolam I designed would depend on how I felt that particular day. On some mornings it was an elaborate welcome to dawn, ambitious and full of snaking grandeur, and my hands would weave a tapestry of blooming flowers and intertwined stars. I would grab fists full of *kolapodi*—one, two, three, even four sometimes—and pour my heart into my masterpiece, my sublime welcome mat to the sun. And on other days it was a hurried note of dots and curves—a snappy, perfunctory kiss of cordiality—achieved with just half the amount of powder.

I have not dipped my hands in *kolapodi* for many years. I can't say I miss the grainy feel of powdered rice and white rock on my fingers.

I am no longer a prisoner of pattern.

THE WALK TO the milk depot, with my ears tuned to the glassy murmurings of the previous day's bottles in the jute bag, was the dreamiest part of those mornings.

I would put on a dry dhavani, fling Amma's maroon shawl over my body and, quietly, with my teeth on my tongue, tiptoe my way through the hall to reach the front door. I would pull the bolt down without a sound and let myself out, like a fleeing ghost. Once outside, I would lock the door behind me, carefully skirt my kolam art for the day and step out the gate.

It was a good fifteen-minute walk to the milk depot, and I would take my own time getting there, stretching those quiet minutes for as long as I could. The tamarind and asoka leaves shimmied and danced in the breeze, and the heady fragrance from the parijatha blossoms filled the air.

Breathe it all in, Janaki. Breathe it all in while you can, I would tell myself, as I filled my lungs with air, as though the perfume were some kind of anaesthetic, a divine drug that would numb me through the predestined drudgery of my day. Occasionally, a cyclist would ride by with a stack of *Dina Thandi* newspapers tied to a wobbly carrier behind the seat. The tinny bell on the handlebar would protest in sharp, shrill notes as the cycle bumped and balanced on the red-earth road. I couldn't have known then that I would make the headline of that newspaper for three days in a row. I had never craved such a populist rebellion.

Cutting across C Block, I would take the route along the temple tank. As I walked along the eastern bank, I would hear the priest recite shivery Sanskrit slokas while he dipped in the tank and performed his cleansing ritual before the morning puja. I would tighten my grip around the bag with the milk bottles, abruptly cutting off their delicate endearments, and quickly walk away from his sight in the direction of the main road.

When I turned the corner, the neon sign of Mahalaxmi Talkies, half fused and flickering, would come into view. Even from where I was, I would see the figure of the night watchman stretched out like a corpse under the hazy fluorescence of the stills showcase.

In the month of Margazhi a group of vagrants and urchins sought warmth around the noxious vapours of a burning car tire or some plastic garlands snatched off the nearby cinema banner. I would avoid them and walk on the opposite foot-path. I would quicken my pace to the milk depot, clutching the four cards for four bottles tightly in my left hand under the shawl. I would dart across the junction of the main roads, pass the Gandhi statue stippled with bird droppings and finally reach my destination.

Kamala from C Block, Revathi from B Block and a few other mamis from houses outside the *agraharam* colony would arrive around the same time as I. We would arrange ourselves in a single line along the milk co-op kiosk and exaggerate the effect of the morning chill as we waited for the delivery van to pull up. Sometimes, Revathi, who had a voice like a river of honey, would sing an alaapana of abstract notes:

Ga–Ma
Ga–Ma–Da–Ma
Ga–Ma
Ga–Ma–Ni–Da–Ma–Da
Ma–Da–Ni–Sa–Da
Ni–Ni–Ni–Ni

Kamala and I would take this to be our cue and quickly join in:

Ga–Ma–Da–Da–Da–Da
Ma–Da–Ni–Ni–Ni–Ni
Ma–Da–Ni–Ni–Ni–Ni

Our voices would float in the mist-cloaked landscape, and little beads of water would creep around the corners of our eyes. We knew the milk van would be there in less than ten minutes. At the latest, by five thirty. And then it would all be over. That hour of girlhood innocence, those moments of rationed independence.

Alaapana

The abstract "scope" of a raga, or the short,
nonmetric (nonrhythmic) prelude

MALLIKA PAUSES at the door and casts one last look at her office.

Everything is in place. The fax machine is buzzing, and there will be reams and reams of messages by Monday. The files are locked. She makes a mental note to remember to bring some tea water for the money plant that sits facing the sun on the window, overlooking the Gemini Flyover. Funny name, she muses, flicking the switch. Money plant.

It is quiet down the corridor, a carpeted, air-conditioned hush. She has met scores of students yearning for such luxuries. Charmed by a humming foreignness. Why does it tug, this desire to be someone else, to escape into the possibility of other beings, other guises? Is it envy, she wonders, or is it something else? Did she, in a still-lost consciousness, really begrudge Janaki for following her heart? Did she resent her sister's sudden fame, and her dignity through it all? Lately, she thinks she hears Janaki inside her body, like a voice from somewhere else, far away, forgotten but always heard.

"She... could have... killed us instead!" Appa told the journalists that day, and the newspapers had added three exclamation marks of their own. He said it with some disbelief, as if he saw the hollowness of such a statement halfway through its utterance but was compelled to finish. He pleaded, "Please let us keep our dignity."

And Janaki kept her distance. She had never been in touch.

But now she was coming back. The reverse of exorcism. A ghost not freed, but forced back into you. Foreign even to priests.

The lights are out in all the cubicles, and everybody is gone for the day. Even Ted Pope, who normally worked late, wasn't around. She had had such a hard time getting through to Berkeley. The fax machine on the other end was constantly busy, and she had forty test scores to send. It had swallowed time. Where did the day go? Mallika wonders, pushing the button for the elevator. I am a woman caught between two worlds in two words—Janaki Asgar.

Mallika reaches into her handbag and runs her fingers over the envelope. She feels the torn edges of the glue-strip. A jagged journey into the past, she mutters as she waits for the elevator on the second floor. When she presses *M*, the steel doors slide like giant razor blades, and she faces herself in the reflection. The image is blurred, yet distinguishable, five foot seven, green cotton sari and a metallic sheen for skin. Once again, another deeper silence envelops her, and the elevator begins to descend. She feels like somebody else.

Dear Mallika, Janaki had written.

I know this letter will take you by great surprise. It has been so long. I only hope it gets to you. I will be in Madras late 20 May. I will be staying at the Hotel Connemara. Could we meet on the morning of 21, if you are free? We can have breakfast together. Say, around nine, nine thirty? I will wait for you. We don't have to tell Appa about this.

Akka.

Why was Janaki coming back? Why now, after all these years? The letter had arrived two days earlier at the United States Information Service, Madras, where she worked. Mallika Venkatakrishnan, Programs Counsellor, her card read, making her job seem important and glamorous when it was really not as important as it would have you believe. For five and a half days a week she sat swivel-chaired in an air-conditioned office on the second floor, interviewing and advising upper-middle-class boys and girls from the affluent neighbourhoods of Boat Club Road and Wallace Garden. Twenty-year-olds who had already begun living their 101 per cent American lives across the seas in Toledo and Syracuse. You could see it in their eyes—and in their easy nonchalance—that they were walking through the early golden rustle of "fall," wearing bright Benetton sweaters and chatting in lispy accents. Their ears—you could tell—already tuned to the distant crunch of maple and walnut under their feet, even in the blazing bazaars of T. Nagar. What could she tell them? Don't go?

At times Mallika found it hard to stifle a laugh and keep her composure in the presence of such wishful eagerness.

She remembers the student from last week. When she asked him, "Why do you think American business schools are better than our very own in Ahmedabad and Calcutta?" he'd shrugged and said, "Maybe they're all the same. But what's so good about staying in this country? Have you read the newspapers lately?" She was stung by his response and terminated the interview soon after that with, "Please let me know where you would like me to send your GRE and GMAT scores as soon as you make up your mind."

Later that night, after that new girl—Rita de Something (why did she wear so much lipstick?)—had wrapped up the news for the day on TV, Mallika felt like calling him for a delayed rejoinder. A cutting sliver of righteous indignation, delivered in a calm and confident voice, "Mr. Vidyasagar, staying means that you have not forsaken!" But she didn't. She always found it hard to let go.

Now Janaki, the proverbial prodigal daughter and runaway sister—the good-at-everything Janaki, the Janaki who played the veena like a goddess, Janaki the Brahmin girl who made them the topic of national dailies—was coming back. Why?

Mallika remembers journalists at the door the morning after Janaki left. That day of a hundred flashbulbs. How quickly the news had spread. How rapidly their lives became fodder for speculation and tabloid sensationalism. Names of shame on a million tongues. A cobra in full-hooded sway the moment the basket lid was lifted. All the way from the Brahmin agraharam where the mamis in their nine-yard cotton lengths wove fictions around the original incident, and right down to the corner shop next to Mahalaxmi Talkies that sold bananas and cigarettes. A scandal even autorickshaw drivers and construction workers chewed on and spat out in all its betel-nut redness, rude and stark on the nearby white wall. That same Janaki, she who was responsible for a deep burn scar the size of a fifty-paise coin in the middle of Appa's palm and a sulphurous smudge on their souls, was coming back.

Janaki still cannot write a straight line, Mallika thought and smiled. Even those few lines went slanting down the bleached blue paper, as though the loopy script of the language were pulling the sentences into a slow and inevitable spiral to the edge. Appa had bought her so many writing exercise books, hoping that her hand would eventually improve, and still the moment Janaki put pen to a blank sheet of paper, something instinctively changed in the spirit of her hand. Her fingers became giddy with the sense of expanse, and the pen danced free from lines and structures.

Janaki had cut loose in her mind long before she actually left the agraharam.

And that other letter, the goodbye-girl one, left between Leo Coffee packets in the kitchen cabinet ten years ago (her choice of place a perfect example of her innate ingenuity), had had the same mocking exuberance about it. You had to follow the lines on the page as they dipped, and curved, and then rose again in what was the shortest proclamation of liberty Mallika had ever read.

THE ELEVATOR DOORS have parted. Down the hallway Mallika hears Gopalan, the security guard, and the buzzy static of his walkie-talkie.

"All okay, madam?"

"Yes, fine, Gopalan," she says, touching her employee identification tag. "I didn't realize it was so late. What time is it?" she asks casually, as though the elevator had only just brought her down.

Gopalan points his torchlight beam directly onto his wristwatch dial. "Six fifteen, madam."

Mallika begins to walk down the corridor to the security booth, where she surrenders her tag and signs out the time she leaves the building. Gopalan follows a step behind her. In the well-lit foyer she can see a few people hurriedly disappearing down the basement stairs to the auditorium.

"Is there some function, Gopalan?"

"Yes, madam. I will give you the information in one second. They are showing American pictures." He takes her badge and turns the sign-out sheet so that it faces her. "Mallika Venkatakrishnan." It takes up the whole column.

Janaki Asgar, she says to herself, feeling the vowels roll. Ja-na-ki As-gar.

"You are having no interest in American cinema, madam?" Gopalan asks as he produces a brochure from under the desk.

"No, Gopalan, I don't see too many pictures. No American, no Tamil," Mallika replies, and for a moment Mrs. Emanuel appears before her eyes. "Nothing can surpass the pleasure of a good book!" Mrs. Emanuel says, holding a copy of *Wuthering Heights*. "Why watch, when you can imagine?" We all have our own secret escapes, Mallika thinks. Hers was English literature. Janaki loved the cinema. Stasis and movement. Is that why it all happened? Was it in Janaki's nature?

Mallika glances over the program. "USIS (Madras) presents Feminism and Film: The New Women of America," followed by a list of names:

Annie Hall
Norma Rae
Julia
Frances
Silkwood
Janaki Doesn't Live Here Anymore...

"Can I ask one thing, madam?" Gopalan is intent on making conversation.

"Yes, Gopalan?" Mallika replies, trying to look attentive. It is getting very dark outside; the buses will be packed.

"What is it, ma, this craze for America? From two in the morning peoples are queuing for visa, you know?" he says, his voice matching the incredulity in his expression. "Is it really very fine country?"

Mallika knows about the queues that wind around the immigration and visa section of the building. They begin at the tip of the flyover and run along the compound wall of Church Park Convent. Everybody, she has heard, arrives with mats and pillows and Thermos bottles filled with chai and coffee. Two in the morning, and a community evolves on the footpath of Mount Road. She has only met students, but she knows that all visa applicants are thrown together in the draw for interviews. And an interview was no guarantee of a ticket to the golden shores of the USA. Only the screening officer has the power to make that a possibility. The expatriate god from the land of milk and honey.

"If I can get a visa, I have vowed to shave my head in Tirupati temple," she recalls a student saying with a chaste glimmer of hope in his eyes. "I am only hoping that it is not that African lady officer for my interview. She is the strictest, no?" Only a rubber stamp between him, his hair and his dreams. The black American visa officer, his moody Statue of Liberty.

And there are other dreams in that lineup, Mallika knows. There are brides waiting to be united with their husbands. Computer professionals looking to snatch H-1s for contracts in Silicon Valley. The notorious Burma Bazaar smugglers hoping for import-export, multiple-entry visas. Even pouring rain does not deter them. They curse and sing and spit and chat as they wait with visions of a distant paradise. And when the gates open at eight, there is a mad scramble for tokens. A free-for-all push and grab for the small copper coins with the engraved bald eagle spreading its wings in welcome. The chance of an interview. The Promised Land almost within reach.

As was only to be expected in any room saturated with mixed emotions and high blood pressure, there were also breakdowns and cathartic screams. Men and women collapsed with "Ammadi, oh, please," and passed out when their application was turned down. Ambulance sirens could sometimes be heard on the northern side of the building. From her office window, Mallika had seen paramedics carrying away people with freshly crushed dreams.

"You are not interested in settling in America, madam?" Gopalan asks, tapping his pencil on the desk and into her thoughts.

"I don't know, Gopalan," Mallika replies, irritation creeping into her tone. "I don't think so. But I know people have their own motivations." She is ready to end the conversation. "Can I keep this program?"

"Sure, sure," Gopalan blusters, a man now unsure if he has crossed the line into familiarity. "Madam has no umbrella?"

he says, relieved that she has changed the subject. "Supermazha is on the way," he says, his "zha" on an expectant curve. He must be from Kerala, she thinks. "Heavy rains, looks like. See the clouds!" Gopalan grins.

For a twenty-six-year-old I get called madam a lot.

"Good night, Gopalan." Mallika pushes her glasses firmly back on her nose and lets herself out through the rotating gate.

Does he know I am Janaki Asgar's sister?

"Good night, madam!"

MALLIKA TRIES hailing an autorickshaw on Cathedral Road. The driver demands ten rupees over the meter. That's of course assuming the meter is not doctored to jump twenty paise every three seconds. Brahmin frugality prevails. She resolves to walk home.

"Why seeing for ten rupees, madam? I will dropping you to house doorstep! Nobody is coming for this climate!" The rheumy eyes of the driver, and the bidi dangling from the corner of his cracked, bulbous lips, make her quicken her step. "Find someone else."

He's not the type to take no for an answer and trails her for a furlong, his voice loud over the humming engine. "Eight rupees, final. Come, na, come, come, nati, go!"

She doesn't look back.

The first drop lands on her nose as she's passing the gates of Stella Maris College. Then the asoka trees in the college compound, tall and gangly, begin to sway like giraffes in lengthy leaf skirts, and a molten yellowness lights up the dark clouds from behind. By the time she reaches the Music Academy the drops turn into long, endless threads of water and come down with great force.

And then there's nowhere to hide.

When she ducks into the little thatched coconut palm shelter between the walls of the Music Academy and Taj Mahal Tea Stall, she's sure there's not a dry spot in the whole city. She manages to keep her hair from getting wet by pulling her sari pullo over her head like a scarf, but the rest of her body is soaked, with her sari clinging to her thighs. Even after all these years she is never really prepared for these sudden downpours, the way they bring everything to a stop, muddling directions and changing destinies.

There was nothing like this in Sripuram. But here, in this sprawling concrete capital, hot, humid afternoons slowly churn the sky as the dust rolls and whirls on the busy inner-city highways. In the intense glare of the sun, if you tuned out the sound of the traffic, you could hear the quiet brewing, the early signals of a storm. Sitting in her office, with the hum of the air conditioner and the UV tint on her windows, she sometimes felt the heat layering the glass. If she peered over the window from her corner of the building, she could see little waves of dust suspended in the air, spinning and moving, and a hazy, blistering carpet of torpor right above them. By evening, the colour of the sky would turn a deeper mauve and the clouds would move in, ready to wail as at a funeral. And then, without a touch of restraint, the wet, sloshy requiem would begin. But that afternoon she had not noticed the storm gathering outside her office window.

Mallika bunches up her sari around her knees and wrings the pleats. She looks around the little thatched shelter and discovers that it is actually a roadside temple for Vinayaka, the elephant god of good beginnings. A few fresh marigold garlands adorn his tar-black trunk, and the small statue glistens with the spray of raindrops. She moves into the far corner of the shelter and rests against the wall. Rain lashes the city, a grey screen of water accompanied by an incessant roll of thunder.

In the adjacent tea stall business is brisk, packed with men—mostly labourers from the nearby construction tenements—slurping hot, steamy chai and coffee. They huddle beside the hot water boiler, listening to film songs from a smoke-stained loudspeaker. The smell of deep-fried masala vadai—pungent turmeric and ground Bengal gram sizzling in cheap, reused oil—filters through the rain screen, and Mallika quickly covers her nose. She closes her eyes.

"Next in *Thaen Kinnam,* your bowl of sweet music..."
That was Janaki's favourite radio program.

On Friday evenings Janaki made sure all the housework was done by seven thirty, and around eight she would sneak into Mallika's room and say, "I know you are doing your homework, but I'll sit near the window and listen to the radio, sariya?" And while Mallika grappled with the many mysteries of algebra, Janaki sailed away on a flotilla of film music. She even sent in her own request to All India Radio, Madras, and they played her song. Janaki couldn't contain herself when she heard the host announce her name with a list of others.

"V. Janaki from Sripuram! My name was the last one, too!" She laughed in happiness. "I wonder if Revathi heard my name? Oh, I only hope she was listening! I told her to..."
Then she began singing with the radio.

Although Janaki's voice did not match the miracle of her hands on the veena, she still enjoyed her escape into film music. She lip-synched with the radio and performed small dance steps, just like the heroines in Tamil films.

When Appa was away in Madras for the weekend, she undid her plait and brushed it till it shone like a dark river in the noon sun. Letting her hair hang loose, she pulled out Amma's purple and gold border sari from the top shelf of the Godrej cupboard and draped it around her without bothering to wear a bra or a blouse. She dipped the middle finger of her right hand into the small rose box of kungumam and circled a huge red bottu in the middle of her forehead. Descending the stairs, she looked possessed by a divine, inner peace.

She pulled out the *jamakalam* from the shelf in the puja room and spread it on the floor of the hall. She placed the veena right in the middle of the paisley-bordered orange rug. After she was certain she had tuned the strings to the right pitch, she began her alaapana. With her eyes half closed, her hair falling onto her shoulders in lush black cascades and her bottu flaming bright and magnetic, she took on an unearthly incandescence. She was a spirit, an enchanting Mohini, from another world.

And then a slow, undulating mellowness filled the air, and her plaintive raga began pleading with the gods in heaven.

"SHE HAS...WHAT?" Appa had whispered on hearing the news of Janaki's betrayal. Mallika can still hear the horror of that whisper, the pain in his voice like the sound made when you stretch the blowing edge of a balloon as air escapes from it. She remembers his slow slump into the chair, a half-stifled sigh caught in his throat, his hands stretched out, his palms upturned, her father-mother guru, Mr. Venkatakrishnan, Assistant Manager, Indian Overseas Bank, City Market Branch, Sripuram-18—suddenly pale. He resembled a man who was either donating blood or had just slashed his wrists.

He sat in his chair for hours without moving, his eyes closed and his lips softly chanting *Sai Narayaneeyam*. He repeated his petition to Lord Vishnu again and again, asking protection in that hour of shame. Then he opened his eyes and looked up at her, his gaze direct and emotionless. "I will apply for transfer to Madras tomorrow. You will finish your studies there," he said, with the absent-minded casualness of a man reading a newspaper headline loudly to himself. He stood up, lifted the chair off the floor and set it firmly against the wall, right below Amma's framed photograph. "Kamakshi!" he cried, calling out to his wife whose name he had not uttered since the day she died.

But Amma, who was tongue-tied for the better part of her life with him, remained consistent and did not come to his rescue. Then he took determined strides towards the puja room and returned with a copper tray, camphor lit and burning at its centre. She can still smell the sick, dense, medicinal odour of that one karmic moment.

He stood in front of her. She remained still, her eyes on the cement floor. And then, before she could fully comprehend what was happening around her, in one fleeting and definite move, he transferred the small glowing ball of fire from the tray onto the palm of his right hand.

"Look at me!" he said with a quiet authority. His eyes were bloodshot when she raised her gaze to meet his. In the soft glow of burning camphor he looked like a tiger, mystical and feverish. "I want you to swear that you will never be in contact with your sister again." Without giving her a chance to respond, he took her right hand into his left, lifted it above the flame and brought it down on the charred blackness of his palm. She felt the icy singe of heat below her ring, and then the fumes curled and died in the air. He released her hand and let it drop. Then he walked into his room and carefully shut the door behind him.

Mallika sat in the darkness of the kitchen, unable to cry and too shocked to move. She sat there expecting him to step out for his dinner, or to use the bathroom, but the door remained shut. The burning sensation under her finger worsened, but she could not bring herself to look for the tube of antiseptic. Around midnight the light in his room went out, and the whole house was quiet, still. A morgue, and a museum. She remembers that silence.

But that was in another place. Not here. Ten years ago.

This was not the original scene of the crime. So, why was the criminal returning here?

THE VOICE COMES to her from a distance. *"Yakko?"* it softly reverberates before it fully registers. When Mallika opens her eyes, she hears the rain, still relentless, but its force somewhat diminished. It might not be long before it completely stops. The boy is around twelve, wearing khaki shorts and a tundu around his torso. He is holding a glass of steaming tea in his hand and is offering it to her. "Saar sent this for you," he says, jerking his head in the direction of the tea stall. Mallika looks up, and she sees the considerate saar behind the cash counter smile and wave to her. Did he really expect her to wave back?

"How much?" she asks the boy, beginning to open her purse for some change.

"Free because of rain!" he replies grandly, and smiles, revealing even gaps between his front teeth. She pulls out a two-rupee note and gives it to him.

"This is for you, then," she says, taking the steaming glass from his hands, suddenly craving its warmth. He quickly pockets the money.

"I'll return the glass, tell saar." He nods and runs away.

Listening to the rain she relishes the dense, hot sweetness of tea and milk on her tongue. She feels the slow fuzziness as it spreads and travels down her throat. Divine. She runs her gaze over her surroundings once again.

The Vinayaka statue is wet and washed many times over, but right beside it, hidden from the road, she now notices a long-abandoned One Way arrow sign pointing towards the sky. "Yes," she thinks, "there is only that after this."

Rajiv Gandhi beams from a poster plastered on the wall. "He is the only Prime Minister for India," Youth Congress claims. "Re-elect him!" Another second-chance seeker. Someone has hand-etched two chunnambu-paste earrings on either side of the face of the country's only future. A buffalo, its tail swatting the rain puddles, sits right outside the shelter completely oblivious to the car horns and the cussing of pedestrians walking past.

Mallika takes another sip and looks at her wrist. The watch, she remembers, is on her desk at home, ticking away forgotten time. It has been a day of that. A rummage sale of memory. There is no way she will find a bus or autorickshaw now. The rain has turned to a drizzle, but the roads are clogged with water. Cars and trucks are lined up as far as her eyes can see, and a few cyclists are wading through a knee-deep river of floating garbage and orphaned footwear.

"*Bejaar pudicha maẓhai!* And now this stupid buffalo!" someone curses as they cross the puddle in front of the shelter.

Mallika finishes her tea and plots her route.

She will circle Alwarpet and get to Adyar Gate. If she can hire an autorickshaw from there, she will; if not, she will continue her walk down St. Mary's Road towards her apartment. She knows she will not be alone in the dark; others will be taking the same measures to get home. Waiting for a bus at this hour, and under these circumstances, would be foolish. Like wishing for mangoes in winter.

Her journey all mapped out, Mallika returns the glass and thanks the tea-stall man. Then, with her handbag securely clutched under her left arm, she steps into the flood, having already imagined the worst.

THE VEENA FLOATS like a gondola on rainwater. It rides the waves, tosses and turns, tosses and turns. When Mallika reaches out, it slips from her hands. She can see the eyes on the lion head, two tiny red beads raging, mocking, as she trips and falls and grabs only water. The veena circles the walls of San Thome church, stopping the congregation in mid-mass, and someone says, "*Aiyyo paavam,* so sad." Then they move away from her, as they would from a madwoman.

She tries to shout, flailing her arms, "Stop it! Catch it!" but the words don't form. That's when the lion head turns around and blows fire in her direction.

"Bring me the kerosene can!" Appa says. He pours all of it over the veena and strikes a match. It doesn't burn. Gayatri Chitti starts to laugh and stubs her cigarette in the ashtray (where did that come from?). "You are so pathetic," she says. "Even your kerosene is impotent!"

Her laughter echoes down the hallway, banging against the walls and entering the quiet stacks of USIS library, where everybody looks up from the books on their desks. "Sing 'Row, Row, Row Your Boat'..." they chorus in a monotone. And the nursery rhyme is played again and again on the internal audio system, "You are listening to a veena recital by V. Janaki," and the sound surrounds her, her head twisting in a whirlpool of random notes and images, and the air filling with just one strum, a row, row, rowing...

The slap stings her face. She misses the bloodthirsty mosquito, and her cheek burns with the tinge of rude awakening.

What time is it?

The ceiling fan has stopped spinning. She can hear the slow, constant trickle of rainwater trailing off the sides of the window and into the balcony drain. She reaches for her wristwatch on the bedside table and presses the radium screw. 3:45 AM.

Power failure.

She rises from the bed and unhooks the chimney lamp hanging from a nail beside the cupboard. She locates the box of matches on the ledge of the door and raises the wick to meet the burning stick. Everything is quiet except for the occasional swishing of the coconut palms outside the window. The rain has finally stopped, and that damp chill of the aftermath is suspended in the air. Mosquitoes couldn't be happier.

Mallika finds the packet of insect-repellent coils in the bathroom, under the sink, and decides to leave it lit in the corridor, right outside the bathroom door. That way the fumes will not be too strong in the bedroom, and she will be able to sleep without coughing herself to death. She places the chimney lamp on her writing desk and sits on the bed, willing the power to be restored. She sits reclining against the bedpost and listens to swamp-water frogs gurgle and croak from fresh pothole ponds, and the crickets buzz and hiss outside the window. The blades of the fan have not moved an inch in fifteen minutes.

Restless once again, she gets up and looks out the window. No lights are on in any of the houses. It is a full power cut. God only knows when the men from the electricity board will have it restored.

Then, before she can stop herself, she walks to the Godrej steel cupboard and opens it. She carries the Nalli Silks cardboard box to the writing desk. It's still there—that bundle of letters and photographs—wrapped and knotted in the parrot green handkerchief. The letter she is looking for is the last one under the pile. Mallika knows exactly where it is. She stares at the melon-coloured envelope and reads the blurred, smudged letters looping in red ink. Five more days and she will meet the author of that turning point in all their lives.

Thangame, my precious. Fading red on bleached melon. History written and placed between coffee packets. Reread and folded into four, more than a million times. Did other families have such letters? Such creased, inexorable paper-pulp ghosts? In the steady glow of the chimney lamp, Mallika begins to read Janaki's manifesto of freedom one more time:

Thangame,
    This is not my suicide note. Dying is too easy. Living is the real challenge.

I won't ask you to forgive me. There is nothing to forgive. Do well in your studies. Find your own happiness. Wish me well. Akka.

And yet, those four lines would change their lives overnight, making them fugitives, forever fleeing one terrible memory. It was a truly selfish trade-off, Mallika had always maintained after that. Janaki had found her space, and they were caught, endlessly, in the arabesques of gossip and notoriety.

But that was in another place. Not here.

Krithi

An elaborate exploration of a
raga through a composition
Sa-Ri-Ga-Ma-Pa-Da-Ni

Wнere do middle-class, Tamil Brahmin girls go when they turn eighteen?

Nowhere, usually.

By the time I was nineteen I had been exhibited for marriage to nearly a dozen men, from Vathalagundu to Palakadu—shipping clerks, tea-estate accountants, LIC agents, even a mathematics teacher from Dubai—all of whom had one thing in common: arrogance with a price tag. Men who came with their mothers and heard me play a short alaapana on the veena. They gorged the vadais and sweetmeats I had spent the whole afternoon preparing with my own hands and sent word two days later, demanding motorcycles and Fiat cars. Men with a monthly salary of no more than two thousand five hundred rupees.

"If she was educated, it would have been okay, you know," the last mami said. "These days two incomes is a must. And she is the one who will enjoy the ride!" Her son, a thirty-nine-year-old shipping clerk in Pondicherry, just sat there and smiled into vacant space as though he were attending a puppet show, his head rocking to and fro.

And if the hauteur was low, and the quoted dowry reasonable, then the mothers, in their sanctimonious silks, ended up not liking me. One of the mamis, I still recall, who turned out to be a violinist herself, summed up my alaapana as "unbearable." She knew I had deliberately chosen a prelude in Raga Raghupriya, a composition with huge, gaping intervals that was renowned for clearing out an auditorium in no time. It worked like a charm once again that evening. She left in a huff to catch the bus to Tiruvannamalai, her son and husband rushing to catch up with her, reminding me of the stray dogs that trailed me sometimes on the way back from the milk depot.

But the thrill of such minor victories wore off quickly. It diminished with every telegram from Madras. Gayatri Chitti's cryptic, cutting efforts to get me out of the way through matrimony. Every time I answered the door and initialled the delivery sheet clipped to a brown wooden board held up impatiently by the postman, my writing spiralled, and my heart rate dipped. I could feel something resembling a metal pin that pierced as it moved all around my chest, slowly killing my spirit, like when there is a power failure and the TV screen suddenly pulls itself into a silver, soundless pall. Chitti's telegrams got shorter and shorter as the pressure built up, two years and counting. One telegram just said, "Get ready!", making me feel like the Meals Served! flapboard that vegetarian restaurants put out around noon, right in the middle of the busy footpaths of the Sripuram main roads.

I was reminded of my fate at least twice a month for four

and a half years. Nineteen to twenty-three-and-a-half. The lines of my auspicious right-hand palm stood fixed between the back well and the temple bell. A boundary decided by others even before I was born. That was the nowhere that happened to middle-class Tamil Brahmin girls when they turned eighteen.

Mine was not a unique fate. And yet it turned out to be.

I WAS NAMED after the wife of King Rama. My father in the myth was King Janaka, and hence the assumed logic of my name, Janak-i. In that story, my namesake, the woman who was the extension of her father's name, walked through fire to prove her purity to her husband. She pushed the concept of obedience to what some would consider ludicrous limits. Deluded, in epic proportions. My father, in the here and now, Mr. Venkatakrishnan, just thought I would follow through. Docile. A woman who could only acquiesce and endure.

I did, too. For as long as was humanly possible. And then one early dawn I was abducted by the voice of my spirit. I wrapped myself in my favourite purple silk sari, hid a little note between the coffee packets and took an autorickshaw out of mythology.

Just like that.

And it was mercurial, my journey from a nobody to news of the day. Make that three days. Splashed across the newspapers in bold letters; an incident that pulled together people from Kashmir to Kanyakumari, as it was when some holy man was shot and killed during prayers, or an Indian politician was arrested on corruption charges and the government collapsed. I was neither.

But I knew this much: being a saint eventually kills you (bullet or no bullet). Then again, why be modest about it? You could say I made history. With just one desperate deed I put Sri Om Shanti Brahmin's Colony, Sripuram, on the Indian map.

Just like that.

I was their first child. My mother had miscarried twice in three years before I arrived. My aunt, Gayatri Chitti, would always remind me of that inauspicious moment right into my adolescence. "Kamu nearly died giving birth to you!" she would say, for no reason at all, right in the middle of *I Love Lucy* or when Mallika and Appa were playing chess in the hall. "The poor girl had jaundice in her eighth month."

She would repeat this within my hearing every time she was visiting from Madras, like a dread-filled mantra. I think it did have an effect. Although I can't prove it for sure, I believed it was something Gayatri Chitti had always secretly wished had happened. It was a mantra of malice, and the source of its power was repetition. The twisted sister of sympathy. I had just turned thirteen when Amma was killed in a bus accident.

There is a small rose-coloured plastic case right below Amma's garlanded picture in the hall. The box always has a small dot of powdered vermilion and a stripe of *chandanam* to accentuate it. A constant whiff of sandalwood and incense permeates that corner of the house. Cloyingly sweet and desperately trying to hide the bitterness that she took with her to her transit grave.

Pretend and it will not exist: rule number one in the Brahmin woman's survival guide. If I didn't know better, I'd say my mother wrote that rule. But I changed it to serve my purposes: imagine and it will all exist.

I know that plastic box is still there, on that little wooden shelf, right next to the copy of *Sai Narayaneeyam*, although I have not seen it for more than ten years. That box contains Amma's toe ring. She was on her way home from the SOSBC Cultural Tour of Nearby Temples when the bus veered off the road, hit the side pillar of the bridge it would never cross and turned over, and the front section burst into flames. "Brake failure, you see," the investigating police officer told the shocked families. Eight people were killed. Amma would have burned to death quickly, we were told, as she was sitting right behind the driver. "Minimal pain," they added, making it sound like a consolation prize. Forensics determined that the toe ring belonged to Amma as it had the letters KV engraved inside it. Kamakshi Venkatakrishnan. My mother had taken her craze for initialling new stainless-steel utensils one step further. Her identity, finally, rose from the ashes. But it was also her goodbye from the edge. She was gone.

It was the beginning of the end for me.

"JANAKI!"

Appa called out to me one Sunday evening. It was the second week after Amma's death. I was sitting on the cold cement floor in the hall and weaving a mallippoo and violet garland for Amma's newly framed picture. Gayatri Chitti had decided to stay back till the fortieth day ceremony.

"*Varen,* 'pa."

I put the half-finished garland on the arati tray, wiped my damp hands on the edge of my dhavani and ran to the veranda.

It was close to sunset, and the rays were mellow around the temple bell.

The crows were lined up on the telegraph wires and would fly away soon after their closing chorus to the day.

Outside, Mallika was playing pandi all by herself, hopping and landing on a flat stone chip, her airplane hurriedly drawn on the morning kolam. There was no one on the street, as everyone was in front of the TV watching *Pilot Premnath*. "Who is the black sheep?" I heard the soundtrack boom at different levels of volume.

"Appa?" I said, knitting my fingers, and my mind racing through a hundred things that I could have done wrong for which I was about to be admonished. I knew it was serious when he called out to me in that tone of voice.

I was not doing well in school. In the last progress report, under the Remarks column, my class teacher had written, *Needs coaching in almost all subjects except music.* Appa had blamed it all on Amma. "You are the one who distracts her!" he hollered. "When you are in front of Vishnu during the temple tour, ask him why he blessed you with a good-for-nothing daughter like her!" That night, after Appa was fast asleep, Amma came to my bedside and said, "Next term don't count on my support." She was right. There was no next term for her.

But things were beginning to turn around at school. I had made arrangements to meet Revathi for two hours every evening for homework. We increased it to three hours for the midterm test. I was also working hard on my handwriting so that the teacher could read my answers clearly. While my memory for historical dates and events was still a problem, I was making good progress in math and biology. I was convinced Appa would be surprised by my marks this term. It would be a pleasant surprise. Did the teacher telephone him at work?

No, it had to be my listening to film songs on the transistor last night. It was forbidden, and I should not have taken such an illicit risk. But how could he have heard that? It was so low even I had to strain my ears to catch every word. It hadn't been all that late either, just eight fifteen. Did Gayatri Chitti say something?

What could it be? Mallika must have told him about my climbing the mango tree in the school playground yesterday. But Revathi had also climbed the tree with me, and when we came down we shared all the mangoes equally. Mallika had eaten two ripe ones herself. If she was a snitch, then it was decided: she was out of the gang. I would warn the other girls to keep away from her.

I stared at Mallika, believing that if she had really told Appa my gaze would make her turn around and look at me, and in that moment I would know that she was a traitor. But Mallika hopped around in her own world and did not once look my way. I began to feel a dull ball of fear form in my stomach, and the sound of my heart echoed in my ears like a mridangam, the percussion reaching a frenzied pitch and ready to burst my eardrums. What had I done?

APPA WAS STANDING at the far corner of the veranda with his back to me.

Gayatri Chitti was sitting on the parapet reading *Kumudam* magazine in the evening light. Her navy blue cotton sari made her look darker than she actually was. Amma was fairer.

"*Va*, Janaki. Sit next to me," Chitti said, and made space for me next to her on the parapet. Then she turned towards Appa. "She's here now. Talk to her." Her arms circled my shoulder.

Appa walked to the single cane chair on the veranda. He picked up his glasses, which were lying on the floor on top of some bank files, and wiped them with the edge of his veshti. He squinted a few times, put on his glasses and artificially cleared his throat.

"Somebody has got to take on Amma's responsibilities," he said. "Gayatri cannot stay here forever."

Chitti sighed on cue, significantly, like a woman finally lowering a heavy sack of rice. "*Eashwara,*" she said, with instant piety, although she had been lost in the scandals and gossip of a film magazine just a few moments ago. She curled up the magazine like a baton in her fist and rubbed her cleavage, which creased her starched sari. She looked heavenward and made three short clucks with her tongue, "Tchu, tchu, tchu," calling out to a celestial dog visible only to her.

"How can I stay?" she said, letting the question hang in the air, as though she knew it meant something more.

"Gayatri will of course come over often," Appa added a bit too quickly.

"Oh, yes, yes," Chitti gushed. "No need to remind me. I will as much as possible." She rolled her plaited hair into a tight knot on her head. I smelled the sweat mingled with Pond's talcum powder from under her armpits and moved a few inches along the parapet. She reached out and pulled me closer.

"You will take Amma's place, Janaki!" Appa announced with all the benevolence of a king donating a vast acreage of land to some poor farmer in a stage play.

I didn't understand what he was telling me.

He added, "You can still go to veena class if you want."

Still go?

Then it hit me. I was being pulled out of school. Needs coaching in almost all subjects except stupidity. "But I am improving in biology!" I screamed, and Mallika came running to the steps of the veranda.

"I have already spoken to your principal," Appa continued, paying no attention to the tears that were running down my face. "He agreed that it is the best decision." He did not look at me directly. His words were addressed to the pink bougainvillea bush about five yards to my left.

"What about Mallika? She will be alone in school..." I was trembling and tried to shake off Chitti's hand from my shoulder. It only made her tighten her hold. "This is not fair!" I sputtered between sobs.

I knew that it would make no difference. They let me cry.

"You are so good in veena class," Chitti said after a few silent minutes. "And I will show you how to do all the house chores before I leave for Madras."

Then she let go of my shoulder. She bent to pick up the coffee dabra that was on the floor, tucked slightly under Appa's chair, and the pleats of her sari grazed against his leg. His eyes stayed with her as she stretched lethargically. "*Eash-wara!* My body is so sore." She sauntered towards the hall. Before stepping in, she turned around and presented her profile to Appa.

"Will you be taking your bath now?" Her voice was a blend of impatience and ennui. Their eyes locked for a brief moment, and a brief half smile lit Chitti's face.

A few minutes after her directive, Appa got up from his chair and walked to the back of the house without glancing at me. Within seconds I heard the jerky squeals of the pulley as the metal bucket banged against the cement of the well and hit the surface of the water with a thudding splash.

Amma's nightly snivels behind the washing stone near the well! Why she had been crying for so many years! It was then that I made the connection. The sound of that splash made me see things for what they really were! Suddenly, it all made sense: Appa's monthly trips to Madras on the pretext of bank work; Amma's sullen mood when Chitti visited Sripuram during festivals; all the arguments when Appa tried to get Chitti her clerical job at the Madras head office . . . and now, Chitti's offer to stay in Sripuram and help.

Moments of clarity, like moments of chaos, come without warning. I joined all the dots of past incidents and saw my dead mother's face stare back at me. I saw that look in her averted gaze, the same, sorry, silent curve of her mouth, once again.

She had known all along!

And there was nothing she could do except cry into her sari pullo. What else could she have done? Announce to the world that her widowed sister was carrying on with *her* husband?

"Don't cry, Akka," Mallika said as she crept up to my side and slowly took my hand. "I will bring you mangoes from school every day. I promise." She slapped my palm gently and pinched the stretched centre to seal her vow. "*Satyam.*"

She snuggled beside me on the parapet—Mallika, my little sister, who was only six—and began to sing:

Row, row, row your boat,
Gently down the stream,
Merrily, merrily, merrily, merrily,
Life is but a dream.

"**B**RAHMIN GIRL in the Ring, Sa–Ri–Ga–Ma!" That's how *Cine-Dust* magazine phrased their highlight of the month (at least they alluded to my music training), but the Tamil newspapers and gossip weeklies concentrated exclusively on my caste. Their editorials debating what kind of message my marrying an already-married *Muslim* (that word always italicized) film star sent out to young, impressionable Tamil girls. Brahmin or not. Their concern was suddenly secular and inclusive. "National Disintegration?" A few learned Brahmin university professors from Calcutta and Bangalore bellowed in op-ed pages of the country's national dailies.

And the film magazines had their own versions of the whole affair.

Asgar made sure that I did not see the clippings file until I was prepared to see the humour in them. "Only when you are ready to laugh at the nonsense," he said, when we honeymooned on his film set in Ooty.

Later, after I had moved into the bungalow on Napean Sea Road in Bombay, after I had settled into my new life and

the reality of having everything done for me, six months after
the initial media blitz had died, it was Zubeida, Asgar's first
wife, who came by with the file one evening and said, "Want
to sit down and laugh together?"

I have that file under my saris in the wardrobe.

And every so often I read the clippings again. After Kabir
and Neelam, my twins, are in bed, and Asgar has called from
Madh Island to say that wrap-up is still a few hours away,
after the servants have retired to their quarters and the security change has taken place, then, in an act that could only
be described as perverse and masochistic, I sit on my bed
and read the clippings from *La Cinema*, *BollywoodNow*, *Star-
Light* and *CineVista*. Tonight is such a night, and I am exca-
vating my past so that I am ready for my first mainstream
interview since I married Asgar. It was his idea: "What's
there to hide?" he said, when I told him about the journalist
and her insistence. "Shame is for those who have a need for
it! Do it, Janu." So, I am researching my past, verbatim, in
other voices. Everything these days begins with "If I could
return to that time. . ." As if I was making a list of the agraharam colony's not so happy endings. For instance, why is
Kamala's story missing? What they all did—the very people she trusted to look after her well-being—and how they
never came to her defence when things fell apart? It would
make a nice sidebar, and here's a good caption: "Kamala:
Another Story from Nowhere." My state of mind paints
everything in the colour of silences. It is the unnatural silence
of hospitals where wheeled stretchers and saline drip hold-
ers sleep in the corridors for a few hours, the empty silence
of concrete buildings with small, unreachable windows in
the corners.

The glossies get one thing right: I now live my life in Technicolor.

Although the stories all have imaginative headlines, I have my own shorthand for those four chapters of commercial sleaze: (1) pregnancy, (2) pregnancy and poverty, (3) poverty and music (the "Brahmin Girl in the Ring" one) and (4) blackmail.

It is the same photograph in all of them—the one Asgar and I posed for after the private ceremony in Madras—before boarding the plane for Ooty. Two of them (in-house art-director brilliance, no doubt) zoom in on my face, blurring it into a distorted, lunatic smile. All four begin with the same facts from the press release put out by Asgar's PR manager—the full consent of Zubeida, my Iyer Brahmin caste and my Tamil Sripuram upbringing—and then dive into their own brand of tabloid muck. The *CineVista* (blackmail) story, by one "CineVista" Vasu (his magazine name worn like a badge of honour), also has a photo of our house in the agraharam, with a crude superimposed arrow pointing to the gate. But it is no piece of investigative journalism. The long slogan under it dispels any such misunderstanding: "House of Desire!" it exclaims. "She played the veena here!"

Yes, I think to myself, whenever I read that particular "scoop" again, talking back to it and its writer, and still, after all these years, unable to explain why I feel the need for such an unnecessary defence. Let's get down and dirty, Mr. Vasu. Let's just...

And she also washed endless dishes there. I feel that other voice within me. I sense it unwind and loop, like my handwriting.

And she cooked for three adults there, and she drew oceans of water in a metal bucket from the well there—go see for yourself, that well must still be there, at the back of the house. And Mr. Vasu, while you're snooping for scoops, you must visit that outhouse near the gate. She scrubbed that latrine with bleach every other day. Look in, please.

That was also the house where she learned about the replaceability of women. Amma out, Gayatri in. Amma out, Janaki in. Janaki out, Mallika in. And, yes, it's also where she played the veena for the gods with her friends Kamala and Revathi, and it was there that she listened to film songs on the roof terrace. You'll need more arrows, so call the art department and alert them.

See that kolam in front of the gate in your news photo? She drew that herself, the morning before she left for good. It was drawn in haste that day, but if you had looked closely you would have noticed that it was a kolam of a lotus opening up to the early rays of the sun. That was a hurried, symbolic thanks to her friend Kamala, the only one who understood. Do you know Kamala's story? Do you know how many such lotuses, kamalams, had opened up to such fireless suns during her adolescence? And why did she still do it? Can you count the times? Imagine the hopelessness of opening up to a sterile sun. She remembers every single kolam even after so long. It was one of the best points of her otherwise eventless day.

But who cares?

That's not the kind of dirt you were looking for now, were you, Mr. Vasu?

To really understand what it means, to grasp the symbolism of it all, you have to go back to the beginnings of the original pattern. You have to live the lives of Amma, Appa, Chitti, Mallika, Kamala and every other life that touched mine, and was affected by mine. You have to see them through me, to see me for who I really am.

Or was.

Nothing even remotely engrossing as blackmail in the House of Desire.

You have to take an ordinary, listless journey and be prepared to map the arid landscape of nowhere—the place that happened to girls like me and Kamala when they turned eighteen. Not very thrilling, let me assure you. Yes, you have to enter into that nothing spectacular, nothing remarkable, falling-into-erasure-without-even-realizing-it life, which is not, you might conclude in the final analysis, really worth writing about. Do you really want to bother? It won't sell.

SA

My market training began on a blistering, muggy day.

Mallika had been shuffled off to school after she had thrown a tantrum insisting that I go with her. "Whom will I have lunch with?" she cried. Appa just stood there and said nothing.

Chitti took control. "Akka will just stay home," she said. "No school for her now."

After Mallika had been coaxed to pillion with Appa on the scooter, and they rode off in a cloud of red dust, Chitti turned around to me and asked, "Where did Kamu keep her saris?"

"In the Godrej cupboard, upstairs," I replied.

"I'd like to take a look before we go to the market."

She chose the green cotton-silk *chinalpattu*—one of Amma's more expensive saris—and set it aside. Then she pulled out an older, printed nylex from the pile, spread it across the floor and began transferring all the other saris from the cupboard. "You are too young for saris," she said, tying them into a bundle. "You have a few more years in the dhavani. I'll distribute these to some poor widows in Madras." She carried the bundle to the other room and placed it beside her suitcase. "This way I will remember to take it with me."

A week later, after she had departed for Madras, and after I had been inducted into the nothingness that would become my life, I would discover that Gayatri Chitti, under all that bitterness and hunger for power, did have a heart. A drawn, pinched one, but still a heart. She had left behind two of Amma's most cherished saris on the upper shelf of the cupboard.

The lavender one I wore on the day I left Sripuram, I took to be mine. The other one I left behind for Mallika.

I had never really been to the market with Amma, at least not for an educational tour. Just the occasional time when she would stop by on the way from the temple and dash into the alley to pick up some last minute mint, or a bag of new potatoes, while Mallika and I waited with Appa, his scooter parked on Clive Road, away from all the hustle and bustle of the market alley.

Amma always insisted that it was better for her daughters to study than get caught up in domestic chores. "They will learn to do them anyway when their time comes," she would say, defending my lack of kitchen skills to the other mamis in the agraharam. "We should give our daughters what nobody thought of giving us," she would declare and go her way, pushing me to veena class, or the tailor shop, pre-empting their response. "That shut them up, didn't it?" she would gloat and give my plait a gentle tug, happy with herself. By the time Mallika and I returned from school, Amma would have already been to the market, and evening tiffin would be well on its way. We would smell fried pooris and chili-cumin potatoes in the air as we flung our school bags on the rattan sofa and dashed to the kitchen. I had sometimes eaten in the kitchen, but I had never cooked a meal on my own.

I was not ready for the nuts and bolts of it all.

After Chitti showered and draped herself in Amma's *chinalpattu*, we set out for the market. It was eleven in the morning. Recess time at school.

I walked behind Gayatri Chitti, carrying two plastic-wire bags, wondering what Revathi was up to. Was she making plans to climb the mango tree again? Does she know I will not be in school forever? FOREVER? I saw the word curve in capital letters before my eyes, just the way they wrote 70MM on the posters for foreign pictures. Chitti had let me wear my school uniform, even though she initially shook her head in bewilderment. "I really don't understand why anyone would want to wear it to the market." She herself was dressed like a guest at a wedding. "You'll be the strange one, so what do I care?"

People on the street did stare at us as we stepped out and took the road behind the agraharam, heading south, to the Sripuram market.

A dark, skinny Brahmin woman in a silk sari, walking like she was the temple chariot that came out at the end of Navarathri, and a sullen, distracted girl of thirteen, in a blue and white pinafore, clutching two plastic-wire bags, and following the matchstick chariot into the market—it couldn't have been an everyday sight.

But that did not bother me. I was too lost in thought to stare back, and the direct heat of the sun was burning my breath away. I was also busy resisting the urge to drop the bags and run back to school. I could be there in ten minutes if I ran fast. But what will you do tomorrow? I asked myself, and finding no answer to that, I moved on to other questions. Will she take Appa away to Madras? Why did Appa not like Amma? Was it because Mallika and I were born daughters? How could Gayatri Chitti do this to Amma? Finding no real answers to those questions as well, my head began to spin.

I stood right in the middle of the footpath, regained my balance by standing still and hated Gayatri Chitti intensely for two minutes. If I had a third eye, like Shiva, I would open it for her. I imagined her begging for mercy as she burned.

"Hurry up!" Chitti looked over her shoulder and glowered.

THE ALLEY LEADING up to the market was narrow and lined with fruit carts on both sides, from end to end. The fragrances and aromas of ripe mangoes, sweet jackfruit, spotted yellow green bananas and tangy sweet limes mingled and simmered in the hot afternoon sun. Fruit flies and bees buzzed all the way down the path, like a dizzy, drunk procession.

"Amma always bought fruits for us," I said, as Chitti navigated her way through the crowd fastidiously so that her sari didn't get tangled in the axle nails of the wooden vendor carts. "On our way back," she replied, dodging a bee that hummed around her left ear, as she walked into the main market area. She waited for me at the top of the stairs that led to a sunken courtyard with a raised, rectangular cement platform in the middle. I had never imagined so many people could pack such a small space, smaller than even the prayer hall at school. Will Mallika remember to bring mangoes for me?

The vegetable vendors were at one corner.

Along the length on both sides of the cement platform, small shops, divided by equal chalk-marked boundaries, sold spices, incense, flowers, *kolapodi,* bangles and kitchen utensils. On the opposite far corner was the fish and meat stall.

"That is the nonvegetarian section," Chitti said, crumpling her face in disgust and bringing the edge of her sari pullo to her vegetarian nose. She pointed to the red animal flesh hanging from hooks in the distance.

"Angey pogathey! Don't go there."

I nodded attentively, although I was suddenly curious to see what real dead fish looked like from up close. The only ones I had seen were at the science project fair last year, when Sheetal Reddy had brought an aquarium to school for her Marine Life demonstration. "The angelfish are my fave," she said. She was definitely nonvegetarian.

Gayatri Chitti spotted what she was looking for and started to descend the stairs to the main section.

I kept pace with her, trying not to step into the little gutters that ran from the platform all round the cobbled courtyard. "Hello! Madam! *Thangachchi!* Hello! Come, nice, new sambar powder! Homemade idli podi! Come, please try!" the hawkers called out to us from behind peak-topped mounds of fresh, brightly coloured spices and *kolapodi,* and rows and rows of bottles filled with curry pastes, pickles and marinades.

They all must have known Amma. Did they know that she was killed in the bus accident three weeks ago? Is this where Amma bought that tomato relish, the one that I liked in my lunch box?

"Palaniappa Pickles," I said aloud, reading the little tin board hanging from the parapet over the platform wall. The smell of green cardamom, turmeric root and raw seafood wafted around me as I picked my way just a few yards behind Chitti.

Right then, in the middle of all the commotion and jostling and trying to watch your step, someone whistled and then a voice boomed over the crowd's—

"Sister! The marriage hall is in the next street!"

Someone else thought Chitti was on her way to a wedding! Her sari had been noticed!

Instantaneously, a wave of snickers and guffaws washed over the southern section of the market. People stopped halfway in their transactions with bunches of spinach and leafy coriander drooping in their hands, and the merchants froze with their weigh-scale pans slowing to a halt. They all looked at us. I stood there too stunned to move myself. The voice had come from the eastern side of the market, which was to our right. Gayatri Chitti stopped midstride and turned around in rage.

A man selling coir mats and bathroom brushes grinned back at her when their eyes met. I still found it all unbelievable.

"Just thought I'd let you know!"

The man then lifted his lungi and folded it up to his knees, the mischievous grin not leaving his face. For a moment Chitti was on the verge of a response, and everybody held their collective breath. *"Badav..."* she began, and then she clipped her tongue and swallowed the rest of the expletive.

"Useless rowdy!" she muttered under her breath in English as she always did when angry. Indignation and intolerance expressed in one word of English, for some unknown reason, made her feel instantly superior. "Low caste!" she spat out for the benefit of people immediately around us and then resumed her walk as though she had uttered a death sentence.

The moment snapped, and everybody went back to business.

I kept looking back at the coir mat man as I followed Chitti. I was so astonished by his casual bravery that as we turned the corner of the cement platform I caught his eye one last time, raised my hand and quickly waved.

He grinned again with a thumbs-up sign.

CHITTI STOPPED in front of the bangle seller.

Two other women were in the small chalk-marked shop. They squatted in front of several wooden sleeves looped with tinkling glass bangles, which one of the two women was trying on for size.

Transparent reds with gold trimming, sapphire blues with silver intervals, oranges and dark greens twisted together, purples, yellows, whites—rows and rows of bangles, stacked on top of each other, dazzled and winked in the melting rays of the sun. I just wanted to touch them.

The shopkeeper abandoned the other customers and focussed all his attention on Chitti.

"Please come, sister, wide variety, please come," he beamed, immediately getting impatient with the two women.

"Come on, come on and make up your mind! You haven't got all day!" he said, getting up from his small yellow stool, which was just like the one Mallika and I had in our bedroom, to wipe it with a rag that lay nearby. Then with exaggerated respect he asked Chitti to sit on the stool, "Sit, please, have it!"

His partiality instantly provoked one of the two women.

"Why all that special respect for the *pappathi?*" Her words sputtered like drops of water in hot oil. She set the bangle sleeves aside. "Does her caste make her money smell better?" Chitti remained impervious.

She was smug about the fact that the women had determined her Brahmin caste without hesitation. A benign look of pride came into her eyes. Was it the Tamil we Brahmins spoke, or did we really smell different—like cold curd rice and spicy lentil broth—all the time? How did the woman know Chitti was a *pappathi?* I wondered, fixing my eyes to the ground in shame.

Chitti preferred such recognition to the coir mat man's bravado a few minutes earlier. She bent and fidgeted with her sandals, pulled at the straps and wriggled her toes farther to the sole's flat edge.

"Why are you simply making a fight now? Half an hour and you have still not bought a single set!" The shopkeeper intervened. "I have to cater to all customers!" He undid the first two buttons of his shirt and started to fan himself with a dried-palm *visiri*.

I stood there clutching my two plastic-wire bags, right behind Chitti, taking it all in without a word. The other woman who was trying on the bangles and who had remained silent spoke as she stood up.

"Then cater the same way to everyone! Brahmin or not Brahmin!"

They deliberately ignored Chitti, who stood there pretending she did not know what the skirmish was all about.

"You can stuff your high-caste bangles! Mannangatti!"

As they walked past, one of the women, the older one of the two who had initiated the argument, looked at me and said, "Maybe your generation will change things!"

In a moment of pure and complete incomprehension, overcome by a sudden panic of being singled out, I blurted, "Don't look at me! I am just wearing my school uniform! But I am not going to go to school FOREVER!" The letters did the concave gimmick again in front of my eyes. The women looked puzzled at my outburst as they disappeared into the crowd without a single backwards glance.

I was sure they had assumed I was mad.

CHITTI SAT DOWN on the wooden stool and patted the mat.

"*Va,*" she said, asking me to sit down beside her, on the floor. I did as she instructed. She then turned to the shopkeeper.

"Show me some Hyderabad bangles."

Her voice was calm, and there was still no trace of a reaction to what had just transpired. She seemed unaffected by the bizarre turns the day was taking. The shopkeeper got to work while other shoppers milled all around us in the different chalk-marked sections.

The noise and buzz of buyers and sellers, *"Kothamalli keere! Venadakkai rendu rooba, rendu rooba,"* haggling and hawking, came in from different directions. I heard the chickens muttering in their straw baskets at the far end of the platform, near the nonvegetarian section.

"Hyderabad bangles?" The shopkeeper searched his memory for a bit, like someone trying to remember the name of a distant cousin.

He then opened a rusty suitcase and brought out two once-white Bata shoeboxes and placed them on the shop floor. From each box he took out four sets of broad bangles wrapped in pink and white tissue paper. Slowly, as though he were plucking petals off a blooming rose, he unwrapped them and slipped them onto a wooden sleeve. I sat mesmerized by the beauty of those bangles, my eyes riveted, as they chimed along the sleeve. I had never seen such bangles!

Amma did not have any like these. She always wore that one gold bracelet that belonged to Patti before her. It would have been mine, when I got married, but the police never found it after the bus accident. Three weeks ago. *"Ponapoch-chu,"* the police inspector said. Forget them.

THE BANGLES the man placed before Chitti were bejewelled circles of magic. Tiny glass diamonds flickered and smiled from rich magenta, turquoise and saffron backgrounds. Each one was designed to outdo the rest, it seemed. One set, which I liked right off, had clear blue stones that crept and curved all around the bangle, like a snake eating itself. At every dip and rise of the serpent's body there were hand-etched little gold flakes lighting the way as it slithered in a lagoon of blue green lacquer. The saffron bangle set was differently from the rest, with a string of pearls running along the rim and studded with tiny red glass rubies in the shape of stars.

I knew we had not come all the way to buy bangles for me, but I still wanted to try on the green set with the serpent.

"Are they my size?" I asked, already reaching for them on the sleeve.

"One minute, *paappa*," the shopkeeper rushed to assist me, worried that I would tip the whole rack.

"I am thirteen!" Don't call me a child.

For the first time that afternoon I regretted wearing my school uniform.

"Janaki," Chitti said, mildly perturbed. "Don't cause trouble."

The bangles turned out to be two sizes too big for me. They rolled all the way along my hand, from my wrists and halfway up to my elbow. I was crushed.

Chitti suddenly took a fancy to the very same ones. She tugged them from the shopkeeper's hand before he could slide them back onto the sleeve and squeezed her fingers into them like a deer's nose jutting through a little loop. Against her skin the bangles glowed like lonely neon coronas in a dark galaxy.

But they were her exact size and matched the colour of Amma's sari, which Chitti had made her own that morning. "How much?" she asked, as she held up both her wrists to the sun's rays. The blue stones lit up as though they were battery operated, and the tiny sparks of azure white light awoke and went to sleep in little winks.

"Sixty rupees, sister, but for you I am giving for forty-five!"

Chitti was still caught up in the dazzling spell of the bangles. I couldn't take my eyes off them, even though they would never be mine.

"Forty-five?" she said distractedly. "I could get better ones for thirty in Madras."

"Ha! I knew sister was not from here," the shopkeeper exclaimed with the familiarity of a long-lost friend. "You can spot a Madras Brahmin lady from miles away!"

Chitti smiled for the first time that day. Her face lost its sharp edges, and her eyes glazed with water as she gave in to the moment easily. "And you should know *all* about Brahmin ladies from Madras!" she said, her voice husky with secret meanings, sliding the bangles off her wrists. She curved her index finger around the bangles like a hook, and dangled them provocatively in front of his eyes.

"What's the final offer? *Sollu?*"

She somehow knew that she had already won the battle.

"Thirty-five last!" the shopkeeper answered. "Only because you are from Madras! And first *boni!* First sale of the day!" In two minutes he had dropped ten more rupees!

Chitti did not bargain with that. After all, he had also taken her side in the recent caste war. She opened her handkerchief in which she kept her currency rolled up like a book of paper mats and gave him a fifty-rupee note. "Wrap them up nicely."

I hated her intensely again for thirty seconds.

"What about one set for your daughter?" the shopkeeper asked as he extended the remaining fifteen rupees to her.

"Oh, she is still too young to wear jewellery," Chitti replied, tugging the notes from his reluctant fingers. "And she is not my daughter. She is my niece," she said, with mock petulance, snatching the notes from his hand in one final tug.

"Adhanai parthaen!" the shopkeeper said in false astonishment, matching Chitti's fake offence every step of the way. "I should have known! You are so young lady still!"

Chitti wiped the beads of sweat from her brow. She wrapped the change in the same handkerchief and quickly tucked it into the bra under her blouse, the left cup her mobile safety case. She must feel like a furnace under that sari, I thought, wondering what made Amma so different from Chitti. Was it her complexion? What was Chitti like when Chittappa was alive?

And then I realized that Chitti had stolen her own sister's husband. Amma's own blood had become the source of her greatest misery. I could not look at her then. I wanted to be somewhere else. With Amma, maybe. I just wanted to leave.

"So how long in Sripuram?" the shopkeeper asked as he wrapped the bangles to put them in a box.

I watched the bangles tumble and roll in his palms as he crumpled white tissue paper around the loops, miracles once again shrouded in darkness. I stood up.

"I am thirsty," I said, holding the bags like a shield against my chest, ready for Chitti's arrows of anger. But she surprised me.

"Yes, I would like a cold panir soda myself," she said, reaching for one of the bags I was hugging. "It is so sultry!"

I gave her the bag, and she carefully, as though she were immersing a baby in warm bathwater, lowered her bangle box into it. She held up the bag by its black plastic handles and confirmed that the box was well supported on either side— that it was held in proper balance.

"*Rombo* thanks," she said indifferently, not really meaning it at all. She had what she wanted. "Is there a nice restaurant somewhere outside this smelly market?"

I was already on the steps of the platform, ready to descend into the gutter courtyard.

Why was everything so prolonged about Chitti? Why was it so impossible for her to just get up and go get a drink? I stood there on the stairs wishing the curtain on her drama would fall soon. She had surprised me by agreeing to my request, and I did not want to anger her with my impatience. I had to wait it out. Maybe she did it on purpose, to prove her authority by ignoring my sudden, wordless agitation?

"Krishna Cool Drinks and Snacks, sister," the shopkeeper announced. "My brother-in-law is owning! On the corner of Clive Road, in the left-hand side," he said, moving his left hand as though he were directing the market traffic. "Excellent gulab jamun!"

He brought his thumb and index finger together to signify good quality, and in perfect coordination smacked his lips, making a slurping sound. The thought of cutting into those sweet syrupy orbs of thickened milk with the edge of a stainless-steel teaspoon made me salivate. The craving lodged in my stomach, and my throat began to parch.

Finally, Chitti made her way to the stairs. *"Methuva,"* the shopkeeper instructed her before she could take the first step. Gently. Chitti looked up and smiled again. Maybe, she had heard what he never said. She had that talent around men.

Chitti descended the steps, holding the plastic-wire bag with the bangles away from her body, her fingers choking tight on the handle so that the contents did not rock. I could feel the shopkeeper's eyes on our backs as we stepped into the courtyard. She walked ahead of me, and I followed in her fastidious footsteps once again, thinking to myself, Chitti's holding the bag like a mousetrap with a mouse in it. Soon, she'll waddle into a lake and open the trap door.

CHITTI ALSO TAUGHT me how to bargain. "Just one simple rule," she said, as we sat sipping Campa Cola in Krishna Cool Drinks and Snacks. "Cut the price in half without shame," she declared. "And don't wear your school uniform when you come by yourself." She sucked the last of the cola into the straw and unexpectedly belched. "They'll fleece you!" The fizz filled her nose and made her sneeze. Her lesson was simple: the shopkeepers hiked the price expecting you to bargain it down. "You are actually fulfilling their expectations. Think of that and you won't have a problem."

I nodded, not knowing then that I would turn out to be really good at it.

"And one more thing," Chitti pushed her cola bottle to the centre of the table as she rose from her chair. "Always dress decently and go to stores run by men. You'll be amazed with what you can do!" She didn't have to tell me. I had seen a stellar example of it for myself at the bangle seller.

I felt like telling her then that I knew about her and Appa, but I couldn't get the words out. "Will we all be moving to Madras?" I asked instead. My words came out smoothly, but I finished the question with less courage.

Chitti looked at me seriously.

I did not look away. I met her eyes without emotion, and I thought for a moment she saw the unasked questions behind mine. "That is entirely up to your father."

Something changed in her manner, a tremor under the skin, as though a chasm had suddenly opened up within her and her soul had dived into a ravine of guilt. She put a five-rupee note under the empty bottle.

"*Aachcha?* Finish up. We still have to go over the house-cleaning chores when we get back." Abruptly, she walked out to the front of the restaurant, without bothering to wait for the change. I finished my drink in one big gulp, spilling the last drops on my uniform, and ran out to join her.

When I stepped outside, she was nowhere in sight. I found her at the junction of Clive and Nehru roads, beside the traffic signal. She looked shaken, like those possessed women I had seen rolling around the temple aisles in high penance, their bodies the husk they wished to shed through flagellation.

Chitti's frame was clumped, and sagged like a cloth teabag. I didn't think she would recognize me as I walked up to her.

GAYATRI CHITTI kept up her instructions from Madras.

She attached typical Brahmin recipes for bisibela bhath, a traditional hodgepodge of parboiled rice and vegetables cooked in a spicy tamarind broth, and podimaas, baby potatoes boiled and mashed with a seasoning of mustard, cayenne and curry leaves, to her letters from Madras. She couriered more complicated recipes with Appa every time he returned from Madras after his monthly weekend with her. "Your father really likes this koottu, so follow the steps properly!" she wrote on top of the page in red ink. Dishes I prepare to this day in my modern, appliance-filled Bombay kitchen as our chef, Khan sahib, watches me do my bona fide Sripuram Brahmin cook act—amused and awestruck at the same time. I don't need to look at the recipes anymore. And this much is true: Gayatri Chitti and my circumstances taught me well.

Even now, when I visit the Bombay markets, say Crawford or Nal Bazaar, I can hear Chitti's voice, faint but still lingering at the back of my head. I can see her picking up shallots in her palm, on our second visit to Sripuram market, and thrusting them under my chin.

"Take a good look," she said. "The colour should be a deep orange and the skin should shine! For all the onions. Feel them for firmness!" And I still do.

Not just for onions. Also for garlic and ginger and brinjals. I know how to spot the best ones in the pile. I can tell a rotten coconut by knocking on its shell with my knuckle and shaking the water inside. I can tell if the bananas have been smoked to ripen fast, before their time. Asgar says that he knows the days I have been grocery shopping by just looking at the consistency of the curry sauces. "You have to thank my Gayatri Chitti for that!" I reply with a sense of accomplishment. "But she might not be very friendly to you."

I feel little crests of pride rise in my heart every time Asgar makes such observations. I feel fulfilled. Appa and Mallika never once said a good thing about my labour all those years. Nothing hardens a person faster than the absence of appreciation. The sense of having been taken for granted. Without say. Amma hid that hard side well. I wanted out before it became rote.

After supper, as I push my chair back and take both our plates to the sink to be rinsed, Asgar begins to laugh. "But I don't think I will be able to tell the difference between your dishwashing and the Bai's," he says, referring to my Brahmin past, which I know will continue to haunt me through habit.

It is this all-consuming struggle between then and now I want to lose. And ten years is still too little time to erase an earlier lifetime.

On such occasions, when Asgar calls me a creature of habit, I turn around and look at my husband with great love and reply in my still shaky Urdu, which I am only just learning to speak in the right accent, *"Adat se majboor?* Remember I was a Brahmin daughter before I became a Muslim wife!" When he weaves his hands around my waist as I am wiping the plates dry and nuzzles his nose in the nape of my neck, just like Mallika used to when I played the veena, I melt and glow. "And this habit is another thing you have to thank my past for! I think you'd better start a list."

MAY 1991

THERE IS A granite slab right below the front veranda, engraved with a name, date of housewarming and *Sri Rama Jayam* that is lost in the black-and-white *CineVista* photo. Every time I see that photo it pulls me back into that house of memory. I can see every single bar on the windows, count every hibiscus on the backyard bush, all by just closing my eyes. My body still bristles with gooseflesh. It is definitely our house in the Sripuram colony, and the arrow pointing to the gate in the gossip story is indeed the gate I walked out that morning. No doubt about that.

But it does not resemble a "House of Desire." In fact, there never was anything about it that could, even if exaggerated, measure up to the imagined erotics of such a phrase. A "House of Desire" conjures images of nubile, silken girls dancing into the early hours of dawn, their sensual laughter echoing down the hallways and spilling into the streets, and the "besh, besh, bravo" of their intoxicated patrons seduced by chimes of salangai bells and craving more than just the dancer's feet.

Vulgar, perhaps. But still an audacious, vibrant example of life. Our house was the complete antithesis of desire. Inside and outside. "House of Discontents" would be fitting. Also accurate. I only have to close my eyes to see it again, a house only I can see. Seeing into its soul.

The house belonged to my maternal grandfather, Srinivasa Iyer, who built it in 1950. His name is on that polished granite slab. Amma was fifteen years old then, and Gayatri Chitti, nine. My grandfather was a successful Brahmin man whose wife, my Pattima, had died one year after Appa and Amma were married. I never got to meet her, but Amma had her old photographs, which she kept wrapped in a green handkerchief, in the Godrej cupboard, and I had seen Pattima in those. She was an austere woman with wafer thin lips and a chin that tapered into a peninsula on a broad, unblemished face. Gayatri Chitti had inherited Pattima's features, while Amma looked like her father.

My grandfather owned and operated a theatre in Madras—Abirami Palace—on the Mount Road cinema strip, which screened popular Tamil pictures made by the Kodambakkam studios. Thathappa, as I used to call him, had a soft spot for mythological and religious dramas. Every Deepavali, he would insist on opening with a new cinematic version of Ramayanam, or a Puranic story filled with amateur magic and ancient morals. Parrots discoursed on the merits of the Vedas in divine rapture within these mythologicals, and gods had fascinating lavender skin, like the soft edges of jasmine buds. The productions were gaudy, over-the-top interpretations of sacred and folkloric myths in which gods and demons clashed and women were given away as prizes in archery contests. Or better still, saved by wild tigers, as the tigers knew them to be goddesses in disguise right from the outset. In the Puranas, I realized later, everything was possible, except common women.

And yet, ironically, common women were the primary audience for these stories, and the enthusiasm with which they embraced them, lost in magic, and lost forever, could turn the picture into a superhit. Just on the strength of the sweat-dripping, *bhakti* matinees. But in the end the heroines always paid the price. They were swallowed up by Mother Earth or disrobed in the royal court; their noses were cut off and mothers were decapitated by their sons on the sagely, stoic advice of their mystic fathers. I learned that you could never be a heroine until you braved and survived elemental catastrophes, and died at least once. In the end there was a boon that brought you back to life, and your head was re-attached to your neck, and everything was all right with the world. The whole exercise only a test for loyalty and obedience. And those were, are and will always be good sentiments. I believed that then.

"Why did Savitri chase Yama, the god of death, and beg for Satyavan's life? We all have to die some day, that's what you've told me before. How come no one says that in the pictures?" I asked Amma after she came home from the hospital with Mallika. The story of a princess winning back her husband's life by debating and arguing inspired me a lot. I had seen the picture just for the final scene in which Yama rides off on his buffalo with a lost expression on his face. Satyavan stirs to life, and Savitri laughs and laughs and her joy turns the whole screen into a glowing pink.

"Because she was deluded and wanted a hundred sons!"

Amma replied, rubbing almond oil into two-month-old Mallika's baby skin.

"Do you want to hold your kutty sister?" she said, tired of my insistent questioning. "Your Thathappa really shouldn't let you see those pictures all the time when you are in Madras! If only you could remember your *two-twos-are* multiplication the way you remember all this nonsense!"

Amma never liked the mythologicals. But I had seen all the sagas during my visits to Madras, sitting in the cozy corner private box beside the balcony seats, which was always reserved for family and VIPs. Sometimes I saw the whole picture from the screening room window, the sizzling, silver arc light of the projector my own shining goddess sword, as Thathappa watched the clock and arranged the reels in the order in which they were to be screened. Most of the time he worried that if he screened reel number nine, believing it to be reel number six, all hell would break loose in the auditorium below. Within seconds claps and whistles would tear the eardrums, and bad words usually involving mothers and sisters would sting and glow like fireflies in the dark. Women, I learned in these exhilarating instances of discovery, can curse better than men, making up on-the-spur expletives, creative when one would least expect them to be. But they also needed the invisibility, a pitch black sari of an auditorium to stay anonymous, so that when the emergency lights came on and the correct picture reel rolled again, their moral, modest side remained intact—untarnished like the heroines on the screen. Pretend and it will not exist.

The "bastards," "assholes" and "shitbrooms" (which was my favourite) were a dark vocabulary that depended on darkness for their articulation. In light they flew back into women, muted, like a bat.

I had seen *Valli Devayanai, Kurukshetram, Ram Seetha Ram* so many times, I knew the pictures backwards, sequence by sequence. I liked the songs, and I was always seduced by the glittering costume jewellery. Also, the soundtrack had veena interludes, and I could quickly identify the ragas they were based on, which, in most cases, turned out to be Neelambari and Kalyani.

Housewives and older women packed the matinees, but the other three shows of the day usually resembled private, two-person screenings. But that didn't deter Thathappa. "My way of attaining purity," he said, turning down the latest potboilers from MGR and Sivaji, and hardening his soft spot for transcendence. And he didn't stop at Deepavali. He took his search for god and selflessness further and further, with the true fervour of a devotee seeking a blessing from a still-indifferent deity and pursuing an ascetic life and salvation through focussed, self-willed bankruptcy. He added other religious festivals, like Krishna Jayanthi and Vinayaka Chaturthi to the list. Before long it also included Indian Independence Day and Republic Day, but never touched on Christmas or Ramadan.

On the first day of a new release, Thathappa conducted a puja in front of the theatre before the premiere screening. Small finger cymbals chimed as he performed the arati, and M.S. Subbulakshmi competed with traffic horns and sidewalk vendors as her Krishna danced out in song from the Philips two-in-one placed on the wooden ledge of the Dress Circle ticket counter. After the ritual, Thathappa always dis-

tributed light orange kanakambaram garlands and chips of
god-blessed coconut to the first few women in the sweaty,
sweltering matinee queue. He then turned on the projector chanting "om, om, om" in three short breaths. He was a
believer of mythological dimensions. Amma always told me
that I had something in common with my grandfather: "You
both despise the real world."

"This makes the idea of giving back to god look stupid!"
Amma yelled at him once, when she came to Madras to fetch
me at the end of the one-week Dassera holidays. "Other
theatres nearby are screening the latest potboilers with full-
house business, and Abirami Palace is performing a thath-
thith-thom for absent gods! What's wrong with you? You are
not the first widower in the world, so don't torture us in your
haste to join your wife!"

I had never seen her speak to Thathappa like that on any
other occasion.

"Why, 'pa?" she then lowered her voice and touched him
on the shoulder. "Why are you slowly killing yourself with
losses? It is a theatre, not a temple, illaiya?"

She didn't tell him that she was not angry with him but fed
up with her husband who was constantly nagging her about
the slowness of cheques from Madras. Appa had agreed for a
life-long dowry—in installment. He expected a cheque of—I
never found out how much—every month, from Thathappa.
And when it didn't arrive on time Amma would hear no end
of it. The grumbling would continue into the nights as I pretended to sleep on the mat on the floor near their bed, hearing each and every word, punctuated with Amma's hisses of
pain as he pinched her at regular intervals to prove his point.

In the morning there would be congealed, purplish blotches on Amma's midriff, right above the waistline of her sari and below the edge of her blouse where Appa had kept a record of the points he scored. They had an argument one day when I left to be with Thathappa. Appa did not say a word throughout the bus ride to Madras, and later he dropped me petulantly at the Abirami Palace foyer and left without saying namaskaram to Thathappa. The drill became routine for me.

THE LAST MYTHOLOGICAL I saw with Thathappa was when I was seven and vacationing with him for the summer and Mallika was about to be born. I had been sent away to Madras on an extended stay that year. Her cousin Kokila had been summoned from the ancestral village to help Amma. *Sarpa Sadhu*, the picture was called, *Snakey Saint*. Predictably, it had a snake that crept up a saintly woman's body and said, "I will protect you all your life!" and the woman, plump already and made plumper by the weight of the jewellery store that glittered all over her body, laughed in pious joy and trilled, "Nagaraja! You are for me and I am for you! You are for me; I am for you!"

Even the housewives—Thathappa's guaranteed audience—kept away from the matinees. And those who did come filed out of the theatre immediately after that scene, which was the snake's introduction into the plot.

"*Aathaadi!* Did I pay two-ninety to see a toy snake pass off as Mahavishnu? They could have at least found a realistic looking one!" one woman exclaimed, as she swore never to see another Jayaradha mythological.

Abirami Palace and its proprietor, however, did not survive that plastic bite. Thathappa had bought the distribution rights for *Snakey Saint* in the urban and suburban territories and couldn't come up with the rent cheque for the theatres that screened it when the picture was declared a box-office flop, just three days into the festival season. He had booked three-month runs in thirteen theatres. He believed it was a godsend. Narayana had finally answered his prayers. Thathappa happily mortgaged the theatre. A year later he sold it for half its market price and retired to a one-bedroom flat on Chalmiers Road. He willed the Sripuram house to Amma as payment for all the absentee cheques over the years and then, having attained his dharma of pennilessness, he died in his sleep—with a smile on his face—the following year. Gayatri Chitti moved into his flat and has lived there ever since. Thathappa was the first casualty of mythology in our family.

A five-storey shopping mall with Levi's and Sony stores now stands where Abirami Palace used to be. I have seen it a few times when I have accompanied Asgar to Madras when he is dubbing at the studios there. And I am not imagining this, it's something that has to be seen to be believed: the mall is painted an uncanny pale blue, as though the colour of snake poison buried in its past was finally fading into thin air.

RI

The house stood out from the other houses in an odd way, although the architecture was neither unique nor aesthetically inspired. The distemper on the outside was fading to a pustule yellow and desperately needed attention, and the dark brown upper window shutters gaped open, forlorn, like the eyes of a dead cow. The best thing about the house, if you really searched for merits, was that it faced the east and was two storeys high. That's what made the structure stand out, like a tall woman in the temple queue for *darisanam*, boringly plain but with the power to look down on the rest, and also see over their heads, to the deity in the distant shrine. Ours was one of the first houses built in the Sripuram agraharam, and, not surprisingly, it faced the temple tower.

The facade was very much in the 1950s style, with a small curving veranda (a bungalow affectation), and two concrete pillars on either side supporting the floor above. The gate was made of twisted iron bars with an overlatch that held the two wing doors in place. The doors of the gate were screwed into two concrete posts with cement-cast lotuses on each head that looked more like ancient, sun-dried artichokes. The artistic impulse ended there.

Amma's sunflower beds are not visible in the photograph as they are behind the wall, but I still remember how eagerly she planted her borderline garden. During summer, sunflowers bloomed and slouched along our compound wall, which began from the posts at the gate, travelling left and right, and ran all around the house before merging behind the well, a boundary just a few spans away from the wash stone.

The windows of the hall opened onto the veranda on either side of the main entrance door and were specifically designed with intervals of iron bars, nine per window, to keep the eyes of passersby from prying in. Amma had made some curtains out of her old nylex saris and hung them over the upper windows, just in case. Inquisitiveness was an active pastime of most of the mamis in the agraharam, and after siesta, a few of the more compulsive ones would take a gossip walk and congregate around the temple reservoir, or the little pooka-dai that sold marigold and rose garlands, exchanging news and snippets—so that they could return to their homes with something to mull over after meals—seen, heard, and most times, entirely made up.

Sometimes, on my way back from veena class, I would see a warren of mamis on Revathi's veranda, where Savitri Mami would be holding court, in all her I-am-the-only-one-with-a-phone-in-this-agraharam grandeur. "Coming back from veena class, is it?" she would ask as I passed the house gate, and I would reply, "Yes, mami," and keep walking. Behind me I would hear them whisper among themselves, catching stray phrases like "doomed karma," and "cursed, ill-fated house" before I crossed to A Block, where our house was. Nothing escaped their scrutiny, and nothing else brought joy like a juicy, communal scandal. Such hungry, middle-aged vultures. Beside the main hall downstairs there was a small puja room, a shrine from where the gods—Lakshmi, Vishnu, Saraswati and Ayappa—watched over Mallika and me when the adults around us let their guard slip. In the agraharam you could never escape a pair of eyes however hard you tried. Air could also stare you in the face.

Next to the puja room was Appa and Amma's bedroom, at the far corner of the veranda. The windows faced the temple gopuram and brushed the papery veil of bougainvillea that fell in cascades into the side alley. Except for the rattan sofa and a small moda, made of jute and shaved, slender bamboo, which was Appa's reading chair—sometimes in the hall and sometimes on the veranda where he did his weekend file work—there was no other furniture in the hall.

When I opened the hall windows—upper shutters and lower shutters—and let the night air in, the cool breeze rustled nothing, and nothing moved, but the whole room filled to the brim with the perfume from the neighbour's parijatha tree, in full summer bloom, just on the other side of the veranda, and the hall turned into a sauna of sweet nausea. Some nights, I did not even have to light an *agarbathi* in the kitchen after dinner had been cooked and served, and the dishes had been rinsed and stacked. I just opened the windows around nine and sat on the veranda and listened to the radio, lost in a Meera Bhajan or a classical program on FM, as the fumes from the kitchen dissolved gradually into a soft, lingering fragrance, and a quiet bliss fell around the house.

But those could only be the nights when Appa was away on his sojourns in Madras with Gayatri Chitti. And I had those once a month, with timetable regularity, starting two months after Amma was gone.

The upstairs rooms seemed like an afterthought. There was a whitewashed bedroom with an attached shower bathroom that we all used, to the right of the stairs. On the opposite side, another room was used as a storage space for rice, cooking oil, lentils and heavy cooking utensils. Right next to the storeroom a door opened onto a flat, cement roof terrace, our private mottamadi, where Amma dried red chilies before they were roasted and ground, and soaked whole sour limes in pickling oil with ginger strips, under the simmering rays of the sun.

After Amma's death I moved out of our upstairs bedroom, leaving it all to Mallika, and began sleeping in the hall so that I could be on time for my new duties, competing with my new-found companion of that hour, the Rockfort Express. I just shared the upstairs almirah for my clothes with Mallika, but otherwise my days and nights were spent in the hall and the kitchen.

And then there was the backyard, not seen at all in the photo. It soon became my sanctuary, my own exile of asoka trees, like Sita's in Ramayanam—only there was no lyricism in my locale. A bitter neem tree spread its scrawny branches in one corner, some stray fronds and wild weeds bordered the compound wall and a hibiscus bush bloomed beside the backyard gate, just beginning to open a few deep red blossoms. A small concrete pillar with triangular openings on all four sides for clay oil lamps stood in the centre of the plot, between the brown brick veranda outside the kitchen door and the scrubbed grey-moss cement well.

That was the entire span of the backyard.

In the hollow of the two-foot-tall cement structure Amma had managed to grow a tulasi plant, the leaves of which she plucked every day to sanctify the water in the small copper puja pot. Immediately after the evening prayer she forced Mallika and me to swallow a few tablespoons of blessed tulasi water.

"It will keep all the diseases away! *Jeeboombaa!*" she would say, chasing all viruses away with her magician's phrase, as we sipped the water without wincing, and then ran out to the veranda after the second tablespoon, afraid that if we lingered any longer she would spoon-feed all of the blessed water from the pot into our mouths.

If I could forget the fact that there was an outhouse with a squatter latrine just beside the backyard gate, the boundaries became a Sahara of misery, or an archipelago of peace, whatever my state of mind at that particular hour. In the afternoons,

I sat in the shade of the overhead asbestos sheet, extended partially to cover the mouth of the well from the neem tree leaves, and wrote my swarams.

The agraharam afternoons were different from the agraharam mornings. A deathly quiet walked the streets those afternoon hours, when no humans wandered. Except for the occasional old mami dragging her worn and tatty slippers with a "varat-varat, varat-varat" sound on her way back from the temple, and the stray horn of an autorickshaw that had just dropped off a customer in B Block, everything was saturated with inertia, as the sun baked a red-earth geography, and faintly, fragile Brahmins slumbered and snored in a collective, sticky siesta. Even the crows shut up for those hours as though their throats were set to an alarm time of 1:30 PM. Soaked in heat, the neem tree leaves drooped with breathless fever, and the green, scabrous branches turned white, like a liar's face. For three hours every afternoon the agraharam became a brightly lit colony with no visible souls. It became a ghost town of the bleached, the fatigued and the nearly dead.

The sunken temple tank defined the agraharam and gave it a landmark status. Brahmin houses lined the four sides from a half-mile distance, and so when people gave directions to guests, friends or strangers, it was common to say, "A Block, west of Narayana temple" or more confusingly, "Temple faces south, you see? We are situated in the east side, but looking to west! So you are in C Block. Your address is in the opposite side!"

And whoever came into the agraharam never left without a *darisanam* of Narayana, which kept the temple trustees more than happy. Regular money in the donation pot was nothing to complain about, and during Hindu festivals the huge brass money pot the priest carried around grinned open, as the saffron cloth lid that covered it with a slot opening was torn beyond redemption by devotees clamouring to make their donations. But afternoons were always a bleak time, seldom auspicious, so there was no *archanai,* no ritual, and the priest went home after the brass pot was locked up in the cast-iron safe of the adjacent temple office. Even Lord Narayana slept between one and three.

Around three or three thirty the alleys around the temple came to life with the flower sellers and incense vendors setting up shop for evening business. That is where the mamis congregated, weaving fragrant gossip as they haggled with the merchants over the pricing of jathi malli, caste jasmine. Then the pigeons wobbled out of their nests, built in the turret openings of the temple gopuram, and fluttered reluctantly in the first waves of the still-warm early evening breeze. Water splashes for the evening kolam began and proceeded like a chain reaction from house to house in the agraharam, and while fresh patterns were being drawn on the ground, a few older mamis from larger families stepped out for the second delivery of milk. A little after four, paamalai devotionals, nasally and annoying, poured out of the temple loudspeakers, and soon the bells began clanging as people announced their presence for an audience with their Lord. "I am here, a believer," the bells said in a coppery shiver. "Look at me."

It was time, once again, to awaken the gods.

THE SUN WAS still blazing that afternoon, just a month after Amma's first anniversary. I was sitting under the canopy of my drying dhavani, which I had on purpose clipped like an upturned umbrella. I had an idea to make a shady spot under the thick cotton, between the parallel clotheslines that ran across the brick veranda. I was picking stones from the ration rice. It was a Tuesday and I had no veena class that afternoon. Everything was quiet around me, as the agraharam was only halfway through the siesta period. It was too hot to sleep indoors and I had to sort the rice sooner or later. Sooner, I determined.

For each stone that I picked from the gleaming copper tray of pearl white grains, I sang a swaram:

Ri
Ga
Ma
Ga
Ri
Ma

And on Ga I saw it.

It was a head looking over the edge of the compound wall. I saw the figure from the corner of my eye, under the billowing dhavani. The head ducked quickly, and for a moment, I thought I had imagined it. A few thudding minutes went by as I pretended to pick stones, my heart racing with fear.

And then the head appeared again.

This time I saw a figure for real as I tilted my chin upwards, not looking directly but still managing a better view. The head ducked again in thirty seconds, before I could identify if the person was a man or a woman. All I saw was a red slash of cloth, and a bush of hair. Someone was hiding behind the compound wall, and there was no one in sight in the back alley. Even the pye-dogs that loitered the streets were not barking. Where were they when you needed them?

Don't panic, I told myself, nothing can happen to you in daylight, while my body erupted into ten million tiny volcanoes and my fingers froze with goosebumps. I slowly managed to put the rice tray down, pretended to yawn and stretch, even though I did not feel like doing either of those two things. Five minutes passed and then the head appeared twice. It was a woman's.

Is she waiting for me to go in so that she can grab my dhavani? Should I just walk up and confront her? I decided against it. I wanted to have a better look at her first, and that was not possible from under the dipping dhavani.

I picked up the rice tray and slowly crept out from under the canopy. Once I was on the back veranda I stood up straight, and without looking back, I went into the kitchen through the back door. As soon as I was inside, I put the tray on the floor, locked the back door and ran upstairs, two steps at a time, to the mottamadi. If I got to the southern edge of the terrace I could get a better view of the intruder, and from up there I could cause a commotion, loud enough to attract attention. I crouched for invisibility once again and quickly moved along the western wall of the terrace, my back scraping the wall lightly, and reached the corner where the two terrace walls met. Cautiously, I gripped the edge of the wall with my fingers and raised my head to peer over the parapet, looking down directly.

"Aey! What are you looking..." I began in an authoritative voice, glaring down at her from above.

The woman did not run. Instead, she raised her hands to her mouth, shook her head vigorously and sank down to her knees, about to faint. A three-year-old boy with a runny nose pulled at the woman's mirror-and-patchwork skirt. He raised his thumb and poured invisible water into his mouth as he looked up at me.

"*Thanni, thanni...*" he said in a raspy voice, pointing to the well.

With a finger on my lips, I let them both in through the backyard gate. The woman looked tired, and I was certain she would faint from dehydration before we got to the well. She was wearing bangles made of ivory and seashells, all the way from her wrists to her elbows. Tangled bead chains and *pasimani malai* hung around her neck. She had tied her hair into a dishevelled, wild-frond bun on top of her head and clipped it with a two-pronged bamboo-stick pin. Her nose ring was a withered bunch of tiny metal grapes, hanging from the bridge between her two nostrils.

"Iru, I'll get some water soon," I said.

I made her sit on the brick veranda in the backyard and ran to the well, praying that she would not collapse in those few unsupported minutes it took me to pull up a bucket of water. I took the bucket to her and poured it, instinctively, down her body. Loose, wet hair stuck to the sides of her face, and the chill of cold well water made her shudder. She sat up suddenly, more awake to her surroundings. "Just sit there." I drew more water from the well. I poured it from above, as she cupped her hands and drank slowly at first, and then in longer gulps, just the way Sheetal Reddy's fish had done at school, when they were lowered into the tank from a plastic bag, their mouths open for what seemed like an interminable stretch of time.

The woman finally splashed water on her face and raised her hand, asking me to stop pouring. She wiped her face with her dusty red skirt, ridden with soot and loose threads, and looked up. Her face was clearer now, and there was a piercing quality in her eyes.

She was dark, and was certainly a vagrant *kurathi*, perhaps from one of the Narikurava clans farther south, but her face did not have strong tribal features. A glowing sheen appeared on her wiped, round face. Water still grazed her lips, and she spoke for the first time in a soft voice.

"Thayi, can I use some more water to give my son a bath? See, he looks like a kutty sand man!"

I turned to look at the boy and realized that he really did need a bath. Oozings from his nose had congealed in the heat around his lips like candle wax drippings, and there was not a single dust-free hair root on his head. He stood beside his mother and looked at me with indifferent eyes. He had saved his mother by gesturing to me in good time. He deserved the clean look of a hero. I couldn't refuse.

"Don't make too much noise or the mami next door will yell at the top of her voice that I have ruined her afternoon nap, *purinjitha?*"

She nodded. "I will be as quiet as I can." Her eyes shone with gratitude.

"*Va*, Sivarasa!" she said, calling the boy by his name and, grabbing his hand, dragged him to the well.

"Here," I beckoned as she was drawing water, and held out the soap dish.

"Magarasi!" she said, as she took it from my hand, making me feel like the Goddess of Soaps.

She worked up the soap into a thick, frothy lather and scrubbed the boy from head to toe. He stood through it all without uttering a word, even though I was sure the soap was stinging his eyes. She poured three buckets of water with great care over him and the wash that leaked into the grass bed beside the well ran brown with soil and red-earth dust.

"Where are you from?" I asked, as she patted her son dry with both her palms.

"Marudamalai, thayi," she replied in her dialect, still calling me her mother even though I was at least twenty years younger in age.

"Shhooo! Keep your voice low. What are you doing here, in the agraharam?" I said, worried that all the water splashing, however controlled and gentle, still might have woken Vanaja Mami next door. I expected to see an angry, bed-marked face at the window on the other side of the compound wall any minute.

"Stop playing with it!" she hissed at her son, who had already tweezed his belly button until it looked like a swollen cardamom pod, and I thought, "He has discovered its presence all over again!"

"I am on my way to Madras," she said, squatting on the edge of the brick veranda. "I went to the temple, and the sami Iyer chased me away. I just wanted to sit in the shade of the temple mandapam for a bit. I have been walking for two days." Then something occurred to her, and she turned to her son and exclaimed, *"Sivarasa, paiyye yenge vechche?"*

The naked boy was spurred by her question. He shook off her hand that gripped his wrist and ran to the backyard gate. Within minutes he emerged with a tattered school satchel filled with all kinds of knickknacks and bulging at the seams. She ran and took it from his hands.

"*En, Rasa!*" she said, relief replacing anxiety in her voice, enough to make her call her son her "King."

She took out a red piece of cloth from the bag and inserted it through the black string around Sivarasa's waist. She wrapped the cloth snugly around his penis and tied the muslin securely to his back.

"What's your name?" I asked.

Something about her intrigued me. I didn't know what it was, but I knew that it had to do with the way her eyes looked at me, her dark pupils holding me in their brilliant spell.

"Neelaranjani," she replied. "And yours?"

"Janaki," I answered. "Itho, Neelaranjani, I don't know what time it is, but I have to go pick up my sister from school in a little while, so . . ." She quickly understood that it was a hint for her to depart. I actually had to meet Kamala, who was getting ready for a proposal that evening, and had asked me to stop by to help her with the violin solo she would play for the "marriage" party. Mallika said she'd walk back from school on her own and meet me at Kamala's. But it all had to be done before Vanaja Mami awoke.

"You've been so kind, thayi," Neelaranjani replied. "A real *magaletchumi*, a true goddess! You saved my life . . . Just one more kindness, thayi, and then I will leave."

I knew what was coming. Ultimately, it all came down to begging. Money.

"What?"

"Give some old soru for my son, thayi. He has not eaten in two days." She emphasized her hunger with three gentle pats on her stomach. "Not a meal here for three! Please, thayi, just a bit of leftovers, and Lord Arumuga will be good to you!"

I had seen Amma take day-old rice and sambar for the beggars who sat near the temple entrance. But no one had been allowed to come into the backyard or the house. All non-Brahmin dealings were conducted on the other side of the gate. Now, all that was required for the afternoon to turn into a minor crisis was a casual glance from the neighbour's window. Brahmins this side, untouchables outside—that was the unspoken rule, and I had already broken it by inviting Neelaranjani into the backyard. One word from Vanaja Mami to Appa, and he would ruin the next few months for me. "Let me see," I said and stepped into the kitchen.

I knew she would not leave without some food. Neelaranjani had seen me picking the stones from the rice. If I said there was nothing cooked, she would have asked for the uncooked rice. I knew that as well. And there was some of the morning pongal that had turned out to be a bit soggy and Mallika had preferred rice cakes in her lunch box instead.

I quickly spread the spare banana leaf on the floor and spooned out all the rice porridge from the pot. I then slipped a newspaper under the leaf and carefully swirled it into a paper-leaf cone. The little timepiece beside the oil bottle on the spice cabinet showed 3:05 PM. I still had some time before I went out to meet Kamala. But I had to get Neelaranjani out of the backyard before Vanaja Mami stirred.

When I brought out my offering, Neelaranjani was waiting near the well. She had plucked a red hibiscus flower and clipped it to her hair, above her left ear. It gave her the appearance of an unassuming warrior princess. Life had returned to her face. Even in hunger, she looked happy. Sivarasa was following a pale cream butterfly that fluttered above his head and around the hibiscus bush.

Neelaranjani ran up to the veranda the moment she saw me approaching. She bowed with respect and took the packet-cone from my hands.

"Iru, thayi," she said, giving my hand a shake before letting it go. She placed the lunch bundle on the satchel and quickly grabbed my right hand again. She selected the red-black bead chain from around her neck and pulled it over her head with her left hand.

"This is for you!" she said. I saw in her eyes that she meant it. "It's not much, I know," she said, without any sadness. "But I can tell you one thing before I leave, which you may or may not remember in the future."

"What is that?"

If she predicts that I will marry a rich, decent, sensitive, young Brahmin man I will have to laugh, I told myself. Astrologers, palmists, clairvoyants, soothsayers all thought that was the first thing on a young Indian girl's mind.

"Don't give up the veena," Neelaranjani said. "There is a *mouna ragam* your fingers will bring to life."

"How do you know I play the veena?" I was stunned. My voice cracked in astonishment. "And what silent raga are you talking about? There is nothing like *mouna ragam* in music!"

"I have felt your fingertips, thayi."

She did not name the raga, but a smile of great warmth and feeling brimmed up in her eyes. "See for yourself."

I immediately looked at my hands and saw that there were indeed a few faint string marks etched into the fingertips. But they were minor compared to the calluses and peeling skin that had stippled my palms, bleached by harsh detergents. I could not feel the veena's imprints myself. Were they only felt by another's touch?

"Now I will go, my magarasi. You have been so kind to this poor soul. Sivarasa, say namaskaram to thayi, come on."

She picked up her satchel and food packet. Sivarasa was still honing his skills of butterfly baiting. He turned around, folded his palms, bowed quickly and went back to the never-ending chase. "My life, my everything," Neelaranjani smiled indulgently at her son. "*Poyittu varen*, thayi." She bowed again respectfully. She took my hands into hers and kissed my fingertips. "If I pass this way again, I will stop by to see you, Magarasi!"

As she stepped out the backyard gate with her son, the temple bells chimed, and the sound echoed in all four directions of the agraharam.

NEELARANJANI'S WORDS stayed with me all through the afternoon. "There is a *mouna ragam* your fingers will bring to life." What did she mean? What was that silent raga?

The evening drifted in a daze with the question marks suspended between my eyes, like an inerasable, stubborn bottu. Mallika and Appa went into their rooms to sleep after dinner and then played a game of chess while I tossed and turned with a phrase in my ears that wouldn't go away. I got up from my mattress in the hall and quietly made my way to the mottamadi. The stars were scattered like sequins in an endless violet sari. And then in half a minute my eyes arranged the little twinkles into another question, "How did Neelaranjani know I played the veena?" I asked in a whisper, expecting that booming voice from heaven that always answered such questions in the mythologicals I had seen.

The skies did not open, and no god with vermilion lips appeared in front of me and asked, "Child, what is your wish?"

I don't recall how long I sat there that night. But this much I remember: when I woke up at four that morning I was leaning against the side wall of the puja room downstairs. My hands cradled the veena. And there were three string marks etched deep into my right cheek where my face had rested in sleep on the jackwood neck of the instrument. Then the Rockfort Express shot into the night with a shriek of triumph, gleeful to have caught me napping once again.

MAY 1991

ASGAR IS IN a meeting with a producer, but I can hear him from behind the closed bedroom doors. His voice is louder than usual, and I worry that he will wake the children, fast asleep in their respective rooms at the far end of the hallway downstairs. Asgar, I conclude, is oblivious to such concerns. I can't read the cuttings file anymore. My eyes burn.

"But Khanna sahib," I hear his voice rise, the "sahib" stretched out into a drawl of controlled impatience, loud and clear.

"The script doesn't make sense! He sees his wife as a goddess each time he wants to make love to her, yet shrinks away? Is he mad? Or is he a hijra?" There is no immediate response. Then I hear a train of short coughs followed by a hard, unstoppable sneeze. I can picture him sitting downstairs, in the hall right below the bedroom. A bald, oily head sporting a trimmed, hennaed moustache, his pot-bellied body trapped in a tight pistachio safari suit. I can see him suddenly flushed and sweaty at the mention of a eunuch, jiggling and heaving in the grips of alcoholic shock, and spraying atoms of whisky into the air that would soon settle on the hall rug Asgar brought home from location in Ladakh last year.

"What Asgar-ji, you are talking?" Khanna manages. "She is Devi!"

Khanna's Hindu sentiments have been hurt, I can tell. Asgar's question has shaken him from the inside out, and his tone is politely belligerent. He believes in goddesses. Asgar, a Muslim, has been spared the real-life workings of Hindu mythology. The way it all creeps up into your world view, turning a man's point of view into a noble law for woman-kind. You exaggerate, Asgar often tells me, I know some liberal Brahmins. You may only have to ask their wives, I think on such occasions, as Amma's face flashes before my eyes.

I don't defend victims of the texts that bind, anymore. I know everything is a choice.

"Khanna sahib, I think you should approach Vinod or Prem with this script." I hear Asgar again, sounding fatigued. "I am too old for this anyway."

I know the meeting is winding down. When Asgar passes up projects by recommending others, I know the move is not selfless, just strategic. A lesson he has learned after twenty long years in a ruthless industry, where today's star is tomorrow's jinx. "Longevity without the fear of the numbers game," is his classic defence. He always says that in his interviews, in one way or another. I have also realized, after ten years of marriage, that he has a sure instinct about such things. He knows success is about luck, and he takes his risks wisely.

"Overexposure is so overrated," he remarked after he received the best actor award from the president two years ago. "I like my privacy. My family is not a film project."

"*Shukriya*, Khanna sahib. Let Remo know what happens. This year is out of the question."

Ten minutes later I hear Khanna's Benz pull out of the driveway, and the headlights flash across the bedroom window before the driver turns and speeds out the gate. Soon there are footfalls behind the door, and then the burnished gold doorknob turns.

"Still awake?" Asgar asks, as he walks to the bathroom, to the far left of our bedroom. "That Khanna is crazy. He expects me to give him two weeks of Riaz's dates for a crappy script! I mean..." His exasperation is met with splashes of cold water and I lose the rest of the sentence. It is late. Almost midnight and I have been up since four in the morning. Since I wrote that letter to Mallika I have had very little sleep. I don't fear the meeting. I fear the returning.

"So how was class today?" Asgar asks as he slips into bed.

"Two of my students will be going to the Melbourne International Arts Festival next year."

"That's really good news," he says, propping a pillow against the bedpost. He manoeuvres his right hand under my back and curves his fingers around my waist, gently pulling me closer to his chest.

"But you seem a bit lost. Are you all right?"

I know I should be ecstatic. Pramila and Sunder Rajan, two of my very best students, will be accompanying the music contingent to Melbourne. What is even more inspiring is the fact that we did not have to bribe anyone on the selection committee. My students will be playing the veena and gottuvadhyam for an international audience, and it will be a raga I trained them for. I should be delirious by now—if I were my usual self.

"I just want this meeting with Mallika to come and go quickly." I can't hear my own words. My mind has been walking those other streets of memory, elsewhere, lost all day in a place called Sripuram.

"I just confirmed the ticket today."

Asgar unwinds his arm from around me and turns on the bedside lamp. A mellow hue spreads around the bed, and the brown and the red woollen tartan is a fuzzy glow, fiery coals from under the forest floor.

"Why not send a cheque if the prospect is so distressing for you?"

"And how long would it take her to tear up the cheque?"

"That's her business. You did what you could."

He pulls out the chequebook from the drawer on his side of the bed.

"How much? *Bolo?*"

I realize he is serious about this. He also knows that returning wasn't my idea, this trek into the past after ten years of complete and fulfilling absence. Why did Gayatri Chitti, her cunning and cowardice intact, send that postcard to Zubeida's address? Isn't pride supposed to go before a fall? Why pull me back, ask me to help when you can't do so with humility? Leaving was easy. It is the leaving behind that one is never rid of.

"I am not dying to return either. And you know that." I turn away from him and reach for the glass of water under my side lamp. He tactfully changes the subject but leaves the chequebook on the bedside table.

"So when are you meeting the editor of *Nisa?* Remo was mentioning that on the set to someone about the big interview of Janaki Asgar. Tomorrow?"

"Yes."

"Are you prepared?" he asks, and I can see real concern in his eyes.

"I think I will be okay. I would rather all this had not come together now."

Asgar is the only man in the world who can still see the other Janaki in me. After all, he married the haunted girl from Sripuram. But he doesn't know the workings of a Tamil Brahmin family. How do I tell him that to know Mallika and Appa and Amma and Gayatri Chitti, to know their past, present and even their future, you also have to know how they think, how they see the world, how they judge it. I can hear their thoughts, I can see their deeds, I can feel their feelings, right here, sitting here on this bed far away from that other reality. What Mallika thinks, how Appa reacts, why Chitti complains and plots—that's inside me. Ten years ago. And now. Nothing changes in that world. But it is something I can never explain to Asgar. It is a bit like an amputee trying to explain the phantom pain and spasm where the limb used to be. How can you approximate that? Can you put that sensation in words? Can you comprehend it? I know what Asgar would say: "Janaki, it is all in your head." And it is. But, trust me, it is not fiction. I know that for real.

Before writing to Mallika, the whole idea of a silence-breaking interview to *Nisa*, the leading women's magazine in the country, for their silver jubilee issue, seemed worthwhile. I was uncharacteristically eager to talk about my veena school, which I opened in the third year of my stay in Bombay, at the age of twenty-six. Now, six years later, two of my students are going abroad as the national representatives of

South Indian classical music. Salima Sikri, the editor of the magazine, has been calling me for the past two years persuading me to talk. After a low-profile decade of self-imposed silence—I have only attended three film parties since my marriage to Asgar—the thought of opening up about my life in Bombay, my talented students, the happiness of being a mother, wife and working woman, all seemed to slowly grow on me. Salima Sikri was thrilled when I said I would do the interview in two sessions, over two days.

At some film party right now, Ms. Sikri must already be gloating about her perseverance and how it has finally paid off. She must be glowing like a silkworm with chunky oxidized-silver earrings, her eyes packed with excessive layers of kohl. She must be on her third whisky soda. I may be having doubts about the editorial coup, but Ms. Sikri, I am sure, is convinced that the interview with Janaki Asgar is publishing history.

Her story. In my own words.

And then my aunt wrote that postcard telling me about my father, and how everything, every spineless act of his from the past had caught up with him. Please, help. She did not even have the courage to sign the letter.

"I have an early call tomorrow morning. Remo will be here at seven." Asgar kisses me on the cheek and turns out the lamp. "Don't stress, Janu. It will be fine."

GADGIL, THE SECURITY guard, buzzes on the intercom to announce her arrival. "Send her to the upstairs lounge," I instruct him from the bedroom phone.

I am wearing a pale lavender salwar kurta with a steel grey dupatta. The diamond and amethyst earrings Asgar gave me on the day Neelam and Kabir were born dangle from my lobes with casual grace. My eyebrows are thinner than that of the Sripuram Janaki, and the pale pink lipstick is just right, subtle and quiet, unlike the flaming red that is the rage these days. It is five past ten in the morning. Asgar left on the dot of seven, and the kids are away at school. Zubeida will send the chauffeur to pick up Neelam and Kabir at three and drive them to her penthouse at Cuffe Parade.

When I look in the mirror before stepping out of the bedroom, I see a thirty-three-year-old woman who doesn't look a day over twenty-seven. She definitely does not look like the mother of two seven-year-olds. The woman in the mirror is poised and totally in control of the ghosts within her. Okay, Janaki Asgar, this is the moment, I tell myself. Seize it. And let the exorcism begin.

THE UPSTAIRS LOUNGE is L-shaped, and the horizontal segment faces the Arabian Sea. After I moved into this bungalow on a two-acre plot, ten years ago, I had the white walls of the lounge painted a burnt orange and cream, and installed three rows of teak planks arranged in the form of a swastika to display the many trophies and awards Asgar had won from the early years of his film career.

"The Brahmin touch?" Asgar remarked when I showed him my handiwork. "I like it." Zubeida later told me that the same symbol, turned the wrong way, was a sign of Hitler's Germany. "Nazis converted a perfectly auspicious Hindu symbol and made it into a sign of racist evil," she pronounced the first time she came around after I had had the room redone. I didn't tell her that my Sripuram textbooks had not mentioned the misuse of the swastika. "I can arrange another pattern if it is so unappealing to you," I had replied, my voice low, and my words fading into an apology. Asgar couldn't stop laughing. "See how she's trying to impress you with all her knowledge of history."

A six-by-nine-foot solarium with palm fronds and jasmine creepers provides a lush green corner and beyond that, through the French windows and the ornate gold-glass doors, the sea glitters in the morning sun, the waves undulating in small curves of crushed, sparkling crystals. The lounge is a very private area, removed from the traffic of the main house, and far away from the telephones, which begin jangling from seven in the morning and continue late into the night. This room is also my refuge when I am restless and unable to sleep, where I can play the veena into the early hours of the morning without disturbing Asgar or the kids with my plaintive raga. My veena rests against the wall, right below Asgar's framed citations on the wall. It is the focal point of the lounge.

"Salima Sikri," she says, as she rises from the beige leather sofa and extends her hand. I had not expected a namaste from the editor of India's leading feminist magazine, and I shake her hand with premeditated ease.

She is wearing no makeup, and her hair curves just an inch above her shoulders. A necklace of garnets dips between her breasts, the maroon stones a stark contrast against her primrose silk blouse. She is wearing a batik print skirt, and the deep brown of the fabric does its best to hide the extra pounds below her waist. I had expected her to be taller than she actually is, but she is about five-seven, five-eight. Her face has a youthful mischief, which is at odds with her otherwise matronly body. She sits back and rummages through her Gucci tote and pulls out a few copies of *Nisa*.

"Some back issues, although I am sure you've seen the portfolio I sent across with Mr. Da Silva?" Her eyebrows arch to highlight the question.

"Yes, I have. May I call you Salima?"

I sit down on the Rajasthani settee, my elbows resting on the bottle green bolsters with silken rainbow tassels. I pull up my legs and slide my toes under my thighs.

"Please," she replies, as she settles back in her seat. "I prefer it to Miss Salima, which is what I get from the bureaucrats in Delhi." She shrugs her shoulders. "Indian men so easily Ms. the point!" She chuckles at her own joke, and continues. "As you can see, Sonia Gandhi, Vijayaraje Scindia, Shabana Azmi and Gita Mehta have all graced the cover of *Nisa* in just the past six months."

"Oh, yes, I did see that," I say to myself. "The wife of the former prime minister, a woman of royalty, a celebrated actress and an international writer. Where do I fit in?"

"But we at our Bombay office are maha-pleased to have you as our silver jubilee woman!" I can sense the pride in Salima's voice.

"I am not in the same league," I reply. I pick up the intercom and dial the kitchen extension. "Those women are all so accomplished."

I am not yet ready to be seduced by her flattery. I am convinced that this is her regular routine with all her subjects. She will have to try another approach.

"Khan sahib? *Khala ke saath ʐara chai-biscuit behjengey? Jee haan, ooperwale Lounge mein.*" I replace the receiver and look up at Salima Sikri. "I'm sure you will have some tea?"

"Of course. How could I possibly turn down chai ordered in such earnest Urdu?"

Blood rushes to my cheeks this time, and I blush. "I could have ordered it in Tamil, which I still speak fluently, but unfortunately my kitchen is not equipped with a translator."

Salima laughs heartily. "To tell you the truth Mrs. Asgar—"

"Janaki would be fine with me," I interrupt, levelling the field of exchange.

"Janaki, then," she smiles in acknowledgement. "You surprise me with your ease and sense of humour. It is not what I expected." Her eyes hold me with a hint of apprehension. "Can I get the whole thing on tape?"

"I will tell you when I want the interview off the record."

"How much time do we have today?"

It is already ten thirty. I have to be at my veena school at three to sign a press release announcing the selection of the two students for the festival in Melbourne. After that I will drive over to Zubeida's, where Asgar will join the kids and me for dinner. "Three hours? And we can go a little longer if necessary the day after tomorrow?"

"Fine." She stands up. "I'll go over to the car and get the Marantz."

When she walks across the marble floor, her kolhapuri sandal heels clack like miniature hooves, and her bob-cut hair bounces off her shoulders in symmetry as though attached to a spring mechanism.

Salima Sikri, at that moment, brings to my mind the plump matrushka doll that stands alone on the top shelf of Zubeida's glass panel showcase.

"MEMSAHIB." Khala is standing with the tea tray on the steps of the lounge.

"*Shukriya, Khala.*" As I take the tray to the coffee table, Salima immediately gathers the copies of *Nisa* and piles them on the floor.

"Thank you."

I pour the tea into the gold-rimmed porcelain cups and look up. "Sugar?"

"Yes, please. Three."

She notices the quick rise and fall of my eyebrows and adds, "My only effort at being sweet." She laughs again at her twist of phrase.

The reel-to-reel is on the floor, under the table, and the cord is plugged into the socket behind the sofa. Salima picks up the microphone and places it on the table, between the teapot and the Johnny Walker ashtray. "Shall we begin?"

The tape spools, and I clear my throat. I place the teacup on the table. Salima assumes I am ready.

"I know this is your first interview in a decade, and can appreciate your nervousness. Let's just forget that there is a tape recorder in the room, okay?"

I nod, suddenly unsure of this whole enterprise. But there is only turning back, and no turning back—now. I take a deep breath.

"This is a question that I am sure everyone would like answered. Tell me, Janaki, is it karma or the veena that has made you what you are today?"

My laughter takes her by surprise. Tears flood my eyes. "That would be a lofty way of looking at the circumstances that have brought me to this point in my life." I can see Neelaranjani grabbing and kissing my hands again. "*Magarasi.*"

"Okay, give it to me in down-to-earth terms then?"

I pause for a minute and take in the silence around us. From under the glass table the two eyes of the recorder spin and stare back at me, unblinking. I lean forward and speak into the metallic mesh of the Sanyo microphone. Of course, I control how this story plays out, how it is received by the world.

"Laryngitis," I say softly. "And a four-by-six photo in a textbook."

GA

Once a month I washed the entire house. All the rooms were scrubbed from corner to corner; the stairs and floors were mopped till a shine came through the dull cement, and the cobwebs were gathered and rolled into a big ball and emptied in the dustbin beside the main gate. I dipped three fingers of my right hand in turmeric paste and drew broad namams on the bottom edge of the door frames and painted a big red kungumam eye in the centre of the fingerprint-tracks to ward off the evil eye. This had to be done during the auspicious hours of the day specified by the Brahmin calendar. Rahukalam—the hours of Saturn—were inauspicious. Yamakandam—the hours of death and sterility—were out of the question. I usually chose the day of the full moon. It was a good marker, and it gave me a month between the sheets of the calendar. Veedu Sutham, I wrote in the broad date column with a full moon circle on the top right-hand corner. I marked those Clean House days as soon as Appa brought the New Year calendars home. And I did not miss a date.

It was eleven in the morning, and I was just about done with the mopping and scrubbing. I stepped out into the backyard to inlay the turmeric prints on the tulasi pot, right below the opening for the clay lamps. I was onto the fourth and final side of the concrete pillar that held the pot in its hollow when I heard Vanaja Mami call my name from the other side of the compound wall.

"Mami?" I said, still squatting, my fingers horizontally flat and held firmly against the cold concrete. Has she run out of sugar again?

"Savitri Mami said there was a phone call from the school. It was the principal, I think. She wanted you to call back."

"When?" I asked.

"Oh? About an hour ago, I think. She told me to pass on the message when I was returning from the temple. *Pathu, pathey kaal irukkum . . .*"

Ten. Ten fifteen. And now she tells me! There was no use in getting annoyed with Vanaja Mami. She kept an invisible log in her head—and vengeance was always hers. She never forgot an inflection of defiance, or a word of anger—even if it was well deserved. Casual revenge was her style. And it was executed swiftly, without warning, always at the most unexpected moment. *"Parungo annah,"* she would begin from her window, as if she were discussing the weather, or the flight of a rare bird, when Appa was drawing water for his ablutions before the evening puja. "Your daughter is so friendly with all the merchants at the market, such an innocent girl . . . Hard to believe how quickly she is turning into a woman." Or, "The other day, I was at the temple and both your daughters were sitting on the reservoir steps and chatting. I know Janaki's laugh even without looking in that direction . . ." As soon as she saw Appa's face tighten in consternation—the effect she was counting on all along—she would quickly add, "Pavam, they must really miss their mother. Kamakshi would have been so proud to see them grow up and get married..." and let her sentence trail off.

A bunch of needles at the heart of a ripe banana. Vanaja Mami's time-tested, time-proven punishment for all sorts of imagined crimes and contradictions. She was very good at it.

"Did the principal say what the problem was, mami?" I asked, trying to keep the terseness out of my voice. I picked up the stained cloth rag beside the turmeric bowl and wiped my pasty hands. I was beginning to get worried. What has Mallika gone and done?

"Illai, Janaki. Maybe you should call back soon. Or better still, go to the school itself, enna?"

I had drained the starch water from the morning rice into a bucket. My next chore was to soak Appa's office shirts and Mallika's school uniform in the bucket and then hang them out to dry in the afternoon sun. That way they would be ready for ironing in the evening. But that chore would have to wait. I changed into a blue cotton sari, locked the doors and latched all the windows, and stepped out the gate.

I envisioned the worst possible scenarios on the way to the school: Mallika had fallen from the school swing and had fractured her right leg. I heard a nurse in starched white whisper in my ear, "She will never be able to walk without crutches for the rest of her life!" Mallika had been caught cheating in the midterm tests, or worse, she had submitted an incomplete answer sheet. Appa had forgotten to pay the monthly tuition fees or the cheque for the amount had bounced. "Please, please," the voice in my head kept repeating, "let it not be something that makes Appa pull Mallika out of school. Let her fate not be like mine. Mallika, what have you got yourself into?" My lips moved slowly, and I chanted slokas, "O, Goddess! Ward off evil. Let good triumph once again."

The school gatekeeper recognized me as soon as he saw me approaching.

"Enna, Janaki? What brings you to school at this hour?" he asked as he searched for the key to the lock. He pulled the heavy iron chain that looped around the centre of the two tall swing doors and gave the NavTal lock a tug after he inserted the key.

"The principal wants to see me, Vellappa. Did Mallika hurt herself during PT class?"

"No, kannu," he replied with a yawn, revealing bidi-stained teeth. "I didn't see anything."

The doors swung left and right, squealing and screeching with rusty exhaustion and reminding me of an old woman with severe arthritis. I ran under the curving arch with Sripuram Vidyalaya (CBSE) written in bold black letters, heading straight for the principal's office, diagonally opposite the flagpole. The corridor of the newly constructed administrative annex was deserted, but voices from the adjacent class-room building crackled like static, and I could hear Sudha Miss's voice above the buzzy waves of nattering back row girls, "An amphibian is a creature that can survive on land and in water—Shailaja, pay attention!"

"Is principal amma in?" I asked the peon who sat on a rickety wooden stool, guarding the entrance to the office. Before he could answer my question a voice from behind the saloon-style doors inquired, "Is that Janaki?"

"Yes, madam," I answered, as the peon flipped the polished overlatch.

Mrs. Manoharan had been the principal for the past three years, replacing Mr. Pillai, the man who had seconded Appa's decision to pull me out of school. She was sitting behind her desk, poring into a file marked Stationery Budget in bold red lettering. She looked up as I entered the room. Sports trophies and merit-student citations lined the wall behind her chair.

"Come in, Janaki."

The room was sparse but clean, and a pedestal fan whirred in the far corner, beside the eastern wall. A stone statue of Saraswati, the Goddess of Learning, stood on the other side. The garland of sandalwood shavings around the neck of the deity had a thin veneer of dust. The floor was spotless, however, and there was a faint smell of phenyl in the air. I had never entered this new office before. Seven years out of school. Had it really been so long? Where did the days go?

Mrs. Manoharan's swivel chair grunted as she stood up and came to the front of the table.

"Is everything—Is my sister..."

"Sit, Janaki," she said as she pulled one of the two visitors' chairs for me. She sat down on the other chair, facing me.

"Don't worry, Janaki, Mallika is fine. But I did not think it appropriate to call your father at the bank..."

My body suddenly felt light and weightless, as though the steamroller pressing my heart had suddenly moved on and vanished. Mallika was all right! "I just got the message, so I came right away."

"I am glad you did," Mrs. Manoharan replied. She looked over my shoulder at the saloon doors. Then she lowered her voice and said in whisper, "Your sister, Mallika, came of age during math class this morning."

Oh, God! Why didn't I think of that? Mallika is thirteen! My time had come three months before Amma went on that bus trip to Nearby Temples, her pilgrimage of no return.

"Naturally, she is upset about the whole thing . . . I am sure you can understand," Mrs. Manoharan smiled sympathetically.

"Where is she now, madam? Can I see her?"

"Of course! She is in the crafts room. Malathi Miss is with her. Do you know where the room is?"

"Yes, madam. Can I go?" I stood up.

"You will let us know if you need assistance?" I ran down the corridor, the flapping of the saloon doors my creaky answer to Mrs. Manoharan's question.

"AKKA, AM I going to die?" Mallika hugged me in a tight embrace and started to cry.

"No, *thangame*, no, you will be all right, now just keep calm. See Akka is here, illaiya? Everything is going to be fine . . ."

I requested Malathi Miss to send for a cycle rickshaw. By the time Vellappa arrived with one at the school playground gate, Mallika had been draped in an old veshti pulled out from the school drama wardrobe and had been coaxed to drink a bottle of almond milk. She still sniffed at regular intervals, her state of disorientation breaking through in sobbing spurts. I thanked the crafts teacher and gave directions to the rickshaw man. He raised himself from his cycle seat and, heaving and puffing, began pedalling across Clive Road, heading uphill and east into the agraharam.

As soon as we got home, I escorted Mallika to the upstairs bathroom. I unbuttoned her school uniform and threw it into the laundry basket. Mallika looked down at her knickers for the first time and shrieked in horror.

"Aiyyyo, Akka, I am going to die." I covered her mouth with my hand.

"Shh! Akka won't let that happen, *thangame . . .*"

I pulled down the blood-soaked white knickers and threw them beside the drain. With a wet towel I wiped her thighs. Then I turned on the shower. Mallika kept her eyes tightly closed, and her face clenched and contorted under the cold spray of water. She did not see the red rivulets that ran down from an invisible source within her. She sobbed as the ripples of womanhood circled her feet and disappeared, sloping into the drain.

"Now listen to Akka, sariya?" She nodded. She still did not open her eyes.

"I will bring something to make you feel better. But you are not to move from the bathroom. *Purinjitha,* understood?" She nodded again. Just make it all go away!

I remembered everything Amma had done for me during my first time. I went downstairs and placed a pot with water on the gas stove. While the water came to a boil I emptied two inch-long pieces of dried turmeric root into the marble mortar. From the puja room shelf I took a sliver of sandalwood bark and soaked the shard in three tablespoons of warm water. I pounded the turmeric with the pestle and mixed the sandalwood together to form a thick, loamy paste. I transferred the paste into a stainless-steel rasam bowl and took the container upstairs. From the almirah I pulled out my starched set of pavadai dhavani. From Mallika's side of the cupboard

I chose a blouse and a fresh pair of knickers. I ran my hands on the upper shelf and located the slab of pumice. From under my pile of saris I pulled out a sanitary napkin.

When I stepped into the bathroom again, Mallika was sitting hunched on the wooden bath stool, her hands folded around her stomach. I scrubbed her entire body with the paste from the bowl, all the while reassuring her that everything was going to be all right. I told her that what had happened to her today had also happened to me many years ago. "And Akka didn't die. Akka is still here, illaiya?"

As soon as the layer of paste dried and parched all over Mallika's body, I took the plastic bucket from the bathroom downstairs and filled it with the boiling water. I gave Mallika a sponge bath.

"Now you are a big girl, Malli. And this is going to happen for four or five days every month. Remember the Stayfree advertisement on TV?"

I placed the pad between her legs and helped her pull up the knickers to her waist. Once she had changed into her new set of clothes, I dampened her face and exfoliated her cheeks gently with the pumice. I towelled her hair dry and wove two short plaits. After her eyes were lined with kohl I made a small red bottu in the centre of her forehead, half an inch above her eyebrows. I couldn't believe how quickly the pavadai dhavani transformed her into a woman.

"Now let's go down and say namaskaram to Amma, okay?"

Mallika bowed in front of the photo in the hall and closed her eyes. Slowly her body relaxed, and her face broke free from panic. After five minutes of meditation she opened her eyes and turned to me. "Don't leave me ever, Akka."

Her voice was still that of a thirteen-year-old girl. *"Ennik-kum."* Her arms circled me once again in a tight embrace. Forever.

Looking back, I now realize that was when it all began in some unconscious way. It was perhaps the beginning of the elusive goodbye note slowly making its way to those Leo Coffee packets in the kitchen.

MA

GAYATRI CHITTI blew in the following week, like a nonseasonal cyclone from the Bay of Bengal.

"Your father knew I was coming," she blustered. "Mallika is in school?"

She did not wait for my answer.

"Yevallavu?" She turned to the autorickshaw driver who had conveyed her from the bus station. Out came the handkerchief from her left bra cup, the currency mats were rolled out and she paid him his fare, one damp, sweaty note at a time.

"Here, take this into the house."

I took the suitcase and carryall and crossed to the threshold wondering if Chitti would remark on my morning kolam. She stepped over the pattern. Four flat footprints between the lotus leaves is all the praise my masterpiece deserved. She glanced around to see if anyone had noticed her arrival into the agraharam. No one had. Not even Vanaja Mami, who was ready for a peek at the slightest commotion. Chitti had not planned such an unimportant entry. She looked disappointed.

"I'm here now, Kamakshi!" Chitti exclaimed with folded palms in front of Amma's photo. "I will take care of your little Mallika."

As though things had fallen apart in her absence. *Really.*

"Bring some water to boil. I'll take a bath."

Why did Appa not tell me Chitti was considering a visit this week? I lowered the metal bucket into the well. I had handled Mallika's transition into womanhood with sensitivity and tact. Mallika was back to her old self in two days, somewhat shy, but definitely over the initial sense of shame and embarrassment. When I told Appa what had happened, his eyebrows crisscrossed with worry. "Hmm," is all he said. Before retiring to bed that night he asked, "You can manage on your own, illaiya?" I nodded. "Yes." Of course I could. I had managed on my own for the past seven years. Did he expect Mallika to be thirteen for the rest of her life?

Appa might have mentioned the incident to Gayatri Chitti on the phone, and she could have made a great fuss. I was certain she had convinced him that her presence in Sripuram was essential—that she had to come over—at least for a few days. Appa never said no to her. Only I knew too well that concern was not what brought Chitti to our doorstep. Any excuse was a good one as long it served her own needs. Chitti's sudden fretting about Mallika was a big whitewash. She did not even remember Mallika's birthday!

I hoped the cyclone would move on after the weekend.

"Bathwater is ready, Chitti."

She climbed the stairs to the bathroom muttering, *"Eashwara,"* at every step as though her feet were tied to a huge concrete block. She ran her fingers over the handrail and looked at them casually. They were dust free. There was nothing to criticize.

Gayatri Chitti unwound her sari, unbuttoned her blouse and unhooked her bra. She pulled her petticoat over her breasts and tied the drawstring behind her back. I poured the boiling water into the bucket and turned on the cold water. Chitti dipped her right hand into the bucket a few times to test the temperature, then turned off the cold.

"Here, scrub my back."

She sat on the wooden bath platform and poured three mugs of water over her body. I took the soap from her hand and lathered her back.

The matchstick chariot had grown into a real one over the years. The flesh above her petticoat bulged like kneaded and rolled chapatti dough. She had also taken to dyeing her hair an unnatural black, and I noticed a field of silver hair roots on the back of her skull.

"Two girls to marry off! *Eashwara!* Tchu, tchu, tchu!" She called out to the gods and her immortal, heavenly dog.

"Why did Kamu leave me with such responsibilities? Why didn't I die instead of her?"

What responsibilities? I thought. What have you done for us these seven years but eat and complain and frolic with your dead sister's husband? I kept the thought to myself.

"And there you are, twenty now, and still chasing away all the proposals I send your way."

She tilted her toes upwards and examined her chipped scarlet nail enamel.

As I poured water over her back, dark skin emerged from under the creamy white lather, like night sky after dusk. Soapy water ran to the drain and made a sucking sound as it gathered on the slotted metal saucer. I put the soap back in the dish.

"Appa did not tell me you were coming over. I'll go down and clean some more rice." I had had enough.

Just half an hour into the house and already Chitti's familiar dirge, like a mattai creaming buttermilk, was beginning to churn gloom around me. I would have happily spent a lifetime with her if she were mute. Her talk always grated on me, like a pin stuck on a record. The worst consequence of Amma's death, I realized, was not my truncated education. It was Amma's unbearable, all-false-notes-guaranteed sister.

She's ringworm suspended between heaven and earth, I said to myself. Reddening into time and space. Yes, I thought. Why didn't you—

My patience with this whole business of respect-the-elders-even-if they-are-eczema was running precariously thin.

When I told Mallika about Chitti's unexpected arrival, her first question was: "Akka, will she sleep with me in my room?"

I said I didn't know, but as that was what Chitti had done during her previous visits I told her she should be prepared to sleep on the floor. I said I would make her bed near the window, and she could wake up to the twittery welcome of the sparrows on the sill.

"Wouldn't that be something wonderful, *thangame?*" I said, trying to cheer her up.

"Akka," Mallika frowned. "Chitti snores like a car radiator! A real pishashu!"

THE BANSHEE WAS waiting for us on the veranda.

She ran down the stairs and opened the gate as soon as she saw us turn the corner of A Block. She was wearing a cotton blouse with red flower-puff sleeves and a light green nylex sari. The diamond nose ring on her face shone like a naked bulb in a dark sea dinghy. Aged thirty-something, she wore her hair in two pigtails with pink ribbon bows and spoke Brahmin Tamil.

"Kannu! Mallika! *Rajathi!* How big you look now!"

And then Mallika was lost in the ghostly embrace.

I watched as Mallika fought and gasped as she sank into strata of fake love, coconut oil, talcum powder and Afghan Snow Cream.

"Soon we will have to find a mappillai for you!" Chitti squealed, planting wet, disingenuous kisses left, right and centre. "What a lucky man he will be!"

"Let me go, Chitti! You are crumpling my school uniform!"

Grabbing the flesh on Gayatri Chitti's midriff with both her hands Mallika pushed with all the force she could summon. Chitti reeled back, stumbled and swerved. For a moment I thought she would fall over the dustbin beside her, but she steadied herself by grabbing the bars of the gate. Straightening the pleats of her sari and refluffing the crushed fabric flowers of her blouse, she let eyes dart quickly to the other houses in the neighbourhood. Her near fall had not been witnessed.

"I don't want your mappillais!" Mallika yelled, wiping the spit colonies on both her cheeks. "I have homework to do!"

"Shh! Just go in and take your bath!" I said.

I was happy that Mallika had asserted herself but also knew that if I let the situation escalate it could have some unsavoury consequences for both of us. Gayatri Chitti and Vanaja Mami were cut from the same cloth. They both loved bananas and loved hiding needles in them even more.

"I'll call you when dinner is ready, *purinjitha*," I said sternly.

Mallika gave me a why-are-you-taking-her-side-now glare. Then she picked up her school bag from the ground where it had fallen and ran into the house.

"She's only thirteen, Chitti," I said. Please don't tell Appa.

"Yes, I know," Chitti replied.

I couldn't gauge her mood. Her voice was flat and dry, but there was no trace of anger. She walked to the steps of the veranda and sat down.

"She's touchy about everything these days," I continued, steering the conversation towards forgiveness.

"Oh, but she has a lot of power, our kutty Malli," Chitti replied.

She flung her pigtails over her shoulders. She arched her back and thrust her breasts into the air. Her elbows supported her body, supine on the top step.

"That chit of a girl will need a real man, a mahapurusha, to hold her down."

I could see what was going through Chitti's mind.

Torsos, and thighs, and a man's erect manhood. Dark silhouettes of passion under a white mosquito net.

I remained silent.

"I am sure she will appreciate it one day."

The pink bows of ribbon curled like newborn snakes at the edge of her plaits. As I stepped into the house, I heard Chitti shuddering to the transparencies in her head.

"Ahh. . ." she cooed.

LOOK AFTER HER well, a voice within me instructed, and she will leave in forty-eight hours.

Endure the weekend and all will be fine.

At the same time something formless at the back of my mind prodded me with morbid images.

I smelled imminent disaster, the way a rodent smells a python near its nest.

I heard the rasp of fire and the numb submission of burning timber.

I reached into my head and pulled the shutters on a chorus of ululating owls.

You are overreacting, Janaki!

Why should this visit of Gayatri Chitti be any different from the previous ones? Just get on with your day as usual and soon she will be gone. Her depressing words can only have an effect on you if you allow them to, I reasoned. Ignore her banter about men and marriage and, before you know it, she will be boarding the bus back to Madras. Be patient.

Gayatri Chitti had rolled out the bamboo mat and was napping on the floor outside the puja room. Mallika had not emerged from her room, where I presumed she was busy doing her homework. It was five in the afternoon—another hour before Appa returned from the bank. It gave me enough time to get dinner ready and cooking.

I went upstairs to the storeroom and brought down the larger copper pots. We had not cooked in those dowry pots since the rituals of Amma's first death anniversary. I rinsed the pots and soaked rice in one. In the other pot I brought water to a boil and blanched snow peas, string beans and bite-size florets of cauliflower.

From the top kitchen cabinet I pulled out a muslin towel and lined a stainless-steel thali. Into the lined plate I emptied the curds that had set like a slab of polished ivory with a lake of yellow water on the surface. Quickly, I gathered the borders of the towel, tied the edges with twine and let the curd water drip and filter over the sink. While this step was not absolutely essential, I was convinced that draining the water made the curds firmer, which in turn made the patchadi sauce creamier and richer.

Although I had assumed the role of a cook without much say in the matter, over the years I had grown to enjoy it. A well-prepared meal, I discovered, was like a finely elaborated raga. They both stirred the soul and evoked emotions that escaped words. If simplicity was the bedrock of the two undertakings, concentration and timing were the two guides to the summit of success. I chose a menu like I would the scale of an octave. The growth arc had to arrive at its crescendo within a preset length of time. You can't collect compliments when what is served up is cold, flat or overdrawn. The blending of spices I realized was akin to nuancing the microtones between the notes—the buzzing gamakams that teased a connoisseur's palate and then lingered on memory's tongue.

Like the *Ma* in Milaghu, the quick burst of black pepper in the soft dome of your mouth. Like the *Pa* in Patte, the sweet wave of cinnamon flooding into your veins.

That evening my culinary raga was already spreading its wings, and the aroma that circled the corners of the kitchen was enough to make the most hard-hearted of gods drool and swoon.

I sautéed the pearl-chip onions to a golden brown and mixed the drained rice into the same buttered pot. A pint of water, a quick boil and then a low-flame simmer with the lid on. Twenty minutes, and the pilau would be ready to gently fluff and serve. The blanched vegetables had been seasoned with star anise and coconut, and the yogurt sauce clung to the green textures like molten sunshine on a leafy bough. All that remained for my symphony to reach its zenith was the fresh zest of mint chutney with pomegranate juice, and the glossy garnish of shallow-fried cashews and raisins for the rice.

I glanced at the clock above the spice cabinet. Six fifteen.

As I was about to step out into the backyard to fetch the mortar and pestle, Gayatri Chitti pushed open the closed kitchen doors and walked in.

"Your father is back from the office and would like to have his coffee."

I had been so lost in the dizzy sizzle of my fragrant world that I had not heard the drone of Appa's scooter entering the gate.

"Itho," I said, stepping back into the kitchen and reaching for the Leo Coffee packets on the cabinet shelf. "I'll bring it out in five minutes."

Chitti stood near the door for a while as I scooped the ground beans into the percolator. I expected her to comment on the sweet smells in the kitchen and I was half ready to turn around with a thankful smile. But she just stood there and stifled a yawn.

"Make sure you don't dent the pots when you wash them tonight. They are more expensive than you think."

Chitti laced the fingers of both her hands together, stretched to the refrain of *"Eashwara"* and cracked her knuckles.

"Dinner will be ready at seven?"

Not a query, but a queen banshee pronouncement.

And then she walked back into the hall, leaving the doors ajar.

I ARRANGED PAGES of an old newspaper in the centre of the hall. On the paper, I placed the pots of rice, vegetables and the bowl of chutney. I positioned four seating mats around the newspaper square and in front of them I laid four evenly cut banana leaves. I filled the stainless-steel glasses with water. When I had finished with the place settings, I went back into the kitchen and fried lentil pappadums in the aluminum wok. With the plate of crispies in one hand, I stepped back into the hall and latched the kitchen door.

"Mallika, come down for dinner!" I called.

Appa and Chitti heard my voice and came in from the front veranda. Appa had changed into his veshti and a striped short-sleeved shirt. He had performed his evening puja, and a small stripe of thiruneer, divine ash, glowed in the centre of his forehead. Mallika came down the stairs and sat in her usual place.

"I'll serve," Chitti said.

"No, I can do it," I replied, picking up the flat rice spoon. My voice held no hostility.

Chitti hesitated for a moment, and I thought she would say something about my lack of respect, or she would start hissing Amma's name and how her daughter had lost all sense of tradition and *sampradhayam*, but she sat down without a comment, across from Appa. He, as usual, was his voice-less self. After Amma's death his vocabulary had dropped to monosyllables. I was sure he wouldn't open his mouth and come to Chitti's defence. He knew that I knew. Nothing parches the vocal chords like shame.

They reached for their glasses at the same time. They poured a little water into their cupped palms and sprinkled the drops over the banana leaves. With their right hands they wiped the leaf clean. I measured equal amounts of pilau, patchadi and chutney onto their respective leaf plates and dropped two crisp pappadums each, on the side. I did the same for myself and sat down to eat.

They ate like survivors of some African famine.

Chitti rolled the rice into small Ping-Pong balls and threw them into her mouth. One, two, three...I watched them slide, bulging like bird eggs down a snake's gullet, before they disintegrated into her stomach. Mallika broke off small bits of her pappadum evenly along the circumference and nibbled on them with her front teeth with the concentration of a squirrel. Appa dislodged a bay leaf from a lump of pilau with his thumb and index finger, and pulled it to the corner of the banana leaf as though he were drawing lice from a single strand of hair.

No one said a word about the food, but they helped them-selves to more.

Except for the intermittent swooshing and swirling of fin-gers on smooth, waxy leaves, and the unavoidable crunch and crackle of pappadum, silence enveloped us in the hall.

Shantham—Quietus, according to our Vedas, was a high virtue.

Prasannam—Joyful expression, in our household, was ugly sacrilege.

I DUMPED ALL the banana leaves into the corporation bin in the back alley. After filling the tin drums with well water, I washed the copper pots and the glasses and wiped them dry. My body reeked of spice fumes, making me feel like a walking bottle of garam masala, and I decided to take a shower.

When I came downstairs in my fresh sari and blouse, Appa was reading the newspaper, and Mallika and Chitti were watching a wildlife program on TV.

"I promised Revathi and Kamala I would go with them to the dance drama at the temple tonight," I said.

Appa lowered the newspaper and looked at me. Before he could utter a word, Chitti turned around and addressed me with tsunami eyebrows.

"Young girls like you should—" she started and I cut her off.

"Kamala's mother will accompany us. You can come, too, if you want. The dance troupe is from Kumbakonam, and on its way to Tiruvannamalai. I hear they are very good."

Assertions were better than requests for permission. I had learned that from Chitti just a few hours ago.

It was a risk, inviting Chitti, but I knew that she would decline. And she did.

"Aiyyo! That bus ride from Madras has given me a sore back. What are they performing?" she asked, and I knew she was just biding time before the final no. I could see her mind racing through possible excuses that might prevent me from going as well.

"Shakti Leela," I replied, grabbing the house keys from the hook beside Amma's photo. Just try stopping me.

"I'll come, Akka," Mallika stood up, "please" written all over her face.

"No, kanna, you have half-day school tomorrow," I said gently. "I've made your bed on the floor near the window. No TV after nine thirty, enna?" Mallika scowled and went back to the jungle on TV.

From the corner of my eye I saw Chitti exchange a quick glance with Appa. He shook the newspaper noisily before turning the page. A coward hiding behind a newsprint screen.

"You'll sleep in Mallika's bed, Chitti?"

It was the wrong question at the wrong moment. The word "bed" startled her, coming as it did right after that quick nonverbal messaging between her and Appa.

"Hahhnn, yes. Oh, this padupavi back makes me miss everything in life!"

Chitti started to massage her back melodramatically. "Mallika, kannu, you will rub some Vicks on Chitti's back, sariya," she said, moaning with every grab and release of her massaging palm.

"If that's what you want me to do," Mallika replied. I could sense the irritation in her voice.

"I should be back by eleven. There's a jug of water on the windowsill if you feel thirsty in the night."

I strapped my sandals, switched on the front veranda light and stepped out the door. I could feel Chitti's eyes burning my back.

As I turned to replace the overlatch on the gate, I saw Appa peering over the closed lower shutters of the window.

I could not see the expression on his face, just the refraction of light from the bulb as it bounced off his reading glasses. He stood there, like a meaningless sentence, framed by two iron bars.

I pulled my sari pullo over my shoulder.

Then I walked to the temple without a trace of guilt in my heart.

REVATHI WAS WAITING beside the parijatha tree in her compound. She stepped out and locked the gate as soon as she saw me.

"Why the delay?" she asked, pushing a tassel of curls behind her left earlobe. She looked beautiful, petite in her cream and red kota silk sari. We were the same age, presumably with the same fate.

"Gayatri Chitti arrived from Madras today."

That was the only context she needed. Revathi knew all about my ever-dramatic aunt.

"Really? I should have guessed."

"Where's Kamala?" I inquired.

"She went ahead to save a spot for us."

We crossed from B Block and entered the eastern alley around the temple. The time was a little after nine, but business in the little thatched shops was still brisk. Women were buying jasmine and kanakambaram garlands, and children stood around the cotton-candy vendor, mesmerized by the fuzzy marvels in pink.

"Want some malli?" Revathi asked, eager for an affirmative reply.

"Reva, we're ten minutes late. We might have missed the *alarippu* already."

She went ahead and bought two jasmine garlands. We hurriedly pinned the flowers to our plaits and ran double-quick to the temple mandapam.

Dance troupes rarely performed at Narayana temple. But when they did, the agraharam swarmed the mandapam like flies around congealed brown sugar. On such nights the pavilion, which stood between the main shrine and the reservoir, stirred once again, thankful for the most fleeting of resurrections.

When Revathi and I entered the courtyard it was a sea of heads. The mandapam stood at the centre with the four stone-horse pillars frozen in time. Bright Petromax lamps with burning mercury bulbs dangled from their raised hooves on each corner. Men and women sat in two sections segregated along gender lines. Children, sleepy but too excited to sleep, hopped between the divide like ambivalent bridges, unable to make up their minds if they liked their fathers more than their mothers.

Kamala spotted us at the entrance and waved.

Revathi and I made our way through the throng of women, ignoring the "ptchu-ptchu" snickers and "Here come the maharanis!" and reached the third row. Kamala immediately withdrew the shawl that lay on the grass as our proxy.

"What took you so long? You missed the *alarippu*," she said, shuffling to her left and making enough room for two.

"Blame her," I replied with a quick dart of my chin in Revathi's direction. "She stopped to buy mallippoo."

"You were late getting to my house, why don't you admit that?" Revathi shot back as she sat down.

"Okay, okay, calm down," Kamala said as she dusted the leaves of grass from the shawl and wrapped it around her body. "The varnam should begin any minute."

We had missed the formal welcome but were in time for the main narrative, the heart and soul of every dance performance.

"Where's your mother?" Revathi and I asked the question at the same time.

"Right at the back, with my niece."

Then the musicians, at the far left of the stage, strummed the opening bars. The male vocalist, his lips stained red with betel-nut juice, began the alaapana.

A few notes into the abstract humming and Kamala piped up, "Raga Bhopali." Revathi, who was always ready with a rejoinder, cut in. "Oh, listen to the Hindustani specialist!" she said, alluding to Kamala's experiments with North Indian classical music on the violin. "We, of the southern tradition, call it Mohanam!"

"They are both from the same source, Mela Kalyani. So nobody wins!" I said, settling the dispute with confidence.

Revathi, who never gave up without a fight, hummed the ascending and descending notes softly to herself. Kamala and I were all ears.

Sa–Ri–Ga–Pa–Da–Sa
Sa–Da–Pa–Ga–Ri–Sa

"See?" I said, thrilled with myself. "I was right! All sharp, suddha notes and no Madhyamam and Nishadham!"

"Shoo! What will it take to shut you girls up?"

Revathi turned around and faced the voice that addressed us collectively.

The woman was sitting right behind us. She was nursing her baby girl, the pullo of her sari lowered over her left breast.

"You make sure you keep that nipple in her mouth throughout the performance!" Revathi snarled, and looked away before the woman could answer. I was overwhelmed by Revathi's audacity and kept my eyes fixed on the mandapam lights.

We heard the chimes of salangai bells on the dancers' feet, and a sudden hush washed over the entire courtyard.

Chaos in the Heavens.

Four bit-player gods with bare chests and tinsel crowns ran left and right in choreographed confusion.

They raised their hands in delicate helplessness and called out to the Hindu trinity:

> *"O Brahma! O Vishnu! O Shiva!*
> *Creator! Preserver! Destroyer!*
> *Mahishasura, the King of Demons,*
> *Is on his way!*
> *Save us now!*
> *Save us, we pray!"*

Their eyelids drooped and their voices rose.

Their voices rose and their eyelids drooped.

Ten minutes of bathos and three shadows converged on the stage.

Left. Centre. Right.

Brahma in the middle looked tired.

THEY DANCED for a few minutes in perfect rhythm.

Then they got angry and got their act together.

"SHIVA IS THE best-looking of the three," Revathi whispered in my ear.

"Shut up and watch!" I said, squeezing her fingers.
Kamala glared at us.

"Let us make our weapon together!
Let us vanquish Mahishasura forever!"

All the gods formed a circle, moving in closer and closer till it got to be too close for comfort. This was the cue for the single spotlight operator to switch on the red. As soon as the light changed, the dry-ice machine spewed thick, artificial fog from the northern interior of the stage.

The vocalist pushed his chords to a pitch.

The gods swayed in a circle, like inebriated but tethered elephants.

Slowly the smoke settled.

Slowly a female form grew out of the circle.

She stood at the centre as the gods transformed into a languorous lotus.

Praises rang. And the heavens rained.

And Shakti coughed, before she sang:

"Shiva, give me your trident,
Brahma, give me your Vedas,
Kaala, give me your sword and your shield.
I am Shakti,
Force of One,
Subject to None.
Lead me to Mahishasura,
I'll make him yield!"

"She's so young!" the woman behind us muttered under her breath.

"Only young girls have the courage to fight back!" Revathi said, spoiling for a fight.

"I think you mean talk back," the woman replied, rocking her sleeping baby on her lap.

"Too bad your daughter has you for a mother!"

"What was that?" the mami raised her voice in anger, missing the last few words.

"She said Shakti is our Mother, mami," I answered quickly, digging my nails deep into Revathi's hand.

ON THE STAGE Shakti rode her lion to confront Mahishasura.

Supreme Goddess. Megaweapon. Twinkle Toes.

> *"Kill him now, O Mother of Gods!*
> *Kill him now with your eighteen arms!"*

Thunder rolled and lightning rippled as Shakti cupped her hands and drank from the Bowl of Life.

She raised the plywood trident with both her hands.

Mahishasura ran around the stage but there was nowhere to hide.

The proscenium turned red once again.

Shakti's eyes burned with murderous rage, and the trident came down in slow motion.

Then, Mahishasura, the bull with a man's head, gasped for life.

The trident sliced through his neck.

His head rolled to the high pitch of percussion.

> *Dheem Tari-Ki-Ta*
> *Dheem Tari-Ki-Ta*
> *Dheem Dheem Dheem*

Shakti danced around the stage, the decapitated head of the demon dangling from her hand. She smiled a bloody smile.

The lion roared. The gods bowed. Rose petals rained.

SHAKTI.

Primal force.

Omnipotent goddess.

Twenty-year-old girl.

WE MADE OUR way to the temple entrance from a cloud of dry-ice smog. All the mamis were lining up to collect their slippers, which we had turned in for a numbered token before entering the inner sanctum. Kamala's mother was ahead in the line, with the little girl fast asleep on her shoulder. Suddenly we felt drained and exhausted, and an irritable calm spread around the courtyard like a feeble virus. Even the tinkling of kolusu bells around the ankles rang like bombardments in our ears. We had had two and a half hours of bells and drums and nothing but.

Revathi and I joined the queue for our footwear while Kamala went over to her mother.

"I don't know where I put my token!" Revathi shattered the silence with a pure note of calamity. She dug into the pink wet-look rexine money purse she had picked up a month ago at Jee-O-Jee, the fancy store on Clive Road.

"Itho, hold your pullo like a net, and let me empty the purse," I volunteered.

I was not in a mood for more drama. A few sleepy mamis snickered behind us and made some noises of annoyance.

"Sariyana nuisance," one use-English-when-bothered mami cussed, and as I turned to look at her she started to rub her eyes as though she had an on-the-spot attack of blindness. I grabbed the silver metal mouth of the purse with both my hands and shook the contents into Revathi's upturned pullo.

Monthly bus pass, two crumpled five-rupee notes, two Halls Mentho-lyptus, one Sai Baba pendant, one hairpin slide, one eyeliner pencil. No token.

"*Aiyyo!* It's not there!" Revathi shrieked. "I must have dropped it near the mandapam!"

I gathered up her treasures once again and stuffed the mouth of the change purse, which was beginning to seem more and more like a bloated pink Dubble Bubble gum.

"I'll keep your place. You go look for it," I said.

Revathi looked at the lineup. More than sixty mamis queued after us, and more were joining in every minute.

"You think I'll find it?"

"No."

"You don't think I'll find it?"

"Reva, you go look. It will be ten minutes at least before we move up, enna?"

There was no chance of Revathi finding that token of cardboard in all the litter left behind after the performance. The older widows and mamis, the ones who swept up the rubbish after temple events, were ready with their brooms the moment the dance drama had ended. I could hear their dried-palm rakes behind the wall, singing in nocturnal penance. But Revathi had to work these things out for herself; till then one had to be patient. Kamala had summed it up quite succinctly a few months ago after veena class: Miss Reaction-Before-Action.

"Maybe I'll pay them for the token. About five rupees maximum!"

Sometimes, it was good to feign indifference and still hold your ground. Revathi snapped her purse shut and looked in the direction of the pavilion.

"That token is not going to walk back and find you, Reva. Now just take your place in the queue properly."

The woman at the footwear booth graciously took the five-rupee penalty and released Revathi's slippers from captivity. We stepped into the alley and quickly caught up with Kamala and her mother. The little girl had been transferred to Kamala's shoulder, and Sundari Mami was walking a few steps ahead with four other women. They were busy filling up on the latest betrothal announcements and word-of-mouth character assassinations. Past eleven in the night and the middle-aged vultures were still hungry for scandal. Kamala fell back with us, taking slower steps. Her heavy burden of loyalty, the five-year-old niece, sucked on her left thumb and drooled all over Kamala's dark green blouse.

"Want me to hold her?" I offered.

"It's okay. I can manage," Kamala replied. "We'll be there soon."

"You want to come and watch the Seshagopalan concert on Sunday? Both of you?" Revathi asked. Her mother had moved on from being just Savitri "Telephone" Mami. She still held the prized place of being the only house owner in the agraharam with a phone, but in the past eight months had acquired another title: "Video" Mami. Savitri Mami was now better known for the music and dance festival videos screened for the seniors of the colony every second Friday.

"Gayatri Chitti is visiting. I can't."

"Don't tempt me with any such things for the next month. I have to carry this girl till my sister has her delivery," Kamala said. "It's endless."

She looked at me, and I saw that her eyes had glazed over and she was silently crying. Kamala quickly averted her gaze and moved her niece onto her right shoulder. The last two proposals had not worked out, and that had made things even more difficult for her with her sister-in-law and brother. To add to it all, her sister had arrived for confinement a month ago. I knew that if I reached out and squeezed Kamala's hand she would break down and cry. Kamala and I had the same life. The only difference was that her father let her finish high school before he decided that her higher schooling was to be as an unpaid domestic. But she could go to music school if she wanted. Our fathers could have been the same spirit, speaking the same words from two separate bodies. Kamala had her older sister, Subhadra, and I had Gayatri Chitti. That was enough discontent for three incarnations as a human being.

But I also had Mallika, my *thangam*, and my hopes for her future. I had that consolation, which made it all worthwhile.

"Why don't you just make her walk? She's five, illaiya?" Revathi said, touching her nose ring as though the ornament were a switch to a secret world of freedom. She then whispered her brilliant strategy with dead seriousness, "Want me to pinch the brat and wake her up?"

The Brahmin exodus that spilled out from the temple after the performance petered out by the time we got to C Block. Most of the mamis and their families had taken the southern alley to A Block, a route I could have taken as well, but I decided to stick with Kamala and Revathi. I was in no hurry to get back to the house.

"I'll see you at the milk depot in the morning, sariya," Kamala said and quietly put the latch on the gate. Her mother was already indoors, and Subhadra stood under the forty-watt veranda light and scratched her head furiously. She looked like a gauzy mothball with her pregnant tummy under a dull yellow sari and the dim fuzz of illumination blurring her into a perfect circle.

"Parthiyo," Kamala said in a low voice, nodding in the direction of her sister. "She's still awake, but she insisted we take her daughter to the show."

I squeezed her shoulder gently. Kamala then looked at me and asked, "What kind of person gets pleasure by making others' lives miserable, Janaki?"

With those words she moved into the domain of duty once again.

Revathi and I stood at the gate and watched her retrace her steps to the threshold.

I don't know, Kamala, I thought as I searched for an answer to her question, and saw her disappear behind the door.

I don't know what forces us to uphold these unwritten laws. And I don't know what keeps us from fleeing this landscape of invisible lines.

CLIVE ROAD had turned into a semidormitory when Revathi and I crossed the alley on our way to B Block. Urchins and ragpickers and roadside families were stretched out on the footpath in inexorable sleep. Children clung to their mothers under tattered blankets, and young men slept beneath the name boards of closed shops, their feet sticking out from the frayed edges of short, dirty bedsheets. How easy it is for them to sleep without a care. How peaceful they look even when they don't know where their next meal is going to come from, I thought, as Revathi and I walked past the Gandhi statue in the small, corporation park. Traffic had slowed down on the main road and, except for the occasional rattling and drone of an autorickshaw or the grunt of an aging Ambassador car, everyone and everything had surrendered to the sleepy arms of the night.

I had had a long day and should have been exhausted like the footpath community of Clive Road. And yet, for some unknown reason, I felt restless and anxious. My thoughts kept returning to the dance drama. It was not the first time I had seen the story of Shakti performed on stage, and the show we had just seen was by no means the best interpretation of the myth. And still, one image kept reappearing in my mind's eye: Shakti dancing with the plastic head of Mahishasura. I could not shake that moment however hard I tried. The demon's head swayed behind my retina, back and forth, like a ghoulish clock pendulum.

"It felt good, didn't it?" Revathi smiled.

"You mean the dance drama?" I asked, wondering if my thoughts were so transparent that Revathi could see the image in my head.

"Yes, the idea that young girls can confront evil and destroy it forever!"

"That only happens in the pictures and mythology, Reva," I answered. "But I agree. It is an inspiring idea."

"There's one thing that I don't understand, though," Revathi said, as we entered the street leading to B Block. "Why does Mahishasura smile when Shakti cuts off his head?

The plastic head in the dancer's hand always has a big smile pasted on it, illaiya?"

Her question jolted me. I had completely missed that single, consistent feature. She was right, of course. Why did Mahishasura smile after being killed so mercilessly? And what did his apparent mirth in the death suggest?

"Maybe," I replied, "he knows that evil will always be part of this world, that it can never be destroyed forever?" It was the best answer I could think of at that moment.

"Or maybe he is just thrilled to be killed by a young and beautiful woman?" Revathi pulled her pullo around her shoulder and winked at me. "You know, men and demons, lusty with their tongues hanging lo-lo like. . .?"

"Yes, that must be it!" I laughed, "Mortal men, immortal dogs!"

"Voiceless Insect, Courage is Your Companion, Only Witness, All Your Requests, Marriage in Heaven, Next Birth!" Revathi raised her right hand and placed it on my head in a sudden blessing.

"What's wrong with you, Reva? Has your Tamil gone to the dogs as well?" I said as I quickly ducked from under her hand and pulled her plait.

"My Tamil is perfect, child," Revathi replied. "Look!" she said, pointing to a row of cinema posters plastered on the walled entrance of B Block. "That is the source of my ancient language!"

She had joined film titles in sequence to make a sentence. I grinned and hugged her.

"That's so eloquent, magamayi," I said, my hand around her shoulder. "But you left out the last bit of your wonderful verse."

I pointed my finger at the final, half-torn poster in the row. "See?"

"Immature Girl," Revathi read. "Vegguli Penn? Ha! Who says?"

THE FAMILY THAT owned the house at the corner of A Block was constructing an extension garage in the vacant plot beside the gate. Stacks of red brick were lined outside the compound wall, and a lorry load of river sand had been dumped next to the cement mixer that jutted half into the road. The street was deserted, and I could see mosquitoes buzzing around the amber bulbs of the municipal lights that stretched into the distance. On an impulse I sat on the sand dune, reclined into the cold mattress of minute grains and looked up at the sky.

My eyes may touch a million stars
But my hands still clutch the window bars.

The lines came to my lips, like a dead language awoken into sound.

Where had I read that couplet? Or had I heard someone recite it on the poetry program on TV? Was it a woman who wrote it? Or was it man's rare insight into a woman's plight? His sister's, perhaps? Or his mother's?

The stars were too far away that night, smothered behind the smoky shroud of the Sripuram Sugar Refinery. The moon looked tired, too, desolate and discarded, like a soggy, half-eaten rice appam. I did not feel like walking home. But I also had no choice, as 4 AM and another eczema-drama day were

just hours away. Let Gayatri Chitti leave without incident.
Please. It was a wish and a prayer. I unscrewed the kolusu
from my ankles and tied them into a tight knot on the edge
of my sari pullo. The bells at my feet would be the first thing
she would hear, and Chitti would immediately wake up and
look at the clock. I was late, but I was definitely not stupid.
After fifteen reluctant minutes I stood up and dusted the sand
off my sari. Then I strapped on my sandals again, and took
slow, heavy steps towards the house.

IN THE PALE light of the distant moon our house looked
dreary and wan, like a bedridden TB patient. The light on
the veranda had either blown a fuse or had been switched
off. Something I will have to check in the morning. All the
window shutters on the ground floor were pulled in and
latched, and the cement artichokes on the gateposts looked
like smudged, forgotten torches from another time. A light
breeze rustled the bougainvillea bush on the far corner of the
veranda, and the creaking of the rusty gate felt like a thun-
derstorm as I lifted the latch and let myself into the compound. I removed the house key from the safety pin hooked
to the *manimalai* around my neck. I couldn't see too well in
the dark, and I was anxious that I would break the thread and
all the beads of Neelaranjani's gift necklace would bounce
down the veranda steps and into the night. I slowly inserted
the key into the front door lock. The snapping sound of the
lock boomed loudly in my body. I shut the doors behind me
and stood there for a few minutes while my eyes adjusted to
the darkness of the hall. In the small, saffron coloured light
that hung from Amma's photo frame on the wall, I could

see the contours of my mattress beside the puja room. The pillows and the bedsheet were just where I had placed them before I left for the temple. Once I was sure that I could move about in the darkness without bumping into the furniture or tripping over the TV stabilizer cord, I made my way to the stairs leading to Mallika's bedroom. The door was half open, and for a moment my heart raced in panic. When I entered the room I found Mallika fast asleep in her bedding on the floor. She lay on her stomach with her face turned sideways, and silver moonbeams danced on the shiny curls that fell around her forehead. My heart rate returned to normal. Then I glanced at the bed against the wall. It was empty! Where is Gayatri Chitti? My first thought was, No, she couldn't be... She must have better sense than that!

Ten minutes went by, and there was still no sign of Gayatri Chitti. I pulled the blanket over Mallika's chest, kissed her cheek gently and stepped out of the room. I took a few quick steps in the dark and ran my fingers on the sliding bolt of the bathroom. It was locked from the outside. My suspicion was confirmed.

Chitti had to be in Appa's room! How could she!

I stood on the landing at the top of the stairs and pondered my next move. I could go to bed and forget the whole thing. Or I could step out on the mottamadi and sit behind the chimney till fatigue finally lulled me to sleep. I could pretend and everything would cease to exist. But my heart rejected all those options. There was only one right way to deal with the situation: you have to put an end to it for Mallika... You have to protect your sister from the discovery and the shame.

Something like blinding rage possessed me that instant. I knew what I had to do.

I went down to the hall and quickly arranged the pillows in a horizontal line on the mattress and covered them with a blanket. With my eyes fixed on Appa's bedroom, I slid against the wall and reached the kitchen door. The bolt fell noiselessly. I waited for a few moments against the closed doors, straining to catch voices. Everything was absolutely still. I grabbed the timepiece and thrust it into the shaft of light that arced through the back window of the kitchen. 12:17 AM. Leaving the clock on the counter, I tiptoed to the back door and unlatched the top and bottom locks.

With the sure stealth of a cat, I crept around the house to the southern end of the veranda and stood under the bedroom window. My feet were unprotected, and dried brambles and twigs pricked my soles. The rough bark of the bougainvillea bush scraped my blouse, and the fabric ripped all the way down to the sleeve. I quickly cupped the torn edge with my palm to drown the sound and crouched against the wall. The top window was slightly open to ventilate the bedroom and within a few seconds I heard a muffled voice.

"What was that scratching sound? Did you hear that?" It was Gayatri Chitti.

"It must be Janaki returning," Appa answered.

"But she came back half an hour ago, I thought..."

So Chitti had heard me enter the house! And she still decided to stay in Appa's room!

"She must be asleep by now then," Appa replied with irritation. "What's wrong with you tonight? Stop this nainainai, or just go back to your room!"

"I was sure I heard a krrreech outside the window..." Chitti insisted.

Suddenly, without the slightest warning, the shutter flew open and banged against the wall right above my head.

My heart went still, and my throat felt dry with fear. Instinctively, my hands pressed down on my mouth, and I shrank down to the earthen floor like a maimed deer.

"There's nothing out there! See for yourself! Even the veranda light is off!"

"Seri, seri," Chitti's voice took on a placating tone. "I must have imagined it. Now come back to bed, en kannille..."

For a few minutes there was quiet again. All I heard was the hurried rustle of a sari being unwound followed by the tinny sound of the gold bangles on Chitti's wrists being quickly removed.

Then the creaking sound of the box spring took over. Soon I heard the bedpost grate against the wall as the mattress sagged and puffed with stale, dead thuds.

"Eeesh..." Chitti moaned, and I imagined her biting her lower lip.

"Innum veynuma... hmm?" Appa grunted. "The only way to shut you up!"

THE BUCKET IN the upstairs bathroom was half filled, and so I did not have to turn the tap. I soaked a muslin rag in the cold water and wiped the scrape on my right arm. From the medicine cabinet behind the stippled bathroom mirror I took out the bottle of Dettol and sprinkled a few undiluted drops on the wound. Holding one edge of the white cloth with my teeth, I wrapped the whole length into a tight bandage in the hope that it would stop the slow but steady trickle of blood. My body still buzzed like an electric bug catcher, and the voices I had heard only ten minutes ago echoed in my ear like hard, endless rain. To calm my shuddering legs I sat down on the wooden bath stool and rested my head against the wall. How could they? How could they? A voice within me kept asking and then slowly, inevitably, my body sank into sleep.

I woke with a start.

I heard Appa's bedroom door open with a squeak and then close again. I got up from the wooden stool and stood behind the half-open bathroom door. This was the revelation I had been waiting for all night.

Chitti's sari grazed the stairs as she came up to the top landing. She stood there for a few minutes and through the narrow gap between the door and the hinge I could hear her catch her breath and exhale. She pushed the bathroom door and located the light switch on the side wall. I stood there, completely hidden from her sight. Chitti filled the plastic mug with water and took it to the ceramic basin below the mirrored medicine cabinet. She lathered her face with soap and scrubbed it with dabs of water. When she was ready to rinse the scum away, she looked into the mirror one more time, and right then the magnetic clasp gave way. The mirrored door of the cabinet cut a short, acute angle, and in the reflecting light of the naked bathroom bulb, Chitti saw me standing behind the door. With the speed of lightning I grabbed the knob and bolted the bathroom door.

"What do you think you are..." Her voice was surprisingly calm.

"Shh!" I said. "Shut up and rinse your face!"

She had no choice. She grabbed the plastic mug and hurriedly splashed water all over her face. With her pullo she wiped her face and then looked up at me.

"Now listen to me carefully," I said, the sudden authority in my voice sounding strange to my own ears. "By the time Appa returns from the office tomorrow I want you out of this house and on your way back where you came from."

"How dare you talk to me like that!" Chitti hissed back.

"Shoo! No need to raise your voice! Leave as I say and save yourself the last dregs of dignity."

"You uppity bitch!"

With those words Chitti lunged forward and grabbed my hand and pushed me against the wall. My head slammed, and I could feel a bump forming instantly on the back of my skull. Chitti raised her hand and was about to slap my face when I buried my nails into her wrist and spat on her face.

She recoiled immediately.

"If you want this out in the open right now, let me not stop you," I said brushing a line of spit from the corner of my mouth. "Let's wake Appa! Then we'll see!"

She did not wipe the blobs of phlegm from her face. She was too stunned to move.

"What can a spineless man like him do? Will he finally tell the world he was sleeping with you even when Amma was alive?" I couldn't resist the taunt.

The words rolled off my tongue like some repressed flood breaking through my lips, sweeping away every moment of hesitation and denial from the past seven years.

Chitti sat down on the bath stool and stretched her legs. She lifted the pleats of her sari and, arching forward, she wiped the caking spit from her cheek and nose. Then she turned and looked at me without animosity, as though she knew that what she was about to say would shatter my self-righteousness forever. She would lay down her cards at her own pace, with the studied deliberation of a seasoned player.

"So that you know," Chitti said, staring and looking through me at the same time. "It was Kamu who pushed your father and me together. She thought she was being magnanimous, taking pity on her widowed younger sister and all, a sister who had no future but was still so. . ."

She did not finish the thought but turned her gaze upwards and looked at the naked bulb. I watched a gleaming tear-stream run from her eyes, move down her left cheek and slowly collect on her imperious chin.

"Yes, your mother regretted it all after a few years, but by then it was too late." Chitti straightened her loose hair and tied it into a quick grocery-bag knot. She continued to stare at the bulb as though it were the source of her slow, shattering revelation.

"Kamu blamed herself for not being able to have a son. Her depression after Mallika's birth and Thathappa's sudden death after selling the theatre was all too much for your father. . ."

She is making it up as she goes along; yes, she is making it all up!

A slow tremor that began at my feet started to spread through my body, a volcano stirring from dormancy.

Kamu pushed your father and me together!

The sentence wrapped itself around my body, like flowing, scorching lava from which there was no escape.

Amma, tell me she is liar, tell me she is a crazy pishashu, please, tell me . . . Amma!

"And what about Appa?" I said, summoning every drop of strength, even though I knew I was fighting a losing battle. "Where was his decency? His morals and mariyathai?"

Chitti's laughter was full of mockery.

"You poor, ignorant girl!" she said and turned to face me once again. "How little you know about the world and how it works."

Then she played that card, that ace of spades that would plunge my heart like a knife pulled out only to thrust and dig deeper.

"Now you listen to me carefully," Chitti said, hurling back my own phrase at me and making up for that slap, which never found its mark.

"As long as a woman is ready and willing, no man—yes, no man—on the face of this earth—will pull back from enjoying himself!"

She stood up from the bath stool and walked to the door. I moved aside to let her pass.

"I will take the eleven-thirty bus to Madras tomorrow."

She raised her hand and brought it close to my cheek. When I looked up I saw that her eyeliner had smudged and there were dark bags below her eyes. She withdrew her hand and reached for the bolt on the door.

"This is not how I wanted you to find out." She tucked her sari pullo into her waist. "But then, there is never a right time for such things, illaiya?" Her voice was soft, and I sensed relief wash over her tired, broad face. It was her moment of salvation.

"I won't say a word to your father. Now it's between you and him."

And then she walked to Mallika's bedroom, an open secret cloaked in darkness, safe once again behind closed doors.

MAY 1991

THERE ARE SOME things about your life you learn not to share. Not with anyone. Like the answers to questions you never summoned the courage to ask, or the inner voice no one else hears. I hold back the distant yet always too close lifetime that throbs and builds its own narrative, while I sit here in front of Salima Sikri, shadowboxing memory. I don't share the feeling of fear that grips my heart before day breaks, even a decade later, when I open the balcony doors and see Kamala's face, blue but serene between the nagalingam flowers. Not even with Asgar. Imagination can never equal lived experience. It also feels strange, to talk in the present tense, while a tape of my past spools in its own world, endlessly tugging and pulling, as it moves to finish on the recorder. Every time I have looked down at the carpet in the last one and a half hours I have caught it staring back at me, capturing every word I utter, in this selective voice I send back into the world. I am fully aware of the fact that I am making and unmaking my own personal mythology.

"I'd like you to pose for a few pictures for the cover. My chief photographer will be here. Maybe, we can get a few with the veena as well, if that's okay. . ."

The light from the sun comes slanting in from the green glass window of the balcony and brushes Salima's garnet necklace into a russet. The beads glow and smoulder, a circle of slow-dying volcanoes. I look away from them quickly, and my eyes catch the clock.

"That can be arranged. Please let Mr. Da Silva know your requirements," I answer and stand up. It is time I got going to the music school to sign that press release. Salima has had all the time we had agreed upon. I pick up the intercom and ask the driver to get ready. I still have to check things in the kitchen before Asgar's lunch is taken to the set.

"Next time we should also talk a bit about your elopement, and all the ruckus and hungama—and all the controversy and allegations in the media. Your marriage was the story that wouldn't go away for so many years! What really happened? You have to give us your version of it!" Salima says, pressing the Rewind button. The reel-to-reel spins with a sudden, metallic jerk that sends a short wave of static up my spine.

"You owe the readers at least that! What is Janaki's truth?"

She has been patient, diplomatic and attentive right through. But she also knows what she wants, what will sell. "Secrets Unlocked, Motives Revealed."

"Janaki's Truth." I can see the headline shouting from newsstands all around the country. Even from that small pottikadai next to Mahalaxmi Talkies, which sold bananas and cigarettes alongside Gayatri Chitti's preferred tabloid, *Kumudam.*

Janaki revisits the roadside stalls with a vengeance. Or is this also destiny?

"Otherwise your advertisers will back out, no doubt!" I laugh and join my palms in a quick namaskaram. Memory, the remembered and the unremembered. That's my truth.

"We can make one up. I am sure your readership can tell the difference between the truth and true-sounding lies. It has been a pleasure talking to you." My dupatta dips below my breasts, and I adjust it so that there are equal lengths over both my shoulders. "I'll ask Mr. Da Silva to confirm our next meeting."

So far I have walked the tightrope of past and present with all the agility of a circus gymnast.

Salima Sikri will not know other lives and tongues that flicker and crackle inside me. That experience is exclusively mine. There are so many stories of Gayatri Chitti and Appa and Mallika from that other narrative, but she will never meet them. She will never know that it was not karma but Kamala, my only real friend in the agraharam, who taught me the most urgent and haunting lesson of my life. Her dreams are now my dreams. But that is a story I don't tell, a raga I don't play.

There are some truths about my life I have learned not to share.

The interview was a success, by all accounts.

Salima had not asked any questions that would have been off the record. She did not probe my past or ask questions about my family. If she wants the sorry details of my agraharam biography, then she will have to dig for it. I told myself: This interview is about who you are, not who you were. I kept the conversation to my life in Bombay. And for a few moments I even forgot that there was a tape in the room, just as she had recommended. Her knowledge about current affairs was expansive ("It is appalling how many kitchen stoves burst in this country and how many woman die dowry deaths that are termed 'kitchen accidents.' How did having a woman prime minister change that?"), and she also had a good understanding of Vedic habits and rituals ("What is it about Brahmins and that song, 'Entharo Mahanu Bhavulu'? And my roommate Radha, at Vassar, was obsessive about the Rahukalam thing. Drove me nuts!").

But it all somehow got back to the status of women in India. And if I thought my marriage to Asgar was really a liberating moment. I had married a married man, correct?

"Many girls from the agraharam marry Brahmin widowers," I said, and thought of Kamala for the first time that afternoon. Dear, dear Kamala. She would have been truly happy for me. She would have applauded my escape. "And most girls pay a high price. Would anybody see that a freedom? I was just lucky."

"But you must agree it is financial independence which makes all the difference? You believe that's what women should think about? You surely don't have to make a living offering music lessons, and still you keep doing it? Why?" Her eyes sparkled, and then she dangled the bait. "Or is it just a star wife hobby?"

I walked across the lounge to where the veena rested against the wall and removed the cover. "Let me show you something," I said, and asked her to join me on the spread-out *jamakalam*.

She watched every move intently.

She saw me cradle the veena and lower the instrument to my lap. Her eyes didn't leave my face as I tuned the strings and put my ear close to the jackwood belly to hear the pitch vibrate.

"Do you know the number of vertebrae in the human spinal cord?" I asked and caught her off guard with the question.

"Why?" she asked, her eyes wide with concern. "Do you have a back problem?"

"No, I don't," I laughed. "But the veena can be a cure for such ailments."

"I do." Salima could not hide her excitement. "How?"

"There are twenty-four vertebrae in the human spinal cord. Now look at the position of my back."

She walked around me.

"Do you see how it is broad at the base but narrows at the top, while still remaining erect?"

She didn't answer, but moved to face me. She shook her head in a gesture of affirmation. It was a slow nod, still puzzled as to what this was all leading to.

"The cervical, dorsal and lumbar are all perfectly aligned, you notice?" I said, and pointed to the columns of the instrument. "Now please count the divisions below the strings."

She began at the lower end of the veena, near the carved lion head, her index finger gliding and dipping into the ridges of the instrument, the wide mansions that shelter sound.

"Twenty-three, twenty-four. . ." She stopped.

"So the veena is like your backbone is what you are telling me." She seemed a little nonplussed by the discovery. She had expected more complexity.

"Yes," I replied. "But the more important question is: Is the veena designed after the human body? Or is the human body a heavenly veena?"

At that, Salima sat down in front of me, just like Mallika used to when I played some new English song she had learned at school and answered all her questions in detail. Does it have a mood or a character? If raga is colour what is the colour of this nursery rhyme when you play it? Mallika is always talking to me, to this day. Only I can hear her.

Salima gazed at me with that same look of anticipation, both her hands under her chin and her face a wide mirror of curiosity.

"You must have heard the phrase, 'That person has no backbone?' Yes? That's because our force is in our spinal cord. In Tamil we call it moolam, which means the source, the home of the cerebral cord or nadi," I continued, as I positioned my fingers to awaken a sleeping raga.

"Between you and me, Janaki," Salima exclaimed with mock passion, "I have met many men with no moolam!"

I've met many as well, I thought to myself, but did not say. My father was the king of the spineless, Salima.

"So you know then what it is to be physically and morally upright? Just think of yogis, or sadhus. You have seen Gautama Buddha's posture under the bodhi tree? A backbone broom reaching up to clean the mind and the worldly cobwebs that clog it."

I had her full attention then. She was no longer merely curious; she was riveted.

My fingers teased the seven notes Sa–Ri–Ga–Ma–Pa–Da–Ni and then quickly slid back into the descending order, Sa–Ni–Da–Pa–Ma–Ga–Ri.

"Each note vibrates in the player's spine and then echoes in the head. Your atma is at that point cleansed and released into pure sound," I said. Then I strummed the first few lines of "Entharo Mahanu Bhavulu." Salima recognized the melody immediately.

"You are testing to see if I was telling the truth, hai na?" She beamed, and a fresh, pink blush spread to her cheeks. I smiled at her lack of guile.

"Music is mainly in the imagination. That's where a true musician hears the sound first, my music teacher used to say. When I close my eyes, the veena is my soul in my own hands, Salima," I said, fading the song slowly. "My breathing, as you see, is imperceptible. My fingers and ears are lost in another world."

"Something like aerobics for the soul or spirit, na?" Salima summed up, distilling the concept of penance and worship, which I was trying to elucidate, into a pithy, modern turn of phrase.

"Yes," I replied, as I put the veena down on the floor and reached for the velvet cover.

"More like yoga," I met her gaze directly. "And to answer your original question, definitely not a star wife hobby."

PA

Kamala looked unusually pleased with herself that day.

We were in the middle of rehearsing Pudhumai Penn that afternoon in veena class, and she kept looking at Revathi and me with half smiles full of meaning. She would adjust the base of the violin, clasped between her shoulder and her chin, and quickly flash a smile. The moment she saw the puzzled look in our eyes she would look away and continue with her solo. We knew something was up. Kamala was hiding something, something that made her happy.

"Concentrate on your *Ri*'s, Kamala, they are beginning to fray!" Nalini Miss kept repeating, but it had no effect on Kamala. She would focus seriously for the next few minutes and then gradually the determined look on her face would dissolve. Slowly the dimples in her cheek would widen and plunge deep, and then the smile would appear again as she pulled the bow, her eyes buzzing and brimming with an undisclosed secret.

We had been rehearsing for two weeks nonstop. Nalini Miss had set the lyrics of the popular Tamil poem to Raga Shankarabharanam, and then, without our knowledge had sent it as an entry submission to the All-India Classical Music Competition to be held in Bombay. We found out that we were participants only after our proposal had been accepted.

"Don't worry, I'll convince your parents, and they will send you with me," Nalini Miss said with confidence. "But for now, just give the composition your best, enna?"

The competition was two months away, but Nalini Miss was already seeing the trophy on the shelf of our music room. She was convinced we would win.

"Your name is going to be on everyone's lips," Nalini Miss kept saying. "Remember, you are going to be competing with the best in India, so it has to be flawless. And practice makes perfect!"

The entire piece was divided into three sections. Revathi was to open with the song, and Kamala and I were to join in after the alaapana. Halfway through the composition I was to perform a solo of the raga on the veena, which would open the second section. Revathi was to resume the vocals right after, and at the end of that section, Kamala was to take over with a solo on the violin. The conclusion had all three of us together—veena, voice, violin—but with a twist. The crescendo was entirely in ascending notes, and there was no fade out. "Pudhumai Penn—the bold New Woman of Music—has to break new ground," Nalini Miss kept intoning. "And you are the trio to do that! Contemporary, strident and full of ambition," she reminded us at every rehearsal. "Just the way Bharatiyar envisioned her in verse, breaking all conventions!"

We nodded.

We would do anything to get a week outside the agraharam. Bombay, to us, was wonderland. How Nalini Miss would talk our parents into sending us, we were not sure.

"We will concentrate on the closing in the next class, and then full run-throughs for the next three weeks. Reva, no screaming, and no ice cream till this is over, enna?" Nalini Miss said. "Class dismissed."

Kamala looked at us with that secret twinkle in her eyes, mischief in one and joy in the other, as she put the violin in the case. I covered my veena and set it in the corner of the music room. I had decided to leave it in the music school for the next little while, till this competition business was over. Eight more weeks, and then I could take it back to the house.

The moment we stepped into the street, Revathi grabbed Kamala's hand and pulled her back. "Haiiya, no running away without an explanation. Tell us what all that sly smiling was about?"

Kamala blushed and looked coy. She pulled her pullo around her shoulder and drew crescents with her toe on the red-earth road. She started to say what was on her mind, and then abruptly broke off with, *"Chee . . . viduviya . . ."*

"Come on, make it quick," I said, faking impatience. "I have to dash to pick up Mallika from school in fifteen minutes."

"My marriage has been fixed," Kamala said in a soft voice. "Twenty-eighth of next month!"

"Adi sakkai!" Revathi exclaimed. "Who's the unlucky groom?"

We sat down on the bench outside the music school gate and made Kamala sit between us.

"Okay, begin at the beginning," I said, as I lifted her downcast chin with my hand.

"He's an insurance broker in Madras," Kamala said, her face turning red with every word. "His name is Rangan, age thirty-nine, one older brother, one married sister, both parents alive . . ."

"So who set it up?" Revathi asked, eager for all the details. "And what about the age difference? You twenty-two, him thirty-nine, like a rose garland in a monkey's hand, no?"

"And what about the dowry?" I added. "Has he said no to that?"

Kamala's face lost some cheer then. She looked a little uncertain, but her eyes still held that irrepressible hope.

"He's my brother-in-law's second cousin, a good family," she said. "They live in Thuthukudi, but the marriage will be here, in Sripuram . . ."

I knew she was not telling me the most important detail. How much money did she have to give in dowry to marry this eligible man? What price happiness?

Kamala saw the expression on my face and immediately read my thoughts.

"It's the most reasonable offer so far, Janaki," she said. "They want us to pay all the marriage expenses and then a cheque of twenty-five thousand rupees."

"Twenty-five thousand for a man of thirty-nine?" Revathi's voice rose in horror. "And you call that reasonable? Has he no backbone?"

It was easy for Revathi to take offence. The only daughter of a wealthy father, she was sure to marry some engineer or doctor in the USA. Her parents also had enough money to pay her airfare for yearly visits from Philadelphia or wherever it was she made her future home. Revathi's was not a middle-class Brahmin fate like Kamala's and mine.

"Reva, you are going to college. I have not even sought shelter there from the rain," Kamala answered. "What do you know about rejection and how crushing it can be? Subhadra fixed this through her husband, and my brother said he can arrange the finances."

"But what about the music competition, Kamala?" I said, changing the subject. We had done enough to dampen her buoyancy. Kamala deserved her happiness, even if it meant having to pay for it. "Nalini Miss has no clue about this, illaiya? And it is just two weeks after your wedding, right?"

Kamala shook her head.

"No, she doesn't. But that will be my only condition. I will speak to Rangan and tell him I will move to Thuthukudi only after this contest."

"Oh, and Mr. Twenty-five Thousand will no doubt agree to that!" Revathi smirked, and her tone oozed sarcasm.

"Shh! Don't be such a negative moodevi!" I said. "It will all work out."

"I know it will," Kamala said and squeezed my hand. The dimples burrowed her cheeks, and she smiled again. "It will be my gift of gratitude to both of you," she said and hugged Revathi and me. "My way of saying thank you for your friendship."

KAMALA WILL LOOK good in a bordered sari, a nice lawn green kanchipuram silk with pyramids of gold rising from the base, and a front-button blouse to match. Yes, Kamala will look like a lotus in a lush, sunlit forest pond.

"I'll be accompanying Kamala for the wedding shopping this afternoon," I said as I placed the coffee dabra on the floor next to Appa's chair. "We'll be taking the bus to Chamundi Nagar."

Appa did nothing to indicate that he had heard me.

As I walked back into the hall I heard the newspaper flop on the veranda floor followed by the steel-on-steel grating of the dabra in his hand.

Over the last few months the conversation between us had been pared to its bare minimum. I kept him informed about household needs. At the beginning of every month I reminded him to pay Mallika's school fees. And on the rare occasions I was away from the house when he returned from office, I left a note with details about my whereabouts and the expected time of return. He, for his part, put seven hundred rupees in a melon-coloured envelope and left it on the small wooden shelf below Amma's photograph on the first of every month. Just as he had done over the years since Amma's death. The money in the envelope was my domestic budget. Anything over and above that amount I petitioned for and explained. He never asked me why—but I still told him: extra for Mallika's new school uniform; or the sudden rise in grain prices at the ration store. The arrangement suited me fine. It kept inviolate the little respect I had for him.

Since that terrible night in the upstairs bathroom, Gayatri Chitti's visits to Sripuram had ceased almost entirely. Even when she had turned up for Amma's anniversary she just stayed for the day and took the last bus back to Madras. I was also successful (if only temporarily) in stalling her machinations to get me married. I did it by playing boring ragas for the prospective grooms and their mothers; by lining my eyes with loads of kohl so that my face looked dark and tired when I served tea to the accountants and math teachers, and by adding inadequate salt and more chili in the vadais, which made it all look like I was a bad cook. When those efforts failed to weaken Chitti's resolve, one evening, after I had served dinner, I stood in front of Appa and told him that I would not put up with the exhibitionism anymore and that he should instruct her to stop sending proposals my way till Mallika had finished high school. He conveyed my message, and there was a brief lull in the avalanche of so-called eligibles. It bought me time for another two and a half years.

Amma, I realized, had blindly subscribed to the male-defined components of femininity. When she finally awoke to the fact that Fear, Ignorance, Shame and Modesty were, in reality, the four prison walls that kept a woman in her place, it was too late. Net result: she took a busload of regrets and a misplaced sense of martyrdom to her grave.

And that was her choice. She might have her own version of things.

But, after that incident with Gayatri Chitti in the upstairs bathroom, I had a simple, quotidian moment of clarity: my mother, Kamakshi Venkatakrishnan, killed in a bus accident eight years ago, and killed slowly for years before that by the betrayal of her sister and her husband, was a traditional, trusting fool. And fools—even if they were of the classical, sympathetic and put-upon kind—in the end, had only themselves to blame. I knew then that I would never walk in my mother's footsteps. My mother, as much I loved her when she was alive, was poor role-model material.

KAMALA GASPED every two minutes.

The three salesmen, high up on the ladder and reaching for the racks near the ceiling, did their best to keep the look of amazement and awe on our faces from fading. They opened the yellow and saffron cardboard boxes, peeled off the white tissue paper and unfurled their masterpieces faster than we could count. Kamala and I sat on a soft, rectangular cotton mattress on the ground, right beside the proprietor of the shop, while silk saris of all colours cascaded from above, grazing our shoulders, caressing our faces and undulating around our laps and toes like waves of the ocean between sunset and moonrise. It was a heavenly way to drown.

"Atho, that one," Kamala pointed to a peacock blue and green sari, and then her attention fluttered and landed on another. "What do you think of the sandalwood and pink, Janaki? Or even this gold and midnight blue?"

"Take your time, chinnamma," the proprietor, a rotund, happy-faced man, kept repeating. "You can see all the saris you want before you decide."

I could tell that he was also thrilled by the looks on our faces. I suppose it was one of the many pleasures of owning a silk-sari shop.

Soon there were little, glowing gossamer hills of reds, greens and purples all around us. Gold borders of paisleys, temple towers, clay lamps and wildflowers shone in the spot-lights of the shop like jigsaw puzzles for the gods. It was a superhuman feat to choose one sari when the heart craved all that the eye saw. And all Kamala could do was gasp.

"You have to pick the one which appeals to you most; otherwise we can spend the whole afternoon here," I said, pushing Kamala to make a decision. "Don't open any more boxes," I said, looking up at the salesmen on the ladders. "Podhum!"

They sighed, filled their lungs with fresh air and then descended, one step at a time, like gymnasts in a synchro-nized circus act.

Kamala took the middle-class route to decision making.

She began flipping the price tags pinned to the back of the inner borders. With every amount her face fell, and the air of excitement around her began to dissipate. Saris from one side moved to the other with such velocity that a fluffy mountain of silk rose to our left, while the many hills to our right flat-tened into a gradual plateau.

"I don't know, Janaki," Kamala frowned. "Maybe we should check out a few other shops, enna?"

"Why, chinnamma? You don't like our stock?" The pro-prietor inquired in a paternal tone.

"Oh, no, they are very lovely," I answered on Kamala's behalf. "She is very fussy. We'll walk down the street, for some variety. We'll be back soon." It sounded like a lame excuse, which I was sure he must have heard innumerable times.

"We'll come by again, annah," Kamala said, and she stood up. "Thank you for all the help. Namaskaram."

The three salesmen, who had arranged themselves as sentinels around us, joined their palms in respect and smiled.

"As you wish, chinnamma, we're open till eight," the proprietor replied. "May you have a happy married life!"

Kamala and I strapped on our sandals, bowed and stepped out into the street.

"Now what? Should we go over to Roopdevi Silks?"

"Maybe we should take the bus back to Sripuram." Kamala's voice was flat with disappointment.

"I thought you liked the peacock blue green one," I said as we took a few aimless steps down the lane. Kamala walked in silence beside me.

Neon store signs winked and beckoned from both sides of the pot-holed, red-earth road. Middle-aged women and teenaged girls stood around the many showcase windows admiring the statuesque mannequins. Their eyes brimmed with dreams of unattainable luxury. I saw envy and desire pull and push in an endless tug-of-war all around us.

"We have to take the next left if we want to make our way to the bus terminus," I said after a few minutes. We were nearing the end of the street.

"It was eleven hundred rupees."

"What was?"

"The peacock blue green. The one I liked," Kamala answered without emotion.

"So? Let's sit here and talk a bit," I said and pulled her beside me on the bus-shelter bench.

"I have only eight hundred and thirty. Minus the return bus fare and that leaves eight hundred and ten."

"I can give you the rest," I said and opened my purse. The four hundred rupees I had brought with me to buy Mallika a new dhavani were still safe inside.

"Where did you get the money from?" Kamala whispered, unable to contain her surprise, and more than a little tempted by my offer.

"Don't worry, I did not rob a bank!" I laughed, happy to see her back in her original mood.

I told her about my savings over the years. The little here and the little there I had collected, like a sparrow building its nest. I explained how I had managed to put away about fifty rupees every month from the domestic budget by switching brands of laundry detergents; selling old newspapers and magazines to the recycling depot by the kilo; buying second-hand textbooks for Mallika; substituting wheat for rice, wherever possible.

"And bargaining at the Sripuram market! The one worth-while thing I learned from Gayatri Chitti!"

"So how much do you have in the bank?" Kamala asked, her eyes two big Os, wide as the black rounds on a tabla.

"About three thousand five hundred. Every rupee for Mallika and her future," I answered. "Not in any bank, but in a secret hiding place in the house!"

"Adeyngappa!" Kamala exclaimed and hugged me. "How did you turn out to be such a wise old woman, Janaki?"

"Wise woman, yes," I grinned back. "But a year younger than you, remember?"

I offered my seat to a mami who had moved into the bus shelter. She sat down, too tired to even thank me for my gesture.

"So, what do you say?" I grabbed Kamala's hand. She stood up reluctantly.

"Will you now fly home on your peacock, maharani?"

NALINI MISS COULD not hide her pride, and a big, jarring smile spread across her face.

"Yes, just play the way you did this afternoon and nobody will be able to touch you! Beshbesh, my girls!"

Kamala and I had just made it in time for veena class. The bus from Chamundi Nagar to Sripuram was packed, but we squeezed in somehow and held onto the overhead hand-bars right through the bumpy ride. Kamala then ran to her house from the bus terminus to lock up the sari box. When she entered the music class, Revathi and I were already rehearsing my veena solo under the observant eye of Nalini Miss. Kamala got her violin out of the case and joined us on the *jamakalam*.

"Okay, Kamala is here now, so straight run-through, sariya?"

And the next thirty minutes had been absolutely miraculous.

Revathi's voice was in top form, and she was off to a brilliant start with her alaapana. The extra fifteen minutes of fine tuning I had had before Kamala showed up also paid off. My *Ri*'s were pitch perfect, and the gamakams gurgled with the tenderness of a newborn. But it was Kamala on the violin who took the composition, and us with it, to the uttermost shores of the sublime. It was as if the happiness in her heart flowed right through the bow and crowned every note with a nimbus, turning the raga into a glowing garland, her devotee soul opening up to her lord. Only when we finished did we discover the streams of tears running down our cheeks, and Nalini Miss's bravos, beshbeshes, signalling our slow descent to earth.

"Have you told Rangan about the contest?" Revathi asked on the way to the agraharam.

"I wrote a brief note and sent it across with my brother yesterday," Kamala replied. "I told him I will be indebted to him for life, and that he had to agree."

"I hope he does," Revathi said, but her tone was still skeptical.

"I am sure Nalini Miss will convince him," I said. "If she says she can convince my father, then she can convince anybody!"

"Just two more weeks and Mrs. Kamala Rangan will tell us everything we need to know about men and marriage!"

"Reva, you're really too much!" Kamala blushed, rosy pink, just like the lotus she was named after.

I HEARD THE nadaswaram and drums the moment I crossed Clive Road and walked towards the marriage hall. The clock on the LKS building showed ten thirty. I quickened my pace. Kamala's mother and brother had come over to our house the previous week to invite the whole family to the wedding. "Please let Janaki come with us to the hall the night before the wedding," she told Appa. "Kamala would like that very much." Appa smiled. "It is a Monday, you see," he said. "A full office and school day." He then thanked them for stopping by. "I will try to make it during lunch hour, and Janaki will be there in the morning before the ceremony, for sure."

By the time I finished rinsing the breakfast dishes and boiling the milk for the curds it was already nine thirty. The auspicious hour, the time when all the stars in the heavens would be at their appropriate and full-of-goodness positions, the moment Kamala would be handed over by her brother in marriage, was exactly at noon. I took a quick shower, hurriedly draped Amma's best silk sari, lit an *agarbathi* near her photo, locked the house and made my way to the marriage hall.

The musicians were seated on a small stage beside the main entrance. Two banana trees were tied to either side of the gate, and someone had drawn a big, coloured kolam on the cement pathway outside the threshold. I stepped into the hall, and a group of girls I had never met greeted me at the welcome table with sandalwood and kungumam. The youngest of the three sprinkled rosewater on my head, and little drops of perfume blotched and spread at random spots on my green silk blouse.

"Welcome, welcome," the oldest one in the trio trilled. "Bride's side or groom's side?"

"Where is Kamala?" I asked as I pinned the rose handed to me by the little girl into my hair.

"Oh, bride's side then!" She smiled and raised the salver with sandalwood paste. I dipped my middle finger and quickly made a bottu on my forehead.

"Yes, bride's side. Where is she?"

"Akka, take the steps next to the kitchen," the rosewater girl replied. "Atho," she said and pointed her finger to the stairs. "They are all there!"

I folded my hands into a namaskaram.

From a distance I spotted Vanaja Mami and Savitri Mami chatting near the official wedding stage. Men and women dressed in brightly coloured silks and pure white linen sat around and talked, their voices rising and falling in competition with the music outside. A few older mamas were reading the morning newspaper. Guests, who had just come in, were lining up on the side to enter the dining hall for their morning tiffin.

As I ran up the stairs the overpowering smell of freshly brewed coffee, quick-fried mustard and semolina and sweat mingled with jasmine and rose filled my nose and made me sneeze. I wiped my face quickly with my handkerchief. The bride's room was to the far end of the corridor, and I heard Revathi's voice as soon as I pushed the door open.

"Now stop blinking or you will smudge your eyeliner!"

"Look Janaki is here!" Sundari Mami, Kamala's mother, said. "*Va*, ma."

Kamala was sitting on a small wooden stool in front of the mirror, and Revathi was holding the bottle with eyeliner liquid.

"Finally the maharani arrives!" Revathi said. "She refused to wear the sari till you got here!"

Kamala stood up and walked towards me. She was in her petticoat and blouse. Her hands were filled with gold and glass bangles and a garland of jasmine and kanakambaram coiled around her hair, all the way to the end of her plait. She looked like a celestial dancer, ready for her debut in front of the gods.

"I was waiting for you," Kamala said with a smile and hugged me. "Rangan has agreed to my request," she whispered. "I will be going for the competition!"

I kissed her cheek. Kamala then pulled out the box from the wooden almirah in the room and gave it to me. "You open the sari," she said. "I want you to unfurl it with your hands."

"Yes, Janaki, you and Revathi drape it around her," Sundari Mami said, touching me on the shoulder. Subhadra, who was braiding her daughter's hair, looked up. I caught a glint of displeasure in her eye. Revathi picked up the reason for my hesitation and came forward with her characteristic boldness.

"You and Subhadra hold the two ends first and then I will adjust the pleats, sariya?"

"Okay," I said. "Come, Subhadra," I smiled and opened the box with the sari.

We draped Kamala with all the care of a jeweller cutting a diamond. After Revathi had adjusted the pleats we stepped back, like the moons of Jupiter, and admired Kamala, the heavenly body that pulled us, shining in the middle. She glowed, like a thousand dreams were bursting in bright eagerness of her eyes. The now blue, now green light and shade of the sari cast a spell of mystery around her, and the temple-tower motif in gold slowly rose from around her feet, circling her knees and then reappearing again above her breasts. In the shimmer of ochre threads dipping below her chin Kamala's face came alive, a lake rippling in the first rays of the rising sun. The pink lip gloss matched the small row of red and white dots that curved around her eyebrows, and her shy, half smile opened like a purse of pearls. She looked at us with nervous joy, and we stood speechless, seduced by her radiance.

"How pretty you look! Let me chase away my own eye of envy!" Kamala's mother said and touched Kamala's cheeks with her palms. Sundari Mami then brought those very hands to either side of her temples and cracked all the evil spirits captured and caged in her knuckles. She thanked the gods and asked for her daughter's protection.

"The pujari is ready and wants the bride to come downstairs," the young rosewater girl burst into the room and announced. She looked at Kamala, and her eyes widened with wonder. "Akka," she exclaimed, "you look like cinema star Sridevi!"

"Great! That makes me the best touch-up girl in Sripuram!" Revathi giggled. Kamala laughed.

"Tell them we will be there in five minutes," Sundari Mami replied. "The bride is also ready!"

The hall downstairs was buzzing like a village fair with the four hundred guests from both the families. Messages were being relayed to the musicians at the entrance to play the getti melam on time, the traditional drumbeat that would usher Kamala into the new identity of Wife. Aluminum vessels and pots clanged and rolled in the nearby kitchen, and the final batch of guests was lining up outside the dining hall for their share of pongal and lentil sambar. Cows called out in blessing from outside the kitchen door, thankful for the used banana leaf plates being dumped in the bin by the assistant cooks at regular intervals. Kamala sniffed the air around her and said softly, "That sambar smells good, Janaki! Did you get some?" I gave her a quick hug and said, "Reva and I were going to do just that! We'll be in the front row in fifteen minutes, sariya?"

"I'll look for you, and you better be in the first few rows!" Kamala said and then Sundari Mami and Subhadra steered her in the direction of the main stage.

Revathi and I made our way to the dining hall and found two seats at the far corner, near the kitchen. I had survived the morning on just one cup of coffee, made immediately after I got back from the milk depot. Even when I packed the lunch box for Mallika, all I could think of was making it in time to the marriage hall. As soon as we sat down and the servers had ladled some lentil and vegetable sambar into my side bowl, I reached for it like a drowning woman grabbing driftwood and gulped it down. Revathi did the same. As we put the bowls back on the table, we looked at each other and burst out laughing. Luckily, the hall was nearly empty, and there were no mamis around to comment on our sudden mirth. Everything—rice, pickles, chili-cumin potatoes, deep-fried pappadum—everything found a place in our stomach, and in record time we finished our meal. It was a wonderful silence, even though the atmosphere around was crackling and singing like wildfire. I wrapped the mysore paak into my tissue-lined money purse, to take back with me for Mallika so that she didn't feel left out of all the festivities. She was also crazy for the sweet, which made me dizzy with a sharp pain of sweetness on my teeth when I ate it. Revathi waved for coffee.

"Soon it will be just us, Janaki," she said, pouring the coffee from the stainless-steel cup into the dabra, to cool it quickly.

"But we still have the competition in Bombay to look forward to," I said, not wanting to think about life with no Kamala in it. "And then Kamala will be back for her delivery soon, I'm sure!"

"What makes you so sure that we will be in Sripuram then?" Revathi said, sipping her coffee.

"Wherever I am, I will come back for Mallika," I said. "I can guarantee that!"

"You're lucky to have a sister, you know."

"And you're lucky to have your mother," I replied. "That's the best excuse to be back, if you need one for your future in-laws, enna?"

"My mother is already dreaming of visiting me in Philadelphia," Revathi pushed back her chair. "She also wants a green-card grandson!"

"Let's not think about all this now, Reva," I said. "It's not like we're to get married tomorrow and move away." I stood up. "Let's go back to the hall."

RANGAN AND KAMALA were busy pouring clarified butter into the sacred fire that burned centre stage. The low flames rose from within a wall of four small bricks. Sacred fire and bricks that will stand witness to a divine contract that Kamala had to literally buy into. I had never seen Kamala so close to a man before. I had never seen her so happy. Every time she fumbled on a Sanskrit sloka she looked up at Rangan, and her lips curved in a coy smile, a smile that had started months ago in anticipation of this moment, this close proximity to a man's bare torso. Quickly, she would then return to repeating after the priest, timing her namaha-endings with Rangan's, so like a young girl in austere company caught out in her spell of delight.

"He looks like a school principal," Revathi said in a whisper. "He has spectacle frames to match!" My own first impression of Rangan had been stationmaster in some place called Mamoor or Thenoor, Tirunelveli Jilla. Dulled by remoteness. But he could also be a school principal. In some place called Mamoor or Thenoor. The faces blurred into one inescapable image. I had seen many such eligibles up until the last fourteen months. I had been up and down that list of Gayatri Chitti's so-called cream-of-the-crop. And every time I was asked to play the veena for them, so that their mothers could evaluate my artistic impulses, I would tell myself, Take a good look, Janaki, that's what a man of twenty-five thousand rupees looks like, all damp and greasy, like wet, stuck-together currency notes piled and dressed up in a terry-cotton pant and shirt. It was a thought I could never shake, and it always appeared in the middle of my alaapana. Contempt seemed righteous; it was all the power I had.

"You know, I think I'll move to the back, these fumes are really burning my eyes," I said and got up. I had to lose that image, which kept coming back every time I moved my gaze from Kamala to Rangan. "You can stay here if you want. I might even use the ladies'." And before Revathi could respond, I waved to the rosewater girl, who came running immediately from the table behind us.

"Where's the ladies' toilet?" I asked.

She grabbed my wrists and literally pulled me to the location. "Hope it's not bedhi bathroom, Akka," she said with soft concern as she turned to leave. "No," I replied, "I certainly don't have diarrhea." I laughed at her cheekiness. "That's better!" she assured me, turning to leave. "Otherwise you will be late for the getti melam!"

I sensed a change in the atmosphere the moment I returned to the marriage hall. It was a quiet buzz, as though static shockwaves were rippling through a barrier of dense fog. The women were chatting, slowly, under their breath, and some men had started to fan themselves with the morning newspapers they had brought along. The priest's voice was beginning to crack with apprehension, and there was a tense look on Kamala's face.

"What's the matter, Reva?" I asked when I got to my seat in the front row.

"I don't know yet," Revathi replied. "But the muhurtham time was ten minutes ago, and still there has been no getti melam." She held grains of rice and flower petals in her right palm, ready to be thrown as blessings at the auspicious hour, to the accompaniment of frenzied beats of the drum. The minutes of perfect planetary alignment were slipping, like the sweat on the guests' foreheads.

"She looks like she knows something is wrong," I said, looking sideways at Kamala, who was trying hard to stay composed.

"This doesn't look like a good sign, poor girl," a mami seated in row two was telling her companion. Vultures, I thought, always prescient of a scavenging opportunity.

Ten minutes went by and still there was no getti melam, and the musicians finally gave up playing. It was only when the percussion and nadaswaram were put away that the volume of whispering became apparent to everybody. Then the priest's chants faded into a slow, syllabic silence. Rangan got up and walked to a man in his twenties who stood near the entrance, right beside the guest reception table. All heads turned from the stage to the conversation being conducted in private, outside the hall. Kamala did not move from her place, but a look of pain had eclipsed her face. Subhadra and

Sundari Mami, united as mother and daughter, wore identical pained looks on their faces, too. Provoked and curious about the abrupt silence in the marriage hall, the cooks in the kitchen took surreptitious steps and emerged one by one to line up alongside the dining hall doors. The cows in the alley began agitating for banana leaf, and someone was heard chasing them away.

Outside, Kamala's brother cupped his palms, begging for some reason, and Rangan stood rooted to the spot. His body was breaking into small shudders every few minutes. His mother, who was sitting in the front row, slowly got up from her seat and walked up to join the group. The man who had prompted Rangan to leave the stage (who, I later learned, was Rangan's younger brother) whispered something in the mami's ear, and Rangan immediately put his arms around her. She let out a blood-curdling scream and slumped back in an instant blackout. A few men and women, Rangan's relatives attending the wedding, ran out and surrounded the swooned woman. "Move aside, give her some air, please, *kaathey viduvela*." A mama in a veshti and jibba assumed control of the situation. Kamala's brother walked back into the hall and pulled up a metal chair from the back row, put it below a ceiling fan and sat down. As soon as he had done so, a minivan pulled up outside the gates and Rangan, helped by the mama, managed to get his mother to lie on the long back seat. Then he opened the front door of the van, got in and pulled it shut. Rangan's brother sat beside his mother. They drove away.

Kamala's brother looked up at all of us and said, "How could I have changed my sister's rotten fate? That's all the marriage she is going to see. Go home."

The last Revathi and I had seen of Kamala was after all the guests had filed out one by one, in utter silence, emptying the grains of rice and flower petals clutched in their palms like damaged blessings, into a silver tray on the reception table. We were sitting around Kamala, who had not moved from her position on the stage. She had not said a word, even though Sundari Mami was cursing the evil stars under which Kamala was born, and bursting into "*aiyyo, mosam poyitiye,* who will marry you now" laments. Kamala's face was relaxed. The pained look she wore a few minutes ago had evened into a vacuous calm. She gently pulled the glass bangles off both her wrists, one at a time, and stacked them all around the four bricks that no longer housed the sacred fire. It had died a long time ago. Subhadra and her daughter were nowhere to be seen. It was Subhadra's husband who had arranged the match, I remembered, as I sat there hoping Kamala would say something. Kamala's brother had not moved from his seat. "Why agree to things you can't deliver on, narayana, why ruin a girl's life? Who was in such a hurry to get my girl married off? Now who has made her an unmarried widow?" Sundari Mami kept up her dirge, and the two mamis trying to console her consciously provoked her into further revelations with their sympathetic "*aiyyo, aiaiyyoo,*" at regular intervals. Revathi and I did not know what to do, so we waited for the elders to make the first move. Even Savitri Mami, who naturally and usually exerted her telephonic power during moments of community crisis, had been stunned into silence.

Then Kamala stood up, lifted the rose garland from around her neck and laid it on the wooden seat she had just vacated. "I would like to be by myself now," she said. "I'll go upstairs and pack my things."

Revathi and I got up and reluctantly left the hall with Savitri Mami.

THE NEXT MORNING the mamis at the milk depot were delirious with fresh, warm gossip. But that is how we were used to finding out things about our own kind in the agraharam. Revathi and I were made honorary members on the spur, because of our proximity to the bride before the marriage was called off. We were Kamala's friends, they suddenly realized. It was not even five o'clock.

"Did you know she knew about the cheque not clearing? She knew all along, paavam, and still hoped it would work out! Did she say something to you girls?"

"We only know what you tell us, mami," I replied, trying to disappear into my shawl to avoid her scrutiny so early in the morning. Revathi was unusually quiet. We were both still devastated about what had happened to Kamala the previous day. By evening everybody in the agraharam, even those who didn't know their family, knew what had stopped the marriage that afternoon. Rangan's father had gulped down commercial cockroach poison, half an hour before the auspicious moment. He was rushed to hospital in critical condition. I could still hear that mami's scream in my spine. Nobody had mentioned a cheque. We knew nothing about any cheque not clearing. Revathi would have to ask Savitri Mami, the telecommunications headquarters of the agraharam, if the milk depot mamis were telling the truth.

"I heard Vanaja saying something about a shortage of five thousand in the money," said one mami who had just joined the crowd. Her source was also reliable. Vanaja Mami knew everything about everybody. I was sure she knew about

Gayatri Chitti and Appa; maybe the mamis in the lineup also knew. "I heard that, too," added the mami who had started the footpath inquisition, unwilling to give up her primacy as information source. "I heard that the boy was agreeable to the discount, but the father was adamant. Cockroach poison! Can you imagine what it must taste like?"

"Maybe you should try some and find out!" Revathi hissed. The mami's jaw dropped for a full thirty seconds. "I must talk to Savitri about your tongue," she replied tersely, and tried to burn us both with her stare. The other mamis in the lineup ahead of her turned around.

"I will tell my mother about *your* tongue," Revathi said, finding the target for all her sleepless anger. "Discount, is it? Are they men or sofa sets? Why didn't any of the mamas drag the groom back to marry the girl? They are no different! Maybe you should share your poison with them as well!" By the end of her harangue she was shaking violently, and I quickly put my shawl around her.

"We are both very hurt by what has happened to our friend," I said, putting my milk-bottle bag on the roadside platform and folding my hands into a namaskaram. "Please, thayavupannungo, we don't want to hear any more."

TWO THINGS WERE confirmed over the next two days.

Appa turned down Nalini Miss's request to allow me to participate in the music competition—I was not going to Bombay. And Kamala's wedding was indeed called off for the want of five thousand rupees. Twenty and not the promised twenty-five. The last cheque had not cleared. Rangan had known of such a probability all along but had kept it from his father. When the principled, cut-and-right father walked to the bank on Clive Road first thing Monday morning, and the teller informed him the cheque had been overdrawn, he became agitated and called Rangan at the marriage hall. We had been upstairs with Kamala when all of this happened, but Kamala's brother had been involved in the negotiations. Rangan told his father the difference in the dowry was not a concern for him and that he was still going to go ahead with the marriage. He asked his father to hurry back to the hall. Instead of following his son's instructions the old man walked to the pharmacy across from the bank and bought a bottle of cockroach poison. Revathi had the whole story from her mother and told me that there was also a police investigation into the suicide attempt by the old man, who according to doctors had missed death by a few drops. They had found him in the hotel lobby where the groom's family was booked, gagging and frothing all over the visitors' room furniture, half an hour before getti melam. All of it thirty minutes too early for Kamala. Revathi and I had not seen her for two full days. She had not been to pick up milk in the mornings, and she had not shown for music lessons. But we heard her name whispered all over the agraharam, like a new taboo, a name of planetary horror.

I was not disappointed about not being at the music competition. In some ways it was a predictable conclusion to our overwhelming optimism. I had known all along, deep in my heart, that Appa would never let me go. A week without the homebound, homegrown domestic was unthinkable. And Mallika was always a legitimate reason, even when she said she could manage on her own. It was a nonissue from the very outset as far as Appa was concerned. Savitri Mami agreed to send Revathi, but Revathi told her mother that she would not go without Kamala and me, and asked her to forget about it. Nalini Miss also lost most of her enthusiasm after Kamala's forgone wedding. Our raga petered out even before we had perfected it. Pudhumai Penn did not matter anymore. It was Kamala, the real woman, and not some mythical, modern woman, who was so easily imagined by Bharatiyar in a poem, that we were concerned about. Sundari Mami and Subhadra would have killed her with their chorus of laments, cursing the constellations and blame casting in divine space, when all of it was just the casual brutality of man. What could men do, if women are born with a rotten fate? Kamala's brother had said it all so succinctly on the day everything fell apart. Rotten fate. They could convince Kamala that it was indeed all her fault, all three of them, brother, sister and mother, each taking their turns, and break her forever. I could imagine Gayatri Chitti's why-didn't-I-die litany, had the same thing happened to me. We had to get through to Kamala.

"God only knows what state she is in," Revathi said on our way back from the temple the second evening. "Her brother came to take all the phone calls." We had kept our distance from the mamis. Everything around us was the same, but everything had changed. In the agraharam everyone cared for the wrong reasons. On the streets of Sripuram people didn't care at all.

"You know, she gets up early to do the kolam and clothes washing every morning," I said, when we stopped to collect our slippers. "I could plan the breakfast poriyal tonight and squeeze half an hour on our way back from the milk depot, enna? It would be better than nothing."

"You think they would still make her do that so soon after all this?" Revathi asked, as we walked down the busy evening bazaar alley, making our way to B Block.

"Who do you think will do the housework then?" I replied, a bit taken aback by Revathi's exasperating naïveté, which only upper-class, moneyed Brahmin girls could afford. She chose to fetch the milk in the mornings; it was not expected of her. "The good-for-nothing Subhadra? Or Sundari Mami with her arthritis?" I had been put to work days after my mother died. It was my duty to remember, not Revathi's. "It will have to be Kamala."

"Okay, at five thirty tomorrow. We'll leave after all the mamis at the milk depot."

KAMALA'S HOUSE was not an easy one to get to from the back. Their yard opened onto an empty wasteland in the agraharam, where cows grazed on the dried, sunburned grass. No wall marked the boundary separating the backyard from the abandoned municipal ground, just a barbed wire fence, which reached up to your waist a few yards beyond the well and the nagalingam tree. I just hoped there were no cows and buffalo to dodge so early in the morning. After we collected the milk, Revathi and I walked towards the temple, just to shake off the other mamis from our trail. They had not said a word to us after Revathi's outburst the other morning. But they took their own sweet time emptying the returns from their bags before refilling them with fresh milk bottles. They were deliberately sluggish. Then slowly they scattered and disappeared, their single file breaking up into separate shards of gossip, walking back to their homes in B and C blocks and also to the other side of Clive Road. We hid behind the pillars outside the temple gates and watched the exit of the last of the mamis. The milkman loaded all the empties in the back of his van and initialled the time and date for the booth manager. He accelerated and moved on to the next neighbourhood. Revathi and I crept back into the alley leading to C Block.

"Let's put our bottles somewhere safe," I said as soon as we entered the agraharam. "I don't want to spill it all over the barbed wire." The streets were deserted, but a few houses already had fresh kolams. The agraharam was still asleep. If we found a kolam outside Kamala's gate, then we would know she was awake and working. I only had forty-five minutes to spare before Appa stirred and called for coffee. "This has to be quick, Reva, I have to be back soon."

The veranda light was on, but all the windows were shut. Kamala's family had closed out the world and shrunk back in shame. There was no new kolam outside the gate.

But that might also be because the house was in mourning. "She's not up, see," Revathi whispered. We ducked our heads just a few inches below the compound wall and took quick steps to the small lane beside the house. It was the only way to reach Kamala's backyard without entering the wasteland. "She is up, I am sure," I replied, "she may have just not felt like drawing a new kolam today! God knows I wouldn't!" Morning dew had settled on the creepers, and I felt the gentle, moist brush of leaves against my elbow as I lowered my bag with the milk bottles on the other side of the compound wall, inside the courtyard edge of the house. I reached out for

Revathi's bag while still peering over the wall and put both bags beside each other, snugly in the space where the side and the front walls met. "They'll be safe here," I whispered. "Now let's make our way to the back, jakarathaiya," I said, hoping stealth and cunning had their rewards. "I'll go first, you follow, enna?"

Revathi nodded. We both needed the reassurance that only Kamala could provide. The third v in the voice–veena–violin sisterhood. And only proof of Kamala's safety could shake us from the paralysis of the past few days.

Cautiously, I moved along the alley wall, surprised by how much litter there was in just that small lane. As I made progress, half a step at a time, in the dim light of breaking dawn and the angled slant from the street lamp I discovered bus tickets, peanut shells, empty supari sachets and an inordinate amount of broken glass, hidden and revealed in the dry sand path that ran all the way to the back. The cows were away on door-to-door milk delivery. The tall and curving branches of the nagalingam tree looked ominous as they cracked and teetered in the early morning gust. But the backyard was still dark, quiet, and the scent of nagalingam, robust and over-powering, swathed the house and everything around it.

"I can't see anything," I said.

"Let your eyes adjust, you will," Revathi replied.

I saw the well first. The small metal tank was filled with water, and the bucket stood on the wall of the well. For some inexplicable reason, it caught my attention. You just had to pull down the rope from the pulley and place the bucket on the ground. Kamala would have known that. And there was no rope tied to the metal handle of the bucket. I crept along the path between the wall and the barbed wire, afraid that should I lose my balance I would have nothing else to grab onto but twisted, rusty metal. Revathi was right behind me. I stopped to dislodge a twig caught in the strap of my sandals, and Revathi, with one hand on my shoulder and the other clutching the twisted wire between the barbs, looked up and saw it first. "J-aa-nakii," she cried in a whisper, her voice throttling and gasping on my name. Her nails dug deep into my shoulder and her body curved as she shrank to the ground. I raised my head and grabbed her wrists in an effort to steady her. And then I saw it, too.

The pullo of Kamala's sari rustled in the breeze. Her head drooped forward, and her body hung from the nagalingam tree, swaying on the fringes of the wasteland. I cupped my mouth with my left palm and squatted beside the fence. Revathi had rolled the pullo of her dhavani into a ball and stuffed it into her mouth. She grabbed my hand, and tremors rippled through her fingers.

Kamala and I had bought coir ropes for our water buckets, the same day, just three weeks ago, at the Sripuram market.

MAY 1991

ZUBEIDA SAYS THAT I should see this return from a different angle.

Not as me confronting my past, but giving my past another opportunity to confront me. An act of generosity, *bas*.

"They need you more than you need them now. You have the upper hand in this, you can surely see that?" she says, pushing her wheelchair over the wooden ramp (I was instructed, politely, the day after I arrived, not to help her in this) and onto the penthouse balcony. She has consistently turned down Asgar's many offers to buy her a swifter, button-operated one from America. "I will feel like I am in the airport all the time, like those indoor buggies they have for the *buddas* and *buddies* at airports. I have not turned into that yet!" she repeats with genuine horror. Asgar doesn't ask her anymore. We finished dinner half an hour ago.

Asgar and the kids are in the hall playing Nintendo, so Zubeida and I know that we have at least half an hour to ourselves. Sometimes I wonder who is more addicted to video games, the kids or Asgar?

"And still she chose to write you that letter," I say, leaning on the balcony bars and feeling the airy susurrations of curls behind my ears, high up here. My house is on the ground and closer to the sea. "Gayatri Chitti didn't have that humility, even a decade later."

Suddenly, after a ten-year gap, just when I am about to completely wash out Appa's words—*She could have killed us instead*—from the hollows of my memory, Gayatri Chitti screws up her cowardly courage and writes a letter to Zubeida's address. Now she is apparently ashamed, and I am expected to jump with joy?

"You know," Zubeida says and pulls out the pack of India Kings from her purse. The cigarette dangles from her lips as she clicks the lighter. "*Sharam* in Urdu culture is a good thing. I think your aunt is just ashamed." She fills her senses with smoke.

"It would be nice if I could believe that."

And, too, if she could believe the gutless, unsigned, pen-held-in-left-hand letter by Gayatri Chitti that arrived at Zubeida's doorstep ten days ago. Did she think of that night when she told me about Amma, how she had known all along about Appa and her, did she think of that when she held the pen in her hand?

Appa in hospital. Sister alone. Financial condition tight. Varavum. Come.

And rest of the postcard was blank. Holding the pen in her left hand hadn't really helped. It had Gayatri Chitti written all over it.

"So your aunt didn't sign the letter, but you still found

out it was her, and now you feel angry that she wrote it to my address. I can understand that," Zubeida says, tipping cigarette ash into the stucco ashtray. There's an ashtray at every turn in this penthouse. "But that is not relevant, is it, Bolo?"

She drags on her cigarette again, and the tip glows like a nest of fireflies in the dimly lit balcony. Smoke drifts and fissures like a gossamer membrane, and the tip crinkles into a burning bottu. I walk to the edge of the railed-in terrace, my favourite spot. The cold iron bars curve under my left hand as I glide it all the way to the end, pulling myself away from Zubeida. From the far corner I can see the lights of Marine Drive, a moving, burning crescent of red tail lights crawling all around the crash of restless waves. The lights stretch all around the bay, bright at first, and then slowly turn into a blurred, wispy ellipsis. I can see them as far as Wilson College. Where was Appa and Gayatri Chitti's generosity when I married Asgar? Who disowned whom? Now I am supposed to be, once again, dutiful daughter to the rescue, rushing to her father who has been locked up in a mental asylum for the past year and a half. I hear Kabir shouting in triumph from the hall upstairs. I also hear Mallika yodelling "Doe, a Deer" somewhere not too far beyond.

"Your sister may be feeling the same way you are, now that she knows you are arriving in Madras in a few days," Zubeida says, steering her wheelchair smoothly and double-parking beside me. "I never knew Brahmin girls could be so stubborn."

"If I hadn't been stubborn I wouldn't be here today, Zubeida," I say and turn to face her. "And you also know what my father told the press after my marriage to Asgar."

"I do. But they also didn't chase you into the paddy fields and kill you. At least your father didn't say a word about Asgar. And how often do Brahmin girls marry Muslim film stars? You could hardly hold his reaction against him. He was in shock." She searches my face in the darkness and reverses her wheelchair. "Sit down, I can't see you clearly in this light."

I sit down on the wrought-iron bench that faces Marine Drive, and Zubeida moves her wheelchair to position herself diagonally from me. My face gets all the distant light and hers just catches the occasional ray, always half dark, like a moon in perpetual eclipse. I am being readied for something resembling a lecture about how I have to face up to things, whether I like it or not. I know this moment so well, this moment when the air between us changes. I can feel frustration, her inability to have the slightest effect on my ability to forget, let alone forgive. She has made me sit down in front of her in this same spot so many times it is hard to remember the exact number. I am also familiar with the growth arc of the oncoming sermon. This is not, she has reminded me time and again, a Cinderella story. There is no stepmother, no evil sister, no glass slipper. You are not that person anymore. So on and so on. Zubeida, like Asgar, also thinks I exaggerate. Too much Tamil cinema.

"But I am going to Madras," I say, with a calm that disguises my urgency, a sheep's clothing for the wolf inside. "I will not be visiting my father at the Kilpauk Mental Hospital."

"Hahn, I know that," Zubeida says and chucks the cigarette butt over the railing. "And you will be seeing your sister after so many years. You should look forward to that!"

"Yes," I reply. "A sister who has not written or called me in as many years."

After our private marriage ceremony in Madras I called Savitri "Telephone" Mami from the hotel room. I hoped Revathi would pick up the phone so I could tell her I was fine, that things had worked out well for me, that I was finally free—and happily so. But it was her mother who answered.

I remember that first sentence, even before the news broke in the press. "Girls like you are no better than *thevadiyas!*" she said. "You are a caste-less whore! Don't call here anymore, *purinjitha!* My daughter is not your friend!" Pariahs were so easily made in Sripuram.

I also wrote a letter to Mallika on the hotel stationery from Ooty. I received no reply. Five years ago, I heard that the Sripuram house had been sold and Appa and Mallika had moved to Madras. This too through the only postcard I received from Revathi informing me of her wedding. She was marrying her aunt's son, Mohan, the software analyst from Philadelphia. She said her aunt, Savitri Mami's sister, was like her mother with all her arrogance and orthodoxy, multiplied by ten. "*Bayangara Sidumoonju!* A horrible frown-face," she said. It also meant that she would not be writing in the future. She would've remained a friend, perhaps, if I had married a Nadar or a Mudaliyar. At least they were meat-eating Hindus. But I had gone a step beyond for her Brahmin imagination. She knew I would never attend her wedding. I had married a man who ate beef but never pork. She just wrote the date, and left out the address. As a postscript she added:

The A Block house was sold. Your sister and father vacated to Madras. You were right. Everything still slips into silence here. With love, Reva

I have not heard from her since.

"I find it funny," I say, wondering why Asgar has not called out to us. He said he had a dubbing session later tonight. I am beginning to feel tired. My ticket to Madras arrived this afternoon at the music school office. It is in my handbag, on the sofa in the living room. I should just accept it as done and allow my memory to work through it all. Zubeida is right. I choose to go back. This sudden vividness of details about how it all played out is only a consequence of a destiny more twisted and rugged than the byways of Sripuram. It is a retracing to the beginning, middle and rising end of an internal raga. A humming of memory. I shouldn't resist it.

"My mother, if she were alive," I say, rising from the bench, "would interpret everything that has happened in the past ten days—my father's illness and my return now, right at this time when I am also doing a high-profile interview, and this Melbourne Arts Festival thing—all of it she would see as some divine plan. One person's contrivance is another person's karma, she used to mutter under her breath, and sometimes even loudly for everyone to hear, like when we heard about her cousin Kokila in Tiruvannamalai, a determined spinster, winning five lakhs in the state lottery. Or when Thathappa insisted on screening *Sampoorna Ramayanam* for a whole week after Rama Navmi to an empty auditorium three times a day. It's funny to think that had she been alive, I wouldn't be standing here in front of you right now. Now it is my father who pulls me back into that life again."

Zubeida laughs. "That sounds like a Madrasi potboiler! Fated by Amma, Baited by Appa!"

"Salima Sikri thinks she might have something like that, with this interview." I begin walking back to the terrace door.

"*Khala, sahib ko bolo niklenge...*" I call out, hoping one of Zubeida's maids will take my message to Asgar. I suddenly feel like taking a warm bath and just going to bed. I don't want to answer any more questions. I turn towards Zubeida and continue. "Yes, Salima wants me to pose with the veena and talk about my marriage and what she termed the 'hungama in the press,' in the second session. She thinks that would be sensational."

"That does sound like Fated by Amma, Baited by Appa!" Zubeida says with a frown. "And I thought she was an activist. Maybe I should cancel my subscription to *Nisa!*"

"Maybe," I reply, pulling the pashmina tightly around my shoulders, "you should wait till this issue is out." Zubeida stops near the ramp and picks up her packet of cigarettes and puts them back into her bag. The echo of high-tide waves crashing on the rocks of Marine Drive rises above the fumy din of late-night traffic. The air up here now has a moist, salty chill. I can taste the tart flesh of the schoolyard mangoes on my teeth as I walk back into the house. "It may just be an independent blockbuster."

DA

Memory is binary.

The moment, and the feeling in the moment. Once we confirmed that it was indeed Kamala hanging from the nagalingam tree, and as soon as our breathing had returned to normal, Revathi slowly uncoiled the stuffed dhavani end from her mouth. "You go wake them. We shouldn't touch her. We should let her brother bring her down."

At first I didn't hear her, for her voice seemed like a droning, a distant whisper of a flute warped by someone on a synthesizer. Then I felt her hand shaking my shoulder. "We can't just sit here, Janaki! You go or I'll go!"

"The milk bottles?" I said. "I have to take them home. Appa will be waiting. . ." and at the tail end of the sentence I caught myself. "Kamala killed herself!" I announced, as though articulating our discovery would make it sink into my consciousness, make fact of a horrible truth.

"Yes," Revathi answered, "but now we have to wake them up! Someone has to get up on that chair and bring her down from the tree. Will you go and wake her brother while I wait here? Or should I go?"

This time I heard her distinctly.

Revathi sneezed into her pullo. She sneezed again. I could feel the dull, fiery buzz of numbness all along my legs. Walking would be a valiant act, I realized, with the blood rushing to my limbs, suddenly released from a prolonged squat. I stood up with my hands holding onto the barbed wire for support. For a moment I had an intense dizzy feeling in my head and was sure I would fall all over the rusty metal thorns. Revathi grabbed my legs with both her hands, and instead I slumped over her crouched back. I took a deep breath and slowly pushed myself back to a standing position. I was tempted to turn back and look again at Kamala. There was a grey brightness of early dawn around us, and the morning mist had disappeared. To turn back, with my legs still stinging with returning life, would also mean losing my balance and risking falling over. I stood there for a few minutes, while my legs hurt like two huge pincushions.

"I'll wake them," I said finally. "But after that I will have to take the milk home. I'll come back after I get coffee ready for Appa. You don't leave!" It came out sounding like a drowsy, fake order, but Revathi nodded all the same.

I could see my way down the alley more clearly this time.

My legs were so heavy, and moved so slowly, that I did not realize my heel had been pierced by a shard of broken glass, a bleeding gash, which had bled all the way to the door. I discovered a rolled *Dina Thandi* newspaper on the coir welcome mat before I rang the bell. There was no echo of its jangle inside the house. I rang again, and then, suddenly overcome by the realization that Kamala was gone, I started to bang on the wooden door with both my fists. "Open! Please *kadhava thirango*, mami," I grabbed the two metal door ornaments and smashed them into the wood, repeating and indenting a random kolam of loss. The tear-stream on my cheeks turned wider and wider and flooded my whole face. Finally, I heard the latches and the locks being pushed and turned on the other side of the closed door. Subhadra stood in front of me in a crumpled, brown sari with the centre part in her hair out of line and puffed up like a haphazard birds' nest.

"Subhadra... Akka..." I said, still holding on to the metal loops of the door. My voice cracked, and the burning at the back of my throat turned sour with dryness. As I grabbed my pullo to wipe the beads of perspiration from my face, I saw Sabesan Mama, the Brahmin Cultural Association's secretary and Kamala's neighbour, walk to the corner of his veranda so that he could get a better view of me. I had seen the lights go up in the houses all around. I instantly grabbed Subhadra by her shoulders and pushed her back a few steps into the house. "Kamala," I began once again, this time looking at her tired face, crisscrossed with bed marks. I gently pushed the doors shut behind me but did not lock them. "Your sister hanged herself from the nagalingam tree," I said, trying hard to keep my thoughts together. "Go wake your brother and husband."

"*Enna penatharey,*" she answered, not believing me. "You must be crazy so early in the morning!"

Then she looked to the floor, and her gaze remained riveted on a particular spot for several seconds. I followed it to its focus and saw a dark pond around my feet. Pushing the shores, the circle widened slowly, like a lunar eclipse on the floor, and only then did I realize it was blood from a gash on my right foot. Subhadra and I looked up, and our eyes locked together for the first time. She was fully awake.

I saw the scream in her eyes, and then the whole house heard it.

The silent raga will be heard.

That was the entire note. It was as if the whole thing was some deluded pattern, unfolding, with a one-line chorus. Kamala had used that same phrase, *mouna ragam,* the one Neelaranjani had, on that distant sun-soaked afternoon. The only time I had heard it was from the lips of a dishevelled and dusty warrior princess in my backyard, and I had cast it aside as a mere two-paise-thank-you-for-the-pongal prophecy. I felt that sun again on my skin, the second house of memory. I felt the hazy breath of heat from that noon-hour blaze flare through me when Revathi showed me Kamala's note. How did Neelaranjani see so far into my future?

"We are not allowed to go with her to the burning grounds, you know that, illaiya?" Revathi said.

"I know," I replied.

We were sitting behind the backyard well, just three feet away from the nagalingam tree. In the full hour that it took me to make coffee, pack lunch boxes, wrap a bandage around my foot, and get back to Kamala's house, everybody from the agraharam—that same group that had cleared the marriage hall without a word of protest or concern—had arrived with convenient horror and disgust, and the place reeked of their "*aiyyo paavams.*" They were in the hall, and in the courtyard. A few mamis sat around Kamala's body, beside her mother who was absolutely inconsolable. While the funeral preparations were under way, the women sat against the walls of the hall, as though they were staring into a mirror that did not reflect an image, blank without a fleck of rage or remorse. Expressionless and vapid.

No one wanted to be near the nagalingam tree.

It was possessed now. *Saniyan.*

An ill omen that had become an instant legend and that would live forever on the tongues of the agraharam gossips. But for all their horror, they couldn't disobey their curiosity. They couldn't resist the macabre allure of the tree, for all the later arrivals made their way to the kitchen windows and stood behind the bars imagining how Kamala might have swayed from the branch facing the municipal wasteland. Revathi and I could see mami–mama heads shaking behind the windows every time we turned and looked over the wall of the well.

The hours ahead seemed meaningless, and the minutes stretched before and within us in a vacuous calm only cowardice can achieve. Appa stopped by for a brief, fifteen-minute condolence visit on his way to the bank. He had the good sense to drop Mallika at school first. He stood on the front steps of the house and chatted with Kamala's brother but did not go into the hall; he did not cross into the threshold where Kamala's body now lay on the cold floor, wrapped in a white muslin length, with a clay lamp flickering a few inches from her head. Had he stepped into the hall he would have had to return home and shower all over again. Wash away the vision of death with cold water and a few slokas. Not only was that an inconvenience, it would have also meant doing more than he really felt. I saw him start the scooter, strap his helmet and ride away in the direction of Clive Road. I heard Sundari Mami's voice calling out to her daughter. Kamala couldn't have been the only girl to commit suicide in the country that day, I thought, as the suddenness of it all slowly began to fade.

There must be other mothers, right at this moment, all over the country, giving birth or mourning a life that came through them. Mothers not allowed to see their daughters burn, kept out of the burning grounds, because they were women born Brahmin. Amma had burned in the bus, and that had made it easier. A low-budget death. There was a small ritual in her name the day of the accident, and after that she was promptly forgotten by Appa and Gayatri Chitti. Amma's words must have come back to haunt her, years before she died: one person's contrivance is another's karma. They were happy reaping the "accidental" rewards of Amma's death, even seven years later. Their memory of Kamakshi renewed their guilt every year for ninety minutes on the anniversary of her accident. All I had of Amma was that toe ring, in that rose plastic box, and her two favourite saris. It had all burned for me as well, in a way, after she was gone.

"I found it on the ground below her feet, when you went to wake them up."

Kamala's suicide note, given its musical allusion, seemed as though it were addressed to us, but did not have our names. It also felt empty, except for the coincidence of Neelaranjani's phrase. I wanted a reason. If death were indeed the foregone conclusion, as it was in Kamala's case, her only way out for being rotten fated, I wanted her to be angry. I wanted a finger-pointing, vulgar letter of blame, in which Kamala cursed the people who had driven her to suicide. I wanted catharsis, not mystery and superstitious poetry. *Mouna ragam,* that exact phrase. The silent raga.

"Does anyone else know about it?" I asked.

"I don't think it was addressed to her family, so I kept it with me. Nobody knows. Except you."

Revathi snatched the note from me, folded it into four neat squares and tucked it into her blouse.

"You think there will be a police investigation?" I asked, still not sure if we were doing the right thing by keeping Kamala's last words to ourselves. When did she write it? Was it just that morning? Did she write the note when she should have been doing the morning kolam?

"I doubt," Revathi answered. "My mother says that when it is suicide the body is taken for cremation within four, five hours." Her eyes were bloodshot and dry. "How's your foot?"

I had soaked cotton wool in Dettol and wiped the wound, and then I rubbed some antiseptic ointment and wrapped a bandage with one of the new muslin towels I normally used for draining the curds. The glass splinter had grazed the skin, and the pointy edge had dug in like a snake fang, two tongued and deep, making me bleed slowly into numbness, until Subhadra screamed when I woke her up. There had been no feeling or pain then, but now I felt the itch, that sterile pulling into rawness of torn skin, which somehow grows into healing. "I will not be requiring stitches."

"What does the note mean to you, Reva? What was she trying to tell us?" I asked, wondering once again why that phrase, *mouna ragam*, has come back into my life, distilled, as the last words of my best friend.

"We could make an exception and show it to Nalini Miss," Revathi whispered, and then we heard a commotion on the veranda. A few mamas emerged from the hall and stood in a straight line all the way to the gate of the house. Revathi and I stood up in our places and walked to the corner of the compound, the place where I had put my milk bottles that morning. Six hours later, Kamala, like Amma, was ready to be burned. Her brother walked ahead of the procession. In his hand he held the earthen pot with burning coals. The pot was held like a handbag with coir rope handles. About the same length of rope it took Kamala to hang herself. Revathi's hand cupped my shoulder tightly as she began to shake and cry. I watched, tearless.

A procession of men in veshtis followed the pallbearers down the street. All the indoor mamis rushed outdoors and lined themselves against the compound wall. We stood silently as Sundari Mami thrashed around and wailed somewhere in the back, inside the house. We watched Kamala fade away, and the slow reality sank in: that this time it was a rope, bought at the south section courtyard of Sripuram market, and not some *mayam*, not some snakey, otherworldly metaphor for the illusive nature of our world. We couldn't pretend it didn't exist.

FIVE HOURS AFTER Kamala was taken to the burning grounds, and here we are, still chasing the morning, and how it all began, I thought, as Revathi pulled me across the road when I didn't notice the signal change. I had prepared dinner for Appa and Mallika after returning from Kamala's house, and I had ironed Mallika's school uniform for tomorrow. When I told them I was going to Nalini Miss's house and stepped out the gate it was already seven thirty. I was late meeting Revathi near the temple gopuram.

Everything was quiet in the agraharam that evening. Dull bulbs lighted the verandas; and lightless souls crouched behind the windows, our house included. The temple alleys were busy with late shoppers and devotees, although the main *archanai* of the day had been performed promptly at six. Revathi and I had rushed to the temple immediately after the funeral and asked the priest to make an offering in Kamala's name to Lord Narayana. Why? I kept asking as the bells chimed and the arati plate in the priest's hand drew circles around the dark god. Revathi suggested we visit Nalini Miss after dinner. She had taken my silence for approval. "Seven thirty, at this gopuram, enna?" she pronounced. Alert and motivated, she still couldn't fully suppress her disgust at everything around her, and her anger broke through her words like the blunt edge of a kitchen knife. It was not the mystery of Kamala's note, not fully that, which propelled us in the direction of Nalini Miss's house, beyond Clive Road and halfway to Sripuram market. It was the need to defer the truth, to desist from feeling. We were like two insomniacs sleepwalking away from day, registering everything, but not sure where and when the nightmare had leaked into reality, had become reality. Reality escapees, I heard a voice within me say, from the land of Pretend.

"No more Kamala and singing in the milk depot queue..." I said, checking off a mental list of where her absence would be felt first, where the cuts would be deeper than the gash on my foot, and would probably never heal. I was always at least five steps behind Revathi, and she had to wait along the footpath for me. "How is finding out what it means going to help—" I said, as I quickly backed up against the wall of the barbershop to let a cyclist pass. "Yes, why don't you run over all of us," I cursed after him as he turned the corner, and then a sense of relief overtook me. Blood rushed back to every follicle on my scalp, as though my own voice had boomed in every end of my body, and I recognized the shudder to be the final convulsion before inevitable exhaustion. Sleep by sleeplessness. I remained pasted against the wall for a few seconds and Revathi stood right in the middle of the footpath, both her hands on her hips, and looked at me with pale annoyance.

"So you don't want to go to Nalini Miss's house? You could have said so when we left the temple."

She looked like somebody else. When I caught myself in the saloon mirror, my own reflection seemed foreign to me. What had gone wrong? Can ghosts feel?

I will not have to read Kamala's horoscope in the paper anymore, I thought, still ticking off that mental list, I will have to just read Leo and Scorpio now—Mallika's and mine. No more Kamala's: I will never again have that thrill of rushing to veena class and asking her, "So has your insight and courage won the day?" and seeing her laugh, knowing in my heart that she would have read mine as well, and just as quickly hearing her reply, "And have your visions and dreams borne fruit, maharani?"—that moment was gone forever. Like Amma's jeeboombaa, and the bitter taste of thyme water, or Thathappa's "om, om, om" and the sudden blast of light from the projection room as he flicked the switch and the film began to roll in Abirami Palace. My three ways of remembering the dead. Kamala's note—*the silent raga will be heard*—was supernatural and indefinable, like a jeeboombaa or an om, and also ordinary and annoying, like the payoff in an otherwise tepid weekly horoscope. And Nalini Miss was not Bala Josiyar, Palmist/Astrologer (Parrot), in Section B of the newspaper.

Also, Nalini Miss's reaction to Kamala's suicide perplexed me.

She had heard about it around the same time as the rest of the agraharam, I was sure, even though her house was at the outskirts of our colony. She had lived there by herself for as long as I was aware, and kept out of the network of Brahmin gossips. Most of the mamis sent their daughters to Nalini Miss for music lessons, and she rented an old rent-control ground floor for classes and school business. We were never invited to visit her at home.

When Nalini Miss came to Kamala's house that morning, Revathi and I were in the hall with the other mamis. I had only just got there myself. Nalini Miss did not say a word to us. She sat near Kamala's body for a few minutes and then got up, walked to Sundari Mami and embraced her. After a few words of consolation whispered in her ear Nalini Miss made her way to the door. A quick, intense glance at Kamala on the floor and she was out of the house. Nalini Miss had been there for all of ten minutes. I did not make much of it then; I did not make much of anything for those first few hours Revathi and I sat near the nagalingam tree. But now, the more I thought of it, the more it seemed strange that Nalini Miss did not stay till Kamala was taken to the burning grounds. She had seen both of us, Revathi and me, but had made no gesture of acknowledgement. Everything about her now seemed so curt and unemotional. So cold.

"Go ahead. I'll follow you," I said, finally, shuddering at my ability to judge people even when I was thoroughly drained. I concluded that Nalini Miss was simply ashamed for giving us false hopes about the competition, and that to make anything more of her manner at the house was simply, as Amma used to say, *vidhanda vatham*. Gratuitous meddling.

"You know she lives in the street beside Medicos Medicals, illaiya?"

"Yes, yes," Revathi replied. I could sense by her tone that she was still angry. "You walk as slowly as you want. And look out for cyclists at the next signal, enna?"

For the second time that evening I saw the note hidden under Revathi's dark green blouse when she adjusted her mustard yellow dhavani. A white paper square with a life sentence hidden in the folds. There was also a question mark, invisible on the page, but pulsing like a heartbeat.

WHEN THE DOOR did not open on the third ring of the bell, Revathi looked at me and arched her eyebrows.

"Maybe she's not in," I said, ready to walk back home.

Revathi pressed the little white nipple in the middle of the black plastic switch once again. There was still no answer. "She must be taking a bath, you think?"

"Let's wait for her, then," Revathi said, and sat down on the concrete steps leading to the front door. "Or I can go and check at the back . . ."

There was hesitation in the suggestion, and I understood why: our entry into another backyard just that morning had revealed something we would never forget as long as we lived.

"No, let's wait here for ten minutes," I said and sat down beside her. "Just ten minutes and then we go back to the agraharam, enna?"

Nalini Miss's house resembled a small concrete toy box with rooms on the ground floor and a flat rooftop terrace. There was no veranda outside the main door like the houses in the agraharam, and the space between the gate and threshold was so tiny that anything bigger than a tablemat-sized kolam would have been impossible. The windows were shut, but from under the frame of the main door I could see the straight streak of a tube light. We sat on the steps without saying a word to each other, our despair deepening like the dark night around us. Revathi sat with her right hand over her chest, shielding Kamala's last words with her palm as though she were covering scar tissue or taking some solemn pledge.

"She's never going to come back, Janaki," she said after a few minutes.

"She has to," I replied, pulling my pullo over my head and my ears to ward off the constant buzz of mosquitoes. "She must have gone to the market or something."

"I mean Kamala," Revathi said, resting her head on my shoulder, "not Nalini Miss."

I did not reply. I felt that dry wave of rage rise up in my chest all over again.

"She really wanted to win the music competition," Revathi continued in a soft, hoarse whisper.

"Yes," I said, raising my hand over her shoulder and pulling her closer to me. "She talked about nothing else, even on that day when we went to the market to buy new rope for. . ." I began sobbing again. Did Kamala end her life because her wedding fell apart, or did she see it as a release, a quick and final escape to a place where her sister's and her mother's taunts would never reach her? I remembered Kamala's face and how it shone a few weeks ago when I offered to pay the extra rupees for her wedding sari. "Okay, I will take it as a gift from you and will keep it with me for the rest of my life," she had said and hugged me at the bus stop in Chamundi Nagar. The-rest-of-her-life. Unable to dodge the silent daggers of memory anymore, I was about to get up and walk back to A Block when I heard the bolts slide and the doors open behind us. Revathi and I were on our feet in an instant and turned around to face the figure of a woman in the doorway. Her hair hung loose and reached down to her buttocks. She held a copper *sambarani* bowl in her hands and was enveloped by fumes all around her. We heard the voice of MLV singing verses of isopanisad on a cassette player inside the house. For a second she looked like another person, a stranger we had never met in our lives, and I thought we were at the wrong house. It took us a moment to recognize that the figure was Nalini Miss. And then my eyes focussed on the one thing that made her seem like somebody else: I had never seen Nalini Miss in a nightie. The light pink cotton gown made her look ten years younger.

"What are you both doing here at this hour?" she said. "Come inside!"

ONCE WE HAD entered the house, Nalini Miss asked us to sit on the teak settee in the corner of the hall and excused herself for a few minutes. "Open that window, please," she said, and went about her evening ritual. The *sambarani* fumes trailed her into the other room, which I presumed was her bedroom. She emerged again and walked with the copper bowl in her hand to the back of the house. Slokas kept pouring from the cassette player while Revathi and I sat on the cushioned settee. Slowly the smoke lifted and slipped out through the open window, and we saw the things in the hall more clearly. There was a footstool and an armchair in the far corner of the room. To the side, near the kitchen entrance, there was a dark brown dining table with two chairs facing each other on either end. On the Formica surface of the table was set a jar of idli podi and two bottles of Ruchi mango and gonkura pickle. Mallika's favourite these days as well. The hall floor had been recently mopped, and a *jamakalam* was spread in the centre of the room, scattered with Nalini Miss's notes, diaries and cassette tapes. Beside the texts lay a tambura, resting on a round, heavy cream-coloured bolster. Had we interrupted a yoga ceremony?

The western wall was lined with photo frames. When I walked from one frame to the other I recognized all the famous musicians of the classical Carnatic tradition, enshrined one after the other. Sri Thyagaraja, Muthuswami Dikshitar, Swati Tirunaal, Syama Sastri, D.K. Pattammal, M.S. Subbulakshmi... all the greats looked back at me. Against the opposite wall a three-foot-high rectangular showcase with sliding glass panels displayed small musical instruments, from the jalra finger cymbals right down to the thavil and mouth organ. They were spotless. Above the showcase there were photos once again, but this time just three. Two of the frames had individual black-and-white portraits of a man and a woman. The man in the photograph I recognized to be Nalini Miss's guru, Subbudu Iyer. It was the same portrait she had in the recital room of the music school. The woman in the second photo wore a nine-yard madisaru sari and looked into the camera with a shy nervousness, her face half turned away from the viewer.

"Must be her mother," Revathi whispered, following my gaze.

"Yes, must be, she has Nalini Miss's nose and chin," I replied. "Who do you think the other girl is?"

The third photo was a colour print, and the girl in the picture looked no older than twenty-five. She wore a light blue sari and a navy blue blouse with puff sleeves. She was laughing, and in her hand she held a single pink rose, which she thrust into the camera so that it looked like an offering to anyone who saw the photo. Two tight plaits fell forward on both her shoulders, and her eyes were wide with mischief. It seemed like she could wink at the person staring at her photo any minute.

"Could it be her sister or cousin?"

"I don't see the resemblance," I answered. "She looks North Indian, a bit like Mala Sinha, no?"

"Yes, she was often mistaken for that film star!" It was Nalini Miss who answered. She walked towards us with a puja tray filled with coconut and rock-sugar prasatham.

"Everyone thought she was from North India, although she was born and raised in Palakadu!"

Revathi and I held out our hands, and Nalini Miss placed some of the sanctified offering in our palms. While we crunched the coconut and sugar with our teeth and quickly swallowed the prasatham, Nalini Miss continued with her introduction.

"She is Prema, my *saki*," Nalini Miss said and placed the offering tray on the showcase. She used the word "saki," which we rarely used in Tamil. It is a Sanskrit word, and her choice implied that Prema was more than a friend or a class-mate; she was a confidante, a soul sister. Nalini Miss picked up a piece of rock sugar and popped it into her mouth. "I took that picture many years ago on the day we went on a college excursion to Kodaikanal . . ." Her voice faltered, and she did not finish the sentence. She stood near the photo and gazed at her friend with a love only loss can bring into one's eyes. Just the way I stood in front of Amma's photo in the hall on some nights before rolling out my mattress in the hall. It was a kind of communion with someone who was not in the room and yet was always present when I needed her.

"Where is she now, Miss?" Revathi and I asked the question in a chorus.

"Sit, sit," Nalini Miss said. "I am sorry I was not able to talk to you at Kamala's house." She did not answer our question about Prema, and we felt embarrassed for prying. She was once again the Nalini Miss we knew at the music school—gentle, but impersonal. "I am fasting for two days as part of my yoga practice. I was about to begin my evening meditation."

We walked back to the settee, and Nalini Miss pulled up one of the dining table chairs and sat in front of us. "So tell me, what brings you to my house?" Her voice had the same authority once again. The delicate timbre that Prema had lent to her chords a few seconds ago was gone. She gathered her hair and tied it into a quick, loose knot.

"Before you tell me, let me get a glass of water." She went back into the kitchen and brought a water jug and three glasses on a tray. She poured herself a glass and drank it in one long gulp, the rim of the glass never once in those few seconds touching her lips. Our way, the Brahmin way, of drinking water, a sign of respect for a life source or an indirect recognition of our contaminated bodies, I still wasn't sure, but that is the way we all drank it. "Athu vandhu... We, that is, Reva and me.... It is actually about..." I began as soon as Nalini Miss put the glass down on the table. Then Revathi took over.

"We found something near Kamala this morning, Miss," she said and pulled out the note from her blouse. Her hand trembled as she gave the piece of paper to Nalini Miss.

"Wait, let me get my specs." Nalini Miss picked up her eyeglass case from the *jamakalam*. She wiped the lenses with the soft cloth from the case and put them on. Slowly she opened the four folds and read Kamala's note. In an instant all the blood drained from her face, and her breathing turned hard, as though someone were pressing her face with a foam pillow. Nalini Miss dropped the note and shook her head in disbelief, like a woman in the grips of a ghostly possession, losing all peace in an instant. *"Aiyyo,* Prema, Prema..." she groaned and ran to the photo frame on the wall. "Please, Prema, tell me it is you, *kannamma,* tell me. What is this game you are playing now? *Aiyyo,* why twenty years later, *ennathukku?"* Kamala's note lay on the floor like a starched white handkerchief.

Revathi and I looked at each other, stunned by Nalini Miss's incoherent outburst. "Miss, we are sorry, Nalini Miss..." Revathi kept saying, as she grabbed my shoulder for support. "It is Kamala's note, Miss, *satyamma,* promise, we found it near her feet... Janaki, what did we do?"

Nalini Miss paid no attention to us, or our anguish. She walked around the room and flung all the windows open. "Prema, *kannamma,* why now? Why my dear?" she muttered, choking on her words as tears ran down her cheeks and her feet picked up momentum. She circled the room as if she were circling the snake pit in the temple courtyard, but in that small room it looked like she was trying to escape something that was pushing her into the corners. "Prema, Prema," she chanted nonstop, but her voice never rose above the pitch of a throttled whisper.

Then she pulled the same chair she had been sitting on five minutes ago and put it in front of the photo of her friend Prema. She stood on the chair and lifted the photo frame from the nail in the wall.

"What did I do, Janaki? What did I do to upset Nalini Miss so?" Revathi began to sob. I sat there speechless, as though my whole body were electrocuted in a split second by Nalini Miss's bizarre response to Kamala's words.

"See for yourself," Nalini Miss said finally. "See how Prema and Kamala used the same word to end their life..."

It was like lightning striking the same place twice. Revathi and I looked at each other, and then we both snuggled closer to read the inscription behind the photo frame.

The faded brown paper stuck to the back had two hand-written sentences:

Silence is not acquiescence.
The raga of my breath is the raga for Nalina...
Prema

THE ROAD TO the mosque is open, and people dodge the little waves as they hopscotch their way to the dargah. It is low tide at Haji Ali.

The driver unloads Zubeida's wheelchair. He hands Zubeida her crutches.

"You're sure you will be able to push me to and fro before the tide rolls back in, na? Or else I can ask Shauqat to come along?"

The driver waits for my answer, wondering, I am sure, if his dreams of a quick bidi and a chai just went up in smoke, right on the footsteps of a shrine to a Muslim mystic. Why did they build the mosque five hundred yards into the Arabian Sea? Was it to prove that faith could make the waters part? What about those who didn't have the patience—would their prayers not be heard if they voiced them at a mosque that didn't demand such elemental subservience?

"No, I can do it. It's not the first time." She knows we have been here together many times, and we've been through these same motions. But she likes to make a fuss; it is part of the ritual. For me, Haji Ali is a stand-in for the Sripuram temple, and I've never said no whenever she's asked me to accompany her. This shrine calms me.

Using her crutches, Zubeida slowly descends, one steep concrete step at a time, and reaches the path leading to the shrine. Shauqat carries the wheelchair and unfolds it.

Once Zubeida is seated, Shauqat takes the crutches and steps aside. I grip the handles from behind and give it a gentle push. The wheels settle in smoothly.

"I'm ready," Zubeida smiles.

"We're not off to the races," I reply with a laugh. "I think your weight has gone up, too!"

"I thought you would say that. Do the best you can. We can return if you feel tired." She seems to be happy about being out in the open air. Sometimes I wonder how she must feel, confined to the penthouse all day, reading all the time. Just like Mallika—the phrase is fully formed before I can begin to stop it. The thought startles me, and Zubeida feels my hands shake as I push the wheelchair forward. The unseen sister, and the always-visible past.

"I hope you don't ruin it for me," she says. "This is the first time I have come to the dargah this month, thanks to your music academy and your prize-winning students."

"You can't be sarcastic when you also want to laugh. It has got to be one or the other."

"Then what about 'laughed sarcastically,'" she says, faking a stage laugh dripping with disdain. It is a short ha, and it means cut-off.

"I've always told you that you can act sitting on your chair. Now you have proof!"

"Watch that pothole," she says with alarm, grabbing the sides of the wheelchair. "I should tell Asgar to talk to somebody at the municipality. This place gets worse by the minute."

"The road is under water at least eighty-nine per cent of the time." I reply, irritated by her suggestion. "How can they possibly do much about it? Even to do patchwork, you need to have low tide for three full days!"

The best thing about being with Zubeida is the thing that is completely absent: my sense of her as Asgar's first wife. She's told me everything about her life before I entered it. "I'd prepared myself for the possibility," she had confessed on my first visit to Haji Ali with her. "I knew that if Asgar was ever going to sleep with another woman, then he would marry her first. We'd talked about it, after the skiing accident." She's told me about that, too. How in their third year of marriage, when she had finally finished her degree and was ready to have children, Asgar had taken her to Nepal for skiing. When she first used the word I didn't know what it meant. I had just substituted skating in its place, for that was what I had seen in the film *Skating Sundaram* during my summer vacation with Thathappa. I did not know it was not the same thing. Now, after seeing her photos on snowy slopes with Asgar before the accident, I know that I will never do something so dangerous. More dangerous than skating, I remember thinking during my first years in Bombay. Everything about Zubeida and Asgar and their lives was fascinating. Back then, before the birth of Neelam and Kabir, I walked around the whole house, making the alienness mine by touching every object and feeling every corner of the house, the entire length and breadth of it, touched by my fingers, like a cat in a dream spreading its scent, rubbing itself into ownership.

The edges of my churidhar and my sandals are wet. I can feel water gently lapping against the bow strap with every step I take. The wheelchair is steady, and I am pushing without having to huff and puff. The lights of the dargah, the black waves at my feet and the smell of seaweed and garbage all around are eerily familiar. It is like going to the Sripuram temple. Seeking peace, just to know that it is still possible for at least thirty, thirty-five minutes. Away. Purity in a planet of dirt.

"The reason I brought you here," Zubeida says, "much against your wishes, is because I want you to buy a murad dhaga and ask them to tie it to the shrine."

"And why do you think I should do that?"

"You always want a reason, don't you?" Zubeida laughs and opens her purse. We are at the footsteps of the shrine. I clutch the brakes tightly, and the wheelchair comes to a slow stop. People around make room, but soon we're surrounded by beggars, all asking for money. Zubeida snaps her purse.

"Who's the oldest one among you?" she asks in a stern, schoolmistress voice. The group falls silent. A girl, wearing a long blue and white men's shirt that falls a good five inches below her knee, raises her hand. Some visitors have stopped at the pillars around the shrine to watch Zubeida's act from above. Mystic Circle seats.

"How old are you? And what's your name?" Zubeida demands, holding a bunch of currency notes in her hand.

"*Sathra, bibi,*" she answers. Her voice is so young, I think. She could be fourteen or thirteen. Her shoulders are already curved, and she has the look of somebody who sees nothing, feels less.

"*Razia jhooth bolti, ine usse bhi badi! Woh dekho woh beti Razia ki,*" an older man smoking a bidi on the top of the stairs points to a young girl in the crowd. I look at the girl in horror. She looks and smiles at me shyly. How could a seventeen-year-old have a daughter who is five? Razia might be lying about her age, but looking at the corner of her eyes I can say that she could perhaps be twenty, not more.

"Here's one hundred rupees," Zubeida takes Razia's hand and presses the notes. "I've counted ten of you, and that should be divided equally. *Samaj me aaya, Razia?*"

The girl's face lights up instantly. "*Ji, bibi.*" The crowd of beggars follows her as she races up to the shrine. The girl who was alleged to be Razia's daughter looks over at us from the top of the stairs and says, "Thank you, madams!" and blows a kiss our way.

"She's already influenced by films."

"And sometimes happy endings are real," Zubeida answers, her smile telling me that I am the point of reference.

"You haven't given me a reason for the murad thread," I say, turning the conversation to the big and yet undisclosed reason for this dargah visit.

"You need a reason and you never forget. That's what makes you so special!"

"I am glad you approve," I laugh. Zubeida has the gift of distilling character essences. About Asgar, she often says, "A well-meaning man in an ill-breeding profession!"

"I'll tell you when you return from the dargah. Now, if you'll just go and do it, I can have a cigarette and enjoy the evening air."

IF HOPES AND dreams and wishes all could be reduced to one single essence, one otherworldly scent, that would be attar, just enough to camouflage the smell of rot just twelve feet away, where crows and pigeons scavenged even at this time of night. The smell around the inner, marbled tomb is so suddenly intense that I feel giddy and panic that attar is all I will be able to smell the moment I step out, my nose robbed of all other discernment. Irreparably damaged. But the bustle all around, the gentle verses recitation of the holy book, and the occasional rise of *sambarani* smoke, which curls in the corner from a silver trophy cup, calms the day inside me. It could just as well be the Sripuram temple with the flies buzzing all along the metal bar barricades on the way to the sannidhi. The thought of my flight tomorrow morning slowly recedes, and all I hear are the verses of the mullah sahib, to my ears the low suprabhatham of my Sripuram mornings, the best hours of my thankless day.

"*Dhaga bandhengey?*"

"*Ji,*" I say, looking up at the latticed arches around the tomb. Every little opening is crammed with coloured threads, dreams and desires fluttering in the gentle sea breeze.

"You can tie on top of another thread," the white-haired matriarch sitting at the foot of the tomb looks at me with a warm smile. She must know this moment; she must see it in many believers, this insistence for a fresh opening in the lattice.

"All wishes are equal in the eyes of Allah, and He hears each and every one."

I quickly tie the thread on top of the others.

"Wait, *bibi*," the woman says, spreading a small towel on the floor. "Come here for a minute, *yahan zara behto.*" She points to the towel, gesturing to me to sit down. The others around the tomb silently nod, telling me I should follow the woman's instructions. The mullah sahib does not look up from the holy book once. He is lost in the Arabic cadences of the ayaths. Nobody else pays much attention; whole families shuffle by. When I sit down, I see the woman's face more clearly. It has fine, intricate lines, particularly around her eyes and her upper lip. So many threads of age and experience, and here she is, sitting under the fluttering loose ends of murad dhagas, guarding a million dreams. Her eyes are big, and the pupils are a light brown shade. The eyebrows have thinned to a pale pencil line. A black burka covers her head, but on the sides I can see curls of pale orange hair, the henna long faded. She smiles, and her mouth opens sideways, revealing only gums, pale pink mixed with tobacco brown. How old is she? I wonder, as I return her smile.

She stretches her hand, and a young man, one of the attendees around the shrine, gives her a wand of long peacock plumes tied together in a thick bunch. The old woman takes the wand.

"Close your eyes, *bibi*," she says, softly. "And think of what your heart wishes fulfilled."

I can smell the attar and the *sambarani* tweaking my nose again. Outside, on the iron railing a crow clutches a plastic bag with prawn shells and pecks unforgivingly. I watch the woman as she leans forward and pats the shrine with the plumes. I close my eyes, and the next moment a velvety softness brushes against my face. She stops after the third time. But I have thought of nothing. Wished for nothing. I know I am living the dream. I can only say thank you.

"Allah pe bharosa rakho, bas teen aur din, sab safal hota phir," she says, and I have no money to give her or to place on the donation mat at the foot of the tomb.

All will be all right in three days. But nothing's been not all right for more than ten years, so please convey my thanks. I stand up.

I look up at the lattice arch and can't remember where I tied the dhaga.

"It has not been forgotten," the woman says.

"I know," I reply. "But it can be. *Salaam, bibi-ji,*" I bow and step outside.

ZUBEIDA LAUGHS when I tell her about the woman at the shrine.

"Well, she just told you what you wanted to know from me. That's exactly why I sent you to tie the dhaga."

"Are you telling me you coached that woman to tell me what she told me?" My exasperation makes my voice rise to a whine.

"No," Zubeida answers, her laughter fading quickly. ""I wished that for you, and sent you to tie the thread. The woman read that thought in those threads and told you what was written on them. Did you give her any money?"

"No, my purse is in the car."

"And I've given away all that I had brought. I was besieged by another wave of fakirs while you were gone. We can pay up double next time around."

I push the wheelchair and face it to the path across the waters. It seems quieter now. The pedestrians have all slowly gone home. The chatter in the air is scattered and feeble.

"Don't forget to remember."

I don't answer, but steer her to the car.

MY MOTHER TAUGHT me a lesson in silence. My aunt taught me a lesson in reality. Zubeida taught and still teaches me lessons of analysis. There are other ways of seeing the world, and you can't deny anybody the right to their version. That's what she told me when I first arrived in Bombay.

"You'll first have to learn to choose between versions, as there will be many about your so-called elopement with Asgar. We need to get you a regular tutor so that you can do home study and matriculate."

Those first few years I didn't know how their world was conducted. Asgar married me, and I could say that he did fall in love with me in his own way, but after our honeymoon and my arrival at the house on Napean Sea Road, I was to discover a world that was really as far away as I could get from Sripuram. Asgar's days were in the hands of the producers and his manager. When he was not in story discussions, he was in front of the cameras at Mehboob or Mauritius. There was nobody in the house on those days and nights when he was away, out of the city or out of the country. He would call regularly after they had packed up, but sometimes the lines were so bad, it would only serve the purpose of aggravating my misery. Initially I was so overwhelmed by the abrupt shift in my life that I felt like I was sleepwalking through one of those dream sequences from my Mahalaxmi matinees.

In the third week of my stay, I made Asgar buy me a brand new veena. And whenever he was away, I played the instrument like somebody who had no sense of time. Early dawn, midafternoon, past midnight, they all became just hours of the day, and there were many to lose in mine. I also ate at odd hours and sometimes slept in until noon. I only lived for the days Asgar was home, which got fewer and fewer. He was nominated for the president's award in the eighth month of our marriage, and the offers just poured in after that. Most of those months he was doing double shifts, working on two films simultaneously, the whole year quartered with fourteen-day breaks at the end of one set of films. Those two weeks were equally divided. One for each of us, though most times Zubeida gave up four extra days to me.

Surprisingly, over the years it never was an issue. We both decided to leave it to Asgar and his discretion. Into the second year, I still couldn't believe that everything had changed so swiftly around me.

The reason I felt the rage of it all only after two full years was not because I didn't care, but because I couldn't bring myself to actually accept that I had married a Muslim film star. It still seemed like news to me, something that had happened to somebody else. But I never had to count the nights after Neelam and Kabir were born. Asgar stopped accepting everything that came his way; he began spending more time at home with the children. He began praying namaz five times a day, as much as was possible. I found out from Remo

Da Silva that there was a *mussalah* in his trailer now, and he excused himself for twenty minutes after lunch break.

Sometimes, when he was home, Neelam and Kabir would stand beside him and perform all the gestures of praise and postulation. I would sit in the corner of the room and watch, my pullo or dupatta pulled over my head, and hear ashktakams in my heart. They never forced me to join them, and I was happy to just watch them, often thinking of note patterns for their geometric moves. Asgar's thigh muscles are stronger now.

Much to my surprise, Asgar wanted sex more, not less, after the birth of the twins. "I've made sure there's another generation. Now I can take pleasure in pleasure." I've been taking contraceptive pills since.

But those early days were unlike any other that I have lived. Not even the last fortnight in Sripuram before I stepped outside the line for good.

Nalini Miss may have taught me music and a way out of the agraharam, but it was Zubeida who taught me how to make a career out of my music and a way into the world.

For three full years, before I miscarried once and conceived right after, Zubeida arranged for a tutor.

"Since you can't pick up Urdu overnight and neither Asgar nor I have the competence for Tamil, it presents us with a unique problem." Those were her exact words. I immediately focussed on what she was telling me.

"I can manage in simple English," I answered. "But for some months, please speak slowly."

She laughed heartily and clapped her hands.

"Simple will not get you very far, unfortunately." Just upfront, full honesty and no trace of mocking. I knew she meant well that very moment. There was real interest in her eyes. "Don't you want to finish what you were not allowed to do?"

I had to say yes.

Zubeida hired Miss Ingrid Gracias, a retired Goan convent school headmistress who also taught English to seniors on TV programs. I had seen Mallika watch a few episodes in Sripuram. So when she walked into the room I shrieked involuntarily.

"You've seen my TV show? I receive lots of letters from girls in South India wanting to know how they can better their English." Miss Ingrid Gracias smiled, but I could tell from her tone that she was going to approach my education with all the accumulated pride of South Indian English girl success stories. It was her tone, one in which pleasantness was also strictly measured. She wore rimless glasses and had her hair knotted into a cone. Not a single strand was out of place. Every rebellious curl had been thoroughly flattened and subjugated. She was slight in frame but held herself up like a walking stick. She did not need one. Her body was held together by poised unemotionality.

"I'd like to begin right away. Shall we go to the study?"

She meant Zubeida's library.

"Yes, I had them put up a blackboard. I also had them collect the BBC tapes you had requested," Zubeida said. "Press Power and all will work smoothly. There is also a Thermos filled with chai and a water jug. Should you need anything else, please call me on the intercom."

That was the arrangement for the next two years. Zubeida sent the car over to pick me up promptly at four in the afternoon every alternate day of the week. I had agreed on the condition that I got Saturday and Sunday off to practise my music. For nine hours every week after that I was Miss Ingrid Gracias's celebrity student.

Grammarized by the televised marm (which I now know to be slang for madam).

In the ten years that I have known her, Zubeida has never complained about her disability. She once said, "Babies would be nice," when I was carrying, but that was more in anticipation than in regret. Zubeida spoiled Neelam and Kabir whenever I left them in her care and went away for a few days to be with Asgar on location. She rented scary videos and watched them while munching popcorn, which was popped in the microwave. She also organized the caterers and the clowns for their birthdays, and supervised all the party games and sleepovers. Her back was damaged for life, but with Zubeida one never got the sense that she was sitting down. To me, she always seemed to be striding.

"SHAUQAT WILL SEE me to the lift and then he will drive you home. That's what you want, na?" Zubeida asks.

"Yes."

"What time is your flight to Madras?"

"Four thirty. But I expect it will be delayed as usual."

"That much you can count on. But it will all be over soon." She says it with her characteristic resolve. But she doesn't know my family. The one thing we all have in common—Appa, Chitti, Mallika and myself—is a stubbornness that has congealed from many years of living with the sense of being wronged.

I know that is why Mallika has not written. I know I wouldn't have bothered if not for the pathetic postcard Chitti mailed to Zubeida's address. That is all one needs to know of how she—and we—saw the world. And I thought I had left it behind all these years.

"Please, whatever you do, don't rent those *Omen* films," I say with mock alarm. "They don't stop talking about it for weeks! The last time Kabir took a comb and searched Asgar's hair for the six-six-six sign!"

"I know. Asgar told me," Zubeida giggles. "But why deprive them the thrill? They are not scared in the least!"

"I am sure they must take these tales back to school and now I worry that the class teacher will call me any day to say that Kabir insisted on being called demon."

"Damien."

"Like a name is going make a difference to the devil." Sometimes I can't help but wonder if Zubeida lives in reality, if she is a real person. She is so incapable of worrying about anything that she could be a character in a children's story.

"Only comedies. I promise." Zubeida grabs my hand and clasps it tightly for a few seconds. "But you have to try and laugh through the next three days of reality, okay? And give my regards to your sister, the librarian." She always forgets Mallika's name.

"Yes."

"And come back to us!" Her face breaks into a smile, and I can see the sincerity in her eyes.

"This the last seventy-two hours I give to my past. Then it's a clean slate."

"I'll stock up on dusters."

"I don't think you'll need too many."

"But you'll still be able to see the difference it has all made."

I give her a peck on both cheeks and then watch the driver push her wheelchair through the automatic sliding doors of the building.

SO I TRY TO see the difference now, before I see it with emotion when I come back to Bombay. Three days in advance. Totalling up before the bonfire.

The most immediate and material difference is the car. A real difference is to have a driver who is Appa's age. But that's superficial and textureless. I've often thought about the unreality of my life. Earlier in the evening, when we were driving to the mosque, Zubeida said something that made me realize that I still, no matter how hard I try, am only half successful at seeing the world around me in other ways. Sooner or later, the Sripuram lens falls in place, and from there everything takes on a pale green and bitter hue. I can read Mallika's and Appa's dreams. I wish I could make them gentle, caring people. Flawless in character. But that would be very, very far from reality. Truth is always a point of view; I have to learn to accept that.

"Asgar also never dreamed he'd have a second wife from South India, or that she'd be a vegetarian Brahmin. The Muslim imagination has a hard time seeing merit in a diet of just salad and veggies. What could have brought a middle-class Brahmin girl into our lives, then? A short history would be your meeting him at the music competition and your dinner with him the following night. A longer version might fit nicely under destiny, kismet or any Raj Kapoor film."

I feel like saying that my version is no different. I would have, in all likelihood, married a man many years older than me. The "second wife" status was probable as well, as I was a thorn in all their sides, growing older and bolder by the day. Appa and Chitti would have none of that—not for too long. So, Asgar's second wife or Anumanthu's second wife, the difference wasn't much as far as marital status was concerned. I would have had children. Yes, Muslim is a difference. But when you see it purely as a form of worship, then the religion issue is a nonissue. Film star? That can be shelved under coincidence. It could have been a Muslim doctor, or a Christian cricketer, or a Hindu scholar or. . . banker, like Appa. A math teacher from Maruvathur or Mannarkudi was a definite dowry-deal possibility.

I feel like asking Zubeida, tell me what's wrong with this refraction? Is it so off the mark? I feel like telling her that she could never imagine my life. Or what it would have been had I lacked the imagination to escape into other lives I saw on the screen at Thathappa's cinema. Imagination was the only barrier between me and a life of nothingness.

Then at the end of the evening she suggests that there's a difference in accepting that I am no longer the girl from Sripuram, and like Asgar and his salad reflex, that I am letting my early history overwhelm my current reality. Denying myself the possibilities of other realities. Imprisoned by a vision of betrayal, guilt and rage, like a tight, scorching plait I knot and unknot again every time I think of my father, sister and aunt. Yes, she is right. I am no longer the girl from Sripuram. From now on, Sripuram and everybody in it is from me.

"*Academy ho kar ghar chalenge,*" I tell the driver as soon as the car merges with the traffic.

"*Ji*, memsahib," he replies, nodding reverently, and I catch his eye in acknowledgement in the rear-view mirror. Shauqat has driven me around this city countless times, and his family has a photo of Asgar and me in their one-bedroom flat in Kalina. "My wife is always telling me to tell you that you and Asgarji are a nice pair," he told me once, shyly when I asked after his family. Asgar bought him that flat, I later found out. Shauqat's father had also been the family driver before he died. I've told Shauqat on many occasions not to address me as "memsahib," telling him that it makes me feel like an angrez lady and that I am from Tamil Nadu. I tried my best Urdu on him, saying, "'Ji' is good. But I am the age of your daughter!" He doesn't pay any attention to it, and I don't make an issue of it anymore.

The shops around Flora Fountain are winding down for the day, but parked bicycles and scooters still circle the fountain's perimeter. The car's window is halfway down, and I can hear men's voices issuing orders and arguing about the sequence in which things ought to be done. I see a few boy employees walking in and out, carrying cartons of mixers and blenders and pushing hanger rows of printed blouses to the back of the store. Metal shutters roll down in sudden release, and I can see a random row of shop owners squatting at shutter edges, locking up the day.

Then the car turns into the narrow lane, and I see the long metal board, the red letters dropping like petals in a straight line on a white background. Ranjani Arts. I step out of the car and wrap my shawl around my shoulders. I walk to the end of the lane and look at the sign from a distance. I give Shauqat the keys to the door and ask him to go upstairs and open the music hall. As soon as I see the lights go up on the second floor, I step into the building and press for the lift. The sliding gates shake as the cabin pulls itself up with a short jerk, and then begins to descend, creaking slowly to a halt. As I pull the shutters and stand back against the panel, Shauqat buzzes from above, and the lift begins to climb. Between floors it occurs to me, for the first time, that neither Appa nor Mallika nor Chitti asked me about the music competition, or how I felt about my prize-winning raga. In fact, the very thing that has brought me here, this moment, to this landing, is my power. This is the only difference, the wild note: a music room that I can call my own.

N I

We couldn't sleep, so we lay facing each other on the two lower berths, trying to identify the rhythmic patterns of the moving train. Everybody else was fast asleep, rocked into dreams of beats and heat. Nalini Miss's seat was in the ladies' cabin, a metal box with six sleepers. It was a mistake in the booking made by Savitri Mami's travel agent, or else Revathi and I would also be locked in there. Even the TT couldn't make the change, as the other women who had been allotted our berths were older Brahmin widows. We both pretended horror but were internally delighted by the change. We got to be in the general cabin, which was definitely more airy, and we could also use the bathroom whenever we chose. No opening and closing of doors, and no murmurs of annoyance from the other women in the cabin.

"Rupakam," Revathi whispered. In the single blue light between sections of the passage the word seemed filled with dusty secrets.

"Right," I replied.

Then we fell silent again. My suitcase was below the wooden length of the sleeper, on the cabin floor. Safe. I had put two locks on both the clips, and I could feel the keys, which I had pinned to my *manimalai*, press again between the cleft of my breasts. But the fever of excitement running through every vein in my body made sleep impossible. Revathi had the same problem, and I was sure that like me, her thoughts were also about the competition the day after. My veena had been specially packed and sent to the fragile luggage section. I wondered what it would be like to play my instrument in a bigger hall, maybe double or triple the size of the school hall in Sripuram. Will there be many people? A thousand, perhaps? What if my fingers froze with fright? Or my raga did not capture the colour of the scale?

I closed my eyes and tuned my ears to the tracks. They seemed to be right under my sleeper, the wheels rolling hollow over a bridge at that very moment. In my heart I knew we had to win the competition. All the hours of rehearsal had to bear fruit. Appa had allowed me to participate. It was a first, and I had to prove myself. Show the world that when I played the veena, I played it with a *bhakti* that quickly found its way to the listener's soul. I had seen the effect it had had during the night rehearsals on the terrace. So many mamis, even the ones that were usually all clipped words and pinched faces, had come up to me in the temple queue and said I was Kalaimagal, the Goddess of the Arts.

For me to have a second chance, the first chance had to be at least close to the best, if not the best. Nothing else would sway Appa.

Revathi did not have the same pressures. I looked across and in the darkness I saw that Revathi now had her back to me. The stillness of her body told me that she had drifted off. I turned away from her and heard the rumble of the wheels suddenly transferred to the other ear, the rush and roll of momentum, piercingly loud, like destiny racing to its destination. My face turned to the sun mica board that divided the sleeper sections, I closed my eyes and willed my brain to give in to the rocking motion of the carriage. I kept thinking of everything that had happened since the day Amma died and how my past had fallen into a pattern of memories—like a raga. Ordinary notes seeking to attain some form of overall meaning, urgent in their need to avoid a solitary existence. Eager to add up to something. Seeking a name through me, chasing an identity in this world.

I fell asleep.

WE WERE TAKEN to our room by one of the volunteers at the music festival. The room was a large, spacious rectangle, with two wide windows facing the canal that ran to the back of the community college. Three thick cotton mattresses were arranged on the floor, and at the far end of the room there was another door, which the volunteer told us was the bathroom. I stood my suitcase on the floor and walked to the windows. The sun was just coming up in Bangalore, and most of the city was still asleep. Our drive from the railway station had only taken ten minutes, so I guessed we were not very far from the city.

"Breakfast is being served right now in the canteen. If you want to freshen up, I will go downstairs and reserve a table for you."

"That would be kind," Nalini Miss replied.

"Does the flush in the bathroom work?"

The girl looked at me and smiled. "That is the first thing that I check when I am travelling," she said. "Yes, it does. I checked. Let me know if there's anything else."

Revathi was down on the floor, pulling a mattress close to the window.

"I'm not hungry. You both wake me up when you come back from breakfast." She quickly tucked the sheets under the mattress on all sides, patted the single pillow and curled up to sleep again.

"Are you all right?" Nalini sat down beside her and touched her forehead. "You've got a fever, Reva!"

"No, Miss," Revathi mumbled hoarsely. "Only stress."

"Janaki, you come here and touch her forehead and tell me if I am a liar."

I squatted beside her. Had we been so overwhelmed by the arrival that we had not noticed Revathi's condition? I had walked with the TT to the fragile luggage compartment to supervise the handling of the veena. I didn't want a scratch on it.

"Nalini Miss is right, Reva," I said, my heart folding in four. The competition seemed to be over even before it had begun. "You have fever."

I turned around to look at the girl.

"I'll see what I can do," she said, and raced out of the room.

NALINI MISS and I asked for directions at the main office and then were on our way to the pharmacy with Revathi's prescription. She had a fever of 103 degrees, and it had turned worse with the journey from Madras to Bangalore. The night air in the train had fanned the fever, or it could have been the kulfi she had made her mother buy at Madras Central. She seemed invincible then. The doctor thought it might be a viral fever. If the fever had not subsided by tomorrow, she would have to be taken to the clinic for blood and urine tests.

"I told that girl not to take a head bath yesterday evening. That, and then all that dust in the train. . ."

Nalini Miss did not mention the ice cream, but I knew that she had not approved by the way she had turned and gone to the bookstall on the platform. Savitri Mami had not noticed her displeasure.

"She'll be fine after she takes these tablets," I said, but my words were filled with doubt. There was no possibility of her performing with fever. That would only serve to give the Sripuram agraharam a bad name.

"But the doctor said she shouldn't strain herself. How will she sing?"

"You will have to play the veena solo."

"That is not what we practised. I am not sure I can do it."

The pharmacist paid no attention to our exchange. He pushed three flat silver strips of capsules into a small brown envelope and took the hundred-rupee note from Nalini Miss.

"Thanks," she said, and tucked the change into her handbag. "You can."

"But we had practised answers to the questions together."

"But you know the answers already?"

"How can I sing the difference?"

Nalini Miss shook her head. Her face fell immediately, and I saw that it was only self-respect that kept her from bursting into tears. She had already done that once, quite dramatically, when we had visited her with Kamala's suicide note. She had been very measured in her responses since then. I knew that she wanted to make something of the competition, too. She had been the one who had pushed us, who had coaxed our parents and who had taken Kamala's suicide note and its message to heart more than Revathi and I ever did.

"You can do it, Janaki."

"Could I play a Dhikshitar krithi in Shankarabharanam instead?" I knew I could do a smaller piece, something tailor-made for the veena, instead of the operatic and modern Pudhumai Penn. I didn't know what she'd say to that. It would be entirely different, except for the raga. I could find a krithi in Shankarabharanam. It had been our first choice after all.

"Will you?" Nalini Miss clasped me by my shoulders right outside the gate of the college. Autorickshaw drivers looked up from their newspaper break and stuck their heads out to see what was going on.

"I know you will do me proud," Nalini Miss said, overcome with sudden relief. "I'll ask the organizers to give you a space in the instrumental solo category. I can tell them about this crisis."

Nalini Miss walked to the festival office, and I went back to our room to check on Revathi. She was to be given her medicine three times a day (after meals), but she had already skipped breakfast.

I opened the door and walked into the room. Revathi was sleeping, her body under a thick blanket and the scent of

Tiger Balm all around. I gave her the capsules and touched her forehead again. The fever had shot up. Her face was wet with perspiration. She could hardly keep her eyes open.

She swallowed the pills without fuss and drained the whole glass.

"Do you want more water?"

She fell back on the mattress and made a small noise in her throat. I took that to be a no.

I locked the room and waited outside the door for Nalini Miss. Something inside me kept whispering that I would not win the competition.

I did not have what it takes to be a solo artiste.

WE SAT UP until four, rehearsing the new krithi. But that was the easy part. It was the questions that I was going to be asked by the judges before the recital that really made me anxious. Nalini Miss and I covered all possible trivia about the raga and the composer of the krithi. We thought up similarities and differences the raga had when played in other scales, which were closer and which differed. Then I had to memorize answers to questions of choice and explain why I had chosen the raga. What made it so special to merit a public recital? Did I know the meaning of the lyrics?

I couldn't understand the need for such a component. Wasn't it enough to play well and win the appreciation of peers? Still, the questions were allotted ten points. The other twenty points were half for clarity and half for technical control. I had to get all ten question points if I wanted to push my score up.

Revathi coughed and threw up two times that night. I mopped up and fanned her for a bit with the festival program.

Her body was as limp and weak as a withered brinjal. Once she was asleep I went back to another round of practice questions. Nalini Miss was determined to give me all the information that I might need. She said my veena recital was spotless.

By early dawn, I was so tired I felt like giving up the opportunity. I couldn't keep my eyes open anymore.

"That should be more than enough," Nalini Miss said, sleepily. "We should at least rest for a few hours."

We checked on Revathi, whose fever seemed to be holding constant despite the three capsules she had through the day. We had planned to tour Bangalore, but it had all turned into a day of nursing and rehearsing. When I turned off the light after using the bathroom, the birds were beginning to chirp in the trees.

REVATHI WAS taken to the hospital at just after eleven that morning. The doctors thought it could be anything, from laryngitis to viral fever, but would only know for sure after they had the test results. She was also anemic as she had had very little to eat or drink in forty-eight hours and was, as a result, severely dehydrated. Nalini Miss called Savitri Mami to ask for permission to admit her to hospital. The doctor also explained the condition on the phone. Soon after, an ambulance arrived and the paramedics pulled out a stretcher. Nalini Miss and I promised to visit the next day. The doctor had the festival manager's personal phone number and said he would call if there was any improvement overnight.

When we got to the canteen for lunch, a few of the other participants came up to us and expressed their sympathies. After they left, in between mouthfuls of lemon rice and vegetables, Nalini Miss kept repeating the questions and I kept up with the answers. We had no time to make friends.

That afternoon I took a long nap. We would be back on our way to Sripuram tomorrow night.

I had only one chance to experiment with change.

NALINI MISS had walked to the auditorium to make sure that we had the right performance time. I was slotted for eight fifteen, the final slot of the evening. I laid out the sari on the mattress and then took a shower. I had chosen the sari for two reasons. One was its colour, a light rose with a gold border. I had bought it with Kamala; it had been chosen by Kamala. A Bengal cotton full length that looked like the evening sky had been starched and pressed on my body. The second reason was that it gave my complexion a lift. I knew my face looked bright and fresh every time I wore it to the temple festivals.

I draped the sari around me and made a red bottu between my eyebrows. I stood for a few minutes with my hands folded and prayed for Revathi's recovery and my success. I asked Amma to bless me, wherever she was. I felt calm inside, but I knew that that could all change the moment I was in front of the judges. I checked my face and hair one last time in the tiny bathroom mirror and strapped on my sandals. The volunteers had come by to take my veena backstage a few hours ago. I locked the door.

Twenty minutes and the Silent Raga would come to life.
Or die.

PANIC STARTS in the feet. I felt my heart begin to pick up speed at the thought of a packed auditorium and other musicians marking my every mistake. The closer I got to the auditorium, the more my confidence left my stride. People were milling around the entrance to the hall. A Sorry! Full house! sign hung between the doors.

"Madam, extra ticket?"

"No, participant," I said, and walked up to the man managing the ticket booth. "I am part of the competition. Can you take me backstage?" I asked. He seemed relieved that it was not a request for a ticket.

"Sure. Follow me."

Nalini Miss was waiting at the door for me. I thanked the volunteer and quickened my steps.

"It will be your spot in fifteen minutes. The previous contestant is just playing his piece on the mridangam."

I quickly touched Nalini Miss's feet with my hands and she said, "May the goddess be with you. She knows what this means for both of us."

We both walked to my veena and unwrapped it. I had tuned it once, but I checked it just to make sure. The volunteer outside the storeroom said he would carry it for us once the other candidate had finished.

"There is five minutes for set up and mike check," he whispered. "You'll do very well, don't worry."

"Has there been any great performance?" I asked.

"So far, so-so," he replied. "You can wait near the wings. I will bring the veena for you."

The auditorium broke into applause, and my spine stiffened. I looked at Nalini Miss, and she must have seen the panic that crept into my eyes.

"Remember, nobody else matters. Just you and your raga."

I grabbed her hand, and together we walked to the stage.

I COULDN'T SEE a single face in the hall. The floodlights burned my eyes, and I hoped I didn't have to play in such harsh conditions. I could feel the sweat break in my palm. The technicians rushed to adjust the mike to the right height for the veena. I sat down and held it in position till they had finished. Then I placed the veena down on the *jamakalam* and stood up. I did a namaskaram to the judges who sat behind a long table that was placed diagonally to the inside right of the stage.

Just then the lights dimmed.

There was a spot on me that also lighted the veena. And the three judges had one broad light overhead. The rest of the stage was dark. The audience stopped chattering as though their mouths and the lights were connected to the same switch.

The moment of the Pongal Prophecy.

A Backyard Destiny.

"Janaki Venkatakrishnan from Sripuram. Guru Nalini Mani. A new addition to the list?" The silver-haired man in a veshti, jibba and a forehead full of viboothi said, peering over his glasses and looking directly at me. He was seated between the other two judges, who looked on without much interest.

"You may sit down."

I did.

"You have chosen a krithi in Shankarabharanam, the king of ragas. Do you want to impress us?"

It was the woman who asked the question. She was about Gayatri Chitti's age, but her face was round and cheerful.

She was also younger and more modern and wore a churidar kameez, like the women I'd seen at the Madras Central Station. She looked like some Hindi actress I had seen many times on TV.

"I chose it because it is an evening raga."

"And ascending and descending order for tonight's krithi is?"

This time it was the man in a Nehru vest. He also looked like a North Indian, or Bengali. He had an inexpressive face, but his voice was soft like the Christian priests in *Vellai Roja* and *Father Satyam*.

"The arohanam, the ascending scale, is $S-R2-G3-MI-P-D2-N3-S$ and the avarohanam, the descending scale, is $S-N3-D2-P-MI-G3-R2-S$."

I played the notes.

They conferred with each other and then nodded in agreement. My confidence seemed to be returning. So far I had answered their question precisely. They seemed to be satisfied with my choice.

"If I dropped Ma and Ni from your scale, which raga will it turn out to be?"

"Sa–Ri–Ga–Pa–Da? That would be Mohanam."

"The raga is called by another name in the Hindustani system. Do you know what that is?"

"Raga Bhopali."

For a few seconds I thought it was Kamala, our resident Hindustani expert, who was asking me those questions. Kamala could be here now, I thought. How do I know she isn't? It is her note that has brought us this far. Thrust me in the spotlight.

"Tell us why you chose this composition."

"The raga and the krithi are both devoted to the same god, that is the first reason. Shankara and Shiva are different names of the same deity. Dakshinamurthi is in praise of the lord in his ascetic phase. This meditative form is one of bliss and knowledge. The krithi says Dakshinamurthi or Lord Shiva the Yogi offers us happiness and eradicates our ignorance.

"The Raga Shankarabharanam can be translated as Lord Shankara's Ornaments. And above all that, I can do justice to the composition in twenty minutes, which is really not much."

There was laughter from the audience when I said that. A few of them started clapping. I was suddenly aware how textbookish and memorized it all sounded. I'd done my best to string along all the details and facts I had rehearsed with Nalini Miss. I turned sideways and caught her figure in the wings. Her bright smile reassured me.

"One more thing before we listen to the krithi. There's a famous Western song in Raga Shankarabharanam. Do you know the one I am referring to?"

"Are you thinking of 'Room of—'" I knew that was not it instantly, and thought I had made a mistake finally. "No," I said, a little too loudly. "*The Sound of Music* is correct. 'Doe, a Deer' is the same scale as Shankarabharanam. I have played it many times for my sister, Mallika!"

All three judges smiled as though they were posing for a group photograph. I could feel my fear and nervousness lift and fade away.

"You may begin your recital."

The lights above their table dimmed until their figures became three grey silhouettes.

I looked up and saw the audience for the first time. Their bodies blurred into smoky rows, rows upon rows all melding together into my eyelids.

In the darkness of my head, I saw the notes rise slowly, glowing like flames on a copper tray.

And then the raga spoke. It was my voice, through my fingers.

Lord Shankara closed his eyes.

Ragam Thaanam Pallavi

Scale Rhythm Chorus
Sa-Ni-Da-Pa-Ma-Ga-Ri

MAY 1991

IN THE AIR, there is that damp, moist assault of rainfall rot.

Mallika knows this smell. She has often thought of its putrid mix and shuddered in moments of private horror or rude awakening, as is the case now. She sits on the bed for a few moments, her head against the wall, hearing the cries of the neighbours' children on the street. Janaki's goodbye letter is on the table, held in place by Mallika's reading glasses. She looks at her wristwatch on the side table. 8:42 AM. What time was it when she had finally gone to bed? Three thirty?

Then once again the smell wafts in through the open window, and Mallika sees watermelon wedges, dog urine, hawai chappals, banana leaf and cinema posters rushing into the open sewers, with special guests cow dung and betel juice here and there, clogging drainage pipes all over the city.

She shudders involuntarily and tries not to think about having to make her way to the bus stop with that recipe rooming in her head. She has to collect her sari from Laxmi Dry Cleaners, the sari she plans on wearing to Mrs. Samanta the senior librarian's retirement party later in the evening. The same sari Mrs. Samanta brought back as a gift from Khadakpur for her. "My daughter Rinku insisted I should buy this for you," she said during lunch hour one day, and produced a packet wrapped in headlines from *The Telegraph*. Inside, there was a pale pink Bengal cotton sari with a gold-lined paisley border. It was hard to believe that Rinku, whom she had met only once in her life, could have felt such an attachment. It was Mrs. Samanta's way of making someone else responsible for her kindness.

A cultured sense of goodness.

Mallika had embraced Mrs. Samanta then, in a moment of unreserved love. She knows the burden of obligation, and Mrs. Samanta has given her more than she would ever be able to repay in seven lifetimes. What would she have done without the older woman's support the day Appa's boss called from the bank three years ago, and Gayatri Chitti was away on her annual visit to the ancestral village? Janaki has no inkling of what Mallika has been through with those two. Mrs. Samanta was always there, right from her second year at the Women's Christian College of Madras.

But now Janaki also knows something. Mallika chases her distraction, rising from the bed to close the bedroom window. Holding her nose as she pulls in the little hook on the wooden shutters, she thinks: Otherwise, why would she come back after such a long absence? It doesn't make sense!

In three days, ten years of separation would either be swept aside or the bitterness would seep in further, deeper.

And she is yet to mention a word about Janaki's letter to Appa or Gayatri Chitti.

The smell begins to dissipate the moment Mallika walks into the living room and unlocks the balcony door. It must be the sewer on the other side of the building.

"Akka, see boat!" The neighbour's older son, Wilfred, yells from below when he sees Mallika gather her rain-soaked petticoat from the clothesline and wring the water over the balcony's ledge. All the children from the apartment building are standing around a puddle that from the second floor looks vaguely like Greenland. Only this time it is a country filled with sinking foolscap paper boats.

"Mine's still floating! Philomena's is *umbayl*!" Wilfred hops from one side of the puddle to the other and lands next to his sister. Philomena stands watching her nautical expedition as it bobs on its side with all the resilience of a defeated INS captain. Without warning, she suddenly lifts her skirt above her knees and stomps on her brother's paper ship with her bare feet. The other children around the puddle pull back from the splash of brown rainwater and then begin clapping. Wilfred stands stupefied by complete rage. Before Wilfred can recover from shock, Philomena quickly jumps to the other shore of Greenland and dashes into the building.

"Amma!" Mallika hears her scream at the top of her lungs, as she rushes up the stairs. "Wilfred took the good boat!" she bawls.

Mrs. Amaldoss, their mother, peers over the second-floor balcony on the other side and says, "Wilfred, *sisteray trouble pannathey*, my boy!"

The children on the street start chanting *"pootakes! pootakes!,"* hoping that Wilfred will either jump in the water and perform a messy dance of fury or at least, to prolong the thrill, chase after his sister. But Wilfred quietly leaves the group and walks out the front gate.

"I'm not coming back!" he booms with all the contrite conviction an eleven-year-old can muster. He steps carefully over the brick-by-brick bridge, a balancing act over five familial puddles. With each step a delicate struggle between life and filth, he crosses over to the other side of the street.

The giggles and taunts from the other children suddenly stop, and the naval exercise ends abruptly. Mallika wonders why Mrs. Amaldoss has not rebuked him for his declaration of independence, his churlish valour.

Mallika feels like laughing and ruining it all for everybody. How long before the buffoon comes back, she wants to tell them, Think!—But she holds back. Wilfred looks indecisive for a few minutes, standing next to the municipal garbage bin.

He wastes time by tucking his T-shirt into his khaki school uniform shorts, expecting his mother to say a few kind words, to urge him to please stay. But there is silence from the balcony; his mother is somewhere else in the apartment. Philomena has been pacified. Maybe mother and daughter are sneaking a feast of sweet basundi and cream. Mallika watches Wilfred give up and run towards the main road.

She clips the petticoat on both ends along the portable clothesline and pulls the whole frame closer to the door so that it gets the best of the sun. What makes Mrs. Amaldoss so sure her son will be back?

Row, row, row your boat, Mallika hums as she walks back into the living room, suddenly remembering how insistent she was, how she made Janaki play that same nursery rhyme, nonstop from age six to seven, again and again, until the desire to hear it on the veena in that regretful, lost voyage tone was completely annihilated. But Janaki played everything so religiously, as if the smallest krithi was a blessing, a revelation. Still, always with a touch of indecipherable pain. That took the fun out of it sometimes.

The only time Janaki used her art as arsenal was when she played those coma-inducing rarities for Gayatri Chitti's would-be husband consignments, sent intermittently with their demanding mothers and inexplicably voiceless fathers, from Madras and Cuddalore. Mallika has not forgotten those evenings of exhibitionism her sister endured. It was art as escape in a very literal sense.

The veena competition changed everything once and for all. Janaki's art had become her escape. And then there was that photograph, that black-and-white moment of truth, and what now, ten years later, seemed to be a truly benign kiss. But the rage that provoked in Appa! How he turned their lives into a doorless, dark room. Was she, Mallika, really the author of Janaki's goodbye note? And Janaki left so easily, too, without looking back, without thinking about anything but herself. She can see that burning camphor in the middle of Appa's palm, silencing her like an accusing third eye. Mallika quickly banishes that thought from her head. She does not want that panic again. She no longer fears that shadow of guilt. That was in another house. Not this one.

Row also means a passionate disagreement, Mallika thinks instead, when she opens the front door and picks up the morning newspaper. And real rebels, she knows, don't announce their departure from street corners like Wilfred. They hide goodbye letters between Leo Coffee packets, and then they just leave.

MALLIKA EXAMINES the border first.

She spreads the fingers of her right palm like a fan under the sari and raises the edge to an angle where it directly catches the light. It is the borders that get ruined in getting on and off the PTC buses of Madras. And then the ripping moves quickly, with just one misstep. She had to give away three good saris last month to Mrs. Amaldoss's maidservant. The sari looks fine. The gold lining of the bright red paisley glistens like a polished mirror. No minute steam blotches either. Murugesan, the dry cleaner—cum-dhobi, heaves a sigh of relief.

"Madam has eyes like microscope," he says, slyly, as he wraps the sari in a sheet of brown paper and slips it into a plastic bag.

"Appa is all right?" he asks, and staples the bill to the bag.

Mallika smiles. "As all right as he can be," she says.

Everybody in the neighbourhood knows her story, or at least some version of it. You don't expect anonymity with a family scandal breaking in the newspapers every five years, as though it were all some menacing horoscope taking its time to unfold in Tamil newsprint. Yet Mallika prefers it like this, everything an open secret. She is touched now by the fact that Murugesan has asked her about her father, even though he has never met him. He has laundered and ironed a few of Appa's bush shirts, which she has brought back from the hospital. He is as old as Appa, if not older, a widower, with a son studying electrical engineering at IIT in Guindy, whom he mentions all the time. Perhaps, he is concerned that he might lose his *buththi*, his ability to discern right from wrong, and like Appa lose all presence of being. But she can also see that he does not seem to have half the dishonesty of her father. He is not lost in some false world of prestige and pride. Who knows? Concern has many faces.

Murugesan moves along the desk to pick up the phone that has been ringing for the past forty seconds, while he locked the cashier box.

"I'll tell him you inquired after him. Varenga..." Mallika says. Murugesan nods his head and smiles. He turns away nodding, to talk to the person on the phone.

Early on, when she first moved into the apartment complex, it was the housewives who had wondered loudly during the prolonged welcome-to-the-building, nice-people-all, but-so-are-you-Janaki-Asgar's-sister? Admittedly, Appa's notoriety was local, and on a much lower scale. It hadn't really caught on two years ago. So she didn't blame them for their curiosity. She herself found out about her sister's life through the slivers of gossip that made it to the *Sunday Hindu,* in the "Mad About Bollywood!" column. She still expects to read "Janaki Asgar's Father and His Dark Secret—Revealed!" as a film gossip item some time soon. It will happen.

MALLIKA PICKS UP her sari packet and walks out.

She knows that Murugesan will also find out about Jana-ki's Madras visit without her having to tell him. It might even be part of their next conversation, flanked on both sides by lifeless, hard-pressed men's shirts on metal wire hangers. Mallika knows someone will leak Janaki's arrival at Hotel Connemara to the film magazines of Madras. A photographer is always around. Janaki Asgar may have kept her mouth shut for the past ten years, and she may have shielded herself in her fortress in Bombay, but that has only added to her mystique. Not a word about her past, or anything too revealing about her present. Every so often there is some talk or speculation about her in the newspapers. "Twins for Janaki!" "Asgar's Wife a Veena Ace!" "Janaki Is a Very Private Woman!" But there is seldom a photograph. The last time she had seen Janaki's picture in the magazines was after her children were born, nearly seven years ago. What did Janaki want now? Mallika found it odd that Appa's drama at the bank did not make it into the national dailies via the Janaki Asgar connection.

For two days a small, boxed item appeared on the fourth page of *Dina Malar* and *Alai Osai*—but after that it was quickly forgotten. The news about Appa in this new neighbourhood was completely word of mouth, trailing her from the Bank Quarters in Chetpet, from where she had to move after the incident, all the way to St. Mary's Road in Luz. The hooded cobra swayed all the way from Sripuram.

After Janaki, and After Appa.

Of course, the agraharam gossips never let you down.

MRS. SAMANTA'S brother-in-law was her landlord.

That December, when she had no choice but to move out of the Bank Quarters and had nowhere to go, Mrs. Samanta had opened her doors to Mallika. "My daughter's room has been vacant since the day she married. Do the room a favour!" she said, when Mallika approached her two days before the official eviction. "Stay as long as you want!" she said. "You should have asked a long time ago!"

But after two months of pampering, dessert with every meal and postdinner discussions of the Marxist party's history in Bengal with Mr. Deb Samanta, Mallika seriously began looking for an apartment. Another thing that goaded her to search for her own place to live was Mr. Deb Samanta's habit of watching Hindi films late into the night. Things got really out of hand when he started to rent Asgar's films and thought it only natural to discuss his merits as an actor with his Tamilian sister-in-law. Mallika still found it hard to accept the fact that Asgar was indeed her Muslim, actor brother-in-law. She tried to watch a few of Mr. Samanta's indiscriminate picks, just out of politeness, during the first month of her stay with them. And then she decided that courtesy sometimes was a terrible mistake.

The films were ludicrously infantile, and she had to resist the dire need to laugh or throw something at the screen whenever they cut to two flowers opening or two butterflies nuzzling (really!) during the kissing scenes.

Nothing seemed to have changed in popular films since those days when Janaki—the film-crazy, music-always-to-the-rescue Janaki, fighting her way to the front of the ladies' queue for two two-rupee-and-ninety-paise tickets Janaki—forcibly dragged her into the Mahalaxmi Talkies for Tamil matinees like *Annakili* and *Penn Jenmam*.

Obliged as she felt to the Samantas, Mallika was also glad to move out of their household and into her own apartment. Mrs. Samanta commissioned the lease with a Madras lawyer on behalf of her Californian brother-in-law. When Mallika asked her why her brother-in-law owned the apartment in Madras, one that he had never rented before, and one in which he would never live, Mrs. Samanta had just said, "For dowry purposes," and left it at that. Mallika did not ask how many daughters. Instead she took the apartment for eight hundred rupees a month. The initial lease was for five years.

It was the first time in her life that she had space all to herself, away from the supervision of an irresponsible father and a self-centred aunt. Appa and Gayatri Chitti were now suddenly out of her life, and she was on her own. She was happy to visit Appa every second week at the hospital for two hours.

His madness had often left her wondering if she should pity him or see his loss of coherence as a fitting end to all the falsehoods. Lost to all truths. His madness had liberated him, releasing him into a world of lost meanings and memories so short-lived that the moments never lasted long enough to become fingers of accusation.

She shared his medical expenses with Gayatri Chitti, who complained about everything in sight as soon as they arrived at the hospital, starting with her own body and how it could take it no longer, and ending with character assassinations of the psychiatric ward nurses who looked after Appa during the week.

Mallika listened to the dirge every weekend when they met during the supervised visiting hours, while Appa walked about the room talking to himself: "Why are all the bank lights on? I must talk to Security Sundaram!" or "Tomorrow, D-Day will win! It will be my. . . Oh, but the race is not tomorrow. Oh yes, next week, for sure, and then I will perform a big *archanai* for my jackpot god!"

He would then smile for the next twenty minutes as he sat down and meditated with a wide grin on his face. D-Day never won. The horse came in fifth.

Gayatri Chitti's voice became background static as she

thought of Appa at the racetrack gambling everything away, even the Sripuram house, in the hopes of jackpot on a horse far away from photo finish. She listened to Gayatri Chitti's woes and losses, but taught herself not to pay attention. It was a skill she learned from Janaki.

But now the last thing she wanted was for Janaki to ruin it all, once again. Their lives had changed so much in a decade. Why reconnect and revive all the dying hostilities? Why believe that one can really overcome it all and get back to that original moment of purity, of blamelessness?

No matter how hard her exit from the Sripuram agraharam may have been, everything after that had definitely been rosy. It was Mallika who had had to live through it all.

Mother, Sister, Father. Newsworthy all.

When Janaki arrives, three days from now, I will meet her, Mallika reasons as she climbs the stairs to her apartment. The children of the neighbourhood have moved to the playground at the end of the street. Mallika can hear Wilfred's voice in the distance. The rebel has returned.

How will Janaki recognize her? What will be her first reaction? It will just be another moment of truth in the dimly lit ambience of the Hotel Connemara reception lounge, she concludes, not wanting to give her thoughts any more significance than what they actually deserve.

She unlocks the door, vigorously rubbing her sandals on the coir doormat, hoping it will stamp out her memories. And it will be over.

She pulls out a wire hanger from the cupboard in the bedroom and loops the dry-cleaned sari. Moments of truth, she now knows, come and go, ceaselessly, for an entire lifetime.

On Sundays, Appa took his shaving kit—a small mirror, scissors, lather brush and barber's razor—outside to the veranda, and shaved his stubbly face with great indulgence and leisure. He never shaved with such care and joy on other days of the week. The mood of the house shifted on holiday mornings. Everything was an hour or two late, even lunch, prepared and ready, but not served until after the noon-hour *archanai* at the temple. Mallika played chess with Appa, if he was in the mood for it, or else sat on the windowsill in her room reading *Oliver Twist* or *The Count of Monte Cristo*. Noises from the kitchen, devotional music on the radio, the rattle and hum of the ceiling fan—everything melded and flowed together on Sunday mornings. Even Janaki was more relaxed—there was no rush to pack lunch, no rush to make sure that the curds set by six o'clock every morning, no picking up Mallika from school. A welcome lull in the morning for everybody in the agraharam, it seemed.

"What do you want?" Mallika heard Appa ask, that Sunday in April.

She set aside the sheets of brown paper with which she was covering her workbooks for the upcoming annual school inspection and peered out the hall window. Appa was standing on the veranda stairs with an annoyed look on his face. The newspaper was on the floor beside his easy chair. He had finished his shaving ritual a few minutes earlier. Janaki came into the hall from the kitchen and nodded at Mallika.

"Somebody?" she asked, in a soft whisper. Mallika shook her head to indicate she did not know. "Non-Brahmin?"

They both stood near the window and stared at the man who had disturbed Appa's concentration.

The man was tall for a Tamil man. He wore an off-white handspun cotton shirt and a dirty veshti. The contrast between his dishevelled state and Appa's spotless banian and veshti was stark and white, like the castes that separated them. Brahmin, and then everybody else. No namam on the forehead, no viboothi either. A total absence of Brahmin markers on the forehead. "Non-Brahmin," she had often heard Janaki whisper when she ran into people they knew outside the agraharam. It is a distinction Mallika learned to make, like everybody else, even if only mentally most of the time. The man lifted the latch of the gate. Mallika noticed a fading yellow turmeric stain below the man's shirt pocket. His face was stippled with salt and pepper stubble bristles, and his eyes were a dry, deep red. Mallika thought he must have conjunctivitis and had stopped by to ask for some eye drops. He wore no footwear. Janaki put her finger on her lips to make a small hissing sound, and silently they watched the man open the gate and walk towards Appa.

"Who are you? And what do you want?" Appa repeated his question, standing fixed in his place on the top of the stairs.

"Saar," the man began in a choked and abrasive voice, haltingly, as though his gravelly vocal chords would suck the breath out of him if he attempted a full sentence. He did not finish his thought but looked over the compound wall towards the neighbour's house. Following the direction of his gaze, Mallika and Janaki knew immediately that Vanaja Mami was back to her sentinel post near her window, watchdog and wagging tongue, a very Brahmin two-in-one.

The man stood on the lower step and cleared his throat. Slowly, with painful deliberateness, he began once again.

"My name is Chellaiah," he said. "I need your help, saar. . ." Then his eyes filled with tears and he abruptly sat down on the step and began to sob. Appa shook his head in disbelief. "Look, this is not the place for this. . ." he said. "It's okay, now what do you want from me?"

The man blew his nose and wiped his face with the edge of his veshti. Mallika thought of all the germs crawling on the fabric and shut her eyes in disgust, but Janaki did not move from the window.

"My daughter Rukku died of typhoid, saar. . ." He pulled out his wallet from his shirt pocket and thrust it towards Appa. Appa did not take it from him; instead, he moved away and walked to his chair. Chellaiah pulled out what seemed to be a photo and showed it to Appa. "Only eight years old, saar, a very bright girl. . . died this morning, my golden girl. . ." he began to sob again. Mallika had never seen a grown man cry before. His body shook and shuddered, and he wiped the rolling tears with both his hands, sniffing and snivelling as he did so. Mallika quickly looked at Janaki and saw a look of pain on her sister's face. "My age, Akka!" she said. What they heard next made Janaki flinch and gasp.

"Why should I believe that you are telling me the truth?" Appa asked without the slightest hesitation. His voice was officious, as though he were ordering a bank peon to sort out a client file. At that moment Janaki pulled Mallika away from the window, and they both sat on the floor. "What a question to ask!" Janaki muttered and shook her head in disbelief. They both strained their ears to hear the rest of the conversation.

"Saar, my only daughter, saar! Why would I lie to you? I just need one hundred rupees so that I can buy some firewood

for her cremation . . . even fifty rupees will help me, saar . . ."
Chellaiah pleaded with Appa. His voice was still shaky and
muffled and his words faded into incoherence.

After a few seconds of silence they heard the easy chair
creak and knew without having to look out the window that
Appa was back to his reading.

"There is no money here," Appa boomed above the rustle
of the newspaper. Appa did not conceal his anger anymore.
"Now if you will leave, I'd like to read my newspaper."

They did not see the man get up and walk to the gate.

They just heard the rusty latch fall back on the iron bars
and knew that the man had moved on. He must have just
walked a few yards when they heard Appa's voice once again.
"Wait!" he said.

Janaki jumped up and looked out the window. The man
stood near the municipal waste bin and wiped his face once
again. Quickly, Janaki walked back to the kitchen to finish
washing the rest of the morning dishes. Appa stepped into the
hall and went straight to his room. Mallika gathered her books
and the brown sheets of paper and piled them on the windowsill. When Appa stepped out of his room, he was wearing his
black office pants and a checked blue bush shirt. "I will be
back for lunch," he said, tilting his head towards the kitchen
so that Janaki would hear him clearly. He went out. When
Mallika looked from the window again, she saw Appa talking
to the man. Chellaiah nodded and then clutched the edge of
his veshti and wiped his face once again. Appa followed the
man down the street in the direction of Sripuram market.

"Appa went with the man!" Mallika announced as she
entered the kitchen, confused by the contradictory behaviour
of her father. Janaki did not respond immediately.

"Did he give him some money?" she asked slowly.

"No, he didn't."

Janaki wiped the stainless-steel plate and arranged it on the top shelf with the other utensils. Her face was drawn for a few moments, and Mallika knew that she was still upset about Appa's question to the man. Then her expression became alert. Something changed in her sister's manner when she perceived some dishonesty on their father's part. Mallika had noticed many changes in her sister in the two years after Amma's death. Janaki's face grew sterner, and her eyes became pools of stone. Years later, after Janaki had run away, she realized there was a war going on between her sister and their father: a cold war of frozen words. Nobody got hurt. Everybody got hurt.

"Do as I say, enna?" she said.

Janaki stood on her toes and locked the back door. She pulled in the shutters of the kitchen window with a lost gentleness, as the thought, whatever it was that she was going to do, finally settled in. A closing and an opening of another window, with a different tonal tug. Latching it in motion. Like she did with the music on the veena. Mallika was always able to see these workings in her sister's head. She was ready. "Go put on your chappals and wait for me on the veranda," Janaki said, finally.

JANAKI DECIDED to take the parallel street, once they had crossed Clive Road.

She kept her distance from Appa and Chellaiah and she crossed the intersection only after she was sure that they had gone ahead. Then she grabbed Mallika's hand and dragged her across the road. It being early Sunday morning, not too many people were on the street, and the temple bells had not been heard for the midday *archanai*. And Janaki would never miss that, Mallika knew. The adventure would have to end soon. That's when Mallika noticed that Appa's left leg was shorter than his right one. It was apparent even from a distance. Every time he took a step forward there was a small jerk of a shoulder, and it made it look like he was flinging something over. The way his neck moved also slightly tipped the balance of his body, something she had never seen before.

"Akka," she was about to say and share her observation with Janaki when the man, Chellaiah, stopped at Medicos Medicals. He went inside the pharmacy, and Appa waited for him on the footpath. Janaki pulled her back, and they hid behind the crowd at the roadside masala vadai stall. Mallika then saw the man put something into his mouth, and the wrapping joined the other garbage on the street. He wiped his face with his veshti one more time. And then he led Appa to the huts on the other side of the railway tracks.

From where they stood they could only see the dead girl's feet and the pavadai up to her shins, sticking out from the door, her toes pointing to the sky. A group of women sat at the entrance to their huts. A few of them stood up and walked away, shaking their heads. That was all that Mallika saw caught between Janaki's crouching frame and a mud wall lined with cow dung *varatti*. Then she saw Appa take out his wallet and drop a few notes at the girl's feet. He walked away, his neck jerking once again, as Chellaiah picked up the money and broke down. Appa kept walking, all the way to the end of the street, paying no attention to the women scrubbing pots near the corporation tap, or the few children following him as though he were the Pied Piper of Hamelin.

Janaki was silent. She did not even get up to rush back home, before the noon-hour *archanai*. Mallika watched her sister's body sag against the *varatti*-slapped wall. The notes of Marudhamalai Mamaniye Murugaiah came in snatches from the nearby shops. Janaki did not say a word, and Mallika watched her breathe, her chest pushed against her crouching knees. Mallika was still confused about the whole adventure. Why did Janaki drag her to see the dead girl? And why did Appa just fling the money and walk away?

"Memorize every detail," Janaki said, pushing her body forward and rising swiftly to keep her balance. "It will tell you a lot about Appa when you are older."

MAY 1991

WHEN SHE GETS there it is eight thirty-five.

Mallika pays the autorickshaw driver and dispenses with him at the main road. From the corner of Avadi Road she begins counting the consul cars, a full side of the road lined with yellow left-hand-drive diplomatic service licence plates. Cars parked with Western dexterity, close to the footpath edge. Chariots of another world. Shiny, and glistening with a metallic Benz foreignness, right up to Mrs. Samanta's gate.

Not altogether surprising.

Mallika had not expected it to be such an important event, but she had been reminded in an internal memo to bring her work card with her, if she were planning to attend. Expect a security check, the subsequent invitation had warned. It was an American Center event, no less. A fitting farewell to one fine lady with great charm and greater influence. She had done them proud, and so they paid for the party. Cultural expenses.

For a few compelling minutes, standing a hundred yards from the gate with her two kuthuvilakku lamps wrapped in crinkly green tissue, Mallika wonders if she should bother at all, if she should simply take the bus back to Luz. She would drop by tomorrow on her way to see Appa at the hospital—it was on the direct bus route—and then she would also get Mrs. Samanta all to herself. By going back she would completely avoid having to talk to the consul general's wife, Dixie Brady.

She would also avoid Mr. Samanta, who she knew from her stay there during those transit days a few years ago played tennis on Sunday afternoons at the Sterling Club. With the national election looming large, she knew he would be full of Marxism and Jyoti Basu, and would loop her into some argument on the Gandhi family and all their corruption.

Mr. Samanta always managed to extract opinions and perspectives from her that she didn't even know existed. She always ended up despising her frankness the next day. She was not given to easy provocation herself, although once provoked she did not tactfully hold back. It all came pouring out of her, as though some inner dam had collapsed and the flood roared out in a crash and tumble of words.

She does not want to see him, not tonight, with Janaki just a few days away and her upcoming moment of disclosure of the return to Appa and Chitti tomorrow. With all the kindness she may feel in her heart for the (manipulative) rhetorical skills of Mr. Samanta, personal state of mind had to trump gratitude and respect, she concluded. She knew she had no need nor want for another discussion on the Cinema and Nationalism or Tagore's cultural renaissance in Calcutta. Not tonight.

She would avoid it all by quickly walking backwards, all for the goodness of self-preservation and sanity. She would need both strength and a clear head for her meeting with Appa and Gayatri Chitti at four o'clock, during visiting hours. That's when she plans to tell them about Janaki's return. Tomorrow. She can already see Chitti's eyes popping out of her skull in horror. But that is still tomorrow, she hesitates.

Would those, her thoughts about Janaki's last days in the agraharam and Appa with camphor burning in the middle of his palm, and that other nightmare—that afternoon when the bank called and she was summoned to the college principal's office halfway through the lecture on the *Sonnets from the Portuguese,* every eye in the room following her on her way out, all the way to the college principal's office and Sister Mary Jacintha handing her the phone receiver—will those events and words disappear for a night? Walking backwards will not help with those ghosts. The day the music died. And her mother died a second time.

Two hours somewhere else, however stuffy, would still be a good distraction.

She hadn't expected that last thought, and it surprises her just as she is on the verge of turning back. Distraction. The easy rationalization disturbs her. How did she get to that thought?

"ID, please."

Mallika clutches her two lamps in one hand and gives the guard both the invitation and her counsellor services card. "And those things in your hand?"

"A gift."

"Please."

She gives him the kuthuvilakku. He unwraps the tissue and checks the two traditional brass lamps.

The difference a few seconds of hesitation makes, and then the lifetime of regret that follows it all. She could have been free tonight. She could have gone to the beach all by herself; she could have stood on the steps of the Basilica of San Thome, watching the evening tide rise and frolic; she could have listened to the chatter of the coastal families out for fresh air. She could have buried all the ghosts in the soft sands of sound. Not an option anymore.

"Go straight, madam," the guard says, scrutinizing her face as he hands her the card. He is a darker man, from somewhere near the coast, she thinks, catching a crucifix on a thin gold chain around his neck. He must be from Velankanni or Rameswaram. Perhaps a Tamil Christian, a security guard she has not seen before, and for a brief moment she wonders if he measures her with those caste markers. Don't we all in this country? Does he know that she is a Brahmin?

Does he think of her as a Brahmin girl, bringing Brahmin lamps as gifts, wearing a nicely ironed Brahmin pink sari, walking Brahminly, demurely indoors to chat and spend the evening among important American men and women and other eminent Indians? She wonders, as she walks towards the portico and the main door, if his eyes see her as a Tamil woman, albeit a *pappathi*, who is suddenly fighting too many other ghosts to give in to the easy allure of luxury and exotic otherness, however tempting it may seem. Sudden ghosts are stronger.

Does her walk reveal the invisible rock of her past, sitting right between her shoulders, heavier than Krishna's butterball, that boulder on a slope on the shores of Mahabalipuram?

Is she slouched? Does she have a limp like Appa that she doesn't know about? Then why does she feel possessed by some restless spirit these past few days? Why does she feel like somebody else is living inside her, shaping her world and everything around it? Could Janaki still exert such control? Even after so long?

She is here because of Mrs. Samanta, and that is the only reason she is here.

It bothers her that even he missed her initial hesitation, her habitual inability to participate without a second thought. Always, at first, biting her tongue.

LAMPS WITH forty-watt bulbs and bright, colourful shades are placed at different spots in the hall. Bulb lighting, another marker of upper-class status, Mallika thinks, standing at the entrance. In her apartment, only her reading lamp has a sixty-watt bulb; all the other rooms have tube lights, maximum brightness for budget living. A wattage line stands between classes all across the nation. The dimmer the lighting, the more important and well heeled you were. Bulb lighting for everyday living was a sign of money and not a care about the following month's electricity bill.

Mallika finds the room to be strangely changed, even though she has spent many days of her past here. It was a different room then, not this turnaround Kapoor Lamp Shade showroom she finds herself in. When she was there as a refugee, an instant casualty of fatherly insanity, back in those days, there were fewer mock chimney lamps with forty-watt bulbs. There is no questioning that.

The dimness of the surroundings does not seem to bother the other guests.

Everybody in the dining room is agog, talking and eating, and she just stands at the door listening to fusion flute music on the sound system, floating in and out with English banter. So different from those days in Sripuram.

And "Row, Row, Row Your Boat." Those days and nights of Janaki.

That's when she turns her eyes to the floor, waiting for the thought to pass, certain she will see the burning camphor in Appa's palm when she raises her head again; but when she looks up her gaze lands on the three-foot-tall brass kuthuvilakku. The most stunning lamp she has ever seen.

It stands in the corner of the welcome room, decked with marigold garlands spiralling all the way down its solid artisan body and ending in a tail in the hollow rim of its golden base. Six wicker flames glow like soft feather plumes from the brass disc cup. Such a grand kuthuvilakku, Mallika thinks, immediately consumed by the smallness of her gift. But the thought passes quickly. I am not here for a kuthuvilakku contest, she murmurs to herself, a recent habit, and walks into the crowd looking for Mrs. Samanta. She knows her way around this house like nobody else in the room.

The house has two big rooms on the ground level, one opening into the other, with the kitchen right at the back. A spiral staircase leads up to the three bedrooms and bathrooms. Her room (or rather, Rinku's, which was hers for those months) was the one on the far left, with a window that opened to Mrs. Samanta's rose and lily garden. Her days here had their charm, Mallika concedes, standing at the foot of the stairs thinking about Mrs. Samanta's concern, and how grateful she will always be for that temporary sanctuary. The kuthuvilakku will always be small. Her sense of indebtedness to the Samantas always greater. She was happy here, during that brief stay, except for those nights when she had forced herself to watch Mr. Samanta's weekly pick of Hindi film videos.

Now she was happier.

Correction: she will be happier after Janaki has come and gone.

Mallika glimpses Sheila, the consul general's secretary, on the other side of the salad table and waves, but Sheila doesn't seem to care. She is engrossed in her conversation with a man Mallika has not seen before. I will never wave to anyone again. This time she waits for a few seconds, making sure she does not even whisper the thought. It is not the lack of response, but the stupidity of the gesture, especially in a crowded room, that really makes her feel smaller. She can see how ludicrous it might have seemed to those watching. The high-ceilinged room packed with more than seventy people, all munching on carrots and celery, and uniformed waiters moving in and out of the throng with trays of bite-size samosas and fish cutlets. She could have knocked a whole tray of *kachori* with that meaningless wave to Sheila. The thought floods her senses like the morning sewer stench, and she sees the embarrassment, the scattering pastry bombs of shame all around. The humiliation, instantly after it.

That glare of eyes. Of flashbulbs. And the right-as-rain gossip. Bye, bye, Janaki.

"LOOKING FOR someone?"

When she turns around, she is face to face with Ted Pope. She really had not expected him to be here, at Mrs. Samanta's retirement party. But Mrs. Samanta knows everybody in that

USIS building, and she was hosting her own retirement party. She knew every American at the consulate. Ted Pope's car must be part of that diplomatic lineup on the street. She tries to curb her surprise with a purposeless smile.

"The hostess, Mrs. Samanta."

"She was here a few moments ago," he says. "Here, let me take that for you." She hands him the gift. She doesn't say "Please hide it," although she is tempted. He takes the brass lamps to a big wooden desk stacked with gifts and finds a place for them near the feet of what looks like a wrapped easy chair. It *is* a retirement party.

Ted Pope walks back with a sense of accomplishment and she notices, for the first time, tiny bristles of golden hair, like baby wheat crests, on his ears. Forty-watt revelations.

"Now, before we find Mrs. Samanta, we should get you something to drink."

Standing to attention, he quickly tiptoes and takes a bow. He sways his arms sideways, his palms joined into a namaskaram—a veritable, white, Air India maharajah—and says, "After you."

SHE KNOWS WHAT he will ask her when he brings her a glass of lemonade.

"How about we make a deal? I'll always bring you fresh lemonade during lunch hour if you take the exchange?"

He laughs, and Mallika sees a sixteen-year-old boy behind that serious facade. He is at least five years older than her. Maybe Janaki's age, or even older. Ted Pope is up there, responsible for all the Counselling Services. She is his subordinate. He is everybody's boss, even Mrs. Samanta's. She should have taken that bus back to Luz!

Why does she need the Maryland exchange, when gifted sister Janaki, shut-up-your-mouth-and-do-as-I-say Janaki, is coming for a visit—suddenly, out of the blue—with a maybe-maybe-not audience with Appa, that is, if she knows about his racetrack D-Day and its aftermath. Of course, she knows. And what new catastrophes does she bring wrapped in her sari pullo? Will she be wearing that purple sari, the one she wore when she ran away on that morning? Is Janaki capable of such irony?

But—I am supposed to have an answer, now, for Ted Pope, as to why I am not eager about spending two weeks in Maryland. This is no time or occasion to ask her about work, he should surely know that. Why does she have to explain the reason she has no interest whatsoever in an excursion into the diversity on North American campuses, with a few courses upgrading her counselling skills at a university in Washington, DC? An opportunity others would give an arm and a leg and a whole head of hair for. Why wouldn't she go, cash in on the free joyride that other Indians of her age would sell their parents for (but who would buy Appa and Gayatri Chitti)? She would also be granted a visa instantly, before you can say Mallika Venkatakrishnan. In the blink of a name, she would be one of them!

She can understand Ted Pope's bafflement even before she has uttered a word.

How does she explain the context of everyday Tamil, Brahmin living, and its everyday (and not-so-everyday) deceits and disasters to a man who seems so unexposed to such realities? Will he understand why her middle-class bank manager father never once gave her permission to go to a school camp or on an excursion, always saying she could work on the following year's syllabus during the summer holidays and always be ahead of her class? And how her sister Janaki never said a word, but always, later, explained everything away with "You will know when you grow up"? Ted Pope might find it all to be a bit too exotic. It was a word that fit all sorts of cultural contexts. *Exotic*.

I'll go, she feels like saying, as she watches him fidget with one of the light bulbs in the decorative string along the trimmed bushes in the garden. I'll go, but can I transfer my dharma to you? Could you please look after my father and my aunt, make sure they don't harm more people in this world, listen to their complaints and put up with their craziness? Take a page from the Indian texts on Obligations of Girls and Women (or Those Who Are Stupid Enough to Suffer and Stay Behind). By the time I return from my sabbatical maybe you would want to start an exchange program in mental hospital administration, or transnational dysfunctionalities and what nations can learn from each other?

Ted Pope has not said another word, and Mallika is embarrassed by the prolonged silence. He is focussed on the loose connection of the adapter. The silence unnerves her. What should she say?

"I did not know I was to consider myself a candidate," Mallika says hesitantly, resting her hand on the garden gnome sculpture and quietly sipping her drink. "There are four of us in the counselling section, and I have been here for only two years. What about Aimee Walia? She is my senior." She feels instantly stupid for saying that. Aimee Walia is forty-three years old.

Would Ted Pope approve if she came right out and said, "Runaway sister is coming back after a ten-year memory lapse; father is, quite simply, insane; aunt is unpredictable at all times. And I know it all—as my sister Janaki often told me—now that I am grown up. Sorry, no exchange. Can't go." Straight up, like the lines of viboothi and one small dot of kungumam on a Brahmin priest's forehead. Lines of fate on an Indian forehead, god destined from birth. That's how Janaki would do things. But she knows such pithiness can only seem cutting in Tamil, of which neither Ted Pope nor Aimee Walia speaks a word. Should she say bad karma (he would know that word) and leave it to him to interpret the rest?

Ted Pope is about to give up with one last tug of the wire when the whole bush bursts into light. Small blue bulbs all along and around the bush like the precious star net for a woman's leafy hair bun. He searches in the miniature wooden safe made especially for garden tools and gloves by the Samantas, and pulls out a rag to wipe his hands.

"Aimee Walia's husband has prostate cancer," he says, rubbing his hands dry.

It is a jarring juxtaposition, just when he has brought the lights back to life. Rubbing his hands with the rag, he has the benign resolve of a doctor stepping out of the operating room, in a grey silk shirt and dark blue pants. With a glass of orange juice laced with alcohol. Is there a name for such a drink? Can it keep the cancer of returning in remission? Can it exorcise undead ghosts?

"I was not aware. Mrs. Walia never mentioned it," she says.

People carry so many other people within themselves. She would never have guessed that the fast-talking, lipstick-wearing, Darling Baba-ing Mrs. Walia, a rambunctious powerhouse of a woman, had such a sorrow within her. A great resolve under all that rattle-rattle of cheer and chirpiness. Does she know about Appa and the hospital? Does Ted Pope know about Janaki and her mad father, for that matter?

He folds the rag into a neat four and puts it back into the tool safe.

"Mrs. Walia told me so last week when I asked her. Of course, I couldn't insist after I found out. I can't think of anyone else. And this is the second time the Madras wing has no representation. One more strike, and there goes a big slice of my budget."

She had met Ted Pope for the first time during her job interview two years ago. He had been surprised that she had chosen English literature as an elective subject, although her degree was in education counselling.

"I see you have written a paper on Reverend Robinson's *For God's Sake*. And what did you think?" he had asked, flipping to the second page of her resumé and recognizing the one contemporary, big American name on the list. He was not interested in Emily Dickinson, obviously, as he completely bypassed her name on the same page.

"Did it work for you?" He prompted, circling the name (or the entire citation, perhaps) with a slender yellow pencil. Reverend Robinson, a world-renowned American Jesuit priest, had spent two years writing on poverty and Christianity in the poor districts of Bombay. His journal, published to rapturous acclaim a year after his return to New Hampshire, was romantic, or at least Mallika thought. Her paper was titled, "On the Road to Dharavi: Reverend Robinson's Poor India."

"Mr. Pope," she had replied, returning to huts on the other

side of the railway tracks of Sripuram in her mind, and seeing the dead girl's feet sticking out of the doorway on that distant afternoon, and the flies still circling her toes. Janaki time. "I have walked through many urban slums, but I have not seen the grace and poignancy in poverty that Reverend Robinson sees. Perhaps such a vision is exclusive to non-Indian eyes? Why hasn't an Indonesian or an Egyptian written about the godly poverty of India? That might be an interesting thought to ponder." Janaki talk. Straight up, she thought even then. Why was she so afraid to speak her own mind?

And at that moment in the interview she was certain she would not hear back from them. Janaki had ruined another future; she'd judged too quickly.

So her surprise had been genuine when they offered her the job.

Two thousand five hundred rupees a month. One-year probation (after security clearance). Four weeks' paid leave. Medical reimbursement (up to five hundred rupees a month for self and family, with receipts). Access to all the USIS– sponsored programs—films, music, literary readings—all free of cost. She accepted. Ted Pope had been friendly ever since, not too familiar and yet affable—but always from a respectable distance.

"What I am..." he begins, until someone from the party inside opens the sliding door to the garden and steps out to light a cigarette. Laughter and loud music slice into the night air. Ted Pope finishes his drink and crunches the last cube of ice. "Time for a refill," he says, and Mallika feels relieved.

He peers at the sky through his empty glass. A light breeze rustles the palms on the other side of the road. There is the thickness of rain in the night air. "Think about it, Mall-i-ka," he says, walking towards the garden steps that lead indoors. "I don't have to send in a nomination for another week."

Mallika pulls her sari pullo around her shoulders. The lemonade has left a bitter taste on her tongue. More sour than sweet. "Yes." And she follows him inside.

NI

"Don't move!" Janaki warned, dipping the rag that was twisted and tied to the end of a long bamboo stick into the tin can of kerosene. Mallika did not move from her place outside the kitchen door, right below the window sunshade. Janaki had drawn an imaginary line and told her not to cross it. "It is too dangerous," she had said. Everything had to be over before Appa got back from the bank.

"I have to do it by myself. You watch from a distance, enna?"

Janaki turned around and said it again.

There was a small fire of twigs and old cardboard boxes, spitting longer and longer flames near the backyard gate. The moment Janaki brought the rag near the fire's perimeter the whole thing burst into instant flames, emitting dark, cloudy fumes.

Janaki quickly lifted her sari fall and tucked the pleats into her hip. She then raised the other end of the bamboo and turned the rag in the air, as though she were balancing a burning turban or crown of some kind in a roadside circus show. Holding the stick firmly with both hands, she turned the stick into a javelin, a gigantic matchstick held diagonally for a good, smooth raze.

"Don't move!"

In a few moments Mallika heard a buzzing, crackling noise, like a million bees trapped in a glass bottle in the sun. Then she saw dark, curvy shapes, like burned onion rings, drop from the bark of the neem tree branches. It had all happened before, but every time it happened again it sent the same minute shiver, a cold sizzle, through every pore of her body. The whole colony of caterpillars that had covered the tree trunk and branches and had turned the tree into a poisonous woollen sweater was falling to the ground, shrivelled and black. Janaki moved the fire rag from one spot to another all around the tree. Mallika felt nothing for those insects and their charred bodies. Good riddance, she thought. Now I will not have to worry about being stung, like last year, and find my whole body in a red, itchy rash. Yes! Akka! Get them! She wanted to shout, "Get them before they get into the bookshelves upstairs and behind the latrine door!" But she held back as it was one in the afternoon, and some mamis and mamas of the neighbourhood were already half asleep after a heavy lunch. Soon Appa will be home. The bank closed at two o'clock on Saturdays.

Standing under the window sunshade Mallika could only see the lower part of the tree and its branches; the top branches were to the other side of the street and were not directly in her line of vision. She tried to stretch her neck and peer over the imaginary line Janaki had drawn. No luck. But she heard Vanaja Mami's voice from the other side of the compound wall, giving Janaki a few directions and strategies on handling the caterpillar crisis.

"Got them all," Janaki said, sitting down on the end of the brick platform. She pulled the tucked part of the sari as she sat down. Her face was wet and flushed.

"Peace for the whole summer!"

"Can I come and watch you sweep up the burned *kambli poochi?*" Mallika asked, itching to move from her spot. It was no longer dangerous to step out. "I can also help you if you want, 'ka?"

Janaki wiped the sweat from her forehead with the edge of her pullo.

"Why do you want to see me sweep the wretched karumam again? Is that some sort of pleasure for you, us burning a tree trunk full of living creatures?"

She nodded. "Come here," she said. Mallika sat down beside Janaki on the floor of the back veranda. There was a faint kerosene scent around her sister—kerosene and Pears soapy sweat producing a strangely alluring perfume.

"You sit here with the pan, enna? No need to step on the ground. I'll sweep them up."

Janaki got the palm broom from behind the latrine and began gathering the burned remains of the caterpillars. Her sweeping was nothing like when she cleared the ground for the morning or evening kolam. It was swift and efficient, and soon all the blackened, charred *poochis* were collected into a sandcastle heap right beside the wash stone. "Give that to me," Janaki said, her hand in the air and her body crouched beside the razed remains. Mallika gave her the metal pan. It took Janaki three trips to the backyard rubbish bin to empty the whole massacre. That was one trip more than the previous year.

"Now let's go to the mottamadi and see how the vadams are coming along, enna? I think they should be nice and dry by now," Janaki said, wiping her wet feet with an old dhavani kept by the well. "Or do you want to read next year's history lessons now?"

"Can I read my English novel in the shelter while you peel the vadams?" Mallika asked, hoping her sister would say yes.

"Is it just a storybook or is it part of your studies?" Janaki frowned as she stepped onto the cement platform and checked her hands and arms for any sign of rash. "So, it is just a storybook?" Janaki was satisfied with the investigation. The caterpillars had spared her. She walked into the kitchen and began filling two pots with cold tap water.

"No, 'ka. It is called *The Guide*. It is about a saint. It is part of the next-year syllabus also," Mallika answered, following her sister indoors.

"So it must be good," Janaki said. "It must teach you good things if it is about a saint. Go, bring it upstairs," she said, climbing the stairs to the mottamadi.

NOTHING WAS different that summer.

Appa had once again vetoed her going along with the school on an excursion to Kuttralam. "Waterfalls can be very dangerous," he'd said. Why was everything so dangerous for Brahmin girls in the agraharam, Mallika couldn't help wondering. All the elders, including Janaki, kept using that word again and again. *Vibareetham*, dangerous. No need for it. Appa never really elaborated on any of his utterances. Her sister Janaki did not raise her voice in protest: You will know when you grow up. She had done just that for the past three summers after Amma's death. "Yes, two-hour typing class would be good, and Akka will wait for you outside the typing institute on the way back from veena class, sariya?" Janaki, indirectly, had agreed with Appa and had always prepared some oversweet kesari those evenings, action that Mallika could never interpret the right way. Why did Janaki always make that semolina dessert whenever Appa turned down her request to join the school excursion? Was it a celebration or a consolation? Victory, or guilt? But soon enough she always abided by her sister's instructions. Mallika seldom protested.

But two small things also made that summer (so far) infinitely more bearable. And they were both good—for her, and for Janaki.

Gayatri Chitti's visits to Sripuram had suddenly stopped. It had been one full year since Mallika's first period and that weekend drama at the gate. It was a relief. She did not have to share her room with the radiator and its droning snoring till dawn. Mallika often caught herself wondering if reaching puberty had some kind of mystical meaning. The forceful way in which she had pushed Gayatri Chitti away that weekend when she arrived from Madras and made a great fuss about her first menstrual cycle had her convinced that there was something else to it—that her maturity was different, and her first period had bestowed on her some secret powers that whole year.

When she turned to Janaki for confirmation (Gayatri Chitti's had not made a trip to Sripuram for Deepavali and came just for the day on Amma's anniversary), her sister's answers were, as always, gentle and ambiguous: "Maybe she has some medical problem. I will send a message with Appa next time." Or, "Maybe she is preparing for a bank exam. She is still junior accounts clerk in Madras, illaiya?" Janaki could make everything sound so plausible. Just in that tone of "please, understand, don't make things any more difficult for me than they already are"—spoken only by her eyes.

Mallika had also noticed that for the past few months her sister looked around first and always lowered her voice when talking about Appa and Gayatri Chitti in the same breath. Everything involving both of them was always a whispered moment. Gayatri Chitti had left that weekend, all red-eyed and mute and had never returned for an overnight stay. Mallika never found out why.

But it was only a matter of time.

She knew there would be an answer to that mystery soon. She would be patient and do everything to keep her secret powers.

The second small thing that was also a blessing for Janaki that year was the unknown intervention that had plugged all the marriage proposals and telegrams from Madras. It had changed everything about her sister, and Mallika was allowed to have her way most of the time. She was even permitted to stay up late, until eleven sometimes, watching *I Love Lucy* and *World Today* on TV. That whole year the radio played on into the nights, later than usual (as Janaki, who never watched any English series, and only sat in front of the TV for *Oliyum Oliyum* and the Tamil feature film on the weekend), or tuned into a Hindi bhajans program, or an interview with some cinema personality. Her veena practices also began promptly at four, right after school, and before Appa returned from the bank. Their father had less and less to say to her sister. And yet her sister was in blissful artistic and domestic control. These small changes were linked. How? That is what puzzled Mallika. There had to be an answer to that as well.

Four cotton tablecloths covered the space of the cement roof terrace. Janaki had squeezed small, saucer-sized spirals of rice vadams in rows of five on all the cotton sheets the previous day. She had also propped up a spindly scarecrow made of sticks and hay and a clay pot for a head, right in the centre of the mottamadi.

The rows of vadams were untouched by the ravens and crows. A whole day and a half in the summer sun had turned the wet spirals into dry, crisp savouries. Mallika couldn't wait to sample them that evening, when she knew Janaki would fry a few just-off-the-terrace-floor vadams in hot oil before serving dinner. But first they had to be gently peeled and stored before there was a supply to accompany a whole year of meals. When and how did Janaki learn to do these things, and do them so well? It was something that always impressed Mallika.

Her sister had taken on the duties of keeping house so easily, so naturally, just like a duck takes to water. She did everything Amma had done when she was alive. Janaki fetched the milk in the morning, cooked, washed clothes, mended her school uniform, packed lunch boxes, oiled and combed her hair, stocked sanitary napkins on the top shelf of the cupboard upstairs, burned caterpillars in the backyard, laid out vadams on the terrace—all just like Amma.

Mallika never heard her sister say a word about missing school. And she never asked Mallika for assistance. She always said, "You study hard and become someone really big, like Indira Gandhi, and make me proud! Enna?"

It was as if Amma's spirit, her *aavi*, had not left the world but had instead made a home in Janaki's body. Amma became Janaki. Janaki became Amma.

Janaki squatted in front of the first tablecloth on the terrace floor. Her kolusu bells around her ankles chimed as she moved her feet. She rolled the sheet, one row at a time, and dabbed the underside of the crispies with a little water. Slowly, without breaking it into bits, she peeled off one crispy at a time, just the way Mallika peeled stamps from letter envelopes.

"So what is the saint's name in your book?" Janaki asked, folding the first sheet and moving on to the second one.

"Raju," Mallika replied, sitting in the shade of the door on the landing of the stairs.

"Raju?" Janaki smirked. "What a name for a saint!" She laughed. "Do his disciples call him Raju Swami?" She dabbed more water under a more stubborn vadam.

"No, 'ka," Mallika said, laughing with her sister. "So far he is only known as Raju Guide! He is not a swami yet!"

"Oh, *appadiya,* is that so?" She urged another crispy from the sheet and dropped it in the tin jar that moved in inches along with her. "So he is like a tourist guide?"

"Yes! How did you guess, 'ka!" Mallika couldn't believe that her sister had nailed the character's profession without having read the book.

"And who is he guiding? Some foreigners?" There was a mocking tinge to Janaki's tone.

"No, no," Mallika said quickly. "He had just met this woman called Rosie and her husband Marco."

"They are not Indian, illaiya?"

"Maybe, Anglo-Indian, but I have not got to that part yet!" Mallika was beginning to be a little annoyed with her sister's questions. She had only finished reading a few chapters of the book, and there was still so much she did not know about the characters. How could she possibly have all the answers so soon?

"It is a school book, correct? Not a lending library book, I hope?"

"Yes, school syllabus for ninth standard, 'ka. But now I think I will go downstairs to read. I have to concentrate," Mallika said, closing her book.

"Sorry, kanna. I was just curious. Seri, you go to your room and study, and I'll call you when lunch is ready. Will you tell me what happens in the story when you have finished?" Janaki was always eager for stories, always hopeful for happy endings. "Maybe they will make a picture of the book and I can see it with you when it comes to Mahalaxmi Talkies. Wouldn't that be great, *thangame?*"

Then, having finished peeling ten whole rows of vadams, Janaki stood up and stretched. Just as she was about to move to the third tablecloth spread at the far corner of the terrace, Mallika heard Appa's scooter approaching the gate. She dashed downstairs to open the door.

"Appa is going on a trip somewhere," Mallika whispered when Janaki came down to the hall. "He took the VIP suitcase from the puja room shelf."

Janaki's face was blank. She said nothing and went into the kitchen to prepare lunch. Appa stepped out of his bedroom, holding his suitcase in his left hand. He locked the bedroom door. He put the bag on the rattan sofa.

"Do you know where the other carryall bag is?" he asked. He seemed excited about something but did not say what it was.

"I think it is on top of the almirah upstairs, 'pa," Mallika replied, holding *The Guide* to her bosom.

"Janaki..." Appa called out to her sister. In a matter of thirty seconds Janaki appeared near the kitchen door. She did not answer him, but merely stood in her place. "Take the carryall from the almirah and pack a few clothes for you and your sister."

"'Pa?" Janaki answered, her eyes widening with surprise. What was he saying?

For a moment, even Mallika was not sure she had heard her father's words correctly.

"You heard me."

Appa strapped on his everyday sandals and unlocked the front door.

"I will be back from the bus station in one hour. I will have lunch later. Be packed and ready when I am back, enna? We are going to Tirukalukundram for two days. Sunday and return Monday night."

He kick-started the scooter and rode off to the Sripuram Bus Terminus.

"Haiyya!" Mallika jumped up and down. "Tirukalukundram! I will get to see the kites now!"

Janaki did not smile. "This is so strange," she said. Mallika also realized that it was very uncharacteristic of their father to take them for a trip to a tourist spot. He was a serious man, a man not given to frivolity or sudden impulses. In February he had said no to the school excursion and had also turned down Janaki's wish to accompany her friend Revathi to Mahabalipuram. But now, in the middle of summer, he was taking them to Tirukalukundram, something he had never done before. But all Mallika could think of was the fun that awaited them. She could already hear the wings of the kites flapping like huge sails in the noonday sky of Tirukalukundram. That was all that mattered.

"Remember to pack your sanitary napkins, enna? It is your time of the month in two days." Janaki went back into the kitchen to get lunch ready.

Why? Mallika wondered. Why was Janaki so solemn when they were about to embark on a once-in-a-blue-moon family excursion? Why was her sister's voice these days always laced with suspicion? Janaki would never answer.

AFTER TWO AND a half hours of sitting in the last row of seats, all the way at the back, where the disrepair of the state highways was really felt, Mallika was happy to be in the hotel room, not alone, but definitely more comfortable than she had been on the bus. That the hotel room overlooked an automobile spare-parts warehouse that announced its name—Wings—with the letters tall and wide, and spelled in overlapping hubcaps, did not matter. Now they were really in Tirukalukundram and this was no fantasy. There were two beds, and Mallika chose the one nearer to the window. It was in the shadow of all the glitter from the name of the auto warehouse. Appa had to take the room one floor below. The hotel had been fully booked and no two rooms, side by side, were available. "Up and down only, season time, bus full, all-India tourist. Overflow from Mahabalipuram. *Jasthi* demand for rooms, saar." The man did not even look at the booking register, but seemed resolute. Appa gently smiled, no words of anger or frustration, and reached for his wallet in the inside pocket of his bank jacket. He was a transformed man, just like Mr. Rochester in *Jane Eyre,* her favourite novel. He seemed happy to take the rooms.

"You both can be upstairs. I'll take second floor," he said, and signed the register.

Janaki seemed indifferent. She just said the common bathroom at the far end of each floor was an inconvenience, but she didn't protest. "As long as all bathrooms, ladies and gents, are properly lighted." The receptionist said nothing about that.

"Two-zero-five, three-one-three." He handed them the keys.

Finally, Mallika was alone in bed.

And the next day there was the visit to all the sights in Tirukalukundram. Janaki could frown her way through it all if she chose, but Mallika was going to go back to school and tell everybody, all the girls in her class, and even write an essay about it—"My Personal Excursion to Tirukalukundram"—for the annual English essay contest. She will write eloquently about the two kites, swooping down from the sky for an offering of pongal, and how they come so close, so, so close.

HOW COULD THE kites land on the bare, burning rock? A rock surrounded by a throng of at least three hundred people? Mallika kept the thought to herself.

"The marvel of Bhagawan; the birds are his messengers," the old woman sitting beside them in the ladies' section kept saying. "Yes, yes," Janaki nodded, sounding annoyed. They had got there early, soon after breakfast and coffee at the vegetarian restaurant next to the hotel. Mallika wore her light green dhavani, and Janaki had pinned a garland of kanakambaram, hastily bought at the foot of Tirukalukundram, where the first of four-hundred steps reaching up to the boulder rock began.

At ten in the morning there were already fifty people, all settled on the towels and bedsheets they had spread on the stone plateau right at the top. The birds will not be there for another three quarters of an hour.

"Akka, is there a bathroom here?" Mallika asked.

"If you leave now you have to go down four hundred steps, and when you come back your place will be gone."

"But . . ."

"Hold it for another hour; then we can both go together."

Janaki pulled out a packet of Poppins from her cloth bag and gave her a pastille. "Suck this. It will distract you," she said, putting one into her own mouth. Appa was in the gents' section and they couldn't see him. But he was there, on the other side of the rock. "You should have listened to me when I told you not to drink the water. Now we just have to wait."

"Once the birds see the priest, they'll know it is time to come down," the old woman kept saying, looking into the sky, which was spotless with no clouds or birds in it. The sun was climbing higher and higher, right into the middle of the sky, and everybody around her was perspiring. Some older women had damp face towels spread across their faces. Even so high up, there was not even the gentlest whiff of a breeze. It was as though people were baked in the heat, nobody moved, nobody talked and the bawling of babies tore ceaselessly into the morning.

When the priest emerged from the adjacent hut with a

copper bowl of water and a stainless-steel tray of pongal, the tray's edge gave off a piercing reflection, the arc of which cut across the boulder rock just as he began to ascend the flight of stairs. Suddenly there was a hushed anticipation in the air. Mallika cupped her stomach and watched him get ready for the chanting, which would be heard by the birds that were still nowhere to be seen in the white sky.

"Garuda, Lord of the Wings, Feathered God of the Heavens, come. Come down for your midday meal. Come down and bless us all."

The chanting began with one quiet voice repeating the mantra again and again. "Garuda Bhagawan, come, my Lord. Come with your Consort."

The old woman sitting beside them began rocking in her place, her hand clasped and her eyes fixed on the sky.

"*Atho,* look," someone said. "There, up there. Can you see?" someone yelped in joy.

All heads turned heavenward. Mallika rolled up her hands like binoculars and looked through the openings. Nothing was visible, just a white heat and voices of excitement all around them. Janaki picked up the edge of her sari pullo and started to fan herself. "Can you see anything?"

"No, Akka. There are no kites still," Mallika replied, her voice still hanging onto the edge of hope.

The priest's naked torso was now glistening with sweat. He was sprinkling water around the pongal tray. He shook off the drops from his hands and began drawing circles in the air.

Soon he was chanting faster and moving his hands as though he were pulling two huge rods of light into his body, or two daggers, one in each hand.

Circles and daggers. His spine stiff and his body wet.

The crowd began to get anxious. "Maybe Garuda Bhagawan is angry today," the old woman said, her voice barely audible. "Someone in the crowd has brought *paavam* with them today. Birds can smell sinners." She kept on rocking.

"I've had enough of this waiting. Ammulu, let's go down," Mallika heard another voice at the back of the crowd. "I told you all this was a waste of time!" When she turned around, she saw a woman grab her bedsheet from the rock floor, plunk her thumb-sucking daughter on her waist and leave the crowd in frustration. "Let me through."

Soon everybody started to look around. A collective restlessness took effect all around them. Families of three and four began moving, slowly, inch by inch, to the stairs, but their eyes were still fixed on the sky, hoping for the final arrival of the birds, hoping they would be stopped in their tracks by the flutter of godly wings.

The priest looked down at the crowd. He curved his thumb into the shape of a sickle and pulled it across his sweaty forehead. His veshti now had huge damp patches all over, and his body was slithery and reflecting, like a piece of dark brown leather. It reminded Mallika of her school bag when it was soaked by the monsoon.

The chanting became louder. The priest's hands kept spinning and stabbing. He is trying to stop the crowd from leaving, Mallika thought.

"Will they come?" she asked, knowing, expecting the answer she was about to hear from her sister.

"Some *paavi* brought bad luck, today," the old woman muttered, a little louder than her last pronouncement. "Someone has sin in their heart."

Janaki stood up, clutching her cloth bag. "Do you still want to go to the bathroom?"

TO MAKE UP for the disappointment of the birds that didn't come down for the pongal, Appa took them for an evening visit to the Tirukalukundram fair. Janaki changed to a rose cotton sari and laid out Mallika's gold border dhavani on the bed.

"No period yet? You're prepared, illaiya?"

"Tomorrow or the day after, 'ka," Mallika replied, drying her hair. She then picked up her fresh dhavani and walked back to the bathroom. *What does she think? I won't remember my dates?* It had been more than eighteen months since her first menstrual cycle, and still Janaki kept reminding her, asking her about her preparedness. She marked everything on the calendar. Mallika resented all the protectiveness, the inquisitiveness of her questions. If she were really a big girl, as Janaki claimed, then why was she not treated like one? Why was she always Mallika *kutty?* Janaki always wanted to know everything. Even Gayatri Chitti had stopped all her questions.

But one image always kept coming back.

The way Gayatri Chitti left the next morning, that week of her first period, without a word; just a formal embrace at the door, and then off with Appa on the scooter. Chitti did not even wave back, like she had done on previous occasions.

After that she had stopped coming to Sripuram for the festivals, not altogether, but less frequently than before. Something had changed, but Mallika didn't know what. Janaki knew. Appa knew. Chitti knew. She didn't.

APPA WORE HIS crisply starched, blue stripe shirt and his dry-cleaned brown, double-knit pants. He was waiting outside his room when they came down the flight of stairs. Janaki handed him the room keys.

"I'll meet you outside the reception area," he said, taking the keys from her and heading off with quick steps in the direction of the hotel office. His shoulder flinging seemed less evident. It goes away when he is happy, and Appa looks so happy today, more relaxed, Mallika thought. Maybe, I will write an essay on Appa and the Tirukalukundram fair for the competition—"My Father's History and My Visit with Him to Tirukalukundram"—she could change the title. And she could also mention their games of chess together, and how good she was at it. She had checkmated him three times last year; she could add that as well. He was, of course, given his age, cleverer, but she was also clever for her age. Mrs. Emanuel, her English teacher, thought so, and she was cleverer than everybody. Mrs. Emanuel would make her read the eloquent essay she had written to the whole class. Imagine.

"Wait here for me," Janaki said, and walked to the end of the corridor on the second floor, where the bathrooms were. She emerged within a few minutes, too quick for even one bathroom, Mallika thought. She walked back to Mallika and said, "Just checking if the flush was working here. Upstairs was not working in the morning. Did you go? I have to tell the receptionist to repair it. Let's go."

There she was again, deliberately inserting a question about bowel movements. And Mallika realized she hadn't been. She was constipated. But mentioning that to her sister would produce all sorts of herbal remedies, and she'll be made to drink endless glasses of hot water every two hours. And then the periods will arrive, and still more annoying questions.

Mallika didn't answer.

When they got to the office Janaki told Appa about her discovery.

"I will send someone to take a look, saar. Don't worry. Enjoy the suttrula fair!" the receptionist smiled and made a note of the complaint on a piece of paper. Appa shook the man's hand, and they left the office. He is so happy, Mallika thought again. Appa didn't care about the birds not coming down at all.

THEIR HEADS WERE still spinning after ten full rounds on the Giant Wheel. After the third round, when the wheel picked up speed and all the lights of the fair blurred into multiple streams of neon liquid in front of her eyes, Mallika had felt a rumble low in her belly. A familiar rumble that signalled a familiar arrival.

"Hold on to me, don't let go," Janaki shrieked above the shrieks from the other cars of the Giant Wheel. "Close your eyes when we go down!"

Mallika kept her eyes closed right through to the tenth spin, counting inside her head, her knuckles all white and bloodless, gripping the thin iron bar of the car, which she was certain would pop open and send her and Janaki flying into the evening air, like exotic birds wearing dhavanis.

But now they were on the ground. It was over. Soon the goosebumps bristling on her legs and hands would be gone. The blood was flowing into her knuckles again, but the strain still left a dull ache.

As they walked behind Appa, who had stayed away from the ride on the wheel and was now leading them to the Udipi restaurant where they had had their breakfast that morning, walking behind him, listening to Janaki's comparisons between the Tirukalukundram fair and the Sripuram Navarathri fair, and nodding at appropriate points of contrast her sister was drawing, Mallika saw a small packet, wrapped in Tamil newspapers, clutched firmly in Appa's left hand.

Janaki never missed anything, and it surprised Mallika that her sister did not mention the packet in their father's hand. She was immersed in her comparisons right up to the restaurant entrance.

That night Janaki slept like Kumbhakarana.

She had eaten like a giant at the restaurant. One full masala dosa, two medhu vadais and then the other half of Mallika's masala dosa. Appa had ordered the uthappam and then went ahead and ordered gulab jamun soaked in rosewater and sugar syrup, for all three of them. Janaki asked for masala chai after all that. Now she also slept like a giant. She had not mentioned the packet in Appa's hand (which went under the table at the restaurant) on the way back to the hotel room. Everything else considered, she had had a good evening.

Mallika lay on her bed, sleep eluding her eyes, staring at the ceiling fan and listening to Janaki's deep, long breaths. They had packed all the clothes into the carryall as soon as they had got back to the room. "We will go back after morning tiffin, eleven o'clock bus. No delay," Appa said before he entered his room on the second floor. What was in the packet?

The glare from Wings still managed to pierce through the slats of the window shutters. It filled the room with a ghostly, grey light and made Janaki's sleeping figure with the sheets pulled over her face look like an inflatable pillow.

What has happened to Janaki? Mallika turned to face the wall beside her bed, closing her eyes and trying not think of the unfair birds, her sister's strange moods and the little newspaper packet in Appa's hand. She started to speak to herself instead, inside her head, mentally writing the essay, which will make Mrs. Emanuel so proud of her.

Mallika felt stickiness on the elastic of her jatti and panicked.

Aiyyo, it is seeping through, was her first thought. She put her hand under her pavadai and tugged at her underwear and her fingertips felt something gummy. Oh, no, I have to adjust the napkin now. With her body still facing the wall, she turned her head to look at Janaki. Should she wake her? If she didn't attend to the napkin right away her pavadai, and then the bedsheet, would both be messy.

Mallika slowly put her feet to the floor and stood up. The room key was on the nail behind the door. The bathroom is just five doors down the corridor, she thought. I can creep out and be back without Janaki finding out.

She reached for the carryall and slowly unzipped the outer pocket where she had put the napkin packet with her underwear and hairbrush. She pulled out one fresh napkin and a fresh jatti, placed it on the bed and pulled back the zip. She was glad for the creaky rotations of the ceiling fan, which muffled the noise of the metal zipper. Quickly she knotted the napkin and jatti in the pullo edge of her dhavani.

She pulled the door and held the handle still as the light from outside rushed in through the narrow opening. Mallika turned around and stood against the door, her body facing Janaki and blocking the thin beam of light. Her sister didn't show any sign of awareness, just the steady breathing under the bedsheet. Mallika opened the door, took two quick steps outside the threshold and pulled the door shut.

The lock fell into place with a click.

The corridor was deserted. She ran to the far corner, the room's key pressed in her palm. She locked herself in the booth and fumbled for the light switch. She flicked it. The booth lit up for half a second and the bulb blew a fuse. *Aiyyo*, she screamed inside her head. There was no time to think, she had to go to the bathroom on the second floor. She could feel more of the gummy sensation now.

Thankfully, there were the back steps and it would be quick. She clutched the ball of napkin and underwear and checked the key. She'd pressed so hard it had dug a shape in the palm of her right hand. There was enough light on the stairs from the hub plates' reflection, although for a moment she turned hurriedly with fear catching her own shadow.

Safe inside the bathroom booth on the second floor Mallika undid her dhavani knot. The light from the bulb was low, but at least it did not fuse. She put the fresh change on the floor and lifted her dhavani, rolled the edges and held it between her neck and chin. She sat on the English toilet and slowly pulled down her jatti.

It was a mess. The running and going down the stairs had made it worse. She placed the new napkin sideways, on top of the other one, sliding the wings into the edges to block the leak. She pulled on the fresh jatti. The sticky jatti she care-fully folded into four squares and stuffed it into the slim plas-tic bag of the new napkin.

She turned off the light in the booth and sat on the toilet seat for a few minutes wondering why the second floor bath-room had English-style toilets when the third floor toilet was just like the one in the Sripuram outhouse. Must be for for-eign tourists who come to Tirukalukundram, she concluded, although she had not seen any fair people during the day at the hotel or even yesterday afternoon when the birds did not come for their pongal.

Foreigners would have been more disappointed. After all, they had come from Australia and Germany and had to go back without seeing the kites. They will return to their country and think poorly of Tirukalukundram. They will tell their friends not to go there. She could mention it as a side point in her essay—the unpredictability of the birds—and how they could let down Europeans as well by not coming down from the sky.

She stood up, wondering how she will make it back to the room. Her jatti felt stuffed and heavy. What was that? She heard something. It sounded like chappals flapping followed by a rustle. She stepped out of the booth and looked around. Everything was quiet. I better get back to the room quickly, she told herself, and stepped out of the bathroom, making her way to the stairs.

Was that Appa? She retreated into the shadow of the bath-room door.

When she looked down the corridor again she saw that it was Appa.

The door to his room was open, and Mallika could see him grab the hand of a woman wearing a head full of garlands.

Her dark sari blurred her figure. Mallika couldn't tell how old the woman was from her place at the far end. There was a muffled laugh from her before the door slammed shut.

Appa and a woman wearing jasmine garlands, silver and bright in the hub plates' fluorescence and all she could think was:

Where have I heard that laugh before?

"WHERE IS Mrs. Samanta?" someone asks.

It sounds like Dixie Brady's voice, but it is difficult to tell in the general melee of people in the room. Ted Pope makes his way to the bar and brings her more lemonade. He has a taller glass with amber liquid and a dense cloud of froth this time.

The bulbs pour their light on full blast, and all the guests are making their way slowly to the centre table. Mallika dreads the appearance of the consul's wife.

Ted Pope turns around and says, "Have you seen our hostess? Or did I rudely hijack your plans?" His voice has an apologetic dip. "No," Mallika answers and quickly adds, "I mean, I have not seen our hostess. I haven't wished her good luck yet."

The food platters are nearly empty, but all the guests are still chatting away, their cars and drivers waiting to take them back when they have had enough to eat and drink. Unlike her, they will not have to wait at Avadi Road for the rare autorickshaw, or put up with haggling about night charge over the meter. They could drink all they wanted, and Mrs. Samanta's retirement was a good reason. Mallika has never tasted alcohol, but she knows the smell well, especially the smell of McDowell's whisky, empty bottles of which she had found occasionally in Appa's room during cleaning, right after the first year of Janaki's run from Sripuram. How everything changed into a lifetime of shame and speechlessness for the next few years. It had been so hard to leave it all behind until she finally left with the job at the USIS. There was a semblance of peace now. But that could all change once again. Janaki was coming back. The past already smells like burning camphor and blended whisky.

Mr. Deb Samanta emerges from a nearby cluster of people and grabs Mallika's hand.

"You've been avoiding a debate all evening, I can tell," he booms, prompting a few heads to turn and glance their way.

"Oh, no, nothing like that." Mallika is surprised by his ability to nail her inner thoughts with a casual remark. He has been drinking whisky, foreign whisky, she can tell by the smoother sourness on his breath. She looks to the floor, suddenly embarrassed.

"I'm the culprit," Ted Pope extends his hand, and finally Mr. Samanta lets go her wrist.

She's glad she is not wearing glass bangles, like Janaki, during festivals. She'd left behind her bangles the day she went from Sripuram into the national dailies. Just one purple sari, and maybe an autorickshaw to the train station. That's all she took. Mallika never felt like wearing Janaki's bangles, the bangles Janaki wore during Deepavali and bride showings.

Gayatri Chitti had packed them in a Nala Sweets complimentary cloth bag and taken them to Madras. Mr. Samanta's grip would have crushed those bangles in the first three seconds. Her eyes fixed on the floor, and the sound around her muted by her instant embarrassment, she can see those pieces of glass hitting the floor with a crash. Yes, a crash. Mr. Samanta was still the same, so unassuming, and so infuriating.

"So, where have you been all this time? Even Dixie was asking about it." Mr. Samanta shakes Ted Pope's hand. "Have you tasted the special snacks our chef has prepared? All vegetarian," he says with a quick glance at Mallika. Then he turns to Ted Pope and adds, "Did you know that the Tamil Brahmins, of all the Brahmin sects of India, are the most particular about their diet and cooking? They will never eat outside cooked food. It has to come from their kitchen only. But Mallika is not like that. She was a good guest with us and ate everything. It just had to be vegetarian."

"I didn't know you were a guest at the Samantas'." Ted Pope has a look of quick surprise on his face.

"Yes, I had a very good stay here," Mallika replies.

She does not mention the Hindi videos Mr. Deb Samanta made her watch, and the questions about Janaki Asgar. The film star wife and veena prodigy who packed it all in four lines and left for good. Who was not there when Appa went berserk at the bank a few years later, just when they had settled into the Bank Quarters in Chetpet and she had enrolled in the Women's Christian College. That phone call—during the *Sonnets from the Portuguese*... What was Janaki doing at that moment, that afternoon? Mallika is now concerned that Mr. Samanta will give Ted Pope all the details about how she ended up being a guest at their house for a few months. And he couldn't possibly explain it without mentioning Appa and his current status as a patient in the Kilpauk Mental Hospital. She had to change the subject.

"Where is Mrs. Samanta?" Mallika asks, taking the opportunity to divert his thinking. "Is she going to cut that cake waiting for her at the table?" Mr. Samanta turns around to take a look. "Is it time yet, is it really that late? There are no candles!"

"Mall-i-ka is just hungry now," Ted Pope pipes up. "She's only had lemonade all evening."

"Where is Bijoya?" Mr. Samanta wonders aloud as he scans the room. Nobody seems concerned. And the clock in the hall, beside the staircase leading upstairs, shows nine forty-five. It is late, by middle-class Brahmin standards. But the consul general is still chatting with a man in a grey suit. Many men are wearing suits, like they are at some reception at the chamber of commerce.

"She may be upstairs. I'll go look," Mallika says, finding her chance to make a getaway.

"Of course, you know your way around this place," Ted Pope nods. He has sensed her discomfort and is making a move to support her departure. He is a very perceptive man, Mallika thinks, as she makes her way to the stairs leading up.

"THE TOILET IS upstairs, to the left," a woman coming down the stairs says. She is wearing a blue georgette chiffon sari and speaks with a convent girl accent.

"Thanks," Mallika mutters and continues her climb.

"And look out for the deodorant. It gave me a sneezing fit," the woman laughs. "Just a friendly warning."

The corridor is lined with old, framed photos of buildings and men. Mrs. Samanta had pointed out her father's photo sometime during her stay. "He was involved in the freedom struggle and knew Tagore on a first-name basis," she said. Everyone in her family was a barrister or a musician or an economist. But Mrs. Samanta was very humble about her heritage. She never used her family name as leverage to get ahead. She married Deb Samanta two years after she enrolled for a degree in library science. She'd recounted her father's reaction, as though she wanted her father to hear every word from behind the glass frame. "He was not very pleased that I was marrying my Marxist politics lecturer. But he kept out of my decision to do so. Deb came from a not so well-known family, so it was fifty per cent all right with him."

"Family is politics, everyday politics," Mallika said. "What else is there?" and left it at that.

Mrs. Samanta's bedroom door is slightly ajar, just enough to hear her voice from the other side. Mallika hesitates for a moment. She hears full sentences in Bengali, punctuated with the two words she can immediately identify in between the run-ons: *nah nah* and *bhalo nah nah*. But her voice reveals nothing. Mallika hears something fall to the floor and then Mrs. Samanta says, "*Kee nah*, nothing, nothing,"

Mallika pushes the door and looks in. Mrs. Samanta is sitting on the bed with her back to the door. A bag of candles is scattered on the carpet. Mallika lets herself into the room and slowly pushes the door shut.

"Oh, it is you. Come in, come in," Mrs. Samanta says, catching her from the corner of her eye, and then speaks hurriedly into the mouthpiece. "Baba will be home in the morning, so call after ten, I must not keep the guests waiting, *bhalo, bhalo.*"

Mrs. Samanta is a small woman. The centre part in her hair is filled with vermilion, and she is wearing light maroon lipstick to match her brown China silk sari. She seems calm, but her eyes are a bit dilated. There is a moist eyeliner smudge under her eyelids. She places the receiver back on the cradle. "See," she says, "I dropped all the candles on the floor. How clumsy of me." She reaches for the candles at the same time that Mallika rushes to her assistance.

"Everybody downstairs is wondering where you are," Mallika offers an indirect explanation for her sudden appearance at the door. "I came in when I heard this packet fall to the floor."

"You are wearing the sari Rinku sent for you," Mrs. Samanta says, picking up the two candles and putting them back into the red and gold Chinese-lettered box. Mallika kneels on the carpet and runs her hand under the bed frame. "That's the last one," Mallika hands the candle to Mrs. Samanta. "Yes, I knew you would recognize this sari. It is really so beautiful." She stands up and aligns the pleats of her sari. In the soft light of the room the sari pleats look like cut rose marble.

"Give me a few minutes. I'll quickly dash into the toilet and then we can go down together." Mrs. Samanta disappears into the attached bathroom.

Mallika looks around the room. The bedspread has a bold print of dried leaves, which look so real Mallika quickly runs her hand over it. A huge black-and-white print of the Eiffel Tower is framed next to the small writing desk and chair in the corner. The room is so peaceful, just the soft buzz of the air conditioner. Every inch of the room is carpeted and all the furniture surfaces shiny, without a speck of dust. Dim lights and dust don't belong together. Fluorescent lights hide everything. On the dresser sits a large lotus-shaped bowl filled with dried flowers and perfumed barks. The whole room is coated in soft light and light incense. Always clean and warm, just the way it is in her memory from her days with the Samantas. Nothing changes in the world of the well heeled. The impeccable touch of three servants, all assigned different tasks for different parts of the house. Dim lights and housecleaning belong together, Mallika thinks. Janaki dusted everything in their Sripuram house every alternate day, but it never looked like this. The rooms of the Sripuram house always looked empty and functional.

"That was Rinku on the phone from Calcutta," Mrs. Samanta says, stepping out from the bathroom. It is hard to gauge her mood, and Mallika wonders if she is trying to read something that is not there. It has become a wretched habit, this need to interpret everything through her personal thoughts, her own obsession for analysis and quiet negativity. She should keep it in check, knowing that she will never really lose it as long as she is alive. Accepting it is the hard part.

"Is she coming to Madras for the vacation?" Mallika asks. My sister is coming for a final showdown, she feels like adding. Everything these days is infused with Janaki. An insular possession. She cannot get rid of the voice in her ears, the voice that keeps telling her, this is not you, it is the antithesis of you. Your days and nights are now not your own, and your words are being composed and conducted by an invisible hand. Janaki Asgar. The Maestro of Misery.

Mrs. Samanta walks to the polished, three-mirror dresser and opens a drawer. She pulls out a small silver box of vermilion and gently retouches the bottu in the middle of her forehead. She retrieves a facial tissue and slowly cleans the small smudge of kohl from under her eyes.

"I can tell you, you are like my own daughter," Mrs. Samanta says, although to Mallika it seems like she is talking to herself. Substituting her for her father's frame in the corridor perhaps. She is distracted.

"Is it about her job at the hospital..." Mallika asks, remembering that Rinku was a pathologist at a hospital.

"Rinku and her husband are divorcing," Mrs. Samanta turns away from the mirror. "Is my face too blotchy with kaajol?"

"No, it's okay," Mallika doesn't know how to react. She lets her speechlessness make itself visible. Mrs. Samanta could surely see that she was tongue-tied. How can she be so calm with such news? How can she talk about it as if it were just a routine housecleaning help crisis?

"I am not really surprised," Mrs. Samanta says as she picks up the box of candles from the bed and smiles. "Rinku always had a problem with Ashish's drinking, and now she's met some visiting Canadian oncologist at a medical conference." She turns off the bedroom light and locks the door behind her. Mallika is now overwhelmed more by Mrs. Samanta's composure. She says everything in a calm and even tone, without a touch of regret or alarm. Not the way Appa and Gayatri Chitti did when they discovered Janaki had flown the coop.

That night in Sripuram when her veena was burned in the backyard, and familial secrets went up in a dark, corroding smog.

The bonfire of the Venkatakrishnans. And more to come.

Rinku, the pathologist at Calcutta General Hospital, and a no-name oncologist from Canada. Dim lights have different destinies, Mallika thinks. Or different mothers, different daughters? A no-name Brahmin girl and a Muslim film actor. Why wasn't that destiny? Would that have happened had their mother been alive?

"Women are entitled to leave a bad situation, I told her," Mrs. Samanta adjusts her sari at the landing. Her conviction is without a false note, and her voice devoid of any giveaway sign of anxiety. "Whatever makes you happy, Rinku, I told her. You can make your own decisions, although it is respectful of you to call and tell me. Only make sure he is not an alcoholic or a gambler, that's all."

Then she laughs, a small, throaty sound muffled more than it is heard, the red box of candles clasped tightly against her chest.

DA

There was no escaping the masala vadai vapours.

They were being fried downstairs, but the burning of spicy oil on the gas stove in the kitchen released short and over-powering blasts in every room when a fresh vadai sizzled.

Janaki had been working all morning. She had soaked the lentils the previous night and had ground it all to a paste; she had added onions and chilies soon after she returned from the milk depot that morning. She had also bought two extra bottles of milk, which she would have done by sweet-talking the depot man whose benevolence decided if there was going to be any almond payasam that evening. He always came through for her.

All of it was in preparation for the arrival of the prospective groom and his entourage led by Gayatri Chitti. They would get there by the six o'clock bus from Madras, just in time for a royal vegetarian feast, all prepared single-handedly by her sister. There had been a lull in the horoscopes and proposals for a brief period. This was the first one since their return from Tirukalukundram, which was already five months ago. But it was familiar, as though everything were set to some never-changing plan, and a fixed menu.

Vadais, and vexed hopes. With leftovers for three days.

"I had a telegram today. She will also be coming," was all Janaki had said the previous evening when Mallika had returned from school. *She* was Gayatri Chitti. Janaki had stopped referring to her by name, just a pronoun. "So please stay out of my way as nothing escapes her eye."

Mallika knew that it was two things for her sister every time these proposal evenings happened, an exhibition and an examination. The groom looked at Janaki, and Gayatri Chitti looked at Janaki's housekeeping. That was another feature that never changed. Janaki did not like to hear complaints from Gayatri Chitti.

"I could help you with dusting the hall?" Mallika offered.

"Seri," Janaki had replied, "but that will not be till I finish the cooking, so you just be in your room with your homework and I'll call you when I am ready." Mallika left the kitchen.

"I'll lock the door to keep out the masala vadai smell, so call loudly."

But there was no escaping the smell. It had crept into the room with the first ball in boiling oil. Mallika wondered if the brown covers on her school exercise books would smell like stale leftovers on Monday, during classes. She was still upset about the essay competition. It was cancelled because one of the inter-school judges had died. Mrs. Emanuel had done her best to get the other judges to agree to her proposal to postpone the date of results, but they had all voted to cancel instead.

Mallika had already finished the first full draft and was ready to begin on the final version. Even Appa had said that it read nicely. She never mentioned that night in Tirukalukundram in the essay. If she was a big girl, he was a grown-up man. He would never be nice to her again if she asked stupid questions. She knew he was not on speaking terms with Janaki because Janaki had asked him something, and Mallika knew that one is not supposed to ask grown-ups about their deeds. What would happen if Appa left them for that jasmine garland lady and never came back? What would happen then? Would Janaki pay the tuition fees for the school and buy her textbooks? Janaki didn't even know *Jane Eyre*.

Soon it will be November, Mallika thought, as she lay on her bed, and then there will be small clay lamps all along the walls of the mottamadi in the evenings. Appa will buy her another silk pavadai for Deepavali. And there was something else to look forward to. No school for four full days.

Mallika heard the latch fall on the gate and looked out the bedroom window. From above she saw Janaki walking away in the direction of Clive Road. This walk was also part of the design, Janaki going to the dry cleaners to pick up her ironed sari for that evening. Mallika flopped on the bed again.

Something else about Janaki had been bothering her for the whole month. Three weeks ago they had been watching the Sunday feature film on TV and when the film was over Janaki said, "Becoming nuns is the best solution for unmarried Brahmin girls."

Ever since, that sentence had glued itself to Mallika's mind. It was more powerful than the smell of masala vadai. She'd been waking up in the middle of the night, just to check if Janaki was still sleeping in the hall downstairs. If Janaki was late by a few minutes to pick her up from her typing class, her mind raced to all the churches in the country and she saw locks of Janaki's hair fall to the floor, like the actress in the picture before she became a nun. Janaki's long, black shiny hair, conditioned for so many years with shikakai and coconut oil, and then her sister's face in a starched white nun's habit walking down the stairs of their house. What will she do if Janaki became Sister Rosanna, or something like that? Who'll look after her and Appa? But when she saw Janaki's figure at the end of the typing school street, Mallika was so relieved, she'd cried.

The marriage proposals were not working out for some reason.

And yet Appa never seemed to disagree with Gayatri Chitti's recommendations. Chitti was stuck on just one refrain: "She is born under Aailyam, so there have to be other ways to compensate. She'll never get married if you don't get a bank loan!" She said so regularly when the groom's party came back with the dowry amount. Mallika had asked Janaki what *Aailyam* meant and Janaki had explained it to her in detail. "There are twenty-seven stars in the Hindu constellation. Everyone is born under a star, which is determined by the time and date of birth. You were born under Rohini, which is a good star. My birth time and date coincide with the Aailyam star. It's a problematic star. My star's special quality is that it can bring danger to my father-in-law's life. So, for me to get married, my to-be father-in-law should already be dead, or my to-be mother-in-law should want him dead. It's a no-win situation."

"So it means you will be here forever, then?" Mallika couldn't contain her joy.

"There is a small way out of the situation. I have to perform some dosham-cleansing prayers to appease the goddess of that particular star. But still there are no guarantees. The goddess might not budge. It could all turn out to be my fantasy."

That repeated answer always reassured Mallika.

Janaki will never be able to get away, unless there was some miracle.

"Do you believe in this, 'ka," Mallika asked, wanting to hear her sister say that she was happy to be there in Sripuram forever, just the way she had promised during her first periods.

"It doesn't matter whether I believe in it or not, for that's the way it is," Janaki replied. "That's what every Brahmin believes. Even my friend Kamala has the same star."

And then a few months later she had talked about the nun solution. She could still turn into Sister Rosanna. Everything about their lives in Sripuram was complicated. Should she tell Janaki about the lady at the hotel in Tirukalukundram, use it as her bargaining chip or her checkmate? Will Janaki agree to stay back then?

Mallika heard the latch fall back on the gate again and knew Janaki was back. She sat up and stretched her arms. Janaki called her down to help with the dusting, and she began with cleaning the edges of Amma's photo frame in the hall.

THE HALL WAS spotless that evening. Every cobweb had been searched and scooped, every bit of sand and every stray hair had been swept up and dumped in the garbage bin outside the gate. Janaki then went away into the backyard to scrub the outhouse latrine while Mallika was dispatched upstairs to tidy her bed and bookshelf. There was no holding back Gayatri Chitti during her visits. Chitti opened all the rooms and ran her eye over all the things. Her eyes always landed on the chipped brim of a new ceramic bowl here, and a new pair of chappals there. Gayatri Chitti had a simultaneous and similar response to both dirt and newness. Both merited her critical eye, and were either followed by caustic snides or excessive adulation. But she had not been the same the last time she left Sripuram.

She can still picture the redness in Chitti's eyes, like she had been crying about something the previous night. Not her ever-watchful eyes, but pools of bursting red veins. Then the proposals had trickled and so had her regular visits.

Mallika arranged all the books according to their shape and size, the tall ones petering out into the shorter ones. She grabbed the dusting rag and wiped the mirror on the almirah. Janaki, smelling like bleach, will soon come upstairs to use the bathroom and change into her sari for the evening. Appa will return any minute from the bank with a ball of rolled kanakambaram garlands, at least ten mozhams, for Amma's photo and to be woven around the veena that Janaki will have to play for the guests. The remaining flowers will be for Janaki's hair. Mallika will get nothing, not even half a mozham, and will be sent to her room before everything got under way. She will have to watch it all from upstairs, peeping discreetly over the landing, as she had done so many times before.

"How do I look?" Janaki asked, as she turned around in front of Mallika.

Her cream kota silk, with its gold chain border curving around her, opened up like a fan above her feet. The evenly lined layers of pleats were sharp, like stacked fabric blades. In ten minutes Janaki had turned her eyes into dark kohl-lined tail fins. She had jimikis in her ears. On both wrists, a dozen glass bangles, which she will remove when she plays the veena. She looked older, and tired. How did she do it?

"You look a lot like Amma in that sari, 'ka," Mallika said.

"Really?" Janaki walked to the mirror on the almirah door and looked at herself. "I don't think so. Where?" She stood at an angle and examined her profile.

"Your nose ring, I think," Mallika said as she pulled up the little wooden stool from the writing desk and stood on it, a few inches higher now.

"Look at yourself. Don't you see the resemblance?"

"Maybe my face is a bit oval like hers, but my mouth is not so prim."

Janaki replied as she wet her lips with a quick circular sweep of her tongue. She is right, Mallika admitted to herself. Janaki's mouth was fuller, a bit like Appa's. But her nose and eyes were just like Amma's, or what Mallika remembered of her.

"Why don't you wear some lipstick, 'ka? I could run to Jee-O-Jee and get you a dark red one?"

Janaki moved away from the mirror and sat down on the edge of the bed. "As though that will finally make me eligible for these accountants! Why does Gayatri Chitti insist on putting me through this—this hopeless ritual!"

Mallika had seen this look before, the sudden clouding over of Janaki's eyes. This was also very familiar, the darkest place in the whole design. She had watched it all from upstairs—all the men who came with their mothers and heard Janaki play a small alaapana on the veena. After that they gorged on the vadais and ladoos Janaki had spent the whole afternoon preparing with her own hands, and then sent word, within two days, demanding cars and motorcycles. Appa couldn't afford one for himself. How was he going to pay for one for the prospective groom?

"Play a horrible kirtanam today!" Mallika said, hugging Janaki. "Full of abaswarams!"

"That'll give Appa something to fume about after they have left," Janaki replied, freeing herself from Mallika's embrace. "*Appuram*," she said with a sense of abdication as she got up and straightened the pleats of her sari. She brought her pullo around her back and tucked the edges into her waist.

"I have to go prepare the decoction. You'd better wash your face as well."

"Why doesn't Appa say anything to her? What does she care if you are married or unmarried?" Mallika wondered why her sister or father never said a word to their aunt. "Why does everything have to have Gayatri Chitti's approval?"

"Why don't you ask them yourself? They should be here in fifteen minutes." Janaki looked at herself in the mirror. "I doubt things would have been different had Amma been alive."

BUT APPA returned from the bus station, sullen and irascible. He strode to his room, leaving Mallika and Janaki perplexed at the kitchen doorway. All the plates had been already arranged, and the coffee dabras ready and waiting. It was usually the time Mallika was sent packing to her room, locked away for two hours, before the grown-ups, who were never to be questioned, sat down and discussed money and terms of exchange, after a raga on the veena, and masala vadais and payasam in their stomachs. But that didn't seem to be the case this time.

The guests had not arrived with Appa.

No sign of Gayatri Chitti anywhere in the vicinity, either. Something like a light flashed behind her eyes, and then she saw things in a different way. Something else was being revealed, something that she could only sense, something like a message unscrolling slowly. She could already sense a quick change in Janaki's posture. Her sister was alert with the eagerness of probabilities, although she could also see that Janaki rested against the kitchen door more casually, seemingly convinced that her destiny had once again been deferred. It was then that Mallika recognized, for the first time, the violence of it all. That was the flash, a sense that revealed Janaki's tight walk on a razor that cut both ways. But what could she do? A few more years and she will have to join the lineup, and that could only happen with Janaki out of the way first. She also will have no say in the whole thing.

Appa stepped out of his room, bare-chested, and wearing a veshti. He had stopped looking at Janaki just around the same time that Janaki had started to refer to Gayatri Chitti as *She,* and so he raised his voice a bit and said to nobody in particular: "They won't be here tonight. There was a lorry collision on the Madras–Poonamalli highway. A cow was killed. I telephoned them from the ticket office and they said their bus never left." His voice was calm but there was a terse quality to his tone, like the buzz of the light bulb in the outhouse.

"I'll just finish my *sandhya vandanam,*" he added, and walked through the kitchen door on his way to the back well.

"I'll get dinner ready," Janaki announced, relief flooding her eyes and the glow returning to her anxious face. Appa was drawing water from the well for his bath.

"Would you like to go to the storytelling at the temple tonight?" she asked. "I'll go and get into my everyday sari before this one gets dirty. You keep out of Appa's way now."

And Mallika couldn't help but notice that Janaki was smiling throughout, at every word. Her sister still liked Hindu mythology and storytelling, so there was no chance of her becoming Sister Mariah or Rosanna. *Aailyam* and dowry would take care of the rest. Janaki would be in Sripuram forever.

That was the magic power Mallika had now that she was a big girl for two full years. She could connect what was said and done in a different way. You had to also hear the unsaid words and see a pattern in the smiles or silences. Reading was her power. People were her books.

MAY 1991

"YOU NEVER TRUST anyone, ma, that's your basic problem," the man booms, loud enough for two rows of bus seats to hear every word. Mallika is sitting diagonally behind him and can see his moustache quiver with passionate disbelief. He is wearing a white short-sleeved shirt with blue stripes, just like the one dry cleaned for Appa. Ironed pants and bush shirts, including seven 750-gram packets of Balaram's Banana Chips—all in the cloth-bag near her feet. Could Appa ever be trusted? Did he trust anyone?

"The doctor is right. You just have to wait it out," he adds with a touch of bass. That finality, like the straight-lined stripes of his shirt, is also like Appa's. But Appa then turned out to be a straight line that curved. Many times. And still he wanted the world to believe that it was unbent—that was his arrogance, his emptiness. Her father—the steadfast banker of falsehoods.

It has been ten minutes since the bus driver turned off the engine at the junction of Sterling and College roads. That's when a dozen policemen on motorbikes lined up, parked their vehicles and formed a khaki and white crucifix alongside the four exits. They turned around and faced the crowd of people and cyclists, all crammed at the footpaths. It looks like they are glaring, from where she sits, but it is hard to tell what they are thinking. Their eyes are hidden and hooded by the reflective silver of their sunglasses. The crowd is quiet with apprehension, and a few voices yell, "*Vazhga*, Rajiv Gandhi, *vazhga!*" A Youth Congress procession is due to pass any moment. All she can see outside the bus window now are photo placards of the former prime minister and his South Indian youth chapter president, Illango—hands folded, and black hair oiled like a Spanish roof tile—rounding up the student vote. Sudden, just like rain.

"Why can't you just accept that?" The man is getting impatient with his mother. He keeps talking to her, but she has not said a word. The standees in the bus are showing signs of fatigue, sighing and shaking their wrists and looking at their watches, each gesture in synchronized boredom. Mallika is glad to have a seat. Imagine being a standee in the bus, waiting for a procession to pass. That was penance for sins long forgotten, a never-complete punishment. It could happen anytime, the standee fate, random and recurring unfailingly, nurtured by the shortage of municipal funds for more buses and every transportation contract sold up the road by corrupt city board bureaucrats.

"What does he mean by 'it has to ripen?' Is it some sort of fruit, like a melon? How can I trust someone who uses such terms? Is he a doctor or a farmer?" the mother finally responds. Her voice is stronger than Mallika had expected—robust and full for her small frame.

The man shakes his head.

The current standee faters close by try to look away, but there is nothing else to see but police helmets, and a cobble of rexine autorickshaw roofs outside the bus windows, and Illango bursting out here and there between the footpath jammed with heads.

"Can you at least talk in a lower voice? Everybody is listening," the man mutters. He looks up shyly at a standee and smiles a weak smile. The couple seated in the row to the side snigger and chuckle, but nobody else seems to care. The eyes keep returning to wristwatches.

"I am not the one who started to yell, it was you!"

Mallika is also glad that the bus is not packed with bodies. Only a dozen people are standing, but all the seats are taken. Sunday afternoon is not a peak time in the city; if not for this procession, she would have arrived at the hospital by now. The mother and son don't seem to care about the ruckus outside the bus window.

"He meant maturity, ma," the man cajoles, in a lower tone this time, just like a chastised boy returning to his forgiving mother. Just like Wilfred, the comeback hero. "The little disk behind your eyes has to grow fully. It is mature in your left eye, but the right eye will take another five months. So by October they can take it out, both at the same time. You can see all the fireworks at Deepavali!"

"I did not like what little I could see of that doctor's face," his mother announces. "He reminded me of my cousin's husband who walked into Marina Beach and drowned. He reminded me of Gundu Karthi." She shudders momentarily in her seat.

"The water, not the beach," the man says, with annoyance. "He drowned in the Bay of Bengal. Marina Beach is all sand; you don't drown in sand."

"He is a ghost," his mother announces. "He is *pei* of Bengal for me. I don't want to see him when I open my eyes after the operation. His voice is also like that Gundu Karthi. I'll ask Sowmya to suggest another doctor, nobody that resembles anyone from my family or my past. Not even like you."

The blaring of loudspeakers fills the air. "Select and elect Illango!" The crowd on the footpath cheers, and the policemen stiffen. Illango drives by in his chauffeur-driven, roofdown Impala car. He lurches and holds on to the raised glass for balance. He performs a quick namaskaram, a two-minute stop right in the middle of the road, waving and throwing a few garlands at the eager party youth. He keeps waving his hand and turns around in all directions. The car stereo is playing a Youth Congress anthem, "Give Us Our Tomorrow Today," breaking all noise pollution laws of the city. The Impala begins to move again. Illango grabs the glass window of the car and grins like a baboon in an open cage, clueless to all the inconvenience and delays he and his similarly greasy acolytes have caused. But it's over quickly. And there has been no violence. That's something.

For the past year there have been student self-immolations, spreading like a fiery suicide ring all over the country, mostly by upper-caste youth protesting the government's

protribal policies, particularly in college admissions and quo-
tas. Thankfully, no student has blazed into the junction this
Sunday. Illango takes it all. That's something.

As soon as the car passes through, the policemen allow the
supporters to join the rest of the procession, all in a single file.
The bus engine starts up, and the standees grip the overhead
iron bar. Horns blast, cycle bells jam, buses and lorries all
suddenly fume and trundle, as though someone had released
the Pause button on a traffic tape recorder. Sooty life bursts
forth again.

"There must be an eye doctor in this city who does not
look like that drowned boy Gundu Karthi?" his mother wonders loudly, as the bus pulls ahead and merges into the lane
for the bridge.

THE BUS IS almost empty at Taylor's Road. Mallika watches
the man and his mother cross the road, his hand holding her
firm at the elbow and their argument still raging. A few of
the standees have found seats, and two full rows in the front
are vacant and losing body warmth.

"They must have sent a substitute bus via the other route,"
the conductor says, walking past her, smiling. He has seen
her on countless Sundays over the years, in this very spot,
huddled by the single window seat (like it was made for her)
at the back of the bus. Sitting without an expression on her
face, a bag of clothes and banana chips at her feet. Mallika
returns his smile. Should she tell him what she really thinks
of the current government and its atrocities? Shock him with
a release of all the pent-up anger and confusion from the past
week, and her complete inability to respond to anything in

her life anymore? They've seen each other grow old without knowing the other's name.

It's a Luz–Kilpauk route bond.

The boundaries between them are speechlessly defined. He always nods when he gives her the ticket, his eyes friendly but blank. He knows her stop and has on many occasions been ready to help her with the bag, holding it while she steps down to the pavement, and blowing the whistle only after she carries the bag and puts it on the vacant seat of the bus shelter. Sometimes he waves and sometimes he doesn't. Like everybody else, he also has his moods and doesn't care to hide it.

"There is nobody at this stop. But if the bus is late, there will be more people waiting, correct-a?" He grins. "I say it like it was some major mathematical solution! Logic Mannan!" He laughs again.

He has never said so much before. Just a smile or a *vanak-kam ma*, or a quick nod, depending on how crowded the bus is when he asks her for the ticket. Today he is unusually forthcoming.

"It's nice like this. Without people," Mallika says.

She watches him collect an empty plastic water bottle from the back row. He dusts the dark green rexine of the back row seats with his palms and quickly pushes a few peanut shells to the floor.

"You're right about that. See this?" He points to the scattered chewing gum wrappers and peanut shells. "Some still don't know the difference between the bus and the beach." Mallika turns around and stares at the shells.

And some don't know the difference between the past and the present anymore.

My father, she thinks, doesn't know anything at all, except horses and numbers and bursts of sobs and laughter at any given moment. And my sister cared only about veena, cinema and multicoloured dreams. But then, what else could she have done but step out of that invisible line, and would the world have cared if it weren't a Muslim film actor? Questions she still asks but is never able to resolve for herself. What-ifs and why-nots that eat up every sane and waking hour.

"Yes, some things are really hard to accept," Mallika lifts her head as the conductor moves to the front of the bus, his whistle setting the bus in motion again.

Everything blurs outside.

APPA'S SLIDE INTO imperceptible insanity had been just that. Imperceptible. A slow-maturing cataract of deviance. She had seen some odd signs, but she had dismissed those moments as a by-product of stress and shame. His palm, where the camphor burned, had healed, but the same could not be said for his pride, which had remained traumatized even after the move to Madras and new Bank Quarters. He got up every morning. He shaved, showered and left for work. He returned to the assembly line townhouse in the evening. Sometimes he went out for a walk before dinner. He didn't smile much.

She knew that he had taken up drinking, but he always did that later, after she had retired to her room and turned off the night lamp. But he could do nothing to hide the sour fumes of alcohol that drifted into the living room the moment he opened his door in the morning. Mallika had rarely found an empty bottle in his room, for he took it with him in a brown paper bag on his way to the bank.

One Sunday, she found him sitting in the living room and reading the newspaper upside down. He was still sitting in the same position, still reading it the wrong way, when she got back from grocery shopping.

"Appa."

Her voice made him jerk so hard the paper ripped halfway down the middle. He looked at her as if she were a stranger who had walked into the living room. He shook his head left and right quickly, like a cat regaining its balance after a landing, and he was alert.

"What is it?" he said, and dropped the paper on the floor.

But Mallika could not tell him that he had been reading the paper upside down.

"Would it be okay if I made spinach dal for dinner?" She had never asked him anything like that before. Her cooking was not as good as Janaki's, but he still ate whatever she put in front of him without a word of complaint. He had never asked for anything particular or special. He had never praised or berated her kitchen skills.

"It is your wish," he replied.

Mallika put the incident behind her.

"THREE VISITING rooms are engaged," the monitoring nurse says. Mallika looks around for Gayatri Chitti.

"No, Chitti, *innum varalai*," the nurse informs her.

Good. Mallika heaves a sigh; it would have been too much to walk into the hospital and have to put up with Chitti's stories about backaches and low bank balances. She realizes that in actuality she will not be telling Appa about Janaki's return; rather she will be telling Gayatri Chitti. Appa will only listen for a bit, smiling, fidgeting, his response lucid for a few sentences and then the horses in his head will start galloping and racing and that will be that. That's the way it has been for the past few years. D-Day always caught up.

Mallika puts the cloth bag on the nursing station counter and signs her name.

"Room will be ready in twenty minutes. Why not finish security check and sit in waiting room?"

This whole ward may as well be her sitting room at the Luz flat. Mallika knows everything about it so well. From the telephone booth where the public phone is always out of order or wheezing when it does work, right to the other end of the V-shaped ward, where the two guards stand at the entrance to the visiting rooms, collecting all bags and handing out a token for checked items. This sanctuary of people who have nothing to fear, this psychiatric ward of the Kilpauk Mental Hospital, this swallower of so many pointless, draining Sundays.

"Seri." Mallika steps back from the nurses' station. "Will you give this bag to Nurse Fathima, please? She knows when to give Appa the banana chips and where to put his clothes."

The nurse doesn't reply but nods absent-mindedly and returns to her paperwork behind the counter.

Mallika walks through the metal detector. All clear.

"Chitti is not coming today?" the guard asks. He smells sour, like mouldy curds. She has never liked him. Standing there and ogling at the women who come to visit their husbands or mothers. Something in his eye, the low dip and brush of his gaze, feels invasive, and predatory.

"Late." Why should he care?

The security screening is a recent requirement. When Appa was first admitted, the regulations were different; even the visiting hours were flexible as long as you called in advance and it was before seven o'clock in the evening.

That all changed a few years ago when Mr. Manickkam, a patient with acute delusional disorder, combined with an acute sense of persecutional paranoia (he imagined himself to be a film hero, brandishing an invisible sword, saving the world's poor), made it all a thing of the past. He lunged at his visiting daughter-in-law (the son was out of town that day), calling her a "third-rate *thevadiya*," who had slept with prominent CEOs to promote her husband's auditing firm. He held her against the wall and yanked the three-inch broad gold *saradu* around her neck so hard, she dropped unconscious. To make sure that she was dead (the villainess and the swindler of the impoverished), Mr. Manickkam used for his final blow the very coffee Thermos from which his daughter-in-law was pouring coffee for him when he decided that she was to be bumped off.

The daughter-in-law was wheeled out on a stretcher, and Mr. Manickkam was sent away for solitary "observation," deemed to be a danger to the other inmates and staff from then on. No jewellery or Thermoses were allowed in the ward or rooms after that. And the visiting hours were fixed for once a week, twice a week with special permit. Then came the old-curd security guards. Two more people in this world you really didn't need to know. Mallika was a few visiting rooms down the corridor when it had happened. Appa, the chief psychiatrist assured her later, belonged to the "delusional disorder" category and showed no symptoms of paranoia. But still, who knew when the horses would assume the form of Janaki and his rage would catch up with his madness? Isn't that why he really went insane? Because of anger and arrogance?

IT IS QUIET in the waiting room.

The ceiling fan is working, spinning warm, stifled air. But still, it feels good to be alone. A day that began with a vision of Mrs. Amaldoss on the stairs in blistering red and green, a rude, rude awakening, is still finding its way through Youth Congress processions and mental hospital metal detectors and slow government ceiling fans. And it is not even half over yet. Mallika picks up a magazine, settles into the corner sofa and pulls up her feet. Every delay is a blessing. Gayatri Chitti must have missed her bus, or else she would be here by now. And that meant another thirty-five minutes of calm and peace. She flips through the magazine, not paying too much attention to anything in particular, her mind still rehearsing her words. Chitti, Janaki is coming to Madras. Tuesday. I received a letter at the USIS. Should I tell her about Appa?

Why does she need Chitti's permission? She would have to leave that out. She could decide whether she should say something about Appa to Janaki when they meet. That was her decision. Leave it at Tuesday. Short. She has not brought the letter with her; she never intended to.

Woman's World is filled with advertisements for creams and creamier soaps. All the models, but for the small, mustard-size bindi at the centre of their foreheads, look like they are from some other country. Somewhere dark-skinned women don't exist. No cream could help them. Chitti still buys her jar of Afghan Snow Cream. "The price of this snow keeps rising and rising," she often exclaims. "But now I can't discontinue. It has been with me all my life, and I am used to it." She never considers for a moment that all the creaming has done little for her face. How could Chitti even think she'd wake up one day looking like the Kashmiri (or thereabouts) model on the label of the jar? Rosy cheeked, with big sparkling eyes, and a headscarf held in place by heavy, skull-crunching silver jewellery? Everybody has his or her own escapes.

Mallika reads the *New Woman* recipes for Curried Potato Au Gratin and Mango–Mint Sorbet and Kitchen Oven-baked Naan with Sun-dried Tomatoes. Colour photos that seem to have moved in the printing and lend a hazy feel to the page accompany each recipe. The contributing chef is Gamo Gomez, a fiercely moustached Goan restaurant owner, who has recently launched his own TV program. He trained somewhere in Switzerland, so his bio in between recipes says. Ted Pope mentioned his show at the Samantas' party and called it "spicy cool."

Can one's own country be so exotic and distant to one's own eyes and ears? Mallika flips the page. Is that why they lined up outside the gates of the USIS such early hours to really go to the land of salads and sorbets? Even if that meant shaving one's hair and mortgaging ancestral property, it was all worth such a diet?

Mallika is ready to throw the magazine on the table again when her eye catches a boxed headline, in the "WomeNews" column: "Runaway success (again!)."

"*Janaki Asgar,*" she reads rapidly, catching her breath and forgetting to exhale, gulping sentences, "*yes, the very veena prodigy who made waves with her elopement and marriage to Asgar the Fabulous (older was never cuter!) is now exhibiting her genius (but seldom her person) in a quiet, so-not-Bollywood way. Still waters, as they say. Two students from her music school have been chosen to represent the country at the Melbourne International Arts Festival. Now, there's a woman who sets and plays by her own tunes! And that puts her in a league of her own! Don't forget you heard it first here. wn Gold Crown."* There is no photo. Janaki has seldom been seen in public since her twins were born. Why was she coming back, and what does she know?

When Mallika was young, every time one of her teeth came out, Janaki would ask her to bury it in the backyard, close to the hibiscus bush. "Make a wish and don't reveal it to anyone," she'd instruct, folding her hands and also closing her eyes. She'd take a quick, underlid glance, out of the corner of her eye, to see if Mallika was following her instructions. Sixty seconds later she would kiss Mallika on the forehead and say, "If you remember what your wish is, it will come true." Mallika just needs a tooth now—a tooth that she could bury and never forget where, and make one last wish, urgent, pushing and very selfish, for a change. Mallika closes her eyes. She'd wish Janaki Asgar, Gold Crown and everything else with it, away.

For good.

PA

"So where were you when I was born?"

Her right hand pushed the soaked rice into the stone grinder's hollow, and her left hand turned the masher, an oval-shaped rock the size of small jackfruit, slowly, with care not to gnash her shovelling fingers. It seemed like a performance, hypnotic if you just kept watching. Scoop, scoop, crunch, grind. Turn the masher the other way. Scoop, scoop, crunch, mash again. Dip right hand in water for a quick rinse. Scoop, scoop. Mallika was about to repeat her question, when Janaki answered.

"Away in Madras."

"So you don't know if I was adopted?"

It was a sunless, dull Saturday afternoon in the backyard. Janaki had soaked the rice and lentils the previous night. Masala dosa on Sundays, those were Appa's orders. He ate at least three potato stuffing–filled crepes before taking his afternoon nap. He was out for the local cultural Sabha meeting. They were the ones who put up the funny skits and temple music programs for Navarathri. Appa, a bank manager, was given the post of supervising treasurer. He had to attend meetings only twice a year. But he was well recognized during festivals, which made Mallika feel proud.

"No, you were not adopted. Here, throw this water on the tulasi plant and bring me some fresh."

That had always been Janaki's method of turning things her way. She offered a curt answer and then right behind it came a small chore, pick up this, or stack that, or hold this bedsheet at the edge. Mallika knew it all now.

"But you don't know that still," Mallika drained the rice water from the stainless-steel pot, pouring it all around the plant.

"Everybody knows. Look at your face, it is just like Appa's. You have his eyes and your chin is Pattima, *saatchaath;* even Gayatri Chitti has the same chin. It is in the family. So you were not adopted!"

"But you weren't even there, so can't be that sure. Maybe you were adopted, too. Can you prove you were not?"

The masher moved faster. Janaki didn't say anything for a few long minutes.

"The best solution is to ask Appa, if you have any doubts. He was there when we both were born."

"But wasn't he also adopted?"

"I don't know what has gotten into you this afternoon," Janaki said irritably, ladling the last of the soaked ingredients into the grinder. She held the masher above the mixture and dropped it with slow precision onto the mixture. She pounded it quickly with a few jiggles, holding the masher firmly in place. Then she began turning it, rotating gently and deliberately at first and then picking up speed, setting a good rhythm on the grains so they were thoroughly flattened.

"What is your sudden interest in adoption business? Is this something you've been watching on TV? Or are you working on some research paper for class?"

"Mrs. Emanuel says that Indians are not curious about their family tree."

"What does it look like, can you say, this tree?" Janaki cupped the ground mixture and ladled it into the pot with the rest. She quickly scraped off the remainder, her palm and fingers sliding against the stainless-steel rim. Her hand dived one more time into the rinsing water. And then her pullo edge wiped it dry.

"It is not a tree, actually. It is about family history. Mrs. Emanuel says Indians don't know much about their past. Have no knowledge about their ancestors."

"So that means we are all adopted?"

"No," Mallika replied. Her eyes were stuck to the masher. Lines of wet dough, where Janaki had scraped off the last bits, were beginning to dry. "It means that we don't know that we are not adopted."

Janaki picked up the vessel with the ground maavu and pushed her flat wooden seat to the side.

"Will knowing it make any difference?"

"We can be proud of our ancestors then. What do you know about anybody before Thathappa? Or of Appa's father? We know nothing. There is only a cinema theatre in our past." She took the pot of rinsing water once again to the tulasi plant. It sucked up the water so quickly she thought she heard the soil hiss with happiness.

"Knowing you were not adopted, guaranteed, should also make you proud. You already know that you were not somebody else's daughter. This is just *vidhanda vatham*."

Pointless argument.

Janaki always put an end to things that in her view did not need attention. She could probe a musical note endlessly, lost in the world of veena strings and distant sounds, but she could never be convinced of anything that she had already decided was of no interest to her. She couldn't reason; she could only react.

That's why Appa never once taught or asked Janaki to play chess with him. He always chose her, Mallika. Meanwhile Janaki would listen to film songs on the two-in-one, sitting upstairs, on the ledge of the window in Mallika's bedroom. Her veena, and her radio, and her film gossip sessions with her friend Revathi, all merged into one for a few hours.

"That theatre was my summer heaven, and Thathappa was a noble and kind man. He was well respected in the Madras

Brahmin community. Be proud of that. That should be enough for your children, too. And plant your family tree in the backyard of this house. This is a good place to begin, and you can tell your Mrs. Emanuel that. Anglo-Indian *sirukki!*"

INITIALLY, IN THE few years that followed Amma's death, their isolation as a family had not seemed that odd. In fact, it was not really all that different from many of the families in the agraharam. Mallika seldom saw visitors or relatives at any of the gates on the way back from the temple, with Janaki by her side, walking with their heads lowered, their thoughts within measured feet. But later, when she moved up a few standards in school, she began to see that their family was indeed different.

First, there were no old women in the house. Every house in the neighbourhood had at least one permanent old person. A widowed mami with her shaved head, maybe from the days of Subhas Chandra Bose (Mallika's favourite real rebel), or an old mama with a *bokkavai*, sitting on a moda or easy chair on the veranda if not standing by the gate with a mug of coffee, smiling toothlessly at all the vendors and merchants strolling the streets. Appa was only forty-nine years old. Mallika had seen his school photo in the pile of photos Janaki kept tied up in a green handkerchief in the Godrej almirah. And he still had all his teeth.

Another fact that made their family different was the complete absence of visitors. Other families in the agraharam had guests and friends over for Deepavali and Pongal—even if they were only two people—but nobody, not one single person, came to their house. Only Gayatri Chitti came often. But she had stopped her visits to Sripuram for the past full year. Neither Appa nor Janaki had explained why. And honestly, Mallika had not missed her at all.

Chitti, whenever she came for a visit, created tension, and Janaki always bristled in her presence. Mallika did not dislike Gayatri Chitti as much as Janaki did. But she was also spared the constant criticism Janaki had to endure. Sometimes it was about the latrine in the outhouse not being clean enough, and sometimes about the dents and scratches on the cooking utensils. Chitti was not a guest; she was like a recurring cough or, as she had heard Janaki say, "Eczema" Chitti.

Mallika could see Janaki seething under her skin, wanting to slap Chitti maybe, or do something violent, like grab a stainless-steel thali and press their aunt's face with it, but Janaki just listened. She did not smile or frown; she stood like a statue and did nothing. She never apologized. "Scratching a scab can only make the scab itch with added freshness," she told Mallika a day or two later. "There is no ointment for it. You have to accept that." And she went back into her silent world.

ALL THAT CHANGED when Appa took off for the Madras weekend. He always had work (her father was an important man; she had seen three telephones on his desk one Sunday three years ago, the only time he took her to the bank). He started visiting the main office at least one Saturday in a month. He only returned later on Sunday nights, after the Tamil picture on TV was over.

She was already in bed on those nights, thinking about the math test the next day, or the upcoming school inspection, when she heard his voice, rising from the cement floor upstairs, slurring and slow. He always said the same thing to Janaki: "I've had my dinner. You can go to bed."

But the Saturdays that he was gone, and right up to late Sunday afternoon, when the second kolam had been made and dinner was being prepared, Janaki was a woman from another, happier planet. Hypnotized by an *aavi*, or some dancer in her dreams. Like that madwoman who threw things around, and released "nerve-tingling" (that was Mrs. Emanuel's description) screams in *Jane Eyre*.

Janaki was a woman possessed by laughing spirits. Even the black of her hair was darker, Mallika noticed, glistening with spirit waves to the very tip.

The excitement began about fifteen minutes after Appa announced his departure for Madras. "Very early," he said, "the next morning." Those statements—the same phrase—were usually made after dinner, just after he had slurped all the rasam from his stainless-steel plate. Then he would stand up and walk to the common washbasin in the small alcove beside the kitchen. It all seemed rehearsed to her.

But to Janaki it was a key to an entirely different existence.

It promised a morning beginning with songs on the radio, turned up a few more dots on the volume dial—so that she could hear it over the running water in the kitchen as she scrubbed and cleaned every corner of this that and everything—and a night with the veena being played on the terrace, under a canopy of stars, late, but not a complaint from the neighbours.

Even Vanaja Mami came up to their terrace and put out her easy chair, right on the other side. After the *katcheri* gathering she said, "You all did a good job—except you!" She laughed when she said that and looked at Mallika, who was sitting at the top of the stairs. It was a different Vanaja Mami, not the surly one.

For the past three monthly Saturdays, the construction man's family who had moved into the agraharam for Sabesan Mama's house renovation sat on the sand dune at the end of the street and had even clapped after Janaki's recital.

Kamala had come just once with her violin, and that night the performance pulled many more passersby on their way back from work at the sugar refinery, a few yards into the agraharam, Mudaliars and Chettiars in a gathering outside the Brahmin colony gates. Many others, the *bokkavai thathas* and Vespa mamas, along with Savitri Mami's cotton-length coterie, gathered along their verandas and compound walls, and listened to a free concert for two full hours.

That night, it seemed to Mallika as though the stars had also come down from the sky and lay about the *jamakalam* where the trio sat. Revathi's voice transistored (it could carry far!) in the air, pushed further by Kamala's violin bow, while Janaki's fingers raced along with the singing voice, hanging a highlight note on every star and slowly pulling them down, just as the raga fell with the descending scale, like stars falling, slowly, and settling on the spread on the terrace.

Appa's absence also meant Janaki's most likely presence at Mahalaxmi Talkies the next day. That was the only part of the freedom wave Mallika hated. She was dragged to matinee shows every so often, to watch Janaki cry at the fate of the rickshaw puller who had developed leprosy and was shunned by his adopted daughter, or a poor blind couple dancing on the streets to earn money for an eye operation.

All the women around were wiping tears. Janaki sniffled throughout, although just as soon as they were out of the theatre, Mallika knew, the criticisms about the clothes and the heroine's cleavage would begin. But now her nose was choking on a kerchief. It was Janaki's way of belonging to a community that was big on tears and exaggeration. She always talked about her summer holidays in Madras when Thathappa was alive and how much fun she had had in his theatre. She could recite dialogues from *Thiruvilayadal* (the whole contest scene between the Commoner Poet and the God Poet) without missing a word, and playing both roles, with just a jump to this side and that side.

Mallika watched the pictures just to be part of Janaki's world but knew all along that it would never be her world. Her eyes were on the screen, but her thoughts were elsewhere. The chess game with Appa that would take place the following week was all she could think of. She planned her next moves, for the following weekend, when Appa would be home.

If the matinee show was full, which had happened last month, then Revathi came over at four o'clock. It was not really a good replacement for being turned away from the cinema, but there was not much she could say or do about that.

Laughing spirits also possessed Janaki's friend Revathi.

Revathi could not stop talking (when she was not singing) and words filled her every breath. But Janaki giggled and laughed along at all the jokes her friend was telling her. She read out aloud from the film gossip magazines she had brought with her.

They sat on the spread-out *jamakalam* on the cement veranda at the back of the house and chatted for hours about

Manjula and Sivaji, their latest cinema gods. Last month Mallika had heard Revathi read something about how the actors had been caught in the same department store choosing toys and ceramic plates.

"Jana, what, you think they are...?" Revathi asked and winked.

Janaki said, "Shoo, shoo," looking sideways at Mallika, and laughed.

Mallika pretended to write in her diary, wishing that her secret powers could actually move Revathi and her mother Savitri Mami, some place far away, like the island of Robinson Crusoe. Where there were no film magazines. She closed her eyes and grated her teeth softly, hoping that those powers that had never returned after their visit to Tirukalukundram will feel her body call out to them and come back, just to take her sister's friend away. They never did.

Janaki did not see any of Mallika's anger. She kept laughing, her loose hair trembling and gleaming around her face. *Mohini.*

Then she and her friend got ready to take their stroll through the temple alleys before the evening *archanai.* The world around them was filled with jokes and laughter. Jokes dangling and dropping from the lampposts, even on the way to the temple. The same walk, but on a different earth. For Janaki.

For forty-one hours, everything and everyone was Cinderella, and everything and everyone was the Madwoman.

JANAKI WAS LATE one afternoon to pick her up.

Mallika stood near the school gate waiting for her to appear but thirty minutes later she still wasn't there. Then she came, stiffer than usual, her eyes just glued to the pavement all the way from the end of the street. Her pullo was pulled so tightly around her back that from a distance she looked like somebody else.

When she came closer, Mallika saw a white face. There was no blood under the skin. Like it wouldn't bleed if you dragged a blade. Her usual, "Sorry-da, *thangame*, I forgot the time," or, "I was late getting home from the market" was not there either. "Let's go," is all she said. For the whole evening she walked in and out of rooms, kitchen to backyard to veranda, as though she were seeking a way out and was confronted by the door marked Use Other Door and a finger pointing in the opposite direction, like the door beside the Mahalaxmi Talkies screen. No word was spoken, no instructions or questions about homework or midterm tests, nothing. Finally, she left with her friend for the temple. They did not chat, and walked away quietly. She came back late.

Then, when she was serving Appa, her hand began to shake, and her fingers released the hot rasam ladle right on his big toe. His leg kicked the plate in front of him, and it raced across the floor spilling rice and kootu and mango pickle all the way to the faucet screw below the washbasin. A few grains flew high enough to get caught in her hair. She did not bother removing them. Appa changed his clothes and drove off on his scooter.

She still didn't say anything.

She mopped the mess, went out to the back well and washed the rag, rinsed the plates and sat down in the backyard, beside the masher where she'd told Mallika to plant the family tree. Two steps down with her toes resting on the third. And started to cry.

When Mallika's shadow fell forward, refracted by the outdoor bulb, Janaki turned around to face the kitchen, and in a voice that was filled more with fear than with sadness, said: "My friend Kamala hanged herself today. With the same rope we bought together at the market."

MAY 1991

"A GIRL BURNED in Teynampet!"

The staff nurse sticks her head in the waiting room and then vanishes. It has taken less than fifteen seconds for her to fling this brutality at Mallika, casually, as though she was only just remarking, "Oh, you are still here," and then there is silence. For a moment Mallika can't help but think that she might have said those words out aloud, herself. But Kamala didn't die of burns; she hanged herself from the nagalingam tree. The tree Janaki could never walk by, the house she could never look up at on the way back from the temple. That was the Sripuram time.

Gone, but never gone fully.

Gayatri Chitti will not be visiting the hospital today. That thought shakes her reverie.

Mallika grabs her purse and steps out to the corridor, outside the waiting room. No sign of the nurse. She walks to the security checkpoint. The two guards are talking to the nurse, their hands spinning patterns of vehemence, and the nurse stands with absolute stupefaction, her fingers two merged peaks of horror covering her mouth.

"Did you say somebody burned in the city?"

They seem startled by her voice, and all conversation ceases. The two guards lower their heads, they are taller, and say something in unison to the nurse. Quick words, and then one of the two men walks to where Mallika stands.

"Youth Congress procession turned into a small riot near Elliots Road, ma. Some are saying a young girl committed suicide, you know, kerosene *ooththi*, pouring and burning in the middle of the road. All buses are stopping after Chetpet. Nurse amma's brother is phoning and telling just now."

Just then, the nurse comes running through the metal detectors and joins them.

"Chitti is coming on bus from Teynampet, no? How will she come now?"

Mallika doesn't answer. What if Chitti is stuck in some bus jam four stops from her origin? That would be Abbotsbury. She will never get to the hospital now.

"Did he say if the police had the situation under control?"

They look at each other as though she has asked them about the existence of God.

"Nurse amma, go and call your brother now, or ask Sridhar to turn on the TV in reception area. Maybe they are saying something on Madras TV."

Mallika watches the nurse hurry back to the other security guard and relay the message. He darts off in the direction of the main reception area, downstairs.

"Sorry," he says. His voice is different now. Not the same voice that had wondered why Chitti was not here earlier in the afternoon. Suggestiveness has been replaced with sorrow.

But sorry for what?

"So many youngsters, *ellam* Brahmin college students. Bloody politicians. Imagine a nice girl burning!"

Now the subtext of the sorrow, Mallika thinks. It's okay for un-nice girls to burn. Was this his way of confessing, just for few minutes, turning her into his confidante, she herself being a nice Brahmin girl? A strange mix of predatory thoughts mingled with palpable, though not genuine, compassion.

"I'll wait another half an hour. Let me know when you have more news. Then I will decide if I want to see Appa or not."

The way the guard had pronounced *Brahmin* and *nice*, stays with her all the way back to her seat in the waiting room. The magazine lies where she had thrown it, split and open, page down on the floor, like a dead bird on the edge of her vision. A dead bird, hiding Janaki's gold crown.

Nice, Brahmin girl, that's what everybody said of Janaki. That was the line that was repeated again and again by Gayatri Chitti when Janaki was made to play an alaapana on the veena. But when the guard said it, it seemed like a vulgarity, something both invasive and dirty. He was lamenting the burning of a luscious young girl, a girl ripe for the plucking; and her Brahmin caste gave that extra pure, nonmeat protein advantage.

Is she reading too much into it? Why is it that she is unable to believe in sympathy anymore? Why does she see betrayal in every utterance? Why does she feel like somebody else this week—somebody who is standing outside of her old self and commenting and directing her to think, dream and judge—all darkly?

If it were indeed a girl, this is a first and there will surely be more, Mallika realizes as she settles into her corner chair. Why choose burning, when there were so many other means of protest? Burning was too personal. It generated a mass outpouring of grief and horror but never changed government policy. The chief minister expressed his condolences to the family on the evening news, and then everybody prepared for and awaited the next one. Even the words in the telecast message began to seem the same, written without sincerity, tepid.

Self-immolation was, by nature, singular. One by one.

That's what sent it to the isolated incident category. And the next one came along, at another student rally, the chosen one all aflame, with their classmates watching and chanting "Stop Mandal Commission, *ozhiga, ozhiga!*" Spectacular waste. Is that what the guard was really hinting at when he said *sorry?* Sorry for the sorry state we are all in, no matter what state it is?

When she had enrolled at Women's Christian College in Madras—after Appa had finally managed to arrange a transfer to the Head Office—there had been no protest burnings or Youth Congress processions. For a few years there had been no drama (barring Gayatri Chitti's ongoing Aching Body serial) inside and outside their lives. Appa's scandal at the bank, years after Janaki's hide-the-note-and-run moment, had put that brief interval of peace in an envelope and mailed it to nonexistence. She should have seen it coming, especially after the minor rehearsal a few months before the grand finale.

One evening, when she returned from work—it was during her first probationary months at the USIS—she found him sitting in the middle of the living room. He had pushed all the furniture against the walls, and four chimney lamps were burning around him. Tube lights and bulbs from every outlet in the house lay arranged in geometric forms to his left and right.

"Appa, what is going on?" She was so exasperated that her voice caught in her throat.

"It is not what you think it is," he said, and looked up at her. "It is a test of memory. I am trying to tell, without markings, which bulb and which tube is from which room. I did not make any notes, and my eyes were blindfolded when I unscrewed them."

"What?"

"But I left the night lamp bulb in your room. You are clear."

The next morning when she confronted him and told him how worrisome she found his behaviour the previous night, he denied it had ever happened.

"You must be having a bad dream. Taking out the bulbs and sitting around with chimney lamps? What are you doing at the USIS? Writing stories?"

How quickly he lied and turned everything around, not only making her question her own eyes, but also putting her on the defensive with that barb about her job?

"I am going to have a word with Gayatri Chitti," she replied. "I am going to look for my own flat." She knew that talking to her aunt about it would only serve the latter's fake drama sensibility, and a place of her own was nice to think of, but unrealistic. She just stood there while he finished his coffee, washed the dabra and walked to take his shower. What could she do with her father? Who could she turn to? She prayed. And she cursed Janaki.

Wretched, self-serving Brahmin girls.

"ROOM WILL BE ready in five minutes, ma. Should I ask the attendant to fetch your father?"

"Seri," Mallika answers. "I'll see him. There won't be buses for at least another hour. Room number?"

"Eleven."

"Appa has been given his sedative?"

"Yes, ma," the nurse says with boredom. These questions and these answers are also another part of the Sunday visit routine. "The attendant will also keep an eye. You are knowing that but you are always asking the same. Five minutes." She does not wait for a reply.

This corridor is so different from the corridor leading to the stacks in the USIS. There it always smells like synthetic air freshener and mothballs. Here it is all antiseptic and disinfectant. Behind locked doors there are other families, daughters and mothers or mothers-in-law, most of them silent, vacant, not very different from their own private inmate. A gathering of wasted, still Sundays. The words return with every step she takes to number eleven: Janaki Asgar. Appa, Janaki is coming back. Daughters visiting mad fathers. Daughters returning to a mad past.

She doesn't have to tell him. What would he, could he, do?

Did that girl who doused herself in the middle of the Teynampet traffic—did she tell her parents and neighbours of her plans? Did she have to steal the ration kerosene, or did they actually give it to her? Did her friends all make a contribution? How many gallons? Did she hide a small note, folded in four between Leo Coffee packets?

Daughters in the middle of the road.

"Only if they want to be," Mallika mutters to herself as she pushes the door.

WALLS DON'T TALK if those within them don't. Appa has not uttered a single sound, not even a sniffle, for the past ten minutes. In the early years of his confinement she had tried to revive his memory, line it with a few more prolonged moments of clarity and coherence, by talking about chess moves, but queen to pawn three only got her so far. Bringing a chessboard might help matters along, she thought, it might make him remember his mastery of the game, revive his lost analytical self—and so she did, one Sunday a few years ago. It had the contrary effect. He pulled his shoulders in as soon as she began arranging the chess pieces, and his breathing became laboured and loud. But still he tried his best. He had managed the first few moves with interest, and then his fingers and hands began to shake uncontrollably, and he started to cry. She tried to introduce it slowly, once again, a few months later, but he had the same agitated response. She concluded that there would be no more chess games between them. It was a bridge between her and her father that had disappeared for good.

The silence today is a result of Gayatri Chitti's being stuck somewhere in the middle of the student riot. There was nothing unusual about Appa's chasing horses, for that is what she imagined him to be doing in his head (most of his utterances danced around horses as well) and she is happy for the peace. The attendant is reading *Pesum Padam* in the corner. Appa has stopped his chatter and is now lost in thought, his eyes closed and his hands making an *X* across his chest. A shield against what? Mallika wonders. He looks like a woman saint.

And what could these walls say anyway? Walls don't know incidents, only aftermaths. The walls of this grey, fluorescent-lit room, with a long metal table fitted to one wall and three folding metal chairs and one stool, was only likely to regurgitate Gayatri Chitti's rants, nothing relevant. And nothing of what she really felt when she sat in front of Appa.

Walls merely absorb. They can feel no pain.

The man in front of her remembers her only in snatches, and that too for less than thirty seconds, at any given time. He could be anybody, even Murugesan from the laundry. Remembering her only when she went back to pick up the ironed shirts and trousers, or the man on the bus with his cataract mother who got off at Taylor's Road.

Appa got off the bus many years ago. And nobody asked what happened. They just accepted it, and all the Sundays were written off.

"Appa," Mallika says. She can see her call travelling into a void that is also her father. He smiles, but says nothing. "Appa, Janaki is coming," she finishes, with a sense of relief, just relief of having got it out of the way, no matter what catastrophes of memory or total recall it may spur and let loose. She faces her father and examines his face for a tremor of sanity.

At least ask, she feels like prompting, ask so that I can answer and tell you about it, ask me, who is Janaki. And I'll take you back to that time, to that point of no return, and return again and again and again. Burning.

MA

The planning had begun six months after Kamala was found hanging from the nagalingam tree.

In those few months, the tree had assumed all sorts of sinister and bad spirit connotations. People came back from their vision of god in the temple and assembled along the compound wall, standing on the opposite footpath, and from a safe distance they gazed upon the Tree of Death. *Marana Maram*, she had heard a few mamis refer to it. Vanaja Mami went all pale when she heard about the crowds near Kamala's house ever since the horrible incident. "It can only spread more bad evil, her atma will never find peace, *paavam*, Kamala." It was always hushed and quick, as though she were wondering what evil might strike. Mallika had seen the tree but had been banned from the funeral.

It was there that they would have hatched the plan. It was a grand plan; Mallika could say that with confidence, although she had no idea what the plan was. She had heard Revathi and Janaki and Nalini Miss, their veena teacher, talking in music terms, on the way back from evening *archanai*.

"I think we should keep it Shankarabharanam. Even without the violin—" and Revathi stopped, abruptly, the word *Kamala* or *suicide* stuck in her throat, stifled before it could spill into the world.

"She had also agreed to the raga," Janaki said with gusto, switching to the third person, working around the evil spirits.

"But I am not convinced it will be appropriate without the violin component. We could make it Bhairavi, with just voice and veena component. *Nanna porundhum*," Nalini Miss, the tallest of them all, said. "But we cannot go on like this as there is a time factor."

Time factor, Mallika kept thinking for the following weeks. Did she mean the length of a raga? Those could be really long, Mallika knew that much, for she had heard Janaki play just one scale, in all its variations, for hours at a stretch on the mottamadi. She did not ask Janaki what it was that made her rehearse her lessons for prolonged periods these days. She just kept it to herself, watching, and matching words and gestures, bits of conversation she overheard walking behind the trio, now Nalini Miss instead of Kamala, and the suddenly gone giggles of Revathi. No jokes, no gossip gleaned from the film magazines. But Mallika was always slow in cluing in to subterfuge, and sometimes never.

She still didn't know what had happened the night before Gayatri Chitti left and why she had never returned for an overnight stay. She had no better idea of the woman outside Appa's door at Tirukalukundram. And the greatest unsolved mystery was the complete absence of conversation between Janaki and Appa. Everything was information or notices, as though the house were an office.

Why was it that she always gave her sister the benefit of the doubt? Why did she lack that judgment in herself, to be able to see everything before it could happen, the way Janaki could? Janaki was always full of strategies and theories. You will know everything when you are a big girl.

It was only when the veena classes were extended, one class added on Sunday afternoons (something Nalini Miss had never done before), and Janaki started to play the veena during all her spare time at home, that Mallika finally put two and two together and confronted Janaki about it.

"You are planning a special for the cultural association, I know that," Mallika announced. "Otherwise, why are you practising so hard?"

"Don't tell Appa, sariya? He thinks I am only performing music thapas for Kamala. Let him think that, *okay-va?*"
She had taken to saying that, too. Okay-va. Mixing both lan-
guages in a very ugly way.

Mallika felt included. She knew her sister's secret, and she
and Janaki were now a team.

THREE WEEKS later, after she had escorted Mallika back from
school, Janaki went straight into the kitchen and, to Mallika's
absolute surprise, started to fry achchappams. Sweet flower-
shaped fritters moulded in a cast-iron metal stencil and deep-
fried until golden brown in a hot oil wok. Janaki had done
this only once before, and even that attempt was more excitement than success, as the flowers had not turned out the way
they should have. The dough had stuck to the insides of the
mould and the flowers fell into the oil, a few circles missing,
which had made Mallika laugh.

"Imperfect flowers!" she had exclaimed, which had not
gone down too well with Janaki. Failure, Mallika had noticed
over the years, made her sister try harder with a determi-
nation that was all consuming. The stove and the silver
screen had become replacements for biology and history,
texts she never touched since the day she stopped attending
school.

"Why are you attempting this again? You were so crushed
last time when it did not turn out right." Mallika then saw the
two packets of Britannia Marie biscuits on the counter.

"What time are they coming?" she asked, sure now, putting clue and clue together, that there was to be another proposal exhibition that evening.

"Who? This time the flowers are falling correctly, can you see? I forgot to oil the *achchu* last time, that's why they did not slide off!"

The star-shaped stencil, its curves glistening with oil, sank into a whole pot of white dough and made an instant imprint of softness; then in a flash it was lifted from the pot and immersed into bubbling oil. When Janaki scooped the cooked appam with a slotted spoon, the flower was perfect. Her sister had mastered another technique, and soon the whole agraharam would know about it. How did her sister accomplish that? How was the good word spread? By one strategic and calculated move. A stainless-steel dish packed with half a dozen murukku, or fresh idli, and now even these achchappam she was frying, would make its way tomorrow to Vanaja Mami's. A telecommunication system other countries only dreamed of. Vanaja Mami would take it on from there, announcing herself as the chosen one for Janaki's delicacies, all over the agraharam. That's how Janaki's idlis became the talk around the temple reservoir: "Janaki, so talented. Janaki, the wonder girl."

"Kamakshi would have been so proud," Vanaja Mami said often. "Janaki keeps the backyard so neat, and how much housework the girl can do!" Comments like those pushed her sister further, Mallika thought. It was her own way of trading, the culinary route to a good name. She was borderline obsessive when it came to having a page in other people's good books. Why bother making achchappams if you really hated all those men who came to see you and who asked for all kinds of machinery as dowry? Did one really have to be good at all costs, even in the face of authorized humiliation? Janaki was a complete enigma.

"When did Gayatri Chitti send word?" Mallika said, moving to the door that led to the backyard. Everything in their lives was so filled with boredom and unnecessary pathos. Just the everyday family games between morning coffee and evening news were enough to make anybody go insane. Or become a martyr. Is that not what Kamala had done by using the wedding tragedy as her ticket out of this life, released from chores and criticisms, and from having to be the good girl forever?

"I thought she had given up some time ago? The proposals stopped last year?"

"It's not a proposal, miss I-know-everything," Janaki replied. "Savitri Mami and Nalini Miss are coming at five o'clock to have tea with Appa."

"Why?"

"Patience has its rewards, Miss Jane Iyer!" Janaki said, as she dropped another appam and watched it sizzle up to the surface of the oil.

IT WAS APPA who let them in that evening.

Janaki had said nothing to him, so he was dressed in his usual veshti and office shirt, but his hands, face and feet had been washed at the back well as soon as he had returned from office. Peering from the kitchen door Mallika could see her father's face expand with surprise. And he said as much.

"How surprising!" he exclaimed, a bit taken aback and still maintaining his bank manager charm. "Janaki never mentioned anything. Please come, *vango!*"

He stepped back into the room and allowed the women to pass.

"Take the *jamakalam* from the puja room and spread it in the hall," Janaki hissed in Mallika's ear, pushing her into the hall. But by the time Mallika brought the *jamakalam*, Savitri Mami and Nalini Miss had settled into the rattan sofa. Appa dragged his moda and sat in front of them.

"Tell your sister who is here and ask her to bring some coffee!" Appa tried hard not to sound terse, but Mallika could sense that he was not entirely pleased by the shock of seeing Janaki's veena teacher and Telephone Mami at the door. He liked to be dressed and groomed for every occasion.

Janaki was ready at the door. "You take the two plates. I'll bring the coffee," she said. "Don't drop it!"

"Why are they here?" Mallika asked, taking the two thalis packed with biscuits and achchappam, with Janaki a few steps behind her with the coffee dabras.

Did she see Nalini Miss wink at Janaki when she took the dabra from her sister, or did she just imagine it?

"Thank you for coming," Janaki said. "I am glad I made the achchappam!" Why was her sister pretending that she was also surprised, although she had known all along? Why lie about nothing? Mallika asked herself, putting the *jamakalam* back on the puja-room shelf.

Savitri Mami spoke first. "You know how talented your daughter is, I don't have to tell you. I've told Nalini here that you couldn't object to such a proposal, that you will say yes." She wriggled in her silk sari and bit into the achchappam.

"Yes to what? No to what?" Appa asked curtly.

"Kamala's wish was to attend the competition last year," Nalini Miss said, putting the coffee dabra on the floor. "But wish was unfulfilled because of her sudden death. Next month there is a classical music competition in Bangalore, and with your permission I would like to accompany the two girls to participate."

"But Janaki never told me!" Appa looked astonished. But quickly he changed his tone from incredulity to resolve. "When is the competition?"

"Next month, third week, eighteenth, Saturday," Nalini Miss sounded like a telegram. Her fingers circled the petals of the fritter, one word, one turn.

"If Nalini is not accompanying, I am also not agreeing. Janaki, *nanna vandhirikku!*" Savitri Mami helped herself to another, and sank back into the sofa. Mallika could hear the fritter struggling under her teeth—she crunched so impolitely.

So much power she had, all just because she had a telephone line in the agraharam. Revathi also displayed the same *thimir*, Mallika concluded. Rich Brahmin *thimir*. There she was, the doyenne and don of the agraharam, with telephone-VCR-connections to the CM, sitting in a house she had never visited, this her first and maybe last time, in her bottle green and gold bordered cotton sari, starched and hard pressed, with her face all made up and her hair tied in a tennis-ball bun, there she was sitting and chewing achchappam, as though every place in the colony belonged to her. *Yaadhum Veede, Yavarum Kelir.* Queen Savitri (undisguised) mixing and munching with her subjects.

Mallika waited to see what Appa would say. He was silent for a long time, cooling his coffee from tumbler to dabra. Janaki stood by patiently, the tray in hand, without any expression on her face. Just the way she had all along, for the past four years, when Gayatri Chitti sent proposals from Madras. Savitri Mami was no different or more arrogant than all those other mamis melded together.

Appa stood up scratching his beard. "I'll be back in a minute. Please excuse me," he said, and walked to the bedroom. He came out with his diary in hand and once again sat on the moda. The only sound during that period was Savitri Mami's chewing and crunching. Right above their heads, through the hall window, Mallika could see that the street light outside was changing. It was already sunset. Soon Appa will want his dinner.

Appa looked up from the diary after making a note, and scratched his beard with the cap end of his pen. "How much will it be costing? And you will have to take the train from Madras, and that will be Friday night? Janaki can't be away for more than three days. I know you can understand that?"

Smiles spread on their faces.

Savitri Mami and Nalini Miss looked at each other and then nodded together. "That is exactly what I was telling Nalini," Savitri Mami said, trying to raise herself from the rattan sofa. "Mr. Venkatakrishnan may be a strict man, but he also is a just man." At first, she failed, her elbow folding unexpectedly and pulling her down, but she managed to push herself more adroitly and stood up. "You can be compassionate!"

"I will be asking my personal travel agent," she announced. "They will make all the arrangements from train tickets to hotel and also taxi from railway station. No need to worry about expenses. Janaki is like my daughter. I am very happy about your acceptance, bank manager, sir!" she said, looking at Appa. She was taller and bigger than him, and older, too, perhaps. "Now, my daughter will stop her petition every day. She was always asking me to ask you."

"The girls will do us all proud, and you will not be disappointed," Nalini Miss joined in; then looked directly at Mallika and added with a smile, something very rare on her face all evening:

"It will also be a test for you to prove that you can manage without your sister!"

IT WAS AS IF an unexpected wave of goodness and gratitude had flooded the agraharam when the Brahmins were sleeping. The fact that Janaki and Revathi were going to the competition was announced at the cultural Sabha meeting. From there, the news got home, and with that the mamis got to work. Janaki and Revathi (with Mallika all but invisible behind them) were stopped constantly on the way back from the temple. Every mami from the agraharam came and said how excited they were that Sripuram Brahmin Colony girls were going for the competition.

"You go and show them what we can do!" they exclaimed. Some older mamis even came up twice, forgetting that they had conveyed their best wishes the previous week. Mallika watched Janaki's grand plan fully emerge. For days after Appa's approval, Janaki walked with a smile on her face and visions of Bangalore dancing in front of her eyes. As if she were in a Tamil film of her own. She even said so one evening herself. "Vishnuvardhan is from Bangalore!" she laughed, folding the bedsheet and pillowcases in the upstairs bedroom. Mallika had not heard that name, but she knew that it could only be a film star. Not a character in a book. Her sister had no interest in reading. "Revathi thinks he will come to the competition!"

And that's all she talked about. The competition, Bangalore, how nobody could match her and her friend when they performed the Raga Shankarabharanam.

Their secret sister pact against Appa was all but forgotten. Put behind.

Mallika noticed how Janaki now smiled when she gave Appa his coffee. How she took extra care while serving food, even asking him, "A little more . . ." something she had never done before. It was as if Appa had waved a magic wand and, by giving her a three-day break from Sripuram, had also banished all past hostilities.

Janaki seemed ready to change her opinion about him. The inmate ready to forgive the jailor.

How quickly things turned around within their Sripuram lives.

One night, after she finished her veena practice, the instrument wrapped and put away outside the puja room, Janaki walked to the hibiscus bush in the backyard, plucked and pinned a large flower in her hair, and, cupping the *pasimani malai* she seldom wore, she knelt down near the gate, her hands folded, and kissed the earth. It seemed like she was at the end of a ritual period. She was always doing something around the hibiscus bush lately. Then she walked back into the house and turned off all the lights. Slowly, Mallika crept back from the landing and got into bed. So it is a *thapas* for Kamala, she said to herself. Janaki had told her the truth, but not the entire truth.

"Come with me to the terrace," Janaki asked Mallika five days before the competition. The whole of last week Revathi had been over and they had practised on the terrace for three hours every evening. Their cause had merit. Hence, there was nothing to fear. All the neighbours were basking in vicarious success and pride, and the news of their selection in an annual Carnatic music competition had pushed all kinds of status buttons, compassionately. And the music was free for three hours.

It was a break night.

Dinner had been served, and the dishes had all been washed and put away in their place. It was dark outside, but the sky was clear and the stars could be seen above the fumes of the Sripuram Sugar Refinery. Appa left right after dinner, saying he had to go to the bank to pick up a file, and from there to the optician's, to get his eyes checked and ask for a new prescription. He had complained a few weekends ago about the chess figures blurring, and how that affected his moves.

"I have to tell you something." There was something secretive in Janaki's voice.

Far away they could hear a radio, the song coming in snatches from B Block. The activity around the temple alleys had slowed, and Mallika could see the vendors from the edge of the terrace, packing their wares and piling their carts with gunny sacks of aluminum utensils and boxes of *agarbathi*.

"One afternoon," Janaki said and stopped, as though she had forgotten what she ventured to say. She dusted a spot on the floor with the rag in her hand and then, after spreading a newspaper page on that exact same spot, she sat down.

"I met a woman called Neelaranjani."

"At Mahalaxmi Talkies?"

Mallika was ready to dismiss it as a story about another ticket lineup brawl, but all the secrecy was inappropriate for something so trivial.

"No, here in the backyard, a year after Amma's death."

They had not talked about Amma in a long time. This new woman's name had brought it back, a vocal presence discovering the house again. Amma on the mottamadi. In fact, their conversation about her had ceased a few years ago, around the time Gayatri Chitti took on the matchmaker role and the proposals started to roll in. Janaki prayed in front of Amma's photo every morning, before and after the silence around her name, and changed the garland every three days. But she never mentioned Amma or her sudden death. Kamala's suicide had also disappeared into that same speechless corner.

"She was a *kurathi*, from Marudhamalai. She and her son spent an hour in the backyard."

"Why tell me this now?"

The revelation both shocked and annoyed Mallika. *Kurathis* and Untouchables never stepped into the agraharam. Brahmins, because they are the people chosen to perform the puja rituals and interpret the Vedas, Mallika had heard the priest intone at the temple, had to maintain their purity at all times. It was their dharma.

Was Janaki making this up, like an incident from one of the matinees? Inserting her presence into a cinematic frame, a mysterious subplot. Was this what Seeing Is Believing meant?

"Because she made a prediction that I will be famous one day. Something my veena will make come true." Janaki started to unbraid her plait.

"Did you pay this woman anything?"

All the *josiars* and palmists were full of such stories, in and around the temple community, doling out daydreams to vulnerable and deprived agraharam women.

Ten-rupee Escapes.

Mallika had said a flat no when Janaki had suggested she line up and have her palm read. "Reality is better than riches," she said. "And I don't want to imagine my future. I want it to be real." Janaki had not mentioned it again.

"I gave her some pongal. She has not come by since. I wonder how and where she is."

"Did she give you that *manimalai?*" Mallika pointed to the chain of beads Janaki had taken to wearing around her neck lately. She touched it all the time, her fingers doing a quick flutter around her neck, as if making sure it was still there. She wore it even when she sat out to do the dosai batter last week.

"And how will that veena make it happen, did she say that?"

Janaki is back to pinning her hopes on her prodigious talent. Mallika watched Janaki's face closely. It had the same look she had seen many times when her noon-show dreams slowly took on shades of personal reality. At such moments, Janaki's eyes had a quick brightness, the light of her visions breaking into day.

Janaki wanted all of that, too, and said so many times.

But then, everyday routine took over, and the dream sequences stopped. After the marriage proposals dissolved, and when she got tired of all the preparation and dullness, Janaki fell silent for weeks.

"The *kurathi* said that I will play something unique, and that will make the country look at me with new eyes." The excitement in her voice was genuine. Mallika could tell that her sister had believed every word of the *kurathi*. She believed that this was her moment, the promised moment.

"What was her name, you said?"

"Neelaranjani."

Rhymes with *veenaranjani*, Mallika thought. Her sister is letting her imagination get the better of her, but there was nothing she could do to shake her out of it.

"Did you play the veena for her?"

"No. But she knew that I was a great veena player by just feeling my fingers."

Janaki looked at her open palm. Her thumb massaged her fingertips in a circular motion, slowly moving on to the next. "She could feel the string marks."

"Oh." That was all that came out. This had to be true then. It was not something Janaki would think of making up. Neelaranjani did exist, just as there were string marks on Janaki's fingers.

The veena was now a power tool. Janaki alternated between the two ways she used her music. The veena was both pride and pathos, and that is how she manipulated it. The instrument was her sign of talent, and also the cross of her martyrdom. That's why all the mamis around said at one point or another, "So talented but..." And stopped with a choke. If you listened carefully, you could hear "...such a waste," even though the sentence was never completed. That is my talent, Mallika thought, the ability to read the unsaid. I can read my sister and the people around us like a book. And I don't need a gypsy woman to come to the backyard to tell me that.

"If it has to come true, it will come true. Can I now go and read for my test?"

"Seri," Janaki replied. "They say things don't come true if you tell them to somebody. But you are my sister, and I know you will wish only the best for me." She smiled and looked up at the sky. "I'll wait here till Appa comes back."

MAY 1991

WE ALL LIVE in the past, a past that is ever-present, every moment of the day, Mallika thinks, only Appa doesn't. We live through habit, through repetition of thought and deed, when we buy brinjals or add Robin Blue drops to whiten shirts and petticoats.

He, like Janaki, has found his escape.

He chanced on it two years ago, one afternoon, when the peon walked into his room at the bank and discovered him urinating on bank files and memos, all arranged to form the visual effect of D-Day over the brick-coloured linoleum floor. It was his ticket out of reality.

What had the psychiatrist called it during a first briefing?

A dissociative fugue.

A disconnect with the world around him brought on by an extreme incident that short-circuits the brain's ability to comprehend reality. It all sounded too much like a literary analysis to Mallika. But her only question then had been: "Will he come out of it? Will he be able to engage with the world at all?"

"Oh, he is out," the psychiatrist had replied, shaking his head as if to say please understand this in the right sense. "He is fully conscious. But he converses with something that is solely in his head. He is functional. Just not thoughtful like we'd like him to be." He smiled. "It can all change, but even if it doesn't he is out of harm's way. He is just in another place."

Appa had aged, but had not improved. Disconnected— she thought often, as she thought right now while recollecting the incident—for all intellectual purposes. Appa is beyond the reach of consequences. Complete outage, to push the doctor's circuitry metaphor.

Still, whether he understood or not, it was definitely a relief to have told him about Janaki's return. Mallika doubts he would have been welcoming had he the ability to step out, this side of delusion, if that had ever been possible. Neither for that matter would he have seen the idiocy and irresponsibility of his actions ever since her departure. What could drive a man to sell his ancestral home, transfer money from client accounts (ST Cycles and Rudra Pesticides) little by little over a period of thirteen months, and throw it all to horses and jockeys? It had to be something else. Not just lunacy or arrogance. It was the complete absence of a concept, a *praknai*, a consciousness of fear.

Mallika knows that there was little pleasure or profit in contemplating how things would have been if Janaki had stayed. Could anyone see a moment of fatality in the ordinary black-and-white photograph, or presage that it could divide their destinies in such stark, nonphotogenic ways? Appa would have been the same, she knows. He would have still been addicted to his self-serving and destructive ways. And they would have both—Janaki and her—walked around the

Sripuram corners, with eyes averting the knowing glances of others and heads bowed to well-known shame.

Sometimes, Mallika couldn't help but wonder, sitting in front of him, muted and stunted by history and rage, if he had any sense of who she was. Did he see her as his daughter, or just somebody familiar who comes for a visit every second Sunday and sits in front of him with a look of disappointment for two full hours? Could he understand disappointment in any sense? Just the essence of it, with no conditions to provide examples?

The attendant gets up from his corner and whispers *"anju"* miming the number five with his fingers quickly pressing an invisible rubber ball.

Mallika rises and touches her father's shoulder. He looks up, but doesn't say anything. *"Poyittu varen,* 'pa," she says, committing herself to return just as she is bidding goodbye. Years of duty and hope and misgivings, all distilled into one phrase: *going to return.* Yes, she thinks, the past is always and already.

THE NURSE LOOKS up from her desk.

"I am waiting for you," she says, when she sees Mallika approaching. "There is no bus; all will be closed because of the riot. How will you go home? Chitti didn't come, no?"

Mallika has forgotten all about the Teynampet incident. She can only think of Appa and his bank incident.

And Janaki's return.

"No, she didn't. Any more news about the riot, Danisha?"

"Sridhar is just finishing duty downstairs; he is coming up shortly with latest news. You can walk with us; we are leaving together."

Mallika doesn't know what to say. Should she go with them? Or should she call the Samantas? They were halfway between the hospital and home; if she got there she could even spend the night. The thought makes her hesitate.

"I don't think Chitti will be coming now. It is too late. Maybe she is waiting for a bus near Pachaiyappa's College."

Just then, Sridhar, the young security guard, now out of uniform, comes leaping up the stairs. He looks freshly scrubbed and smells of Lifebuoy.

"All closed, ma. Nothing is running, we have to walk at least to Taylor's Road, and maybe buses are having special service. But TV announcer is not telling the time." There is a touch of excitement to his voice. He seems eager to get out on the street and see all for himself.

"I want to make a phone call to my office colleague," Mallika tells the nurse.

The phone rings and rings on the other end, but nobody answers.

The Samantas could be stuck in traffic, too, just like Gayatri Chitti. As she puts the receiver back on the cradle, Mallika hopes her aunt is not caught up in another self-made catastrophe, like criticizing the rioters and getting a black eye or a tight slap from a fellow passenger on the stranded bus. No more drama, please, she pleads silently. I am very, very tired.

"I'll walk with you to Taylor's Road now."

It has to be endured. Everything about the past week had been like walking into an inferno. Since the day Janaki's letter arrived at the USIS it seemed her whole world had moved into a corner of misery and memory. It is like some strange penance, she thinks, penance before the purging, a washing away of *dosham*. Even this walk to Taylor's Road due to a sudden riot is part of the process of cleansing. Next week it will be done. The assault of recurring nightmares, ghostly letters, bitter mornings and twilight burnings will be over. Janaki would have come and gone. And the national elections will be over.

The thought was salvation enough.

"I will walk with you. Sridhar can walk in front," the nurse says, and holds the door open till they pass.

MALLIKA DOESN'T KNOW the answer. How does one answer such a question: why all this division between us? For that is the question, the first six words Danisha has uttered in the last twenty minutes of the walk. Sridhar, gripping a thin, rusty metal rod from a hospital lamp, walks a few yards ahead. Thankfully, there has been no accident or broken glass on the road. She wonders why the thought of violence and the breaking of glass go hand in hand. Danisha has pulled up her sari to her shins and tucked it into her waist, reminding her of Janaki and her preparation for the caterpillars on the neem tree in Sripuram. Danisha is shorter and walks on her toes. She intuitively knows that there could be reason to run at any given moment.

They have walked past the Kelley's neighbourhood and are turning onto Balfour Road when the nurse breaks the silence with a question to which there are no quick answers.

"There can be divisions between families, so why should we be surprised by these things? Don't you watch Maha-bharatham on TV?"

Sridhar has stopped in front of a group of men waiting at the intersection. So far there has not been a single vacant auto or cycle rickshaw. The two battered taxis that have trundled by in the past few minutes have been stuffed with human bodies, seats and laps all full, with people's heads and spines curving against the Ambassador ceiling. To her surprise, not many people are on the street.

"We should wait here for a bit," Mallika says. She stops midstride. Sridhar is still engaged in his conversation with the men. Mallika can see that one in the group has a transistor to his right ear, and all the others are listening attentively to the audio spill. Then two from the group disengage and resume their walk down the road. A few moments later Sridhar turns around and walks towards them.

"Students at Pachaiyappa's College are blocking the bridge nearby Chetpet. The police are using tear gas. The radio is telling that waiting at Taylor's Road is not advisable."

"We can't wait here all night!" The nurse says with disbelief. "Everything in this country is going mad!" She can't seem to stop herself, and her sentences follow with fully formed rage. "Mad people in the asylum are sane by comparison to those who are outside! All the politicians siding with the rowdies."

Mallika waits for Sridhar to say something. He is still smiling.

"Nurse is right. We can't wait here all night. Can you call somebody or should we walk back to the hospital? How did the other shift staff get to work, then?"

"By staff bus, ma. But then driver is taking bus straight to servicing. Otherwise we are able to get dropped off," Sridhar says. "Danisha, don't say too loud, ma. It can become problem for us!"

"I can call one more time. But I have to find a phone first," Mallika says, reaching into her handbag. She pulls out her USIS department directory. Sridhar doesn't answer but looks up and follows the telephone line to its nearest installation. "That house with the black metal gate is having phone." He thrusts the metal rod into Danisha's shocked hands.

"You hold this and wait here. Be calm! I will give signal from gate if success." Leaving them in the sodium vapour haze and buzz of the single street lamp, he runs to check on the availability of a phone.

"YES, IT IS A local call," Mallika tells the man of the house. His red turban seems to float in the yellow front door light. Two children, about four or five in age, are watching Donald Duck cartoons on TV. The sound from the banter is so loud, Mallika wonders if he has heard her.

The man casts his gaze to Sridhar and Danisha, both standing right behind her.

"Why is he carrying a metal rod?" he asks.

"He was expecting some danger. It is just for protection. They both are hospital staff." She looks at Sridhar, and he nods. "Only protection," he says and smiles, as though that was the only proof of his goodness that was needed.

"I work at the American Center," Mallika gives him her directory.

"Oh, I see." The man is suddenly relieved. Then he calls into the house and says something in Punjabi. She catches the word *cha*.

"Come in and make your phone call. My wife is preparing fresh tea for you and your companions."

"COULD YOU PLEASE connect me to Mr. Ted Pope's residence," she says to the operator at the USIS. She identifies herself as part of the Programs Counselling section and reads her employee number from the directory.

"Is he expecting your call?" the voice at the other end asks. "We are not permitted to forward calls to consulate homes. Is this an emergency?"

"Yes, it is. I wouldn't call him otherwise." There is silence at the other end for a few seconds.

"I'll have to put you on hold for a bit. Please wait."

Mallika nods at Sridhar and Danisha, two eager faces watching her face as they sip tea brought out by the lady of the house. The TV has been turned down, and the children are in the bedroom with their mother. Mr. Hardip Singh is sitting at the dining table, sipping tea as well, right under the picture of Guru Nanak. A wire of coloured bulbs is the highlight of the room with its bare walls and a faint smell of urine. And the drone of a voice recording in her ears announcing all the services offered by the USIS, voiced over an instrumental rendition of *The Star Spangled Banner*. Why has everything turned out to be such a calamity, all reality and routine spinning completely out of control?

She has not touched the tea.

The operator comes back. "One moment please."

"Mall-i-ka, are you all right?" he asks.

WHILE THEY WAIT for help to arrive, Danisha and Sridhar fall silent. Both of them seem lost in their own thoughts, or maybe just exhausted by this variation on their everyday dealings with insanity. Mr. Hardip Singh has stepped out to use the bathroom. Mallika can hear the hum of the ventilator fan, with its drone of everyday exhaustion.

She can also hear the voice of a woman singing something in what she assumes is Punjabi. The mother in the bedroom singing a lullaby, her children safely tucked into bed and hidden from this lunatic world. Mallika follows the melody, the tune familiar yet foreign. It sinks into her being, massaging her head like a burning balm. She shudders with her eyes closed as she realizes that the woman is not singing in Punjabi but in English. And she keeps repeating it over and over again.

Rustic sounding, thick with age and accent, but unmistakably, inexorably, "Row, Row, Row Your Boat."

GA

After the competition, Janaki, Revathi and Nalini Miss stayed on in Bangalore for three more days. The doctor had advised them to postpone their return. Revathi was only just getting better after the severe laryngitis. Savitri Mami herself brought the news.

"And Janaki won best performance for Carnatic! My poor girl was not able to sing, that is my only regret. But, Mr. Venkatakrishnan, they are both the pride of this agraharam, and I will ask the Sabha secretary to organize a congratulatory function for everybody. Revathi can sing for that!"

Appa accepted the news with a tired smile and didn't comment on the way Savitri Mami was flaunting her influence in the colony, or the real reason behind her cultural generosity. On every occasion, Mallika had noticed, she made it a point to sing her daughter's praises. The name Revathi crept in, no matter what. Even if it happened to be just a brief conversation, for they did run into her on the way back from veena class or typing class. Savitri Mami would promptly drop the daughter name and its varied associations—from the constellation to the dirty screen of Mahalaxmi Talkies.

"Revathi is the name of a star, you know?" That was her best one, and she used it many times.

"Yes, mami," Janaki would say, quickly giving Mallika's wrist a tight squeeze, their agreed-upon signal for such everyday agraharam calamities. "She is also very pretty." Just then, it would be Mallika's cue to say, "Akka, one bathroom, *varudhu, vaa seekiram.*" Even when she had no urge to visit the backyard latrine just then. Savitri Mami would never offer them the use of her toilet, Janaki had been certain about this all along, and so far Savitri Mami had done nothing to refute that prediction.

It was the easiest getaway excuse, and Mallika knew why Janaki had agreed on it—Brahmins never allowed strangers, even if they were from the same caste—into their personal and private spaces. No matter what, the kitchen and bathroom were beyond the reach even of best friends' sisters. She was also rich and had a telephone, which meant that she could afford to be above niceties and courtesies. She even charged two rupees for allowing families in the agraharam to use the phone, which was pulled way out from the hall, its long cord curving around the edge of the front door and placed carelessly midway on the veranda floor. There was no way she was going to allow anybody into her house. Only Janaki and Kamala were allowed inside, and that too only for music rehearsals.

But now Savitri Mami had arrived at their door, journeying all the way from B Block to A Block by car. Happy horror.

"I hope they are sure about returning in three days," Appa said.

He did not look too pleased about being disturbed, having just returned from work. Luckily, he was in his office clothes: full white shirt and ink blue pants. He was standing in front of the mirror above the washbasin, and loosening his tie, when Savitri Mami had arrived. He had splashed a few hurried scoops of water from the basin tap and opened the door, still wiping his face with the white cotton towel. His face looked haggard and his eyes were blank like dark, glass marbles.

"I am glad to hear that Janaki won the first prize. But train reservations will not be a problem?"

"Appa, I'll make the coffee," Mallika said, closing her book and rising from her seat on the windowsill. *The Bostonians* could wait. Revathi was never nice to her, but she had to be nice, or there would be some criticism from Appa about insolence and ill-mannered behaviour later on.

Appa looked to Savitri Mami to ask if she would like coffee or not. But she just continued with her weight throwing, ignoring the offer. Appa shouldn't have mentioned the first prize and Janaki in the same sentence. Although he was only just repeating what she had said a few minutes ago, Savitri Mami did not take to the reiteration too well. She was not going to step down from her high horse.

"I telephoned my travel agent in the afternoon. He will call the Bangalore branch to make all arrangements for travel. The date and time he will confirm tomorrow."

She said this and made polite noises for being in such a rush. She had a charity meeting to attend ("I am very busy" suggested but not said). She waved to the driver to open the back door even before she got to the gate. He ran like a mouse, all intent and servitude, and opened the back door of the car. Savitri Mami flopped on the seat and, gathering the hem of her sari into a bunch, quickly pulled it in. The driver pushed the door shut. He ran again like a mouse and got behind the steering wheel. Appa stood at the door, watching the car leave and turn out to the main road.

Back to her seat at the window, Mallika watched Appa pull up the easy chair, loosen his tie and pull it slowly to one side and then fold the length into two and then one more time. He released the collar button and sank into the chair. He sighed so loudly she could hear it clearly as she turned the page of *The Bostonians*.

And all she could think of was Janaki winning first prize at the competition. But for some unknown reason she was not happy about it at all.

THE FIRST THING Janaki did when they returned from the music competition in Bangalore was to frame her first prize certificate. She searched high and low for some nails, having already located the hammer kept under the kitchen sink, and once she found them, she strode into the hall and nailed the frame on the side wall of the staircase. She stood back between chores, for the whole of the following week, and admired her certificate from all angles.

"Neelaranjani was right," she exclaimed one day, clutching the *pasimani malai* tightly in her hand as though she were sucking some power out of the beads. "There are people who can see the future."

"Do I have to go for the function? I have a class presentation tomorrow, so—" Mallika was not allowed to finish. Suddenly there was a chill around her, and it was that look from Janaki. It was a look that occurred at selected moments, when she could stare into the deepest chasms of your heart and shine a spotlight on the truth. It was a look that she had used and practised to perfection with Appa. A whole history of suppressed rage in a span of thirty seconds.

"Why don't you wake up early and study? The Sabha celebration will be over by nine thirty. You want me to iron your blouse?"

AN HOUR BEFORE the event for which the planning by Savitri Mami had started three days before their arrival, Janaki stood in front of Amma's photograph and prayed for a full fifteen minutes. Standing beside her, in her freshly pressed green blouse and turmeric yellow dhavani, Mallika couldn't help but notice the passage of time. The ant that had started at the edge of the floor was now steadily making its way to the top of the puja room door frame. Mallika closed her eyes again. Now it was on the top edge of the frame, creeping upside down but still with purpose and direction. Janaki never once opened her eyes.

She could have been a mannequin in the sari shops on Clive Road, wearing her Proposal Is Coming kota silk, and an extra span of mallippoo in her hair. Mallika always found the smell of jasmine too sweet to bear, but did not say so when Janaki had pinned a smaller length to her hair and clipped it with a hairpin. Something had changed in Janaki. There was a sudden burst of superiority and spirituality from the day she had stepped off the train. Bangalore Mail had delivered a transformed female: Janaki, with all excesses to the power of ten.

Finally Janaki opened her eyes.

"Appa said he will come straight to the hall from the bank. I'll check the kitchen windows one final time, and then we can leave."

When they stepped into the school auditorium, which the Brahmin Sabha often rented for Tamil dramas and dance programs, everybody was in his or her seat. Savitri Mami was already on the stage, talking to the Sabha secretary. The school principal, Mrs. Manoharan, was talking animatedly to Nalini Miss.

"Late or not coming. Maybe not coming," Janaki said. No name or role was mentioned. Mallika knew from that signature tone that Janaki could only be thinking of one person. Their father.

Appa was not there or else he would be right in the front, smiling, nodding and being his official self with all the important people from the agraharam. Whenever he was outside the house in his work shirt, pant and tie, he was always in control. He had a show-off quality, although lately it had all begun to seem a bit over-rehearsed and overproduced. Like those children's programs on Sunday TV. It had taken Janaki only minutes, with a quick glance, like a panopticon gliding all over the auditorium and seeking something amiss. How did her sister weigh, judge and dismiss all that mattered only to her?

Gayatri Chitti too had a similar manner, but hers was more self-serving. Janaki, on the other hand, manipulated situations more selectively, making sure that all the emotions were perfectly balanced, but you still saw the spearhead in the sentence, definitely burning. And Appa was her favourite target since Gayatri Chitti had stopped her overnight visits to Sripuram.

"Janaki is here now! We can begin!"

Mrs. Manoharan clapped her hands, the way she did to quieten the student assembly before the morning school prayer. Janaki quickened her steps to the stage. The Sabha secretary directed Mallika to the two seats reserved for her and Appa in the front row.

As soon as Janaki had taken her seat next to Revathi on the stage, Savitri Mami walked up to the mike and started her "grand welcome to everybody to this function of pride for the Sripuram Brahmin community..." and then the sound began to vibrate and the mike screeched, sending a shiver up everybody's spine.

Savitri Mami took a few startled steps to the inner stage, as if she were under attack by a swarm of bees.

Revathi got up from her seat and boomed, "I want no trouble during my song. Make sure about that, Secretary Mama!" With a voice like that why would she need any more amplification? Mallika thought. She was surely over her laryngitis.

Soon, the school electrician, who had stepped out for a bidi, came into the auditorium from the fire exit beside the stage, bringing with him a strong tobacco stench. He fiddled with a few wires, and adjusted a tuner knob, and then said something in the Sabha secretary's ear.

"He says it is okay now, but asks you to stand a few inches away from the mike, and not to speak into it loudly."

Savitri Mami couldn't contain her anger.

"There's is nothing wrong with my tone," Savitri Mami said, this time standing back from the podium as instructed. "This mike is from Ali Baba's time!" Everybody laughed.

Janaki laughed as well, touching her forehead, her three middle fingers pressed half an inch above her eyebrows. Sitting in the front row, Mallika discovered, made all gestures on the stage more pronounced.

The angle revealed all sorts of details and visual deformities that were never possible when you spoke to people face to face. She could also see the white petticoat under Savitri Mami's dark red sari, and Nalini Miss's snapped strap in her black sandals. Then Janaki touched the same spot above her eyebrows again.

Ever since her return from Bangalore, that quick press and release of fingers meeting forehead had become an unconscious reflex. Or maybe it was conscious, just like her spirituality and belief in her supreme powers, as though she were Joan of Sripuram who kept hearing a *kurathi*'s voice predicting greatness of self and glory of God, rationalized and assumed to be a virtue. And the three-finger gesture was perhaps actually a salute. All part of the new, triumphant, invincible persona that was picked up on the tracks between Bangalore and Madras, and the bumpy highway bus route to Sripuram.

What had happened to Janaki in a matter of seven days could be summed up as the birth of a new movement with an unspoken but clear slogan, Winning Changes Everything.

Savitri Mami told the whole audience of Brahmins and their friends about her daughter's plight and suffering, and how because of bad *shani*, the agraharam was deprived of another gold medal, for had Revathi been able to sing at the competition, there could have been no contest. Saturn factored, now it was all the agraharam's misfortune, all their collective, crazy stars, but Mallika was yet to hear a sentence praising Janaki, who had won the prize and had come home all powerful.

At least in her own mind.

Tired of the proceedings already, Mallika looked at the vacant seat beside her. There was still no sign of him. Was it deliberate, this snub? But why would he, after being so out of character by allowing Janaki to go in the first place? He should only be happy that she'd returned with the trophy, and made him great by association? She'd given up following the exchanges and cold fronts between Appa and Janaki. It fluctuated from tolerance to amity, impasse to hostility, all so rapidly that sometimes it was hard to tell if it was a truce or an icy snap. They never really talked to each other the way Mallika and Appa did.

But there was silence, too, on those chess nights in the hall. Maybe, he'd noticed Janaki's new airs over the past two days. And if it was the big framed certificate hung on the wall, Mallika agreed that it was something to be upset about. Janaki should not be so vain, or she could have at least asked Appa for permission to hang it before doing so. But she had never asked him for anything, just knew what to do and what not to do, full paragraphs of instructions encoded in his body language. Mallika always marvelled at her sister's tact and composure, only now the balance had tipped. Now she had made up her mind that she was not going to play the intimidation game anymore. And she had her certificate to prove her worth.

Appa arrived five minutes into Revathi's varnam, which had taken fifteen minutes to get going (after Savitri Mami's long-winded speech in which she accused the local Tamil press of having an "anti-Brahmin bias" and how her request for coverage had been politely turned down as "unsolicited"). Mallika had given up on Appa making an appearance. But just as Revathi was moving into an exploration of the first line of the krithi Nee Dayaradha, Mallika saw his figure at the side door.

The doorman pointed to the metal chair, for that's what they were, of the folding type, multipurpose, so that the same chair could be used, rearranged, for staff conferences and then folded and stacked up when the school's science fairs, yoga practice and music rehearsals resumed every term. In fact, their fate seemed to be more and more stacked up than used.

Mallika was still thinking about the chair vacant beside her when from the corner of her eye she saw Appa—crouching along the edge of the stage while holding his briefcase in one hand and his tie in the other—come running to his seat. She could smell the sourness of his day as soon as he sat back in his chair.

For the following twenty minutes they sat silently and listened to the whole composition. A brief murmur settled into sudden wordlessness. Revathi sang her Rehearsed But Cancelled Because of Laryngitis raga, and soon everything and everybody was touched with a fleeting sense of calm.

A WEEK AFTER the event, on their way back from typing class in the morning, Janaki stopped by to visit Nalini Miss. "I won't be long, just have to pick up some music notes from the competition," she said quickly. "You wait near the gate. I'll be back soon." Soon was nearly fifteen minutes. Mallika clicked the stopwatch she had been carrying to time her typing speed. She was managing to type a balance sheet, debtor and creditor sections and figures perfectly tabulated as per previous exams, but still all in little over an hour. That was not good enough. She had to get it down by at least ten minutes. The exam date was coming closer by the day.

"Let's go," Janaki said, rushing but blushing a little. She had a manila envelope, which she held with both hands clasped against her breasts.

"What's in the envelope?" Mallika asked.

"Just what I told you before. Notes."

And Mallika watched as Janaki rubbed the spot on her forehead with the edge of the envelope. She did it as though she were shielding her eyes from the sun's glare. But the gesture gave away more than that. It had a cluster of stamps in the corner, and bold letters that read —SONAL. By the time they stepped into the agraharam and turned into the block Mallika had guessed what the preceding three letters could be.

Fate is a fish on a fisherman's hook. Fate is a formula that never fails. Fate is an opening and a trap door.

In an eight-by-eleven-inch manila envelope, it can be a secret that was bound to spill out.

There was no other way of looking at the event after it had occurred.

What else could have prompted Appa, at that particular moment, to walk in from the veranda that Sunday morning, while Mallika and Janaki had walked to the temple for the morning *archanai*, to look through Mallika's notebook for a blank page to scribble an address from the newspaper, and instead discover a photo of a film star kissing Janaki on the forehead, right above the left eyebrow, and Janaki's obvious pleasure in the moment. Fate is a black-and-white photo she had hidden from the rest, just to see it again and again pretending she was reading her school notes.

And it was fate that fell to the floor when Appa lifted the notebook, and it was the voice of fate he heard in the line at the back of the photograph:

I'm already yours. Asgar.

AFTER DROPPING Danisha and Sridhar at the corner of Arts College and Mount roads, Ted Pope drives to the marina, taking the circuitous but safer route to Mylapore. He knows this city, just like a local person, although under normal circumstances he would be chauffeur driven. It was the driver's day or evening off, presumably. Mallika was just thankful somebody had come to fetch them. The lullaby had made the last half hour at Mr. Hardip Singh's house unendurable. When Ted Pope had opened the door so that she could sit in the front seat of the car, for a moment she had wondered if Danisha and Sridhar read more into it. The ability to amplify simple and meaningless gestures into sagas of scandal and honour was culturally generous in its sweep across castes and class. That much one could safely assume. The melodrama of it all only varied in degrees of effect and interpretation.

Street lamps, for it is already dark outside, fall into luminous pools on the windscreen as the car glides through Mount Road.

"Was there really a riot in the city?"

The main road seems normal, and there are few cars or autorickshaws on the road. It is already eight in the evening. Mallika hopes Gayatri Chitti is back safely in her apartment. She'll have to use Mrs. Amaldoss's phone to call Chitti's neighbour and request them to go around the corridor and knock on the door to make sure. Maybe Chitti never left her apartment, decided not to go to the hospital because of arthritis or some sprain on her left knee, which had been bothering her for the past three years. Can there not be something called Fatal Default? Or Wisdom by Chance?

"On my way over to pick you up it was under control in the hot spots. There was a bit of arson, looting, around Nandanam." He slows on the word, but gets it right.

"My aunt was to meet me at the asylum. She lives around there." Where was Gayatri Chitti?

"Who's in the asylum?"

"My father." She wonders if she should go on or wait for another question. Ted Pope doesn't ask it immediately. He waits for a few seconds, and then says, "I must confess, I didn't have a clue."

"It is not the sort of thing people go about telling people if there is no need."

"You got me there."

Mallika does not fully understand what he means, but she assumes it must be an American phrase for *that's true.* Last week, one of her interview candidates had asked for the full university fall *skeddule.* Then also she had not been sure if she had heard right. Why would somebody named Krishna Prasad, raised in Coimbatore, sporting an inch of viboo-thi between his eyebrows, feel compelled to say it like an

American? Was it the USIS environment that prompted such mispronounced desires?

"Would you mind if we stopped here, near this upcoming statue to your right? Just for a few minutes?" The air conditioning in the car, after the breezeless confines of Mr. Hardip Singh (he had jotted down her work phone number and said he would call next week to check if everything was fine with her and Gayatri Chitti) suddenly makes her feel cold.

"Sure," Ted Pope says, and parks the car close to the footpath off the main road.

"I'm sorry, but I was feeling a chill from the air conditioning."

"Oh, you should have said so," he says, with genuine alarm. "Would you like me to roll down the windows so that you can get some fresh beach air?" He turns off the fan.

"That would be nice, if it's not an inconvenience." Is she losing all sense of proportion? Ted Pope is the head of the whole department, and here she is treating him like a driver. Stop here, do this, don't ask.

The breeze, blowing in from the Bay of Bengal, carries with it a salty, sand-scented punch. The car is at least a mile away from the beach, but snatches of conversation drop into the silence like broken glass bangles into a pond.

"Feeling better?"

"Yes. Much," she says. It would be wonderful if somehow she could just move, prolong, lease the night into a few days or months, she thinks. Suspend everything in her life, lock it all in a steel-reinforced chest and drop it halfway into the bay, and then sit, endlessly, or at least till all the sands of the beach slip through an hourglass, and listen to lapping of the waves.

"Why is she pointing to the buildings?" he says without warning. "I mean that statue, what's her story? Is she angry about something?" Has Ted Pope read her thoughts of escape? Why would he otherwise ask about the statue, a moment in his life that might never have occurred had she not asked him to stop the car five minutes ago? Was it his way of saying a little peace and distraction would do you a world of good; you've had a day from hell?

"That's Kannagi," Mallika says. She lowers her head to get a better view of the statue from the car windshield, stretching the straps of the seat belt. "She's a celebrated heroine from Tamil literature. Known for her chastity and her fidelity."

"Which period?" He turns down the car radio, and presses a button on his side of the door and the back windows go down automatically.

The breeze rushes in and fills the car with a new layer of saltiness. Behind the statue, down on the sands, a row of vendors grills fresh corn and peanuts and hawks coconut mango chickpeas with tamarind chutney.

She remembers coming to this very spot, just once with Appa during their first months in Madras. It seemed like a ceremony now, like losing their Sripuram history in the damp sands of the Marina. He had let her stand in the water till she had had enough.

"The Sangam Period. Third century A D." She presses the seatbelt to release, but not hard enough. Ted Pope reaches for it with his hand. "Here, let me do it for you." It snaps, and the straps slide back across her breast, the metal making a small sound against the door panel.

"Would that be during the Cheran Dynasty?" His knowledge of Tamil kingdoms surprises her.

"I'm not an expert, but I had to read a few books on South India before my posting here. Actually, only two books. And I only remember the kingdoms and the corresponding centuries. Nothing about Tamil literature."

His face breaks into a boyish grin.

"I have a T-shirt that says *Don't I Look Like I Know It All?* But I'm not wearing it tonight." He laughs.

That's a fact. He is wearing a dark blue shirt, grey pants and a brown cut-sleeve vest, maybe a gift from some Indian politician. She can smell some aftershave cologne and wonders if that's what got him through the crowds and barricades on his way to meet them.

Did the crowds part, and if so, how much of it was due to this musky foreignness of smell, hair and Coca-Cola English?

"I am not an expert either," Mallika replies. "And I know the story well because my si—" She stops. "It is a story that every young girl in Tamil Nadu is taught from a very early age. It is based on a local myth, not very well known by girls from other states. Surprisingly, it has held on to its power inside the language."

"So it will be like Homer or Milton?"

"Homer is a closer parallel," she says, wondering why he seems so genuinely interested. What did she really know about Ted Pope's interests? He knew her active passion had always been reading. It was all there under a tabulated heading on the resumé she had typed herself one afternoon in the Bank Quarters of Chetpet.

Ted Pope falls silent. He presses a button again from his side of the door, and a glass opening in the roof pulls back smoothly to reveal a rectangular piece of the sky above. A crow lands on Kannagi's pointing finger and begins to caw. Lost in the night, and looking for signs of a companion or scavenging colleague.

"As the crow flies," Ted Pope shakes his head. The light catches his hair, and it looks like a mesh of tinted gold straws, fine and long.

"So am I going to know what makes her so angry?"

"Kannagi was a merchant's daughter married to another merchant's son, Kovalan."

"Is the beach named after him?"

"No, that ends with an *M*."

"Carry on."

Mallika closes her eyes and sees those evenings, two years after Amma's death, the nights when Janaki told stories, filled with all sorts of musical and mythological elements, verbatim screenplays of her days and nights in Abirami Palace. Relived under the canopy of a smog-filled night on the Sripuram terrace.

How many times had she heard different, more embellished versions of Silapadhikaram and Kambaramayanam?

"For a few years Kannagi and Kovalan lived a happy, prosperous life. Then one day, on a visit to another city on business, Kovalan falls in love with a courtesan named Madhavi. She becomes his mistress, and he lavishes all his wealth on her. He abandons Kannagi and begins to spend all his days and nights with Madhavi."

"Oh, it's one of those hell-hath-no-fury-like-a-woman-scorned stories," Ted Pope says with clever certainty.

"Not quite," Mallika says.

"Oh. But I shouldn't interrupt."

"During a romantic moment with Kovalan, Madhavi sings a song to please him. However, the song is about an absent lover. Kovalan accuses her of having thoughts about another man and leaves her in disgust. He returns to Kannagi, who is filled with happiness to have her husband back."

"Nice," he smiles. "I mean, this is so much like Penelope accepting Ulysses after he's romped around with all those sirens."

"Kovalan wants to restart his business, but he has been such a spendthrift, he has no capital. They both decide to sell one of Kannagi's anklets. He goes into the city of Madurai to find a customer around the same time as the queen's anklet goes missing. All the guards are sent out to find the thief, and the chief commander, who is the real hand behind the robbery, points to Kovalan in the market place, Kannagi's anklet in his hand, and arrests him."

Mallika pulls her sari around her to keep warm. She speaks in a low voice, audible but not too energetic.

"The king gives his orders, and Kovalan is beheaded. News of this atrocity reaches Kannagi, and she walks into the court of King Nedunchezian with her other anklet in hand. She is actually pointing at the king," Mallika says, ducking once again to take a look at the statue. The crow has flown away.

"So how does it end?"

"Kannagi asks the queen to break her anklets, for therein lies the truth. These ancient anklets were hollow and filled with gems and pearls," Mallika explains, showing him the breadth of the ornament with her fingers. "The queen has pearls in her anklets. The first one shatters on the royal floor and reveals pearls. The second one breaks into a scattering of rubies. Kannagi looks up at the king, fiery eyed and all full of righteousness, and breaks her other anklet in full court. Rubies. The king, realizing his hastiness and the miscarriage of justice, dies instantly. The queen, shocked by the king's sudden death, dies soon after. But Kannagi is not satisfied. She walks into the city and burns whole neighbourhoods by just staring at the buildings. Soon a good part of Madurai is up in flames. A divine goddess intervenes, calms Kannagi and takes her to heaven to be with Kovalan."

"For a story like that to become a myth for young Tamil girls..." he says.

"It's about the purity of being a faithful married woman. Otherwise there is no way the violence can be justified. And Kovalan would not be martyr."

"Surely nobody lives like Kovalan and Kannagi anymore."

"Living like them can send one to the asylum," she says, thinking of Appa. "Could you please drop me at my apartment? I should be back." She reaches for the seatbelt and this time it locks in without a problem.

"I really don't know how to thank you," she says. Ted Pope starts the car and presses the panel buttons to roll up the windows and close the sunroof. He leaves the front windows open.

"You can," he replies, turning the car right onto the road to Mylapore. "Take the exchange. Save my budget. And see the world." He chortles at his own simplicity. "That sounds like an ad slogan for some airline co-op or something."

Mallika does not respond. She smiles. "Left turn here," she says, directing him to her street.

"I will not be in on Tuesday. I have already had a word with the head counsellor," she says, unbuckling her seatbelt and opening the car door. "And I will give it some serious thought."

She waits at the apartment gate and watches his car turn onto the main road. Then she climbs the stairs to the second floor, the voice of Lipstick Rita and the nine o'clock news buzzing through the neighbours' doors.

A CRIMINAL, selfish, mad father and a caustic, egotistical and irresponsible aunt: why do they have to be her burden? As difficult as it was to say the word, that's what they were—only their pleasures, pains and losses mattered. A responsible man till the day his first daughter had skyrocketed from zero to heroine, Appa had not tapped into his subconscious until then.

Janaki's departure had lowered a ladder into those depths, one rung at a time. After the bank scandal, the magistrate in the Madras high court had ruled that Mr. Venkatakrishnan had demonstrated "irrationality beyond words" and would be put under psychiatric observation. The bank settled for half the sale of the Sripuram house (already a collateral submitted by Appa in another scheme with a rival bank), and the police closed the file. Appa was sent to the Institute for Mental Health, better known as the mental hospital.

Chitti had no subconscious. Or if she did, it did not manifest any newer shades that hadn't been previously visible. The physical was her only domain. The alpha, beta and meta in her life were also about the physical—aches, tingles and chronic cosmetic addictions. It was a small mercy that she had given up patting Nycil on her face, which, with the sweat-congealed, prickly heat powder stippling her face, made her look like a science-fiction bad seed. Now she applied minimal makeup, just pencilled brows and eyeliner eyes. A statement, if only to an audience of one, that she had sacrificed her "worldliness" (by giving up the Nycil foundation) and taken on something resembling selflessness.

Even without the mask, nothing changed.

Except, after Appa was confined to the hospital, she agreed to a percentage cut from her monthly salary (which she now regretted), which was only fair since she had been an accomplice in Appa's schemes and gambles. A darker-in-complexion-and-paler-in-ambition Lady to Appa's veshti-wearing Macbeth. Her last demonstrated selfless moment had been when she voluntarily went out of her way to share his medical expenses.

Mallika had been thankful. It gave her two hundred rupees to put away in a savings account every month. Something she had never told Chitti. But for that, she got used to Chitti's ways. It was like having a relationship with a woman who was always around but could easily be made invisible and shut out. Soon Chitti's complaints and commentary became banter, and soon forgotten. Chitti had not been a liability, just a persistent itch. You learned to live with it.

Janaki was right on that, too: Eczema Chitti.

The neighbour comes back to the phone to tell her that there is no answer from Chitti's apartment, but that she can hear the rattle of the pedestal fan from behind the door. "Maybe fast asleep. I'll leave a note saying that you called. Don't worry!"

Mrs. Amaldoss repeats the same phrase with added religiosity. "Don't you worry, my girl," she says, seeing Mallika to the door. "Jesus is taking care; all is well. You can come and telephone any time!"

THE COLD WATER, falling in uneven streams from the lime-clogged shower, still is calming. It chills the thoughts of the day and releases her skin to a tingling freshness. She imagines Appa, Chitti, Revathi, Ted Pope, The Girl Who Burned in Teynampet, Kannagi, Kovalan, All of History of Current Consciousness—everything washed and scrubbed and lathered, and slowly leaving her body, like grime from under a roadside hawker's wok, Mysore Sandalled from every pore, and draining into the municipal gutters.

Except Janaki.

Neither washed up nor washed away. Yet.

Whatever the case may be, there was no possibility of her arrival trumping her departure.

And it will be over soon. Mallika turns off the shower and reaches for the towel. Goodbye, sister.

R I

Kausalya Suprajarama...

Sri Rama, endearing son of Kausalya, wake up my dear! The day is here, and you have duties to perform, so please wake up, dear!

It began like every other morning with the pristine invocation of M.S. Subbulakshmi, spooling from the tape recorder low but clear in every corner of the house. It began at six AM on the dot, the same way, the first alarm of the morning. By seven, breakfast would be ready, lunch boxes would have been packed and the tape recorder will be turned off. She could lie in bed, or she could revise her notes for the class presentation on the Swaraj Movement later that afternoon. But her head feels heavy. Suprabatham fades into a faraway place in her ear.

Eeshathprapulla Saraseeruha . . .

Dawn is here; the flowers are opening to the day. . .

Mallika drifts into sleep, just one more hour, I'll be up by seven, her head sandwiched between pillows, pressing into quiet once again.

When she wakes, at ten, her world, their world, is a furious place. But she only knows and wants more sleep now; just one more hour feels good.

THERE WAS NO music.

She remembered being awake for a bit, hearing the distant voice of M.S. Mami, and then she remembered her head being heavy and a pillow pressing on top of her ears. Now it was in her arms, and she doesn't remember how it got there.

Mallika clutched her pillow, squeezing every ounce of comfort she could draw from the rectangular cotton cover. She had to be at school! She jumped out of bed and rushed to the bathroom. Why hadn't Janaki awoken her? The room was bright, the sun pouring in from the window and across the bottom part of her bed. Her feet felt warm on the cold cement floor. What time was it?

When she stepped out of her bedroom, all showered and uniformed for school and her hair woven into a rush-hour plait, she was convinced that it must be nine o'clock. The clock in the hall showed ten minutes after ten.

There was no noise from the kitchen. That was the reason for the silence. And Appa's door was still closed. The morning paper sat, untouched, on the hall moda.

Mallika walked into the kitchen, and the smell of coffee decoction welcomed her. Janaki must be in the backyard, doing something around the tulasi plant. She was doing more and more of it since the day Appa discovered the secret photo.

Everything had turned into such a big house arrest for Janaki since, and Appa had become another man. Gayatri Chitti had arrived last Sunday, and there had been severe arguments between the two. Appa burned the photo and agreed to get Janaki married to the next proposal that came her way. Janaki kept saying that it was not what they thought and that note was what a film star would write to please a fan. It had no meaning, she kept repeating, it only takes the meaning you put into it. But they had not listened. Appa had even gone to Nalini Miss's soon after and had a heated exchange with her. Janaki was ordered to bring back her veena from the music teacher's home, where it had been all along—as the prize-winning instrument—garlanded every day.

Her music lessons were terminated, and she had been under the surveillance of Vanaja Mami while Appa and Mallika were away. Janaki had only been able to go out in the morning to the milk depot. Gayatri Chitti had decided this: Vanaja will keep an eye during the day. Four in morning was too early for Appa, and Mallika was young and that was that.

They had both also been instructed to keep a constant vigil till she ferreted a proposal from somewhere. We've got to get her out of the way before the word of her kiss with a Muslim man spreads. And it will, Gayatri Chitti intoned, standing right in the middle of hall downstairs, for there will be copies of this photograph, and film magazines will soon find it.

To which Janaki shot back: "You should talk! You didn't even spare your sister!"

That's when Appa had slapped Janaki right across her face.

"If it has no meaning what was it doing under the mattress where your sister found it? Isn't that where you found it?"

Mallika had just stood there. She had started to cry, sobs shaking her whole body. And then she was instructed to go to her room.

After Gayatri Chitti left, vowing to return soon with a made-to-marry man in tow, Janaki had fallen into a long, calm silence. She hadn't said much, had not even accused Mallika of stealing the photograph that had made everything so miserable for everybody. But what could Mallika do now to make the photo go back into the envelope and find its original place under Janaki's mattress? The photo had fallen from *her* school notebook! She couldn't think of anything else. Janaki had brought back the veena and had never played it again. All the happiness on winning the music competition was now a distant memory. Janaki had not even stepped out to buy the groceries. Appa did that for the past few weeks, stopping by the Sripuram market on the way back from work. Janaki only left the house for the milk in the morning.

By five thirty, if Vanaja Mami didn't see a kolam in front of their gate, she had been instructed to come by immediately to wake Appa.

That had also been Gayatri Chitti's thinking, and she had found a willing ally in Vanaja Mami, who was all for keeping young girls under control. She blamed cinema and film magazines for every social decadence, and it was proof, she'd agreed during the contract signing and duty-appointing meeting in the hall, after all, this "Asgar-gisgar" is a Muslim actor, illaiya? She'd conveniently forgotten all the free concerts on the terrace that had been enjoyed by everybody around without reservation. Not to mention all the extra bowls of ladoos and payasam that Janaki had taken across to mami and her lively-as-damp-firewood mama.

She must be in the backyard, walking around the tulasi.

Mallika peered through the back window. There was no movement on the cement platform. Janaki was not at the gate either. The kitchen door that led to the backyard was latched and bolted. In the hall, an *agarbathi* burned at Amma's photo, and an easy lotus kolam decorated the usual spot on the ground outside.

Janaki must be at the temple; that's why she is not here. Mallika gave up on making it to school till after the lunch break. Students were not allowed to walk into class at their will, and if they did so, they had better have a good reason. Her Swaraj presentation was not until two thirty, the second hour of the afternoon. By then Janaki would be back. In fact, if she were indeed at the temple, she should be back by now. It was nearing ten thirty, and the morning *archanai* would have been done by nine thirty. Even if Appa forgave her going to the temple, he would never forgive her casual arrival. Janaki should know that. What was she to do? Mallika sat down on the moda, deciding to give it ten more minutes before she woke Appa.

Mallika knocked on Appa's door. She heard his groggy but still rude *"Aahn, Varen!"*

Appa opened the door wearing his knee-length, blue and white–striped underwear and a vest worn the wrong way in a hurry.

"Vandhu . . . Janaki," Mallika was suddenly terrified to utter the words.

"Where is she?" Appa was fully awake. He immediately focussed on Janaki's whereabouts.

"She's not in the backyard, but the coffee is made," Mallika said, her gaze on the floor, not wanting to look up to him and see the Tantex label of the vest.

"What time is it?" he said, walking to the washbasin. He turned the tap and splashed water on his face.

"Ten thirty, 'pa," Mallika answered, "and I'm already late for school."

She resented having to be Janaki's guardian. Who was the older one here?

"What?" Appa scowled. "I am also late for the bank!"

"She might have stopped by at Nalini Miss's, after going to the temple," Mallika offered.

"I hope that is not the case," he said, subduing the anger in his voice but failing to control it fully. "It is that headstrong woman who has instilled all this *thimir*, this stubborn attitude. Don't you forget who gave your sister the photo from that disrespectable man!"

He squeezed some toothpaste onto his pointing finger and quickly wiped his teeth, too much in a rush to squeeze it onto a proper brush, which was sitting on the small ledge of the mirror above the wash basin. Mallika turned away but did not move.

"You will have to stay here and look after the house until she gets back. I'll have a word with Vanaja before I go to the bank."

He showered and dressed and drank a quick dabra of coffee in the kitchen, his mind fully alert. Mallika went back upstairs to her room, got out of her uniform and unhooked her home clothes from the hanger behind the door.

Just as she was tucking in her dhavani and bringing its edge around her hips in a semicircle, she heard Appa open the gate and push his scooter out the gate. When she looked out the window, she saw him open Vanaja Mami's house gate.

He returned in a few minutes and started his scooter. Without being told a word, Mallika knew that the first thing he would do on arriving at the bank would be to place a call to Gayatri Chitti. And then there would be no escaping yet another, full blown—and coming to blows—argument between Janaki and their aunt.

Janaki had better be back home by then.

BUT SHE WASN'T.

Minutes slipped into hours, and soon the inevitable happened. Vanaja Mami came to the door.

"That girl is determined to give the whole community a bad name," she said, all her caste concerns released into long fingers of frustration, which she kept clasping and unclasping like two irreconcilable realities.

It was as though the whole house had gone cold all of a sudden. The walls looked damp, even though they were not, and every corner, from the cement terrace right up to the bougainvillea around the veranda, seemed stifled by an air of certain calamity.

"Your mother is lucky she is not alive to see this," Vanaja Mami said, positioning herself in front of Amma's photo. She scrutinized the photo with a long stare. If Amma were alive everything would have been different, Mallika had felt like saying, but what did she really know about Amma? Hadn't it been Janaki who taught her everything, from multiplication tables to the preparation of morkolambu? What will happen if Janaki did not come back? Who will forgive her and love her again like nothing had happened?

"I will go to Savitri Mami and see if she has any news. Does she know about this? Did your father talk to Revathi?" Vanaja Mami started to rehearse her questions as she walked out the door. Putting the latch back on the gate, she took a moment's breath and said, "I can't believe that last night she brought us some *payasam*, and this morning she is nowhere to be seen. This must be what they call *kaliyugam!*"

Why do these women all talk as if they were reading from the same script? Mallika thought, bolting the front door and giving up on the possibility of the afternoon and the Swaraj Movement presentation. Appa will have to write a letter explaining why she had missed classes.

THE BELLS AT the temple started to jangle for the evening *archanai*, and still there was no sign of Janaki. Mallika had spent the whole afternoon at the window. She had unpacked her lunch box and eaten the curd-rice prepared by Janaki that morning, all the while seeing Janaki at some bridge, ready to jump. For a moment she even thought that the ghost of Kamala, to whom Janaki had dedicated her prize at the competition, has possessed her sister.

But that seemed impossible. Janaki had not said too much at all.

And Mallika knew that *aavis* talk through the possessed person. Her head hurt, and she felt nauseous whenever she laid her head on the pillow. So she sat near the window, waiting for the gate to be unlatched, waiting for Janaki to walk back into the house, and say, "I forgive you, *kutty*. Come, I'll walk you to school and explain everything to Manoharan Miss."

Vanaja Mami came by once again at around four, right after the second delivery of milk. Mallika saw her talk to a few mamis at the gate when she opened the door. The other women had walked away and then she said, "Savitri tells me that Revathi says she knows nothing about Janaki's disappearance. She tells me to tell you to tell your father that he should go to the police if she is not returning by evening *archanai*. Are you listening?"

The bells kept clanging.

The key! Mallika thought, and her mood changed. If Janaki had taken the spare key with her, then it would mean that she had every intention of returning. She took the spare key with her in the morning, on her round to fetch the milk.

Mallika looked at the clock. Appa would return in twenty minutes. She ran to the kitchen and opened the rice and spice cabinet. Neatly lined stainless-steel boxes with lids. Janaki kept the key under one of these. Mallika quickly lifted each dabba and looked under the lining. The key was not there. Janaki could have changed the place recently. She ran into the hall and picked up the moda. That should give her the height she needs to reach the second shelf, where Janaki kept rice, lentils, wheat flour and dried chilies, all wrapped in individual plastic bags. Mallika stood up on the moda and ran her hand under the bags. No key.

As she climbed down from the moda, her eye caught something on the lower shelf she had missed the first time. It was a melon-coloured envelope, folded in two and inserted between two packets of ground coffee in the corner.

Mallika pulled out the envelope, and the spare key fell to the floor.

After Appa had burned camphor in his right palm, and the whole house had fallen still, Mallika crept into the kitchen, hungry and holding Janaki's letter in her hand, and drank a full jug of water. It did not satisfy her hunger, but it drowned the fear that had lined her stomach the whole day.

Appa had gone to his room and bolted his door. There was nothing to eat, except really sour curd rice, which had already done its bit to churn her stomach that afternoon. Mallika refilled the jug and drank more water.

What would happen now? Would it be her turn to give up school and start cooking? She still couldn't believe that all that was happening was actually happening. From where had Appa picked up the camphor-swearing act? Had he seen it on TV? Or had he made it up on the spot? His palm must be burning by now, she thought, as she put the jug down. If he didn't apply antiseptic soon, it could turn infectious. But he had turned and walked away and locked himself in his bedroom. Mallika hoped there was a tube of something in his bathroom cabinet. Such excess, she thought.

And such fear.

Padham

A light, semiclassical exploration of a raga
through the verse and song of saint poets

MALLIKA WAKES UP ten minutes before the alarm clock. Five twenty. She has to pack a few things into the carryall for Janaki. The Goodbye and Comeback Letters. The Notation Books and Diaries. Back issues of film magazines and clip books.

She'll pack them after the shower. It will take a carryall.

RI

Janaki, this is the day when you confront it all, and the rest is up to you, I tell myself that morning.

I inform Kabir and Neelam that they aren't to rent any videos, just do their homework and read their Famous Fives. They both look at each other and smile conspiratorially. I will never be part of this secret language they share. I repeat my instructions. "Understood?"

"When will Abbu be back?"

"Tomorrow."

"And you?"

"The day after that."

"So, we can go to the club with him to swim?" Kabir finishes and looks at Neelam. "Yeah, can we?" she says, slurping the last of the milk from her cornflakes bowl.

"Abbu will decide that. Now shower and get ready; Badi Ma's driver will be here soon."

The bags are packed and are waiting at the door and will be taken to the car soon. Samsonite Medium.

Upon arrival, unpacking will be a breeze.

GA

There is nobody in the lineup for number eighteen, but the bus is parked in the first spot. She sits near the window, the carryall at her feet, trying to see Janaki before she really sees her.

"This bus broke down, the bus at the backside is leaving now." The conductor points to the bus behind her.

"In ten minutes."

Why say now when you don't mean it?

Mallika picks up her bag.

MA

"Have a safe trip, Janaki memsahib." I smile and tell Khan sahib to take the next day off, and ask him to give a list for groceries and *aatta* to Khala. Asgar will find out all about my visit with my sister over a dinner cooked by me. If Mallika turns down the offer of financial assistance, so be it. I will have done my dharma. Isn't that what's considered important? Wasn't that Appa's favourite word for all of his actions and inactions? Melodharma, if he'd seen it that way.

I will not give myself up for rejection once again. Whatever the outcome, I know I will not allow it to affect my view of the world. I am lost to that other world of the agraharam.

When I come back I know I will still feel as light as a poori.

PA

Now there's not a single vacant seat on the bus. The woman sitting beside Mallika reeks of Chandrika soap. By the time we get off we will all be united by common sweat and frustration, she thinks, looking down at the brown rexine bag bulging with Janaki's things. When the conductor comes around for the ticket, she says, "Arts College," and gives him the seventy paise.

"If the bus is full, driver is stopping only at select stops. You can get down at TVS?"

She nods.

Lady Chandrika looks perturbed as she pays for the ticket. "Bus is stopping at Church Park Convent?" Her gruff voice startles the other standees.

"Yes, yes, stopping, stopping," the conductor moves to the seats behind them.

Mallika lifts the bag and puts it on her lap. She clutches the rexine handles together into a tight grip. Her Burden of the Past ready for dumping.

Krishna's Butterball ready to roll.

DA

The woman behind the check-in counter recognizes me and waves me to the front. "Janaki-ji, how nice to serve you again!" she beams. She asks why Remo Da Silva had not checked me in as he does on the other occasions I have flown.

"I am going on a personal pilgrimage. Remo is with Asgar on location."

"Pilgrimage to Madras?" She thinks I am joking.

"I like your new uniform sari," I say, taking the boarding pass and baggage check coupons from her.

She lowers her head and says in a quick whisper, "Cheap art silk, bought wholesale in Taiwan."

I am suddenly conscious of my boutique-made churidar kameez, a gift from Asgar last year for our wedding anniversary. The dupatta is embroidered with semiprecious stones, and I know it would cost over five thousand rupees at least. I am Janaki Asgar. I don't have to feel apologetic.

Twenty-five minutes to take-off.

NI

Mallika walks to the guest phone in the lobby and picks up the receiver.

"Janaki Asgar, please," she says, and waits for a response.

Thillaana

A rhythmic piece that brings
together the high points of a raga

IN ALL HER imaginings of this morning, she has left out the bellboys, the trolleys and the husky, Western pop music of the hotel lobby. Seeing them, and hearing the bustle of guests and wheeled luggage—and not seeing and hearing them at all—Mallika's eyes seek only one face in the crowd. Nothing else matters but this final face-to-face, the moment of truth and then a traceless dissolve. Her burden—this carryall at her feet filled with Janaki's things—unburdened. Without guilt, her soul fresh and dry cleaned, like the girls in their teal uniform saris behind the reception desk. That thought, the desire for a complete and final cut, has travelled with her from the moment she got on the bus. It has sat behind her, like an invisible stranger, prodding her with just one question, all the way from Mylapore to Arts College: What is the real purpose of this encounter, and why are you making the effort?

When Mallika buzzed the reception from the lobby intercom and asked for "Janaki Asgar," one of those girls in the sari uniform must have answered her call. "She's expecting you. I'll convey your message."

Tell her it won't be long. Mallika kept the thought to herself.

Ten minutes have gone by, and her heart has not stopped pushing—punching—inside her chest. Mallika lowers her head and stares at the small marigold buds on the border of her pale brown sari. Whatever it took to be inconspicuous, she had reasoned when she chose it, anything to make things less than ordinary.

Janaki should be down any minute.

As she turns to make way for a trolley passing behind her towards the taxi stand, she sees a woman step out from the elevator at the far corner of the lobby. It is the duppatta that catches Mallika's eye, even from such a distance, as though the hem were laced with a border of diamonds. Mallika looks directly at the woman and her heart freezes.

It is Janaki!

The Janaki Asgar.

Shoulder-length hair, high-heel shoes, the same erect walk—but wearing a churidar kameez. The vision stuns and stings Mallika. So this is her new Bombay avatar?

Mallika picks up the carryall and walks towards Janaki. She crisscrosses through the guest sofas and reaches Janaki with decisive steps. It is Janaki, the same hide-the-letter-and-leave-without-thinking-of-the-consequences-of-your-actions Janaki. She had nothing to lose, did she?

"Here are your things," she says, ignoring her sister's smile and open arms, her tongue touching the roof of her mouth on "Malli . . ."

Mallika puts the carryall right next to Janaki's silver, two-inch heels. Those are indeed small diamonds on her duppatta. Forsaker's fortune.

She looks up at the face that she has tried to imagine for the past ten years, but always with a bottu, and never like this. There is no red dot in the middle of her forehead. Mallika's voice is steady, but her body feels suddenly cold and rigid. She watches Janaki's rounder face distort into a look of incredulity, while she senses the eyes of the other guests on the lobby sofas focussing on the two of them.

"Go back to your life of selfishness."

The thought is complete.

She spins around and tries to walk, but her legs don't move to her command. I am going to trip on my sari, she thinks, hobbling in small, hurried steps towards the entrance, with her handbag clasped under her arm. Janaki remains rooted to the spot.

"Mallika! Wait!" Janaki's voice—that voice of the past— but Mallika does not want to turn, to be pulled in, to be seduced by it. How dare you! How dare you! The phrase in her head carries her beyond the taxi stand and out onto the main road. Full rush hour, with the sun moving quickly to the centre of the sky. It is hot outside, and the air is filled with smog from autorickshaws and transit buses. Mallika dodges cyclists and people hurrying to catch buses at the junction, and walks, her heart still punching her chest, but her head light and vacant.

I've met Janaki Asgar. It's over.

It is the ordinariness of the meeting, and how easy it had been for her to tell Janaki what she had been meaning to say for the past decade, without anger, but every word meant fully and truly. Goodbye, Janaki.

And it has actually happened. Two minutes into the average, insignificance of it all. All the rage has disappeared, every minute of those days and nights that had congealed into hard, immovable years, finally put away by the truth.

She crosses the bridge to Ethiraj College and walks in the direction of the Madras Museum.

I don't have to see her again.

"Mallika, get in!" The voice comes from a green Ambassador that has pulled up so close to her at the traffic lights, Mallika jumps to the side footpath.

It is Janaki at the back-seat window.

The pedestrian sign is flashing, and cars and vans stretch like a trail of ants, glistening in the morning sun, all the way across the bridge. Mallika runs across the road before the light drops to red and ducks into the lane circling the college. It is a one-way street. Janaki will not be able to turn around quickly.

"I'll listen to you. Please get into the car, Malli. . ."

It is Janaki again, circling the college from the other end and trailing her with hands folded at the back seat. The car is moving in reverse gear. Two cyclists get down from their seats and begin walking behind the slow-speed Ambassador. Mallika turns and glares at them. They push their bikes to the nearby tea kiosk, but their eyes are still curious about the car following the woman down the college lane. What should she do?

"You can tell me everything over breakfast, Mallika. . . *thangame!*"

To ordinary ears it would be an ordinary endearment— precious—and after its utterance, precious little. But to Mallika's ears it is a melody, unstruck for more than a decade. The cadence of Janaki's voice, her face beaming and bright like the light of day, that's the way she looked sitting on the ledge of the front veranda, while Mallika hopscotched to her sister's "My precious, listen first before you start. It is Ri–Ga–Ma–Ri–Ga–Ma—you have to land on *Ma*," like a mother to a child. How she has longed to be her sister's precious again. How many times had she read the letter and not heard the word, written at the very opening, but always muted, always invisible?

Mallika feels the icy sheet around her heart, a wafer-thin accumulation of ten years of anger, resentment and bitterness, she can feel it all fissure and break and melt away inside her. Janaki's voice, like the river Ganga, washing past sins away with a word. Yes, the power of Janaki's voice. Nobody else can call her that, like that. Nobody has since the day she left, taking her warmth with her to another city, another life.

Mallika opens the car door and sits beside Janaki.

"How you've grown!" Janaki says, wrapping her arms around Mallika, her eyes filling with water, and kissing Mallika on her face and head.

"Look at you, look at you," she pushes Mallika a few inches away from her chest and looks at her face, examining it through her tear-blotched eyes, as though, like Mallika, she too can't believe this moment.

She is older. She is a mother now, Mallika realizes, and that's why her contours have curved generously around her face and her waist. Her eyebrows have been plucked by a beautician in Bombay, but there is no bottu in the centre of her forehead. Now the strangeness has an ethnicity: Janaki is a Tamil-speaking North Indian!

"I have planned a surprise for you."

WHEN THE CAR circles the statue, she asks the driver to slow down and shows Mallika the building where Abirami Palace, Thathappa's cinema theatre, used to stand many years ago. "The best days of my life," she said, while her eyes glazed, just like those photos in the papers the day after she had left for good. "He was so kind to me. I've told Kabir and Neelam all about their great-grandfather."

Have you told them about me, the sister you raised only to leave behind? About Appa and Chitti? It must be so nice to be able to pick and choose selected episodes and people from your past, so that everything looks magnanimous and ideal. But the questions are a whisper at the back of her mind, not the boom and crash of the past week, when they seemed incessant and unendurable. She feels that strange speechlessness, a lavish calm of surrender. For the first time that morning, Mallika realizes that what she has not admitted during the years of silence and resignation, the one thing that now prompts her to forgive, to change, to leave it to Janaki, is just that—her willingness to put herself in the hands of her sister, to have her decisions made for her. The luxury of trust, that's what Janaki really took with her. Could it ever return in a day?

She suppresses the urge to point out her office as the car speeds on the Gemini Flyover, heading towards the airport. She has not asked Janaki where they are going or what the surprise is. The real surprise is that she is sitting next to her sister in a car—and she feels no regret. The scenarios of rage and dismissal she had turned and folded and expanded every time she read Janaki's goodbye letter over the years seem irrelevant and jejune now. The ghosts of the past have vanished into broad daylight.

Ted Pope must wonder what made her take the day off, something she has never done during all these years at the USIS. She was the sort who stayed through Saturday afternoons at her desk, while the others had packed and departed promptly at one.

Appa would have been served his breakfast at the hospital. Would he remember her telling him about Janaki's visit? This meeting with Janaki has a lot in common with her telling Appa of the prodigal's arrival. While she had agonized equally about disclosure and closure, caught in the divide between "Janaki's coming" and "Goodbye, Janaki," in actuality, as it happened and after, all she felt, still feels, is a lifting of exhaustion and the rush of relief.

Gayatri Chitti will be at her bank desk, signing her initials behind draft cheques before handing them over to the peon to take them to the teller. Janaki has not mentioned them. Then, why is she here? Why now and not last year or next year?

"I told Appa, but—"

Before she can finish, Janaki takes Mallika's hand into hers again and holds it in her lap. She draws small circles in Mallika's palm with her index finger, but she does not answer immediately.

"At least he let you do what you wanted to do. According to my husband, that makes Appa a not entirely bad person."

"And according to you?" Mallika asks, her tone more curious than curt.

"Tell me," Janaki says, closing the palm and stopping the circles. "Can we stop being his daughters even if we wanted to?"

"Is that why you are here, Akka? Because you are his daughter?" She has to know so that she can truly believe that this sense of happiness, this preciousness, is above and beyond the wounds of their selfish histories, wholly metaphysical.

Janaki's face is washed with a sense of accomplishment, and the soft smile remains sincere and permanent.

"I am here because Chitti wrote a letter to my sister Zubeida Asgar's address. I don't know how she got that address, but I know her handwriting. The letter said that you were feeling burdened and that the financial situation was bad. Why didn't you write me, *thangame?*"

"And about Appa? Did she mention how sad it is to see him without any sense of—of who he is? How could you not think of what would happen to us before you left? Do you know the humiliation we suffered in the agraharam? All those photographers and microphones . . ." She can't control her tears, and she finds herself right in the middle of the everyday horrors of the past decade. She wants to fill in that fear with words. Can she shake those flashbulbs and burning balls of camphor in this life? And why her?

"I've been so alone these years, Akka, so alone. And you think you can make it all go away by showing up for one day after how many years? Do you know what it is to be alone and helpless?"

She had never meant to say that. That was the last thing she wanted to accept, the fact that she felt abandoned by her family, feeling all these years as though her mother had died twice. She had kept that reality at a distance, never allowing it to break through the invisible steel wall she had built around herself. But those words have come bursting through that forted silence.

Janaki reaches over and pulls Mallika into a tight embrace, and at that moment Mallika feels as she did on her first day of womanhood, far away in Sripuram. That day when she felt dirty and bewildered and tearful, while in her heart she knew that Akka was all the protection she ever needed. That bond of trust, that knowledge of safety, her sanctuary bathed in sandalwood—Akka will make everything all right.

But that afternoon Janaki had not cried. This morning she does.

JANAKI SEES A school playground at the foot of St. Thomas Mount and asks the driver to stop. She steps out of the car and adjusts her dupatta. The stones catch the sun in a sweeping flash and for a few moments Mallika is blinded by a shade card of pink. The driver steps out right after her, and Janaki says something to him, pointing to the school gate. The driver runs to the watchman. "He is saying it is okay to use the playground bench to serve breakfast."

The driver opens the trunk and takes out the plastic bag holding the tiffin carrier. He walks ahead with the bag, a newspaper tucked under his arm. While he arranges the paper and unlocks the carrier, Mallika walks with Janaki to the school gate. Is this the surprise? Breakfast at Sundaram Pillai's?

"*Nandringa,* we are grateful." Mallika watches Janaki quickly do the namaskaram and tilt her head forward in a nod of respect.

"Thanks, sir." Mallika follows Janaki to the wood bench. The driver has placed two stainless-steel plates and two plastic cups and bottled water on the table.

"I placed the order last night, just after I had checked in. It was packed and ready this morning," Janaki says, making it seem as though this was part of her routine. And who knows?

She would have taken over the kitchen and the general management of her house in Bombay—but now she must surely have servants? She seems so easy with her affluence, and so fully at ease in hotel lobbies and rental cars. Janaki has not said a word more than is necessary to the driver. In fact, she has not said anything to Mallika that might reveal her new, rich, film star wife life. Everything is made visible through the unsaid.

"It is so quiet around here. Is it some state holiday?"

"No."

"Here, have one more idli." Janaki picks one from the tiffin box with a plastic fork and drops it onto Mallika's plate. She takes another idli and plonks it onto hers. Mallika does not resist. She had a quick dabra of coffee before heading for the bus stop in the morning, and that was more than three hours ago. She helps herself to more sambar.

"So she didn't tell you?"

"No." The third person can only be one person. Gayatri Chitti.

"I am not surprised." Janaki answers her own question. "She must have felt ashamed to tell you."

"That's not such a bad thing, Akka. We have to accept her for who she is."

Janaki dabs her lips with the paper napkin. She reaches for the bottle of water and unscrews the cap. Holding the bottle with one hand, she washes her fingers with the water—all but half a cup. She places the bottle on the table but does not cap it.

"You do remember what they both did to me during those final days? What would have happened to me had Asgar turned me away? Did that occur to you?"

Mallika hears no accusation in the tone of the question. It is asked in the same prompt of curiosity with which she had noticed the absence of school children and the quiet all around.

"Appa can't remember, so there's no shame. Chitti can, so there is."

Janaki pours water from the bottle while Mallika washes her fingers, and quickly, out of habit, she dries her palms with her sari pullo. The driver repacks the tiffin carrier and takes it back to the car. Janaki stops at the gate and thanks the watchman. She pulls out a hundred-rupee note from her purse and gives it to him.

"Why no children at school today?"

The watchman, wearing a white shirt and khaki shorts, grins—appropriately—like a schoolboy. This must be the first time he has been given a hundred-rupee tip, Mallika thinks, watching his face turn from surprise to suspicion: the lady looks genuine but the note could be counterfeit? Does he know that Janaki is Hindi film star Asgar's wife? Does he read the *Dina Thandi?* Did he, ten years ago, for three days in a row? But this is not that Brahmin girl.

"Pounders Day-nga," he answers in Tamil, shoving the note finally into his shirt pocket.

Janaki turns around and looks at Mallika, her chin raised and her eyes drawing a question mark with a flutter and glace.

"The school's founder. . ." She looks over the watchman's head and reads the school's name written on a small board hanging from the watchman's booth. "Shanmuga Sundaram Pillai."

"Aamanga," the watchman nods excitedly. "Avanga Pounder, yes."

"Buy some flowers for your wife, sariya?" Janaki folds her hands into a namaskaram. Does she do this in Bombay, too? Folding her hands like a dancer, for waiters and liftmen? For that matter, why do all these older men grin in that shy and peculiar way when they talk to young women?

When they get to the car, Janaki opens the door for Mallika to get in and says, "I am not here for them. I am here for you." Once they are seated and the driver has turned on the ignition, she holds Mallika's hand in her lap again. Mallika looks down at her hand in Janaki's and sees the Hyderabad bracelet, blue and green, with small, snaking diamonds. It looks like a peacock plume curved to fit Janaki's wrist. "My husband bought that for me a few years ago, when he was in Hyderabad city." Janaki says, looking directly at Mallika.

"Chitti had a set that looked a bit like this, so I was surprised for a moment."

Mallika quickly realizes that she has reintroduced her into the conversation. Why does she keep doing it?

With the half smile that has not left her face since the minute she walked into the hotel lobby, Janaki giggles. She leans forward and tells the driver: "Drive to Sripuram."

"BUT...BUT THE bank took the Sripuram house and auctioned it a few years ago—" Mallika is alarmed by Janaki's "surprise." She hopes her intervention will persuade Janaki to drop her plans and ask the driver to turn around and drive back to the hotel.

"I know that."

"What else do you know?"

"Revathi got married and moved to Philadelphia, and Vanaja Mami moved to Bellary to stay with her son after Mama died. Nalini Miss has settled in the U.S. and has started her own music school."

"I have not been there since we left. Gayatri Chitti finalized the transfer, and I had nothing to do with the selling of the house." She feels like she is justifying something, without knowing what it is or why. Janaki falls silent for a few minutes, and Mallika hears the traffic and car horns for the first time that morning. So long the inner world had cancelled out the outer world, but now the real world wants in, honking and nasty outside the grey tint of cold glass.

"All I can see is Rajiv Gandhi! Is he coming? Or has he come and gone?"

Without knowing it, Janaki has formulated Mallika's own thoughts into words—she can still do that. She can say things that startle with their prescience. Answer: She has come. And she will be gone. Back to her Bollywood life.

"I was stuck in a Youth Congress procession. The bus I was on was blocked for more than forty-five minutes. Let's hope he has come and gone."

Janaki laughs. A half throaty, half knowing laugh. Like a short siren, loud and stilling.

"As my sister Zubeida often says: I know what you mean." Mallika wonders if Zubeida is also the sister who has taught her the skill of distraction with a short laugh. Without doubt a post-Sripuram manoeuvre.

As soon as the driver stops at Arcot to fill up with petrol, she interrogates the boy holding the long, metal-coil hose.

"Rajiv Gandhi, *vararaa? Vandhu poytaraa?*"

Mallika still can't believe how intact her Tamil is. She speaks it the same way, with that perfect Brahmin stress on each syllable. Who does she speak to in Tamil in Bombay? How has it stayed so inviolate?

"I don't know." His eyes are fixed on the numbers on the pump.

Janaki sighs with disappointment.

"There are posters all round, and he doesn't know a thing! This lack of curiosity is what keeps us the way we are!"

Next time you see one, ask the driver to stop so that we both can read it and put an end to this lack that keeps us the way we are, she wants to reply, but now it feels likes an empty barb. She keeps her thoughts to herself and takes another sideways look at Janaki. Not all that foreign. Face a little rounder, no nose ring, bottu-less forehead. *Exotic Sister*, in enunciated Brahmin Tamil subtitles. Would it show up as a screening at the USIS?

"Let's just hope it is not Sripuram!" Janaki says. She does not tip the boy.

NOTHING ABOUT THE agraharam is the same. There are new stores all the way along Clive Road that she does not recognize, stores with shop spelled as "shoppe," and a few with "boutique" behind the names. All the walls along the buildings are defaced with the faces of film heroes, heroines and Rajiv Gandhi. The road is packed and congested, and Mallika counts an inordinate (at least for Sripuram) number of Maruti cars at the junction of Clive and Nehru roads. How much has changed in Sripuram in just a few years since the house was sold! Mallika turns around, and she catches Janaki peering from her side of the window, her words—"Look, look!" and

then "Where is Mahalaxmi Talkies?"—more a shriek under-
scoring a fact, a lost time, lost permanently now to Sundaram
Chit Funds and Karur Vysaya Bank.

"I have not been back since the house was sold, so I don't
know when or what happened to the cinema theatre." The
look of disbelief on Janaki's face—that she can't bear to see.
It is ten years later for Janaki Asgar.

The driver turns around, more perturbed. Did she tell
him she is a film star's wife? What does he think of all this?
Two Brahmin girls who look like they might be sisters, sitting
in the back of the car, one south, the other (maybe) North
Indian (how?), speaking in chaste Tamil, stopping at vacant
school playgrounds for breakfast and then taking a car ride
three and a half hours out of Madras. He must hear it from
his wife: "The girls these days." Taking to the highways, or
burning in the middle of them.

"That's not our—" It is her turn now. The house looms
out of nowhere and it is not their house.

"Of course it is!" Janaki smiles. "I knew you'd be
surprised!"

The lotus torches at the entrance are freshly painted
and look like lotuses for once. The exterior of the house is
bathed in a primrose yellow, and the window and doors are
olive green and new. The bougainvillea bush is packed with
pink flowers, and the pillars of the veranda are a deep red.
The gate has been replaced with a sturdier and broad black
metal single sheet, and there is no rubbish bin next to it! But
there is a small kolam in front of the house. Who lives here
now?

Janaki asks the driver to turn the car around to the
alleyway.

"Don't worry, the telecommunications department relay station has closed down!"

She can still laugh about it all.

As soon as the driver steps out of the car, an old man with watery eyes and shrunken shoulders appears at the backyard gate. A few minutes later, the driver opens the trunk and starts to unload the luggage. One large suitcase, one small vanity case, one handbag, two tiffin carriers. They carry it into the house. What's going on?

"Come," Janaki says. "We're home."

THIS IS WHERE they burned the veena, Akka, right here, but that place is not here anymore. Here, right here, beside this tulasi plant. Here is where she stood and gave Appa the kerosene. These steps of the backyard, this very same one, now nicely painted with limestone, Vanaja Mami watched it from here. The bonfire. They called you names, Akka. Not cheap names, but horrible, horrible names. Appa, Chitti, everybody. Even Savitri Mami, who came by the next day, after the news broke in the papers. She chided Vanaja for not inviting her for the veena burning. For two full weeks this house was dark and dead. The words stick in Mallika's throat, and her legs turn to stone.

"I can't. . ." She hears herself saying, but stops. Janaki turns around at the backyard terrace, her heel shoes off, ready to step indoors to inspect the house, eager like when she was at school climbing mango trees—how many times has she imagined this return? How many times has she relived this moment in her Bombay house, wanting to step back into the world of the agraharam, her mind on lentils and the tiffin adais? That Janaki is intact. Her sister did not want it to turn out this way. She did not will it. Appa did. All these years and a week she has been standing at the crime scene framing the wrong person. The real criminal will never visit this scene again. Nor will his accomplice.

But Janaki is home. And she has proved everybody wrong.

Mallika says it again, her words forming slowly: "I can't believe it."

THERE ONCE LIVED a family here, once, a decade ago. A father, a mother, and their two daughters. Their lives were filled with music and ritual, and then, one day, everything fell silent. That silence is still here, Mallika can see it, but she knows that Janaki can't. In the corner of this changed blue living room, there by the shelf where the *jamakalam* was kept with the veena, the camphor still burns on Appa's palm a foot from where the photo fell and lives were ruined. How did his rage help? What would have become of them had Appa taken Janaki's words—it only takes the meaning you put into it—seen the maturity of her response and trusted her? These walls, behind the new blue coats of paint, hold those words. Polished floors, gleaming sink and bathroom fittings, prefab kitchen cabinets, a new colour for every room—nothing can disguise those scars of denial and hubris. The sad and destructive wrath of a man named Venkatakrishnan.

Still, Mallika obeys Janaki and, holding her hands, stands in the four corners of every room while her sister recites slokas usually summoned during housewarmings. She leads her into the backyard again and walks around the tulasi plant, muttering a few more verses. The driver and watchman stand and stare at them. Why is she doing all this? We don't live here anymore. This is not our house.

"Has the doctor from Colombo ever lived here?" Janaki asks the caretaker. Mallika stands astonished by her sister's ability to dive right into her thoughts.

"No. Only for three months when house was being renovated."

"I am going to use it for a few hours. The owner knows about it. This structure is new."

He is standing next to a long, four-foot-by-eight-foot concrete structure along the compound wall. It is as high as the outhouse, two feet away from alleyway gate where the neem tree used to be. Janaki has not mentioned the hibiscus bush. It is in full bloom. A hard plastic shield covers the mouth of the well, and a small metal bucket sits under a dripping tap below the kitchen window. Was it there when they lived here?

"House owner built this for me to sleep at night. You are beautiful."

Janaki laughs heartily. "This is my sister. She is younger and prettier. Is the milk Thermos in the kitchen?" She looks at the driver.

"Yes, madam."

"Has Rajiv Gandhi come or gone?" She is as insistent as ever.

"Not coming here, madam. He is going Sriperumbudhur, after next two villages en route to Madras. Thirty miles this side."

"I know where Sriperumbudhur is. I hope all this political circus does not delay my flight to Bombay tomorrow!"

Back in the kitchen, she empties the milk into a brand new saucepan pulled out of the brand new kitchen cabinets. Mothballs and insect repellent have conquered the space originally under the rule of *agarbathis* and *sambarani*. The whole house reeks of artificial lemon and half-dead memories.

Janaki says a little prayer over the boiled milk and pours it into four stainless-steel tumblers. She calls out to the driver and gives him two tumblers with steaming milk. He takes them to the cement terrace and calls out to the old man.

The scene is so surreal, and yet it so resembles those evenings of proposals and disposals that Mallika can't say if she feels sad or incredulous watching Janaki in her element. Everything is, at least to Janaki, just the way it was back when. At that moment, Mallika decides not to tell Janaki about the backyard bonfire and Appa's self-destruction. Not to mention a word about the hospital visits or the medical bills or the slow depletion of the bank savings account. This is not the time for it. And why now, when she knows that Janaki was not responsible for any of that? She doesn't have to hear all the details in just one day. This day belongs to the Janaki who is back, not the Janaki who left. Her resolve releases her into a world of lightness.

"You want to go to Tirukalukundram?" Sheer insanity, but she can't stop from smiling at the abandon of the thought.

"But the kites would have come and gone by now!" Janaki laughs.

"So what?" Mallika can't hide the excitement in her voice. "We can be together a little longer." Say yes, Akka, say yes.

"Let's!" Janaki takes Mallika's face in her hands and kisses her forehead. "We'll freshen up and leave. I forgot that you had the whole day off!"

THIS JANAKI, the sister now sitting beside her in this sweltering Tirukalukundram sun, with her hair centre-parted and tied up in a rubber-band ponytail, a small red bottu in the middle of her eyebrows, this woman, wife and mother of two, is on rent for one full day as my mother in a lavender cotton sari, speaking sweet-as-nectar agraharam Tamil. How amazingly contrary to all the imagined dramas and traumas of discontent!

"You don't have to write the essay. You can tell your Anglo-Indian teacher you got there at two thirty, long after the kites had come and gone!"

Janaki's laughter draws the attention of a few tiffin-time patrons in the restaurant. Do they recognize her? So far nobody has walked up and asked for an autograph. Even up in the hills, amid that melee of women and children, nobody had noticed or stared at Janaki. How easily she has transformed herself from Bombay to Sripuram, with just a comb, bottu and sari!

"You have not told me about your job, Miss Jane Iyer!" She holds the past in that mispronunciation. She remembers asking if the character in the novel was an Iyer Brahmin. She laughs with the memory.

"How did you know I worked at the USIS?"

"The same way I knew about the house being sold to a doctor in Colombo." She opens her purse and looks up. "Should we walk up and pay?"

When they step out of the restaurant, the car and the driver are nowhere to be seen.

"Where did he disappear now?" Janaki walks to the end of the street and peers left and right. "What do you do at the USIS?"

"I advise students who are applying for higher studies in America."

"Have you visited America?

"No."

"So how can you advise them?"

"I might be going for some training to the U—"

"Sorry, madam!"

"You were inside the restaurant?" Janaki confronts the driver who has come dashing through the doorway, rubbing his washed hands ferociously on white trousers in an effort to dry them. He grins like a mouthwash model.

"Parking is available in the back. I am waiting there after finishing meals!"

"Seri, Seri, you can bring the car to the front now. Look at the time!"

"Akka," Mallika says while they wait for the driver to come through the main gateway. "Thanks for coming." There is no better way to say it. Nothing can match the ordinary exuberance of the day.

Janaki wraps the sari pullo around and over her shoulders. She looks so much like, so much like—

"And I always will. Whenever you need me," Janaki replies. "But, *thangame*, don't ever forget that it was not I who wanted to leave. I was also forced to give up everything I loved."

She sits on the red stone steps of the restaurant entrance and begins to cry in small sobs, just like when Mallika had found her on the backyard terrace the evening of her friend Kamala's suicide. Looking back, wasn't that the point when love truly left the agraharam? Why has Janaki not mentioned her best friend?

Mallika sits next to Janaki and takes her hand into hers.

"Everything that I am, I owe to you. Remember how you would tell me—after playing 'Row, Row, Row Your Boat' on the veena—remember how you would tell me that saying thank you makes the person saying it feel happier than everybody else? That is how I am feeling now."

"Then listen to me," Janaki says, wiping her face with her pullo. "We go back to Sripuram and pick up the bags. You are staying with me at the hotel tonight. The driver will drop you at your flat in the morning."

Janaki stands up and shakes the pleats of her sari. She bends to pick up her handbag and the Ambassador pulls up in front of them.

"Say yes and I'll accept your thank you!"

ON THE WAY back she asks the driver to take the car around to the Sripuram temple. It is already seven in the evening, two hours past the evening *archanai*, but she still insists on seeing the flower-shop alley and the gopuram before leaving for Madras. "There is nothing like this in Bombay!" she exclaims, as though that made it a particularly horrible city. She buys incense and *sambarani* from the first stall at the edge of the road.

"Want flowers?"

"No."

Dusk has dissolved into night by the time they reach the Sripuram house.

"Akka, we still have to drive for three hours!"

Had they not left their bags in Sripuram, they could have continued up north from Tirukalukundram, and that would have saved so much time.

"You go up and pack the bags. I will join you soon."

When Mallika comes downstairs with the packed bags and clothes, Janaki is standing in front of the wall where Amma's photo used to hang. Her eyes are closed, her hands folded, and her lips move to the soft cadence of Sanskrit words. On the floor, right below the absent photo, Mallika sees a red hibiscus.

Janaki opens her eyes finally.

"We can leave now. Here, put this envelope in your handbag." Mallika takes the broad manila envelope from Janaki. The photograph that set it all off?

"My handbag is in the car." It feels more like a stack of papers clipped with a stapler. Can it be Appa's medical bills? But, how did Janaki get those?

"Open it after I have gone back to Bombay."

Passing through the kitchen door to the cement terrace, Mallika notices that the milk pot and tumblers have been rinsed and lined beside the sink. All in the time it took her to use the bathroom upstairs, stuff the clothes into the bags and bring them down. Does she still wash dishes in her Bombay kitchen? At the backyard gate Janaki stops to have a word with the old caretaker.

"Who draws the morning kolam?" she asks, opening her handbag and unzipping the inside purse. Mallika stands near the car and waits for Janaki.

"My daughter comes sometimes and does it." He sees a few currency notes in Janaki's hand and his smile widens.

"One hundred out of this is for *kolapodi*," she says, giving him the money. He takes the notes with both his hands and bows. His head keeps nodding throughout the exchange.

"Ask your daughter—what's her name?"

"Susi."

"You tell Susi she has to come every day to do the kolam, sariya? And ask her to draw bigger ones!" Do her eyes miss anything?

"Akka, it is late." Mallika folds the envelope and slides it sideways into her handbag.

"You take good care of the house and say thank you to the landlord from me."

"And you are? *Unga peyru?*"

"Janaki Asgar."

IT IS DARK BLUE outside the window. A deep, dark blue that stretches into light, pulling with it a flutter of wings, the shrill gargle of morning birds. She hears a broom sweeping up the dust from the front of the house. It is a music she has not heard in a long, long time. How good it feels, half asleep and half awake, and the sound of Akka sweeping before the kolam. Soon she will be off to the milk depot. Another hour before the agraharam fully wakes up. It is not dark blue outside the window. It is pitch dark. She looks over and sees that Janaki has nodded off as well. She's still holding Mallika's hand in her lap. The driver has turned off the car radio, and there is just the buzz of air-conditioner fan.

"Akka."

Janaki is fully awake with a whisper. "Yes?"

"We'll be in Madras soon."

"Driver, where are we?"

"Just crossing Ranipettai, madam." He does not take his eyes off the road. "Turn off AC, madam?"

"We're both so tired," Janaki's mouth opens into a yawn halfway through the declaration. "What time is it?"

"I can't see clearly." Mallika wipes her glasses and wears them again. "I still can't see the hands."

"Yes, turn off AC."

"Nine forty, madam." He quickly unwinds the window to let fresh air in. It is a mild, warm whip, bringing with it the smell of kiln-baked bricks.

"You must be so hungry," Janaki says, pulling out a Cadbury's bar from her handbag. "I always have to carry these things for Kabir and Neelam."

She breaks the slab of chocolate into half and offers it to Mallika.

"They love fruit and nut! It is so late; I told them I would call tonight!" She does not eat the chocolate.

The two-lane highway is dark except for the headlights of the traffic racing past them in the other direction. Mallika can't tell how many cars or trucks are ahead of them, but the journey has been smooth so far—despite the sorry state of the roads—for them to drift off for an hour. The driver has kept within the speed limit, and that makes her feel safe. She is happy to have Janaki by her side once again. Time doesn't matter anymore. She has missed this security of being with her sister, and she doesn't want the day to end. These hours will never return, not like this, not again.

"Dammit!" the driver exclaims, as the speed drops to a slow crawl. Within minutes the car grinds to a complete stop. Through the windshield Mallika can see the tail lights of the car ahead.

"Maybe lorry accident!"

There is no traffic in the opposite direction. If the driver's hunch is right, it could be a truck carrying bricks or cement bags, turned on its side across the highway. It will be hours before they get to the hotel. Cars are lined up behind them. Drivers—men—stand between half-open car doors, the engines rumbling in the stationary gear. Their driver has not stepped out, and Janaki has not remarked on his prediction. Mallika knows that a U-turn will take them back to Sripuram. How would she get to work in the morning?

"This is inconvenient so late in the night!"

"They can't keep the road blocked for the whole night. They'll clear it soon." Janaki unwinds the window on her side, but leaves it halfway up.

"Driver, turn off the engine and get the fruits from the back. Now I wish we had taken the other route to Madras!"

He does as he is told and knocks gently on the window glass. Janaki unwinds it all the way down and takes the plastic bag from him. "Here, have an orange while we wait." She gives him one, and offers Mallika the rest. "Let me peel it for you."

The driver walks a few steps to the car ahead and strikes up a conversation. It is difficult to see in the dark, and only the voices of men break the crickety silence. Women and children, if they are passengers in the cars behind and ahead of them, are uncharacteristically quiet. Janaki digs her nail into an orange and pulls back the peel. The car immediately smells of citrus oil.

Something had to ruin all the cheerfulness of the day, Mallika tells herself. Like a big dhrishti bottu, a black smear on the edge of a precious object of beauty. She knows it is fatigue and nothing else, and nothing, not least of all a truck carrying cement, can ruin it at this juncture. She is pleased with Janaki's invitation to spend the night at the hotel. Her only hope now is that it comes to be.

"Here." Janaki drops two orange crescents into Mallika's palm.

SHATTERING THE PEACE of the road, two buses decorated with the national flag and streamers, and packed with men yelling "Congress Party Zindabad!" at the top of their voices, race ahead of all the stalled cars and buses, daringly, on the other lane.

"It is not a truck accident," Mallika announces. "It is that Youth Congress rally at Sriperumbudhur!"

"See, it will be over soon." Janaki smiles. She has not lost her composure one bit—the same determined sister, strengthened by all the haggling at the Sripuram market!

"What are you doing?"

Mallika reaches across Janaki's lap for the winding handle and rolls up the window. She arches over the driver's seat and spins the lever on the door. She moves back to her side of the seat and pushes the inside lock.

"Akka, one of those men has to recognize you, and we'll have all the drama we don't need!" She is surprised by the stiffness of her command.

"*Sabaash!*" Janaki claps her hands. "How those students must shiver!"

She removes the membrane. She pops the seeds onto the peel on her lap, and in one poised move the fruit disappears into her mouth.

"When are the elections?"

The driver opens the car door and settles back into his seat. His face has a worried look.

"What's the problem, driver?" Janaki demands.

"Police, madam. They are checking all the cars, one by one, from the main junction."

"Why?"

"Something is happening at the political meeting."

Twenty minutes later, a policeman approaches the car. He lowers his head, and his eyes scan the back seat, the torchlight quickly moving from Mallika's face to Janaki's.

He instructs the driver to step out of the car. Mallika moves closer to Janaki. The policeman walks around to Janaki's side of the car and taps on the window glass with his torchlight. "I'll answer," Mallika tightens her grip around Janaki's wrist.

"Rental car booking for Madras–Sripuram roundtrip, correct?"

"Yes."

"Driver is telling car rental is by Bombay party?"

"Yes."

"Why?"

"It is booked in my husband's name," Janaki answers. "Hindi film actor, Asgar."

"Oh, I see."

The policeman steps back and waves to the driver. "Why you didn't tell me about film star status?" He spits on the tar road. The driver claims ignorance.

"Madam, there was bombing at Sriperumbudhur rally," he says, his voice taking on a tone of respect and recognition. "No car is passing for at least one hour more. I will sending information to you first when road is open."

As he is walking away, three cars zoom by in the opposite lane, heading to Sripuram. The policeman registers their licence plate numbers—*"Daridhirathaẓhi! Losers!"*—and moves to the cars behind them.

The dashboard clock shows 11:15.

"What does he mean he is going to send information?" Janaki throws the orange peel into the plastic bag and ties a double knot. "Where is he going to send his information from?"

"Akka, please don't step out of the car! There were riots near Pachaiyappa College two days ago. It has been like this the whole week."

They see policemen in white helmets, with their sirens blaring, rumble past them on their motorcycles.

"Something is happening in the back," the driver says.

"My children would have left so many messages at the hotel." She stretches and yawns.

They sit in silence, waiting for the policemen to clear the road and let the traffic through.

"Driver, tune to All India Radio," Janaki instructs. There is static on the frequency for a few minutes, and then there is Sarod music with a voiceover: "We are sorry for the interruption. Please wait for an important announcement." Ten minutes of that droning voice, and Janaki is impatient once again.

"What's going on in this city? There's nothing on the radio, and nobody has any information!"

Car horns puncture the night, and the rumble of police motorcycles has not ceased.

A motorist behind them does not let up on the horn, and a group of men surround the car, arguing about the time and the unnecessary hold up.

Mallika rolls down the window fast and sticks her head halfway out into the open air to get a view of the commotion in the lineup of cars behind them.

"Ladies and children are in passenger seats. How late can they wait?" she hears a man talking back to the police officer.

That's when the obscenity is hurled at her—at all of them on the road—from a car with four men in white, wearing tri-colour bandanas, swerving past at high speed, the words loud above the engines, stabbing into the dark night and leaving a bloodless wound behind:

"Rajiv Gandhi killed in bomb attack!"

The wind blows Mallika's hair in her face, and she falls back into her seat as though electrocuted. It seems like a perverse joke, as if somebody were venting their anger in a cruel and insensitive way. The phrase slices through her brain like a cold, sharp knife.

"What?" Janaki's voice is hoarse. She heard it, too.

"Can't be!" The driver shakes his head in disbelief. He steps out of the car and leaves the door open. Horns from the cars ahead and behind of them start blaring, a chorus of wailing automobiles.

Shock eases, and Mallika says the word softly, her eyes staring into shapeless space.

"Amma."

"What?" She can feel Janaki shaking her arm, but it feels heavy and distant. People have spilled out of their cars, and suddenly there is a whole procession of men and women on the road. Everybody is shaking their head, like people who have suddenly lost all their possessions in a flash flood and don't know how to put their grief in words. Mallika sees them walk past their car in silent, huddled groups, their eyes vacant and lost. Where are they going? What is at the end of the road?

"Mallika, are you all right, *thangame*, is something wrong?"

"He must have felt like Amma on the bus." Mallika can barely hear her own voice.

Amma is gone. Janaki is here. But she will be gone tomorrow. The words arrange themselves noiselessly in her head.

"Our Amma."

Janaki touches her face as Mallika leans back and rests her head on her sister's shoulder. She feels Janaki's lips on her hair and hears her agreeing between short, muffled kisses.

"Yes, just like Amma. Just like our Amma."

Mangalam

A coda, a "thank you gods and listeners" conclusion to the concert

Bethesda, Maryland
July 2, 1991

MY DEAR AKKA,
You would have received the post-card I sent you three weeks ago. I hope there is no crisis at the hospital. I had given them your number as you had asked me to.

Today was the last day of my two-week training program. I learned many new things about career counselling that will make me more effective during the student interviews. It has been a very rewarding experience.

Before we met in Madras, the week prior to your arrival, I was afraid that our reunion would open all the old wounds and scars. It was impossible for me to see it any other way. Now, five weeks after our day in Sripuram, I know that you did not come to rake our past; you came to give me the gift of our history. My heart fills with pride when I think that you bought back the Sripuram house (how could you keep it to yourself right through that day?) with your music academy lessons and savings. Did you have to get the property deed using my name?

My supervisor, Mr. Ted Pope, will be arriving this evening from Madras. He has invited me to spend the American Independence Day holiday (day after tomorrow) with his family in Richmond, Virginia. I am told the fireworks are really amazing.

Your sister,

Mallika

ps: *Have your children any interest in meeting their aunt? And, yes, a hibiscus bush can be a fine family tree!*

I leave Mallika's letter on the coffee table and take out the veena from its velvet case. I roll out the *jamakalam*. The house is quiet and still. It is Khala's first day off in months, and there is absolute silence from the kitchen. Kabir and Neelam are at the Bombay gymkhana for their swimming lessons. Zubeida will send her driver to pick them up, as Asgar has taken his car for an unscheduled dubbing session in Andheri. He won't be back until dinner. It is a good time for cleansing.

I draw the curtains and open the bay windows. It will be night soon. I light a few *agarbathis* and stuff them into the holder on Asgar's trophy shelf. A gentle jasmine creeps all around the room within a few minutes.

I lift the veena onto my lap, and I position my fingers on the strings. When I close my eyes, Amma smiles inside them. My raga is alive.

Sa is for Sarpa, the serpent around your neck, my Lord. In its skin we see our world reborn eternally.

Ri is for Rudrakhsa, the necklace of tears on your chest, my Lord. In every purple bead is our worldly breath.

Ga is for Ganga, the heavenly river in your wild hair, my Lord. Her waters cleanse our world of sin.

Ma is for Mriga, the deer you hold in your hand, my Lord. We realize the world is just an illusion.

Pa is for Pushpa, the lotus you dance on, my Lord. That is our world at your feet.

Da is for Damaru, the rattle drum of creation in your hand, my Lord. It is the music of our inner world.

Ni is for Nisakara, the crescent crown on your head, my Lord. In it we see the time of our world.

MY RAGA RISES and dips and dances with the dappled gold of the waves.

I am my song, and my song is the red of the sun.

AUTHOR'S NOTE

I AM NO EXPERT on Indian Classical Music; nor do I play any musical instrument. All my learning (or lack of) comes from various sources, and these are some of the texts I have consulted while writing this book:

The Illustrated Companion to South Indian Classical Music by Ludwig Pesch (Oxford University Press, 1999).

What is Carnatic Music? by Vidya Bhavani Suresh (Skanda Publishing, Chennai, 2002).

The History of Indian Music by P. Sambamurthy (The Indian Music Publishing House, Chennai, 1998)

The Ragas of Karnatic Music by N.S. Ramachandran (Trinity Music Book Publishers, Chennai, 2003)

The couplet Janaki recites is by the Tamil poet Mu Metha.

I HAVE ALSO benefited greatly from the theoretical articles by E. Gayathri, which have appeared periodically in *The Hindu*.

I have dramatized some of these theoretical points in the novel.

I have used the Sanskrit word "Raga," as it cuts across both Hindustani and Carnatic classical music traditions of India. The music in the book pertains to the South Indian (Carnatic) Classical Music tradition. Tamil speakers refer to "Raga" as "Ragam." The Sanskrit word is equally acceptable and understood all over India.

All the technical errors and inaccuracies (if any) in the text are my own.

ACKNOWLEDGEMENTS

THERE ARE MANY without whom—
Indhumati "Akka," for teaching me Tamil, for showing me the infinite riches of the language, and for leaving me with one question to which I've sought an answer for twenty-five years: *What happened to Janaki?*

The inspiration for this book belongs to her.

Edna Alford, for her faith in this book, for being with me at every stage of the writing, for her nurturing spirit.

She is the true mother of this book.

Paul Bowdring, Daphne Marlatt, Peter Oliva, Rachel Wyatt and the Writing Studio at the Banff Centre for Arts, Alberta, where early chapters of this book were written. Thank you for the good care.

Alana Cymerman, W. Mark Giles, Chelva Kanaganaya-kam, Ruth Krahn, Leilah Nadir and Kathie Wayne, for shared "struggling writer" stories, for their unflagging support.

Yasmin Assur, Shahnaaz Jeena, Javed Merchant and Munir Merchant, for all the long-distance affection and warmth, for being family.

Ann-Marie Metten, for her copy-editing expertise.

Hilary McMahon, for her efficiency and good judgment, for being my agent.

Steven W. Beattie, for his editorial guidance and encouragement.

Scott Steedman, my publisher, for giving my book a good home, for his wisdom.

Alan Buchanan, for a love that's a discovery every day, for letting me belong to him.

JANE "JANAKI" WEITZEL

AMEEN MERCHANT was born in Bombay and raised in Madras, India. *The Silent Raga* is his first novel, was shortlisted for the Commonwealth Writers' Prize Best First Book Award and was published in India, where it was an acclaimed bestseller. Merchant lives in Vancouver, British Columbia, where he is working on his next novel.